where we have to go

T0204699

where we have to go

LAUREN KIRSHNER

Emblem
McClelland & Stewart

Emblem edition published 2009

Emblem is an imprint of McClelland & Stewart Ltd.
Emblem and colophon are registered trademarks of McClelland & Stewart Ltd.

LIBRARY AND ARCHIVES CANADA CATALOGUING IN PUBLICATION

Kirshner, Lauren
Where we have to go / Lauren Kirshner.

ISBN 978-0-7710-4490-8

I. Title.

PS8621.I78W54 2009   C813.'6   C2008-904231-X

We acknowledge the financial support of the Government of Canada through the
Book Publishing Industry Development Program and that of the Government of
Ontario through the Ontario Media Development Corporation's Ontario Book
Initiative. We further acknowledge the support of the Canada Council for the Arts
and the Ontario Arts Council for our publishing program.

The epigraph on page v is from the poem "The Waking" by Theodore Roethke,
from *The Collected Poems of Theodore Roethke*. Published by Anchor Books,
a division of Random House, Inc.

Typeset in Fournier by M&S, Toronto
Printed and bound in Canada

ANCIENT FOREST
FRIENDLY

McClelland & Stewart Ltd.
75 Sherbourne Street
Toronto, Ontario
M5A 2P9
www.mcclelland.com

1   2   3   4   5   13   12   11   10   09

This shaking keeps me steady. I should know.
What falls away is always. And is near.
I wake to sleep, and take my waking slow.
I learn by going where I have to go.

Theodore Roethke, "The Waking"

1

The night before my eleventh birthday, I dreamt I was five feet off the ground and flying through the No Frills grocery store on a royal blue Schwinn. My handlebar streamers whipped behind me, lighting my trail with shiny electrical sparks. I zoomed up a wall and across the ceiling so all the blood rushed to the top of my head. The floor was the sky, the aluminum carts cramming the aisles silver spaceships, and the shoppers little Martians. I rode back down and pedalled to the in-store bakery, where the lady in the dented puffy white cap was squeezing pink letters out of an icing bag and onto the top of my birthday cake, first an *L*, then a *U*, then a *C*, and finally the *Y*. It was my first store-bought birthday cake, and I was riding my bike up the deli wall to celebrate when my front wheel got caught on the round security mirror, leaving me hanging in space just like E.T. frozen against the moon.

When I opened my eyes, Lulu was kneading my blankets and purring at the foot of my bed, but I was too excited to play cat games in my first minute of being eleven. So I kissed her on the mouth, sprinkled some sunflower seeds into Charlie Sheen's cage, and walked down the hall to the bathroom, Lulu following behind me. Some people thought it was strange that my name and my cat's name were so similar. It peeved me when people said, "You have the same name as your cat!" Most of the time I'd explain that *Lucy* and *Lulu* are actually 50 per cent different. But if they still weren't convinced, I'd say that like everything in our house, there was a story behind it. Mom said that when she was pregnant, she and Dad had argued over what name to give me. Dad had wanted to call me Lulu. "Frank, don't be a nudnik. We're not giving our daughter the stage name of a showgirl!" She wanted to call me Lucy. For six months there was a draw. "Then I was in the backyard a few weeks before you were born, and out of nowhere, I see this kitten chomping on your dad's tomato plants. We did a compromise. I let him name *her* Lulu." Still, Mom sometimes mixed up our names. "Lucy," she'd yell, standing on the sundeck, dinging a can of Turkey Feast with a fork. "Dinner!"

As I brushed my teeth, I parted the curtains and looked out the window to the backyard. My new Schwinn bike wasn't on the sundeck yet, but Mom was crossing the yard carrying a red bucket and her magic bag stuffed with clothes from the 1970s. She was going to wash and dress her mannequins for my party. This meant I had at least half an hour to sneak a peek at Dad's Glamour Shots album before she came looking for me. I shut the curtains, spat in the sink, and went to my room to get dressed.

Dad kept his Glamour Shots album in his study, on the highest shelf of his closet. "Location is everything," Dad told me. "People on vacation want access to malls, beaches, and nightclubs. If you want to know what a package is worth, don't look at the price tag. Look at the location." Even though he'd been talking about what he called the "science of selling packaged tours," I thought Dad's keeping his album on the most secret shelf in the whole house said something about what it was worth to him.

Before Dad became a travel agent he had been a photographer. The lower shelves of his closet were filled with old Kodak cameras, including the 1954 Brownie he'd snapped his big-break picture with – Elizabeth Taylor and Richard Burton stepping out of the Windsor Arms Hotel in 1964. He once showed me the photo he'd taken of himself moments after: he was seventeen, pimply, skinny like me, and wearing a striped jersey with a Lacoste-type alligator that he'd drawn in ballpoint pen above the breast pocket to "attract girls of a higher class." He'd used the money he made from selling the Taylor-Burton photograph to the *Toronto Telegraph* to open Glamour Shots Limited, "the hot spot for head shots and more." It went under in 1989, when I was seven. Now all that was left of Glamour Shots was this plastic-covered album on my lap. It was beginning to stink of mildew even though I sometimes sprayed it with strawberry air freshener.

If she was in a good mood, Mom would say that Dad's old photos were art*ish*. "Who says that girls in tassels can't be as tasteful as Greek statues?"

If she was in a bad mood, she'd say, "I used to think it was Glamour Shots, but now I see it as Glamour Shits. That stuff was one step away from burlesque."

"What's *burlesque*?" I'd say. "Is it a kind of desk?"

I turned the pages of the album slowly, pausing for the girls in bustiers and fishnet stockings, the girls with shellacked beehives and red lips and halved-cantaloupe breasts popping out of bikini tops. The showstoppers. When I asked Dad about the women who came to his studio, he said, "Lucy, they were all young and stunning.

High-quality models. Lots went on to have important roles on TV." But Mom said, "Don't listen to him, Lucy. They were just university kids with crunchy hair, looking to make extra cash by rubbing themselves against cars at trade shows."

The girls in the Glamour Shots album were the most beautiful I had ever seen. I loved looking at them in the same way I loved admiring the peacocks or shiny snakes at the zoo. When I flipped through the album, it sometimes made me think that if I was that beautiful, everyone would listen to me when I spoke up in school. I wouldn't be the last girl picked when we had to make up teams in gym class. If I was that beautiful, everyone would want to come to my party.

I loved to imagine that Mom had once been like the girls in the Glamour Shots: brave, beautiful, and confidant, as bold as Tarzan's Jane, only better, because she wouldn't need to rely on a man. But I couldn't know for sure. In our house of cameras, there were only two photos of Mom from before I was born. And for all the stories Mom told, the stories from before she moved to Canada and met Dad never made the cut. The only clues to her old life were the packages that her relatives in Bulgaria sent her twice a year, wrapped in brown paper and tattooed with stamps the colour of Monopoly money. Inside the parcels were jars of prune jam wrapped in even more layers of stinking brown paper, tea-rose perfume in wooden canisters, and disc-shaped lucky glass eyes meant to be hung in windows but that we ended up using as coasters instead.

In Mom's photos, she looked fearless and energetic, happier than I'd ever seen her. In the first photo, from 1974, she's standing on a stage in front of quilted gold curtains, holding a bouquet of orange flowers. She's the first runner-up in the Miss Sophia West Beauty Pageant, and her dress has a fringe of peacock feathers hanging near the cleavage, deep and full Eastern European cleavage that at the rate I was going I'd probably never get. In the other photo, this one larger, as if she wanted to remember every detail of the moment forever, she's wearing a green Mary Quant dress and gold grape-cluster earrings, and posing by the "Arrivals" sign at the airport. She's waving. I could picture her flagging down a total stranger to take the photo as soon as she got off the plane. Six months later, she started working at the Eaton's Department Store on Bloor Street, in the Petites section. That's where she met Dad. He had been looking for "inspiration" for one of his clients, and because Mom was the same height, he had asked her to try on the dress he was consider-ing. Then they went out for coffee and the rest, as they say, was history. Actually, it wasn't history because Mom told the story of how they met again and again, though the details changed depend-ing on how she felt about Dad at the time.

Sometimes their first date was lousy: "He was wearing a striped T-shirt that reminded me of a prison uniform, and Lucy, I swear to you, my instinct was to say no."

But sometimes it was two stars coming together: "All the cos-metics girls were eyeing me in an envious way when he came up to *me*. He looked just like Omar Sharif, but with blue eyes, like you." From what I could tell, Dad's remembering to water the bonsais and empty the dishwasher was all it took to make their first date dreamy.

When Lulu started scratching on the door it was almost ten, which meant that Mom would be finished washing the mannequins soon. I flipped forward to the very last page of the album, to my favourite girl. She was wearing a shiny white toga and a lopsided crown of laurels on her head. Unlike the showstoppers, whose pouts made being beautiful seem a real serious business, she was laughing as if she thought the camera was a joke. The handwriting on the bottom corner of the photograph was loopy and careful: *To Frank, Lots of Love, Allie. August 29, 1977.*

I closed the album and put it back on its secret shelf.

▬

It was steamy hot when I stepped out onto the sundeck, but I didn't care because our backyard in July was a magical place: the sides of the yard were wild with trumpet flowers, daisies, and ferns, and at the foot of the sundeck were Dad's tomato plants. There were more tomatoes than I could count, and every June Dad planted more. Mom didn't garden anything except her mannequins. There were three of them – a man, a woman, and a child – and they were naked except for the plastic dollar-store vines she'd glued in palm-leaf formations onto their private places. Mom had found the mannequins two months ago outside a fabric store near the high school where she taught English as a Second Language to new Canadians. After she'd dragged them home, she leaned them up against the back fence and planted their feet into the soil.

When I walked over to Mom, she was on her knees scouring the man mannequin's feet with a toothbrush. His detailed toenails, right down to the faint arc of cuticle, were always caked with dried mud. I didn't like him at all. His body had been built at a wrong angle, so he always seemed to be leaning toward the gate, the Gingerbread Man ready to make a break for it. But because his chest was as sculpted as a bronze Herculean breastplate, and his feet firmly planted on the ground, he was Mom's ideal man, second only to Julio Iglesias.

"Happy Birthday, Lucy." Mom kissed me on my head and handed me a rag and a spray bottle. "Now, come help me."

Mom loved her mannequins. Every morning, while Dad cleaned his car in the garage – a private ritual involving a Roy Orbison cassette, many shammies, and Kiwi wax – she would gaze out at our plaster counterparts as she drank her morning Nescafé. Sometimes, her mouth opened into a tiny *o* of pleasure, like the women on *Dallas* we used to watch fall in love, week by week, with a different set of men who all looked suspiciously similar: boomerang-jawed men with thick dark moustaches, lots of arm hair, their gun-coloured top-down cars idling on a circular drive. Every Monday night, while Dad went to his AA meeting and I watched *ALF* on television, she filled the twist-mop bucket with sudsy water and go outside to wash them, sponging them in the same way I'd once seen a nurse bathe my grandmother in the months before she died.

I pretended not to care about the mannequins when Mom was home. I told her they were creepy. "How about we get a bird bath instead," I'd say. "Or a swing set?" But when she was out I'd walk up and admire them, especially the woman mannequin, whose exaggerated beauty impressed me. Her Icelandic eyes were the pure blue of glass cleaner, and her feathery eyelashes were long and blonde to match her wig. Her lips were as fat as a Pink Pearl, and she had the kind of anglo-goddess nose that Dad would admire on celebrities and celebrity look-alikes – "Look at that Jessica Lange nose!" he'd say. My nose had just got to the point where it would never be cute again, so I saw her as a wish fulfillment packed into twenty pounds of plaster. But every time I looked at the child mannequin, I worried that in a few years I would pass for her sister. She had the prankster face of Dennis the Menace, and her lips were thin and unkissable.

When Mom asked me why I was always glaring at the child mannequin, I lied and said it was because I had more freckles than she did.

Mom laughed. "Are you joking? People shell out big money for freckles in some countries. They line up and get under these sun beds. And it costs plenty. Remind me to show you a picture of those fake freckled people. You need to see it to believe it."

"Oh," I said. "Okay." I knew she didn't have a picture of people who had paid to get freckles. Mom told stories all the time, but some of them were made up. Sometimes she made them up to make me feel better. We were a seesaw. When I was down, she brought me up. When she was down, I brought her a glass of orange juice mixed with soda, her favourite drink.

When we finished washing the mannequins, we dressed them in the party clothes Mom took out of her bag. Then Mom gave me five dollars and told me to walk to the convenience store and buy some soda pop for my party. It was so hot that I changed into my bathing suit and a pair of shorts.

The convenience store was six blocks away, with two streets to cross and neither of them busy. While I walked past the thicket of lilac bushes at the foot of our street, their perfume sugary as maple syrup, I thought about my birthday present. A few weeks ago I'd left a catalogue picture of the Schwinn on the kitchen table for Mom and Dad's "information." I was only allowed out of the house by myself for half an hour at a time, which meant I could only get as far as the convenience store and back. If I had a bike, I'd be able to travel long distances and go to places like the grocery store, where I could buy shiny gold jewellery for a quarter from the plastic machine near the rental vacuum cleaners. But I couldn't be sure Mom and Dad had got the hint about the bike, though. In our family, you couldn't come right out and ask for what you wanted. Mom thought that was rude and against the spirit of gift giving, but I didn't understand why that was any worse than pretending to be ga-ga over a gift you really hated.

The bell chimed as I opened the door of the convenience store. Estelle Pomper, who had been in my grade five class last year, was standing in the candy aisle, using a pair of plastic tongs to load jelly feet into a paper bag. In the tongs was a jelly foot. I didn't have a sweet spot for Estelle Pomper. She'd told Jilly Rhodes, whose family went to the food bank, "Maybe you should quit eating the toothpaste and actually wash your teeth with it." That's how I knew Estelle was a lousy person.

"Hey, Bony," she called, "why're you wearing your bathing suit? Someone sue you for the clothes on your back?"

Estelle's parents were lawyers; she was always saying something about lawsuits. But all last year I kept hearing "lost suit," which made me think of Grandpa's dry cleaning carousel moving round and round, with just one lost suit on it.

"It's not a bathing suit," I mumbled, moving away from her and toward the pop bottles lined up underneath the flats of puffy white bread. I thought of telling Estelle that it was my birthday, but I didn't think she'd really care.

"Well, if it's not a bathing suit, what it is?" Estelle said behind me.

"It's a girdle of course!" I wouldn't be apologetic with girls like Estelle anymore. I would be bold. "What? You never heard of a girdle?" I didn't know what a girdle was exactly, only that every morning I watched Mom lie down on her bed and stretch one over her butt, and it was tight.

Estelle bit a candy ring off her necklace. "You need a reverse girdle," she said. "To give you an ass. If that's not invented, I'm going to go invent that."

I picked up two bottles, one Coke, one orange. "You should do that." I was desperate to think of a better comeback, so I stood there for a minute longer, but all I could come up with was "Who died and made you boss?" and that didn't really work here. So I just paid for my soda and left.

On my way home I tried to think of better comebacks. *You're so sad, you've got teapots coming out of your eyes.* No, didn't make any sense. *You're so dumb you were still carving your jack-o'-lantern at Christmas.* No. Not good. Too serious. When I got home, I put the soda in the fridge and went to my room to change. Every time our family came over, I had to wear clothes that made me look like Anne of Green Gables, even though they usually wore jeans or jogging pants. I wanted to wear my Indy 500 sweatpants and my St. Augustine T-shirt with the lucky dog bite out of the collar. Instead, I tied the sash of my grey flannel dress and fluffed the depressed princess sleeves.

"Come on," I said to the mirror. "Get pretty."

I slipped on my scuffed Mary Janes, snapped my fanny pack around my waist. Inside it I kept beautiful possessions: my scratch-and-sniff stickers, Lite-Brite pegs, and my house key. Downstairs, Mom was in the bathroom revolving herself in front of the mirror as if she were a hotel dessert carousel. She was wearing a green wrap-dress and her beige Dr. Scholl's sneakers with the bloated toes, which I called her Big Ugly Shoes. Her hair was fastened behind her ears with plastic tortoise-shell combs that matched her glasses.

"I don't know what happened. I looked totally different yesterday. Didn't I look different to you yesterday?" she said. "Now remember, if Grandpa gives you a gift that you saw him open at his birthday party, just smile and say thank you because your dad's side isn't well."

"I know."

"They're here," Mom said. Then quieter. "I can hear their cars."

▶

At the far end of the sundeck, the picnic table was laid out with delicacies of the Black Sea region and the frozen foods aisle of No Frills: spinach and feta triangles, moussaka, and pigs-in-blankets. My aunt Florence, Dad's sister, was sitting on a deck chair beside the table. My cousin, Hyman, was sitting on her knee, even though he was the same age as me. Grandpa was stretched out on a cushiony lawn chair with a newspaper over his face. I was playing hostess because Mom and Dad were probably off somewhere wrapping my present.

"You want me to make you a plate?" I said, pointing to the food. I knew Mom would feel insulted if no one touched it.

Hyman shifted on Florence's lap and made a sulky face as she raised her eyes from her magazine. She pulled at the waist of her romper. "No snacks for me, Lucy. You see how tight this is getting? I like it looser."

Florence was Mom's closest friend, but she wasn't like Mom at all. She was single, drove her ladybug car on the highway, and wasn't afraid of making left turns, even without an advance light. Once a year, she left Hyman with a babysitter and spent a week on the Mexican Riviera. She came back with photos of herself holding lime green margaritas and laughing against the arms of men whose faces the camera had cut off.

"She's my Other," Mom would say. "Florence is the butterfly and I am the caterpillar in the cocoon. Or the underground worm."

It broke me when she said this. "If you're a worm, I'll call you Slouchie and build you a dirt castle in the backyard."

"Thank you," she'd say. "Thank you."

When nobody was watching me, I grabbed a handful of the cheese cubes and dropped them into my fanny pack. That way, Mom would think people had eaten and Charlie Sheen could have a banquet later. I couldn't bring Charlie Sheen out when Florence came over because she was convinced that he was a rat no matter how many times I tried to tell her he was a Chinese dwarf hamster and there was a difference.

Florence squeaked forward in her chair. "Lucy, could you get your grandpa some soda water? He's schvitzing."

I was glad to have an excuse to get off the sundeck. I was already tired of being the hostess and my party was only thirty minutes old. I walked across the deck and was about to open the door to the kitchen when I saw Mom and Dad through the glass. Mom was standing behind the kitchen table wearing oven mitts and holding a cake pan. The top of the cake was brown, almost burnt, and instead of icing there were only raisins, which reminded me of Charlie Sheen poop. Mom's cheeks were pink and she kept biting her lips and blinking hard. Dad was slumped in my chair and picking at his nails, what he did when he was anxious. Then he got up, and I could tell he was upset by the way he started talking with his hands. Mom began to cry, her shoulders shaking.

I took my hand off the doorknob. I couldn't believe they were fighting at my party.

I turned around and marched down the sundeck steps into Dad's garden, stood on my toes, and glared at all the daisies, measuring them with my eyes. When I found the tallest one, yellow with a flower the size of a yo-yo, I didn't even check behind me before I grabbed it and lopped its head off. I was ready to knock off another one, but then I remembered my present. On my Schwinn, I would ride away whenever Mom and Dad fought. I would ride for a full half-hour wearing all the gold jewellery I bought from the machines at the grocery store, and when people waved at me, I'd do a beauty queen wave back, with my fingers closed and my hand cupped like I was holding a lemon. That was my birthday wish. Big, but not impossible.

When Mom carried out my cake, I stared down the eleven candles plus one for good luck, squeezed my eyes shut, and pictured the pink icing spelling out my name across my dream cake. I imagined myself on a mini Schwinn leaping over the flames as I blew the last candle out as hard as I could.

Hyman wrinkled his nose. "You slobbered all over the cake."

When it was time for me to open my presents, Mom made me sit on the edge of a lawn chair in the centre of the deck so everybody could watch. She didn't look sad anymore, but the corners of her eyes were still red. I opened the gifts from Florence and Grandpa – a set of satin-covered clothes hangers and two library-discard copies of *OWL* magazine – and smiled until my cheeks were sore.

Then Mom handed me a box wrapped in plain white paper. I waited for Dad to get up and go down the steps so he could bring out my real present from underneath the sundeck, but he stayed planted in his chair. "Dad, don't you need to go somewhere?"

"Where would he go?" Mom said, frowning. "It's your birthday party."

I shook the box. Faintly, I heard the sound of spinning wheels. Maybe they'd got me one of those foldup bikes? Still, did they fold up this small?

I tore off the paper in strips. The box underneath was a shade of yellow that always made me think of a time machine because it was a yellow that probably started off being white. The box was taped shut. The backyard was so quiet all I could hear was the hissing of the sprinkler on our neighbour's lawn.

"You said you wanted to be independent . . ." Mom said. "So go ahead, Lucy. Don't keep us in suspense."

I lifted off the lid. Inside the box, surrounded by balls of scrunched-up newspaper, was a pair of scuffed metal roller skates. I kept staring at them, waiting for them to change into something else. I looked up at Mom to see if this was a joke. She was smiling at me. "They have an adjustable footbed. So you can use them for a long time!"

"When I was young," Dad said, "I wanted my own set of wheels too."

"Well?" Florence said. "Try them on. We'll all go to the road and watch you."

But I don't know how to roller skate, I wanted to say. But everyone, even Grandpa, had shuffled out of their chairs.

Although I had an audience for the first time in my life, I had no clue what I was doing. I sat on the end of the driveway and jammed my feet into the skates. I buckled the straps around my ankles, stood, and wobbled five steps forward. Our street looked a hundred miles long. I held my arms out on either side of me and clopped forward a couple of feet. I wouldn't let anyone see me fall. I took a few more steps, then a couple more. When I was ten feet away from the driveway, I looked back. Mom was waving at me. Grandpa was dozing against Florence's car. Dad was busy combing the ferns that grew around the maple in the front yard. Hyman stuck out his tongue and clapped his hands together very slowly, as if he were a mechanical tin monkey. I waved and then I kept going.

I wasn't really skating – it was more a combination of walking and trotting – but I pretended I was skating faster than the speed skaters I'd seen on TV. I passed the lilac bushes at the end of our street and said, "Goodbye, lilacs." I skated past the houses on the next five blocks and said, "Goodbye, neighbours." When I reached the convenience store, I stopped. I was panting and swaying like a weeping willow, so I leaned over until my hair flew in front of my eyes. Then I rolled myself up slowly until I was looking up at the sky. There was a cloud in the shape of a bicycle, and I used my finger to spin one of its wheels until the sun shone through it.

I had never gone farther than the convenience store on my own. Six blocks ahead of me was the grocery store. I could keep going. If I made it there, I would jump the sidewalk, speed skate through the main doors, and slide a quarter into the jewellery machine. The machine would malfunction and a hundred plastic bubbles filled with beautiful gold jewellery would pour out. Then I'd put it all on and do eleven victory laps around the cars in the parking lot. Only I had been gone for a long time. Mom might worry that terrible things had happened. She might think I was lost or that I'd fallen on the sidewalk and cracked my head open like a melon. I didn't want her to worry.

I looked down the street again. It seemed so much longer now than it had before. I turned around and made my way back home.

2

Every Friday night Dad took Mom and me to visit Grandpa, a twenty-six-mile trip up Bathurst Street. We'd drive past Pearl's Glatt Hutt, where butchers the colour of slow-cooked brisket gathered outside on the sidewalk to smoke and gaze out onto the road. Past Brooklyn Furniture, which had had the same bedroom set in its display window for as long as I could remember, the head-board padded in red leather like a barstool. Past Isadora's Wigs and Electrolysis, with its neon sign of a single strand of hair like some-thing out of our fifth-grade sex ed slide show. As usual, at the halfway point of the trip, Dad pulled into the parking lot of the Sea Dragon Chinese Restaurant Plaza, across from the video arcade with its giant clown-head sign, the great mouth open dentist-wide with laughter. In the sign's shadow, a group of teenagers was sitting on the rain-slick bike racks, smoking. I could tell they were smoking marijuana because of the way they held their breath after they inhaled, as if it was something precious.

"Hoodlums," Dad said. "Wasting time."

Mom closed her calorie counter booklet and slipped it back into her purse. When her hand came up again it was holding a lemon Danish wrapped in a diet bread bag. "Relax, Frank, at least they're having fun," she said. "That's what kids are supposed to do. That's what you were doing when you were young."

It was hard for me to imagine Dad young, without his grey moustache or the bald spot at the back of his head. Or his adult-man habits, like how he was already sealed inside his enormous brown parka, its massive fur hood framing his head, even though it was only October. He wore the parka for six months of the year like a uniform. When he finally stored it away at the end of March, he looked shrunken. Through the bird-shit-streaked window, I watched him bending down to inspect the flowers outside of Sue's Blooms. Mom and I knew it would always be the $2.99 special, the five white and red carnations, blooms closed up like tiny fists. They were the flowers you buy for someone you don't know very well, or don't need to impress.

"Sixteen years," Mom said, flipping down the sun visor so she could check her lips in the mirror. "For sixteen years I have watched him buy the same cheap flowers."

"It doesn't matter if the flowers are cheap," I said. "Grandpa hates flowers."

"But I love flowers," Mom said. "And he buys me the same kind."

The carnations Dad bought would sit in a Mason jar on Grandpa's kitchen table until the following week, when we returned to find them stinking and brown, the stems wrapped in threads of cottony white mould. Although we spent longer driving to Grandpa's apartment than we did in it, this was our only regular outing as a family, and lately I'd started to worry that, just like the flowers, it wouldn't last.

Dad came back to the car and passed me the cone of carnations wrapped in silver foil. At the same time, Mom handed me a tissue. "Your face is bleeding a bit," she said.

Dad pushed the key into the ignition. "You shouldn't pick at those pimples unless you want to get all pockmarked," he said. "Things heal if you just leave them alone."

As we drove, I fastened my eyes on my ALF shoelaces, on his cartoon smile, as wide as the smile of the woman who turned the letters on *Wheel of Fortune*. My plan was to look like her by the time I turned sixteen, but even though I had five more years to go I was kind of losing hope. "She's pretty, sure. But people make too much of pretty," Mom always said. Then she'd use the horrible C-word. "You shouldn't compare yourself, Lucy. Better to have a face like yours, with lots of character."

When I took the tissue away from my face, it was freckled with blood. But I knew the truth about just leaving things alone. It just made them worse. I tied my shoelaces in big floppy loops. Then I untied them and tied them again.

"Oh, I almost forgot," Mom said, removing a plastic sleeve of photographs from her purse. "Lucy had photo day."

She held up the 5x7, the wallet-sized, the magnetized tree decoration, the glossy 8x10, all of me in the Salvation Army cowboy shirt with my bangs parted sideways across my forehead, greased and hardened like chow mein. I knew I'd used too much gel because while I was combing my hair in the photo lineup, Estelle Pomper, who had a perfect French braid, had sidled up next to me and said, "Hey, Bony, quit fixing yourself up. It won't make a difference." I'd been dreaming about pulling on her braid like it was a chain attached to one of those old-fashioned toilets we saw at the historical home

— I'd use her perfect braid to flush her down the toilet — when the photographer told me to say "pepperoni" seconds before the flash went off. I'd felt my loose tooth edging out between my lips.

Mom pulled the photo order form from the plastic sleeve and checked off the "no, thank you" box. "Those photo men are robbers," she said, pushing up her glasses. "Dad can take better photos of you in the backyard. Near the mannequins or by the tomato patch. We can even get you a special outfit. You're getting too old to wear funny tops." She turned around and her eyes passed over my T-shirt. "What is that thing anyway? A schnauzer?"

Underneath my unzipped jacket, I was wearing the official ALF from Melmac T-shirt: sprouting from the top of ALF's snouty alien head was a tuft of auburn hair, and shiny drops of black paint filled his human-like eyes. *ALF* was my favourite television show in the history of TV and me. It was on every Monday night and I never missed an episode.

"With a neck like yours," Mom continued, "you'd make Audrey Hepburn jealous. You ought to wear keyhole-neck sweaters. And if I had your long legs I would show them off. Even before you were born, my legs were shaped like guitars."

I didn't know who Audrey Hepburn was. I thought she was maybe another teacher from Mom's school who never did enough work and broke pencil nibs and let the geraniums die over the Christmas break.

Dad cleared his throat. "I was really lanky when I was your age too," he said. "And if you want to see a dermatologist, you can."

I pretended I didn't hear him and rearranged the tomatoes inside the green plastic bag beside me. Every week we brought Grandpa tomatoes from our garden patch. "Grandpa must be tired of these," I said. "I think we should bring him something exotic. Like an avocado."

"Not an avocado," Mom said. "It would just scare him."

"She's right," Dad said. "Tomatoes are the best gift you can give him." He pumped the steering wheel emphatically. "You know why that is?"

I knew he was about to tell me. It was the same story every week.

"Your grandfather, he is not a normal man," Dad said, "and I should know. I'm the one who grew up like an orphan. While all the fathers were taking their sons to carnivals, to baseball games, and on fishing trips to Muskoka, do you know where I was? I was in the basement of a dry cleaning shop, listening to him tell me how he survived the Holocaust by hiding in a feed bin. Listening to his goddamn stories while the other boys met girls and got good tans."

Mom reclined her chair back and shut her eyes. "Don't forget to tell her how you would've been a famous art photographer if your father had loved you more."

Dad made a noise with his mouth like he was spitting out an olive pit. Then he knocked his hand against the dashboard. "Lucy. Your grandfather would say to me, 'What do you think the air is like in a box meant for barley?' And if I didn't get it right he would tell me the story again. So now I'll ask you the same. What was the air like in a box meant for barley?"

Dad would always get confused partway through his story. It would start off as a rant on how the old man had held him back, and then it would turn into a defence of him. "When your grandfather finally climbed out of that cavity," he continued, letting go of the wheel, "his skin was green from hunger." *And each of his legs was the circumference of a maypole.* "Are you listening? Each of his legs was the circumference of a maypole. Okay? Just picture that. Now. When you think of not loving that old man, think about what I just told you."

▬

At Grandpa's building, Dad parked the car under a weeping willow and rolled up his window, turning the lever until I heard the sound of it jamming against plastic. He was afraid that someone would steal his car by sticking their arm through an inch of opened window, some spaghetti-armed criminal with a thing for 1987 dusty rose Corollas. Dad always worried about losing property. That's why he didn't like me staying home alone for more than twenty minutes at a time. He thought I'd get hungry, turn the stove on, and burn our house down. "But I don't cook," I told him. "Still," he said, "it only takes one mistake, one little screw-up, and there goes your entire life."

We moved in single file across the parking lot, Mom carrying the carnations and the three No Frills bags, and me following behind with the tomatoes. Dad walked ahead of both of us, swinging another green plastic bag filled with three jars of jam, the kind that were two for a dollar – quince and pineapple flavoured. At home, the only way I could get it down was if I pretended I were in prison. I ran a few steps ahead to walk alongside Dad and held out my hand.

"Let me give the jam to Grandpa," I said. "Let me hold the bag."

"You'll drop it." Then to Mom he said, "Joy, you know she drops things."

"I can do it."

"Frank, let her hold it," Mom said. "Don't deny her everything."

Dad gave me the bag as we entered the lobby vestibule. I picked up the phone, which smelled like dog food, and dialled Grandpa's extension. He answered as if he'd just woken up from a terrible dream, his voice quavering.

"Grandpa, it's Lucy. We're down here. Waiting for you to press seven. And buzz us in. Press seven, Grandpa."

Nothing.

"Grandaddy, press seven. Number seven."

I could still hear the door buzzing as we walked into the lobby. On the coffee table was a copy of the *Great Hadassah Wizo Cookbook* and old issues of *Chatelaine*. Since it was Friday night, only one elevator was in full service. While Dad and I waited by the elevators, Mom went to sit on the crushed velvet couch to rest her feet and change her shoes. She took off her Big Ugly Shoes and put on her one-inch heels with the red bows on the toes, her Lady Shoes.

"Your doctor said if you lost thirty pounds your feet wouldn't hurt," Dad said.

"I like cheeseburgers," Mom yelled back. "So screw you."

When the elevator doors opened, standing inside was a skinny woman wearing a tight denim jacket and tapered jeans. The rosy scent of Charlie perfume wafted out at us. My eyes travelled across her body and settled on her feet. Her high heels were grape-gum purple and I could see the tops of her toes. *The cleavage of her toes?* Then I turned to Dad. He was staring at this woman with the bleach-blonde hair, staring past the sapphire eyes of the broncos embroidered onto her jacket and at the pointy tips of her breasts.

A funny thing happened then. My hand went slack and I dropped the bag of jam. The woman walked out of the elevator, and her heels made powerful noises on the marble as she passed us. I heard the sound of breaking glass after, when Mom came to stand beside us, before stepping over the glass and into the elevator.

"It's okay, Lucy," she said. But I didn't think it was because behind her foggy glasses her eyes were two pieces of charcoal. Then she turned to Dad. "Don't just stand there, Frank. Get the janitor and tell him."

The elevator doors closed. Mom was gone. The woman had left too, but her perfume still hung over us. Dad was staring at the lobby doors. A draft had come in. Finally, he turned his attention back to me. "Jam is expensive," he said, sounding very disappointed. "You can't just toss it around like that."

The door to Grandpa's apartment was unlocked, and when we went in, the first thing we saw was Mom sorting through Grandpa's mail at the kitchen table with a Mickey Mouse coffee mug beside her. Wax was sliding down the red Sabbath candles.

"Where is he?" Dad said. His voice was all soft now, so I could tell he was trying to make up for the losing-weight comment. Grandpa's apartment was a no-fight zone.

Mom pointed down the hall and then she went back to sorting the mail. She didn't even ask me to sit with her. Usually I got to drink one sip of coffee.

Dad hung my coat in the closet but kept his own parka on. He never took his parka off when we visited Grandpa because it was his insurance that he could leave soon. We found Grandpa in the laundry room. He was bent over behind the washing machine, hiding bananas in a crawl space, but as usual he was doing it in style. He was wearing a pair of salmon-coloured pants, a white snake-skin belt, and a mint sport jersey. Except for the faded numbers tattooed on the inside of his forearm, he looked like the kind of gin-and-tonic-sipping country club members I recognized from watching *Dallas* and *Dynasty* with Mom.

"Oh, is you," he said, casually dropping a bunch of bananas on top of a box of detergent. "Joy's in the kigzen and I already tell her, 'I ate dinner.' So I've gut nuttin for you."

"*We're* not hungry," Dad said. I could tell he already wanted to leave because the vein in his forehead was bulging out. "We're here to help *you*."

Grandpa followed us back up the hall into the kitchen. On the counter were canisters holding rice, beans, and pasta from when my grandmother was alive. Nothing had been moved, or removed, from this place since she died five years ago. Even her plastic pillbox still sat on top of the microwave. Masking-tape strips labelled *Kigzen* and *Offal* and other words that I didn't understand were stuck to the heating vent, the breadbox, and the fridge. Once I'd asked Dad if the words were Yiddish. "Not Yiddish," he'd said, "just Gibberish."

Mom was still going through Grandpa's mail, making piles of bills, flyers with good deals, and garbage. She hadn't said a word since we came in, and I hated the silence. It made me feel as if Mom and Dad were standing on opposite sides of a volcano. To keep it from erupting, I got up and switched on the television that sat on a shelf to the side of the kitchen table, above Grandpa's black trundle sewing machine. Draped all over the machine were pairs of pants. Even though Grandpa had closed down his dry cleaning business years ago, he still took in clothes for alterations from people in his building. Survivors got half-price.

Geraldo's handsome face filled the TV screen, but his moustache was a dirty green and his skin the drained yellow of an old egg. "Hey, Grandpa, I think you need a new tube for this thing." Grandpa ignored me and padded to the table.

Dad pulled a bunch of shallots and a sack of potatoes from a No Frills bag. "See," he said, "plenty of everything. I even got you the long tomatoes you like. The expensive ones you like to eat on cheese sandwiches."

Grandpa opened the cabinet under the sink and yanked out a bag of tomatoes. Usually he only hid cereal or bread, not perishables, so I figured this was a bad sign. Through the plastic, I could see the dark red skin spotted with white nubs of mould.

"I had tomatoes," Grandpa said, and then he went to spit in the sink.

"Okay. So now you have more," Dad said. He looked to Mom for help, but she was staring at her Mickey Mouse mug. "No big one. You should keep them in a bowl where you can see them. That way they won't rot."

"I had plenty of tomatoes," Grandpa repeated. He took a tomato out of the bag and pressed its mould-pimpled skin to his nose. "This tomato is a piece of gold," he said, biting into it like it was an apple. I concentrated on tying and untying my shoelaces, but I still heard the sound of juice squirting.

When I looked up, Mom was holding a napkin out to Grandpa. "You've got something on your face, Sol. Wipe it." It was the first thing she'd said since the elevator.

Grandpa ran the napkin over his face without effort, as if it were a feather duster.

Dad picked at his nails. "You like your flowers?" he said, trying to change the subject.

Grandpa stared at the television, transfixed by the animated Mr. Clean flying across the kitchen in a yellow flash of light.

"Dad?"

Mom brought her coffee mug down on the table hard. I untied my shoelaces.

"Of course he doesn't like his flowers. You've given him the same ones every week for the sixteen years I've known you."

I knotted my shoelaces twice, three times, four times, until there was nothing left to hold on to.

"Well, maybe he appreciates the gesture, Joy. Not everyone goes around checking price tags like you do, adding up all the good and bad in a ledger to see what the final tally is –" Dad stopped. "And there's nothing wrong with coronations."

"They're carnations," I said quietly. "He's not Queen Elizabeth." I stared at the canisters on the counter and thought of how when my grandmother was alive there'd be chicken soup and liver dumplings and enormous turkey thighs that Dad devoured in a way that made him look like Fred Flintstone eating the choicest brontosaurus cut.

When my grandmother was alive, these visits reminded us that we were a family instead of four paper dolls held together with glue.

Mom stood up and moved out from behind the table. "Maybe he just wishes your gestures didn't look so – so cheap. And that you would for once take off your coat!"

She strode out of the kitchen, and I imagined her going to the living room and calling a lawyer the way I'd once seen a woman do on *Dallas*, pressing her lips into the receiver and muttering, "Send that jerk the papers." Dad began collecting the empty No Frills bags, balling them up, then he looked at me and nodded – the cue that we were leaving. But I didn't want to leave. Not while they were still fighting. I turned to Grandpa. He was staring at the box of Betty Crocker cake mix that sat on the table and running his index finger along the side.

"Who's that?" Grandpa asked.

"Who's who?" Dad said. His voice was quiet but edgy, like it was squeezing through the thin spaces between his clenched teeth.

"That woman." Grandpa pointed to the tiny oval picture of Betty Crocker on the front of the box.

"That's the woman who makes the mix," Dad said. "Who makes the recipes."

I switched off the television and went into the front hallway to get my coat from the closet. In the mirror, I watched them stare at the cake mix like it was this valuable family heirloom.

"She's beautiful," Grandpa said.

"She is beautiful," Dad agreed. "Too bad she's not a blonde. Blonde girls just have a certain quality to them. It can't be denied."

Mom came out of the bathroom and her eyes looked red. She took her black suede coat out of the closet, and I watched as she sucked in her stomach to get the waist button done up. Mom never wanted to buy the next size up, which would've meant that she was a plus size.

"Don't laugh," she said. But I wasn't laughing. "You try having a baby and fitting into your old things, Miss Make-Me-Fat." She opened her coat and pulled down the waistband of her skirt. The scar the size and shape of a white worm squirmed in a loopy line down her stomach. "Or should I call you Miss Give-Me-Scars?" She closed her coat and kissed the top of my head. "I don't want to talk to your father now," she said. "Get him and tell him that I want to leave."

When we were all standing in the doorway with our hands shoved into our pockets, the sound of hunger gurgling upward from our stomachs, Grandpa pushed past us to open the door. He cleared his throat. "Is a shame," he started to say before Mom put her hands over my ears. I wiggled out from underneath them.

"Is a shame for a girl to see her parents acting like children –"

"Dad, you don't need to tell –"

Grandpa cut him off. "Be a mensch," he said. "Be a man. Is a shame. Now go, and I see you next time."

When we got home, Dad slapped the house keys into Mom's open palm, his keychain fat with its rainbow of AA tags. Mom never brought her own keys when she went out with Dad.

"I need some air," Dad said. "I'm going for a walk."

"Okay," Mom said. "So see you in six hours."

"Your keys," I wanted to say, but he was already walking down the steps, his fur hood bobbing up and down away from us.

Dad came home long after Mom had gone to bed. She hadn't left the lights on so I was sitting in the dark, between the stair railings, listening to Dad clunk around blindly. Even in the dark, I could make out the silvery ALF keychain dangling from his hand. I'd left my key under the *Welcome* mat for him twice before: once, last year, when Dad had come home late two nights in a row and Mom had locked him out; then again, three weeks ago, when he wouldn't answer "any more of her questions" and he'd walked out after dinner. He hadn't come home until after midnight then either. I heard the closet door open and close, and then the sound of his parka thumping to the floor. I stared down at him, my hands pressed into a pile of jacks. I'd lost the ball in a sewer hole during the summer, but I was beginning to think it was a waste-of-time kind of game anyway.

I called down to him through the railings. "Dad?"

He turned around and grabbed the door frame to keep from swaying. His shoulders looked stiff, and although his mouth was open slightly, he wasn't taking in any breaths at all.

"Where did you go, Dad?"

His shoulders fell. "Why are you still up?"

"Where did you go?" I repeated. I wanted him to go to the closet and take out a can of tomato soup from his coat pocket because he'd been clearing his head by walking through the 24-hour grocery. Or better, tell me that he had one of those midnight psychiatrists that I'd once seen in a movie, who charged a lot and lit the whole place with candles. Anything so I could feel he wasn't staying away from us on purpose.

"I went walking," Dad said. "Don't you ever go walking?"

I squinted down at him, at his dry moustache, his white, warm cheeks. "Are you drunk?"

"No," he answered. "Are you?"

I wouldn't let him make a joke now. "I don't believe you were walking," I said. "It's too cold to just go for a walk."

"Yeah," he agreed. "It is."

The next morning at breakfast, I came downstairs wearing two watches to be funny. One was an ALF watch and the other was a broken hand-me-down Swatch from Florence. Mom was standing in the doorway of the laundry room, holding up a dented box of muesli cereal that looked yellowy, faded by the sun. "You know where I found this?" she said to me. "This is from the Seventies, I swear to you. Look at the girl on the box. No one irons their hair like that anymore."

I didn't say anything. I just went to the freezer and pulled out a cello-wrapped package of smoked meat and a jar of mustard. I was going to make sandwiches until they stopped arguing, even if it meant making a hundred sandwiches. I would use all the bread in the fridge.

"I found this cereal behind the dryer."

Dad was reading the *Star* at the kitchen table, and his cheeks were spotted with one, two, three bits of toilet paper stuck to shaving cuts. I slathered goopy yellow mustard on my first sandwich and looked down at my sneakers, at ALF's face staring up at me, and took a deep breath. I heard the sound of Mom slamming the cereal box down on the table.

"I'm reading!" Dad said.

"You're hiding food again. Just like your father."

"I was storing it there. Don't do this back and forth. You're free to eat anything you want." He set the newspaper down. "But you know what your doctor said." Two sandwiches, now I was on the third. I brought the knife down hard on the soft white bread, slicing it diagonally in one motion.

"Lucy," Mom called to me. "I want you to ask your father something now. I want you to ask him if he's cheap or if he just wants to starve me so I can look like one of his shiksa goddess fantasies."

"Lucy, don't ask me anything."

"Ask him."

Then they went upstairs to fight. But they weren't even using their heads because they left the door to their bedroom half open.

Out in the hallway, I crept in between the giant fronds of the Schefferella plant, where they couldn't see me, but I could see them. Mom was bathed in the tropical orange glow of her bedside lamp. In her hand was a rolled-up Sunquest Vacations catalogue, thrust out at Dad like a sword.

"You're a goddamn travel agent," Mom cried. "You book vacations for the entire city, so why don't you ever take me anywhere?"

Dad paced in front of their big brass bed. "I work. I go to meetings. What else do you want from me?"

Mom made little choking noises. "I want to go places!"

"Okay, I've heard this before. You want to go away. You think you'll go and discover yourself. Or meet someone more like yourself. I keep asking you, What is this person like?"

"Someone who . . ." Mom began and then she burst into tears.

I reached out and grabbed a hold of one of the big, spotted Schefferella leaves. Whenever Mom and Dad fought, I made war between the leaf splotches. If there were more light green splotches, my parents would stay together. If there were more dark green ones, they'd split apart. If I lost count, or started worrying about Charlie Sheen choking on sunflower seed shells in his cage, or Lulu choking on grass snakes in the backyard, I had to start counting again. Lately I was still counting the spots long after their fights had ended.

"Go places?" Dad said. He had stopped pacing. Now he stood in front of the curtains, wrapping the cord around his wrist. "Go all the places you want."

I lost count of the dark spots at 126. Then I took a deep breath and began again. My heart was pounding so hard the sound of it seemed to be coming out of the walls.

"I will. I am," Mom said. "I will show you that I can do things by myself. That I don't need you to live. I'm going to register for a cake-decorating class at the community centre starting in two weeks. I'll be there on Monday nights from now on. I will not," she sniffled, "become dependent on you."

Dad shook his hand free of the curtain cord and pulled on it. The long white curtains parted and white sunshine flooded the room. "Not Mondays. That's the meeting I like in Rosedale. I can't miss it. No way. You have to be here with Lucy and anyway, Monday's the night she watches that ALF thing on TV."

"I'm going to the class. I am going. You can go to some other meeting, on some other night. It doesn't matter anyway. Same church basement, same old speeches." She wiped her eyes. "I am going. Lucy can stay home alone. She's not two years old."

Dad lowered his voice. "Listen to me now, I don't want her home alone. She'll burn the house down or worse." They stood with their arms hanging slackly, their faces the grey colour of lifetime coal miners.

I finished counting the spots. There were more dark green ones than light ones. Terrible things were going to happen.

I went downstairs. The foyer near the front door was covered in fake marble tiles. One day, after my parents had been fighting for a long time, I had this urge to go there and count the tiles. I didn't want to, but my legs just carried me down the stairs. There were twenty-seven whole tiles plus six halves, and quarters. Then I had the idea to walk on the tiles in a special pattern. I put one foot on a tile stained with a dark blob shaped like Canada and the other foot on the tile marked with a scuff the shape of Japan until I had covered every blob nation once. If I did that every morning, keeping my mind absolutely clear, things might not get broken.

I stepped around the marble tiles, but still the worries swirled in my head. What if the next time Charlie Sheen was rolling around in his plastic ball, the door came off? What if he ran out and died in an air vent? I'd be ruined. Everything could be broken. Charlie Sheen would get caught in the spokes of his wheel or choke on a sunflower seed shell and die gasping, his tiny heart-shaped mouth hanging open. And when she went outside, Lulu would park herself under some car and not even notice when the wheels started rolling over her. Everything would be broken. They were going to split up. I would be to blame. I, Bony the Bug Eyes, I, Miss Give-Me Scars, was to blame.

When I looked up, Mom was standing above me. "Are you doing calisthenics?" she said. "That's so healthy."

"Lucy!" Dad called from the kitchen. "You're going to be coming with me to my meeting on Monday nights. Your mother is now going places."

3

It was Monday night. Usually I would have been downstairs with Mom, propped up on three pillows in front of the television, drinking a glass of chocolate milk with the spiral straw I used in every drink – sometimes I tasted apple juice in my milk, sometimes milk in my water. But now Mom was at the community centre learning about how to make pink sponge cake and something called chiffon icing, and I was in the upstairs bathroom with Dad, watching him run a mini comb through his moustache. He was wearing what I liked to call his hunting scene sweater, with its design of two deer knocking their antlers together and a couple of leather almonds sewn onto each sleeve. Dad splashed Jovan cologne on his neck, then lifted his sweater and daubed some on his stomach. I looked out the window, down at the rotting tomato patch and the three mannequins leaning against the back fence. Now that Mom was going places, there was nobody to wash the mannequins, and I was worried they'd get covered in dirt and spiderwebs. If ALF from the planet Melmac were here, he wouldn't let the mannequins be neglected like that.

Last week I'd written a letter to Mom and Dad about ALF. I wrote about how ALF's spaceship had crashed into the Tanner family's house in California, and how this lonely little alien, some might even say an ugly one, found a mission on Earth: he made Kate and Willy Tanner love each other again. Because before ALF arrived, they fought all the time. *I love ALF because no one expects him to make a difference. I love ALF because when he sees a problem that needs to get solved, he takes responsibility. So please let me stay home alone. Don't worry, Dad, I won't turn on the stove.* When I finished writing the letter, I slipped it under Mom and Dad's bedroom door, but no one mentioned it the next morning.

"Lucy?" Dad was holding a pair of gold-plated scissors from his moustache-comb set. Mom and I had bought it for him three years ago for Chanukah. At first, he'd thought it was gross. "Who uses used scissors? Who knows where these have been?" Then Mom sterilized them in boiling water and he stopped complaining. "I need you to trim my sideburns."

Dad sat on the lid of the toilet seat as I carefully clipped the tiny white hairs from his earlobes and straightened his sideburns. He drummed his fingers against the knees of his corduroys. I stood back to check my handiwork.

Quietly I said, "Do you always get this excited before a meeting?"

He jerked his head. "Why are you asking that? Did Mom tell you to ask me that?"

"She didn't tell me anything. I can see it for myself."

"Well, I'm not excited. That's the totally wrong word. I antici-pate these meetings. Like you anticipate your show. Mom doesn't understand the program and how hard it is to take it one day at a time. Your mother sees things in black and white only. Do you know what that means?"

I cut another curl from the back of his head. Cutting his hair made me feel like I was removing the lousy parts of him, the ones that made him come home late and have to go to these meetings, or think blonde girls were the chosen creatures on earth.

"It means you don't like her. That you don't think she under-stands you. That you don't want to take her on vacation."

Dad checked his reflection in the bathroom mirror, wetting his fingertips to smooth out his sideburns. "I would love to tell you it was that simple." Then he got up and turned to the window. "That garden. It's festering. I'm going to need your help with it soon."

We were in the car ten minutes later, listening to Dad's favourite station, which played oldies all the time. One song was about a boy who walks along the railroad tracks and dies trying to rescue his sweetheart's ring. The next one was about a guy who needs to wait until September to see his baby again. Another guy can't see a thing. Smoke gets in his eyes.

When we pulled into the church parking lot, Dad killed the engine and put his hand on the top of my head. "It won't be so bad. There's lots of kids there and you can do puzzles and play games."

"Is there a TV?"

"No," Dad said, taking my hand, something he hardly ever did. "But there's a cat."

But there wasn't. When we got down to the basement, there were just a dozen empty chairs set up in a large oval, and a buzzing light bulb dangling overhead. At the far end of the room was a stage with a set of steps on wheels in front of it. To the right of the stage was a table with a coffee urn and a few plates of cookies. The only time I got to drink coffee was at Grandpa's house, from Mom's Mickey Mouse mug, so I wanted to get myself a full cup here. I'd put tons of sugar in it too. I tried to pull Dad toward the refreshments table, but his hand suddenly went stiff.

"I'm thirsty," I said, tugging on his arm. "Please, can we go get something to drink?" When I looked up at him, his forehead was all wrinkled, the way it got when people cut him off in traffic. He wasn't listening to me. He was staring at the two men and the woman who were standing beside the refreshments table. The men were tall and stood on either side of the woman, their bodies angled toward her as if they were protecting her from the wind. She was thin and blonde, and while she spoke, her hands stayed on her hips in the authoritative pose of the ladies on the covers of Mom's exercise tapes. Her calves were little twigs, her feet tucked into blue plastic heels. Dad's face was glowing with an expression I'd never seen before: he looked *interested*. The woman's hands flew around like tiny confetti bits as she talked. Then one of the men must have made a joke, because she laughed, throwing her head back and then rolling forward until she was bent at the waist, her whole body rocking like a crashing wave. I let go of Dad's hand and moved a few steps closer to them so I could hear what was so funny.

"Ken, you don't have to worry about that. Just be straight with her from your gut. Or if you're still stuck, you can always go with flowers. Go big. Hydrangeas maybe. If you come into the store, I'll help you pick something out. Give you the wholesale rate. How's that?" She stuck out her tiny right hand and the man held it, kept holding it, even after she tried twice to wriggle her hand free. Finally, she stood on her tippy-toes and patted the man first on the side of his arm, and then on his shoulder, so she was kind of pushing him away, but gently. "Good, Ken," she said softly. "You're good."

When she went over to the refreshments table, Dad put his hand on my shoulder. "You want some water before it starts?"

"That's what I've been trying to tell you."

He didn't answer me. He just took my hand again and pulled me over to where Crashing Wave was standing. She was stacking pamphlets beside the paper plate of cherry crème cookies, and when she saw us, she came forward and patted Dad on the back as softly as she'd patted the other man, only her hand stayed on Dad's shoulder, spread open like a tiny starfish.

"Hi, Frank," she said.

"Evening, Alicia," Dad said. "This is my little one, Lucy."

I couldn't stop watching her hand, the nail polish at the tips of her fingers as red as the ends of matches. Then her hand dropped away, and when I looked up she had turned her eyes on me.

"Look at you," she said, her voice husky like a tiny engine, "and here I was imagining you as a little kid. But now that you're in front of me, I'm gonna bet you're at least twelve and a half."

"I'm eleven," I said. Then I remembered. "And a half. How old are you?"

Crashing Wave laughed, throwing her head back and then rocking forward again so her hair fell over her eyes. She pushed it away and looked to Dad, her large fleur-de-lys-shaped earrings tinkling. Then she grabbed a few cookies with a napkin and held them out to me. "Have a cookie," she said, winking. "You and me, we've got that natural Twiggy figure, so lucky for us we get to eat whatever we want. Oh, you're too young to know Twiggy probably. She was like Cindy Crawford when I was your age."

I could feel my cheeks burning red. Was she saying I was like Twiggy? And Twiggy was beautiful like Cindy Crawford? No, I had made some kind of mistake. Or she was making fun of me? I turned to Dad. He was picking at his nails again.

"No?" Crashing Wave pouted. "But they're so good."

"I'm on a diet," I said, pretending to be Mom. "But thanks anyway."

"You're funny. And I like your shoelaces too. My niece watches that show all the time. Come with me, sweetheart, I want to show you something."

Crashing Wave carried a plastic chair up to the stage and set it down for me before going to rummage through a basket of children's books. I could still smell her perfume, which made me think of green soap that you squeeze out of a bottle. When she turned around she handed me a book I'd already read. It was about a guy who cooks so much rice that it ends up filling his whole house and almost kills him. It smelled like pee.

"I know," she said, "you'd rather be somewhere with your friends. Or reading *Seventeen* magazine. And usually there are other kids here, I don't know what happened. And the cat, there used to be cat here, but he must have eaten a bad mouse or something . . . Hey, what about this –" She opened her purse and pulled out a silver tube of lipstick. "Why don't you have this?" she said, holding it out to me. "The colour would be good on you." She touched my ear. "New lipstick and now the best seat in the house. Not bad, Lucy Goose."

I felt special. I felt so special.

Crashing Wave left me on the stage, sitting on the plastic chair facing the assembling oval. People were pulling out chairs, sitting with their books opened in their laps. I was out of breath. Then I uncapped the lipstick and rolled it up – the smell of oil and caramel mixed. *Jason's Vitamin E Lipstick* was written in black loopy letters on the side of the tube. On the bottom of the tube was a tiny sticker: #472 Sweetheart. *Come with me, sweetheart. You look like Twiggy the model. The colour would be good on you.* Tomorrow I'd go to the library and say to the lady at the desk, "Hello, could you please tell me where I could find *Seventeen* magazine?" Because I look like Twiggy. I felt special.

The meeting began at exactly eight o'clock, just as the opening credits of *ALF* would've been flashing across the TV screen at home. I tried to ignore the sound of the group discussion, that oval of voices coughing or stumbling when they spoke, apologizing for not being able to find the right words.

"Sorry, folks. It's a tough November, this one."

"The way my boss won't quit stepping on my tail is a bitch —"

I stared at the guy in my book drowning in rice, drowning in his supper. Everyone knows half a cup is good for three people, or at least that's what Dad always said. I tried to catch Dad's eye. But he'd turned his chair toward Crashing Wave, who was sitting at the head of the oval.

Crashing Wave was the only person who wasn't slumped in her chair, but sitting upright, and unlike the other hands around the oval that scratched at knees, arms, elbows, scalps, hers stayed folded in her lap. This made me think she was the leader. When a guy in a green suit began stumbling over his words, he looked at her and she smiled back and mouthed, "Keep going." And when the heater in the corner started making a chugging noise, she was the one who got up and went over to give it a kick with her blue plastic heels so it would stop. Even though she had knobby knees and little wrinkles on either side of her mouth, she tossed her hair as she walked, not arrogantly, but as if she was used to people watching her. When it came time for her to share, I opened my ears wide.

"Hi, everyone," she began. "I'm Alicia and I'm an alcoholic."

"Hi, Alicia," said the oval.

"Hi," she repeated. "Thanks for coming out. Uh, well, probably a few of you know that tonight I get my medallion, one year, clean and sober, the big one —"

The guy in the green suit interrupted. "Keep coming back, Alicia."

"Thanks, Paul. Well, I don't have any big speech prepared. My mother's coming to town tomorrow, to celebrate, and I guess that's what's on my mind right now. I love my mother, but she's like an army of one."

I moved my chair to the very edge of the stage. Crashing Wave talked about how she had been trying to find something for her and her mother to do in the city. She finally settled on taking her to see a live taping of a local talk show, because that was the kind of thing she liked to do. "I asked my mother, 'Why do you want to be on TV so badly?' and she says, '*I* don't want to be on TV, I just think you're so beautiful that you ought to get of your shell more. You have grey hairs, Alicia.'"

The oval laughed, and some of the women rolled their eyes.

"Anyway, we'll go to the CN Tower and I'll buy us each a CN Tower snow globe because I love snow globes and then we'll eat in the revolving restaurant and talk about why I'm not married." Crashing Wave wiggled off her blue plastic heels. "My mother cleaned houses since she was seventeen and never bought herself anything that wasn't practical. I have to remember that when I get irritated. How hard she worked. Because I know how it feels to be running on empty. I know that now."

The oval murmured a series of "uh huhs" and "yeahs."

"Anyway, thanks for letting me share. I'm glad that I got to spend the last year with you. All of you."

The oval began to clap. Crashing Wave motioned for them to stop, but they didn't, so she joined in the clapping too.

When the meeting ended, Dad came up to the stage to get me and then we went to say goodbye to Crashing Wave. She was folding chairs with Ken, but when she saw that we were leaving, she stopped and came over to us.

"Happy anniversary," Dad said. "It's a good thing."

She nodded and raised her hand as high as her waist, like she was going to reach out and shake Dad's hand, but then she dropped it back to her side. "It was nice meeting you, Lucy. Twiggy Lucy."

Dad took my hand again and we walked toward the stairs. But when Dad and I reached the door, I pretended I needed to tie my shoelaces so I had an excuse to stop and turn around. I wanted to see Crashing Wave one more time. She was hugging a man in blue sweatpants, pulling him close to her, patting him on the back. Behind him, I saw four other people waiting. Nobody was talking. They were all watching Crashing Wave, just like I was. She made me think of a light bulb, the way everyone flew to her. It was her anniversary, and people should have been hugging her, comforting her. But she was hugging them.

In the car on the way home, I felt the tube of lipstick through my jeans pocket. I couldn't wait to try it on in front of the mirror. None of Dad's other friends had ever given me presents. "Your friend was nice," I said. "The lady with the snow globe. Who's going to the CN Tower."

Dad put on his windshield wipers and I watched them skid back and forth, leaving the flurry triangle at the bottom of the window. I wanted a snow globe for Chanukah now. When I got tired of shaking it around, I'd crack it open like an egg, but in the sink, and check if the white flakes were real snow or coconut. If they were coconut, I would eat them. "Dad? Do you like snow globes?"

He signalled and turned right onto a busy street clogged with cars, their white head lights twinkling. "I don't know about snow globes," Dad said. "I'm just glad she's got her medallion. This was her third try. She always fell off the wagon just short of twelve months. It happened three years in a row."

"Oh," I said, but I had no idea what wagon we were talking about.

The only wagon I knew was the one I rode on at the Chudleigh's apple farm. "Did you meet her on the wagon?"

"No, I met her a long time ago. She used to be a dancer. I took her photos at Glamour Shots."

Now I understood why she moved like that, with her whole body, every muscle alive like a cat. Maybe she was in Oklahoma. Estelle Pomper did musical theatre and tap and was always talking about Oklahoma.

"Where did she dance? A tap dance theatre?"

"No. Not like that. It was called The Right Spot. It used to be a cool place. Back when I still had hair." I'd never heard Dad using the word *cool* before. When I looked over at him, he was smiling.

"That's a weird name," I said. "It sounds like a bar."

"It's a men's bar. Alicia was a . . . well, men used to pay her to . . . they used to pay her to dance."

"Sick," I said. My lips trembled.

"Not sick. Alicia was the most beautiful dancer there. She wore a crown of laurels on her head, and a toga. Like a Greek goddess. I never went there, I mean, I never saw Alicia there. She wore her costume once when I took her photos. Lots of girls were trying to be models then."

All of a sudden I remembered the girl on the last page of the Glamour Shots album, laughing in her shiny-looking toga, the crown of laurels sitting lopsided on her head. *Lots of love, Allie.* It was Crashing Wave. I squeezed my eyes shut and saw her asking to borrow Dad's pen so she could sign her photo for him. *To Frank, lots of love.* "I thought she was sweet, but we came from different places," I heard Dad say. "We stayed on as good friends. I'm the one who helped her find the meeting. That's what a friend does. A friend helps and doesn't judge. Sometimes we all need a helping hand."

Later that night, I lay in bed holding Lulu against me, listening to Charlie Sheen running on his wheel so fiercely it was as if he were trying to drive it straight out of his cage. But behind that sound I kept hearing those voices at the meeting, chanting the serenity prayer, the voices rising up from the oval, clashing against the tinny sound of the wheel, turning and turning: *God*, I heard them say, followed by the long pause. *Grant me the serenity to accept the things I cannot change, the courage to change the things I can, and the wisdom to know the difference.* Just once, I'd heard the grunt of Dad's voice rising above the rest, throwing itself up high like a bird, straight up into the pipes that ran across the ceiling of that basement. The words were *cannot change*.

▶

Wednesday after school, Mom and I took a trip to the Salvation Army. I trolled after her as she pushed the cart, piling it high with "practical" items like military-style sweaters with sewn-in labels that read "Made Specially for You by Grandma," no-name purple jeans with Popsicle stains on the crotch, and some large floral vests. She had it in her head that vests were really "in." Mom wanted to buy me a new outfit so Dad could take photos of me in the backyard beside the tomato patch. Before it got too cold, she said, and all the plants died.

"But they're already dead," I told her. We passed the lamps section, where everything smelled burnt. "I can smell them stinking up to my window."

"That's the smell of regeneration," Mom said. "Next year, we'll have better tomatoes than ever."

I was installed in a musty little changeroom, where I pulled off my T-shirt and stared at myself in the tiny mirror affixed to the pipe on the wall. The big mirror was outside and Mom always made me come out so she could decide for herself if the clothes were "working or not." I channelled ALF from Melmac and transmitted a message: No sign of breasts. Please send immediately. Sincerely, Bony the Bug Eyes. Over and out.

"Lucy," Mom called through the curtain. "How's it going in there?"

"Okay, but I wish we could go to Zellers." I wanted to sit at the speckled Formica luncheonette counter at Zellers and get served a hot chicken sandwich with fries by one of the glamorous waitresses who wore frilly uniforms in a shade of pink that reminded me of watermelon bubblegum.

"Don't be spoiled. Some kids your age just wear shirts made from rat hair. When I was a kid in Bulgaria I wore a smock made from camel's ass. Not so pretty." Then, after a moment, Mom said, "Anyway, did you hear about the neighbour at seventeen? Her husband went out last week to get an attachment for their blender. He didn't come back that day, or the next. On day three, she gets a priority letter. Guess what it is?"

"Bad news?"

"Yes!" Her voice rose with excitement. "Exactly."

Mom loved shocking bad news, the reversals-of-fortune type that cheap tabloid news shows liked to feature. In Mom's stories, someone was always getting divorced after thirty years of cup-cakes. Someone was waking up paralyzed after running a marathon the day before. Someone was getting a routine checkup when his doctors find a cancer the size of a basketball in the stomach.

"He'd sent her divorce papers," Mom continued. "The guy, it turns out, was a big homosexual type. The note he attached said, 'I need to feel men on my skin.' Can you believe that?"

"Gay," I said through the curtain, "is what they like to be called."

"Okay," Mom said. "So now you're an expert?"

I slipped on a pullover vest embroidered with dogs wearing glasses. The glasses were attached to the dogs' heads with real mini strands of pearl. Mom had raved about this piece when she'd plucked it off the rack, insisting that "they" – her unnamed group of fashion experts – would be wearing ones just like it come next week. I came out of the changeroom and stood in front of the crooked mirror. Mom came and stood beside me, taking me in distractedly.

"Having your husband leave you, just like that," she continued, "it must be pretty devastating. Especially when it's for another man. What do you think?"

"I don't know." I shrugged. I wanted to change the subject. "But I've heard of worse. Like the girl at number eleven who got a bad thought in her head and didn't know what to do. Her family was very rich but never home."

Mom handed me the next outfit. A matching pants-and-top set with a pattern of electrocuted cats. Behind the curtain, I took off the vest and threw it into the "passable" heap. I'd made three piles: Passable, Disgusting, and Ultra Grotesque.

"So this girl," I continued, "she's the type of person who naturally has a lot on her mind. But now she's not coping. Her parents are totally absent. She's so upset that she stops watching TV. That's serious, isn't it?"

"Lucy," Mom sighed, "are you making this up?"

"Listen. One day out of the blue, she starts collecting sticks and dirt. Like, she starts going hunting, like a hound, and for what? For sticks. And all over the place – schoolyards, sandboxes, squirrel lots. The whole bit." I tightened the drawstring of my pants. "All this dirt makes her feel a bit better. She's suddenly got jars of it stacked in her room. Buckets of mud –"

"Her rich parents didn't notice buckets of dirt in the house?"

"They had a cleaning lady," I explained, "who was used to how rich people act weird. Anyways, this girl's got a room filled with dirt. Rocks, sticks, mud, fibres from animals. Disgusting stuff. When she starts building the free-range ant farm, her parents wise up. They make her sit down with a shrink."

"I would've just made her clean it up. And sent her to one of those science camps for special people."

"Mom," I sighed. "You're missing the point. This girl was sick. She had a disease in her brain. You can look it up. It's when you can't stop collecting dirt and everything that's in it. It's a coping mechanism. Geraldo did a show on it."

"Well, please don't invite this girl over is all I can say. I have enough problems in the house as it is."

I came out of the changeroom.

"My turn now," Mom said. "But don't think I'm crazy."

I revolved in front of the mirror. "I won't."

"Your dad," she began, "I think he has another woman."

I remembered Dad in his hunting scene sweater, his face frozen in concentration as he stood in the entrance of the church basement, where he'd stopped to watch her – Crashing Wave, in her blue plastic heels, laying her hand on another man's shoulder. I remembered how they had laughed. She'd given me her lipstick and told me "You and I have that natural Twiggy figure." But Dad said they were just good friends.

Mom stared back at me, her mouth open, her hands folded over the shopping cart. Once upon a time she'd been Miss Sophia West, the beauty queen of suburban Bulgaria. She'd worn peacock feathers and posed in front of gold curtains, smiling with shiny red lips. Now she wore huge tortoiseshell glasses and had hair in her armpits. Now she wore lipstick only on special occasions, because she said it was boiled pig fat marked up 1,000 per cent. It belonged with all the other "rip-offs" – hairspray, leather shoes, and fashion magazines – she didn't need now that she was "out of that game."

"Lucy?" Mom said. "Did you hear what I said? Do you think he's seeing another woman?"

I didn't understand why Mom was asking me these questions. Or why she had so many doubts and worries. If she spent less time worrying, maybe we could do more fun things, like eat hot chicken sandwiches at the Zellers luncheon counter, instead of hanging around this changeroom wearing other people's clothes and talking about crazy things.

"No," I said, "Dad wouldn't do that."

The next day at school, Estelle Pomper and her crew of popular girls were hanging out in the changeroom while the rest of us were getting ready for swim class. Estelle went to stand in front of the mirror and pulled her fingers through her long wavy hair. "My mom says I can get highlights when I turn twelve. Because her mom let her get highlights when she was twelve."

"What's highlights?" I said. "You mean, when there's dye in just pieces and not through the whole head, or just on the top?" I knew I sounded nerdy even as I said it.

Estelle ignored me and took an eyeshadow palate out of her knapsack, rubbing her finger into the violet shade. I took out my towel and wrapped it around my waist and then began to undo my pants.

After a minute, Estelle spoke up. "Who's bleeding today?" Her eyes travelled over her three girls, who were lined up on the bench facing her.

Missy Lakakis raised her hand. "I am." Around her wrist she wore three Slap bracelets. She lowered her hand and continued rearranging the photos of her "boyfriend" in the plastic sleeve in her wallet. Nobody questioned why he was one of the actors on *Beverly Hills 90210*.

"Well," said Estelle officiously, "I am too." She leaned against the mirror and pressed her lips into it.

I slipped off my pants, still holding the towel around my waist, and looked at Estelle. Her skin was peachy, her eyebrows round arcs of beige. In the yard I sometimes saw boys, mean ones who stuffed pebbles up other peoples' noses, stopping to stare at her as she jumped up and down for double dutch, her perfect French braid bouncing on her shoulder blades like a soft whip.

"I am too," I said. "I'm bleeding."

Missy burst out laughing. Her braces were neon green and orange. She got the colours changed every month. "So why are you taking off your pants, Bony? You wanna show us your tampon? You can get a pass if you're on the rag. School policy."

Estelle shook her head. "I don't believe she's bleeding. No way. Look at her tits. They're a pirate's dream."

"Why's that?" Missy snapped.

"Sunken chest," Estelle snapped back. "And did you notice that her shirt smells like cat piss today?"

Kelly Peters, the principal's kid, looked over at us. She was the kind of person who would climb a mountain in high heels if she thought it would make her popular. "Yeah, Lucy." She laughed. "Why does your shirt smell like cat piss?"

I ran from them and locked myself inside a washroom cubicle until I heard the whistle blowing from the deck and the sound of the changeroom clearing out. Then I unlocked the door and went to stand in front of the mirror. Bony the Bug Eyes stared back at me, a pirate's dream. I lifted up my T-shirt and squinted into the mirror, imagining what it would feel like to have real breasts. I squinted harder. I could almost see them —

The swimming teacher, all red legs and whistle necklace, burst into the bathroom. "What's going on? Why aren't you on the deck?" she barked.

I dropped my shirt. "I'm bleeding. Don't make me go."

I got a pass to go sit in the cafeteria. Before going in, I stood outside the door and peered in through the glass squares to make sure that Estelle and her crew weren't there. The only person in the room was my cousin, Hyman, who was sitting in the corner. Hyman could never go into the pool. He had a phobia and a doctor's note to prove it, and lots of snacks and comic books to fill the hour.

He had a cheese-string wrapper hanging out of his mouth cigarette-style, and he was telling me about how pot made you feel like your chest was full of cotton candy, although his mouth kind of spasmed when he lied. "It's like being in an envelope that's always on the way to a place you love."

"Where do you get it?" I said. "I mean, you're always talking about it so why don't we just go and do it for once?"

He shrugged his shoulders. "How about this game, then? I name a country and you tell me the capital of that country. Then we switch and you ask me. You start."

"Fine. Bulgaria."

"Sophia," he answered. "That's easy. Your mom's always going on about how she had to wear a camel's ass because she had no other clothes."

"Rat hair, it was rat hair." I smeared extra egg salad from my sandwich onto the edge of our table. "And over there, whenever it rains it means a bear is getting married."

"Sure," he said.

"Also, if you've got hairy arms, it means you're going to be very rich."

Hyman snorted and inhaled a load of Nerds from his double-sided candy box. "So I guess you're going to be a billionaire."

We sat there in silence for a moment. Then his eyes narrowed as they travelled over my matching shirt and pants, the best I could manage from the Disgusting pile.

"What's that smell?" he blurted.

▬

My eyes were still stinging when I got home and found Mom in the living room, sitting on the couch, calmly eating a pepperoni stick. The television was tuned to the Home Shopping Network, a segment on vinyl winter boots. "Rip-off," she muttered. "They say it's a waterproof product, and on day one the water starts pouring in like a deluxe shower. Then when you try to do a return, they charge you for the shipping, and boots are heavy, that's what kind of charlatans they are."

I went to stand in front of the television. "Why didn't you tell me?" I pulled at my shirt and grabbed at the drawstring of my pants.

"Tell you what? Move out of the way."

"This is a uniform! From a veterinary clinic!"

It was the first time I'd ever raised my voice at her, and as she muted the TV I thought she looked pale.

"How would I know that?" Mom cried. "You think I follow fashion? You think I'm the kind of woman who goes to the hairdresser and reads silly magazines and spends a fortune on cosmetics?"

I wanted to scream at her, to tell her how she should have told me about periods, taken me shopping for a bra. She should have made sure I knew what highlights were and bought me a lipstick instead of letting me go around accepting them from strangers.

"You don't tell me anything," I said. Then quieter, "You don't."

"But you didn't ask," Mom said. "You never asked about any of these things."

Everything would return to normal as soon as Friday came around. We would all take the twenty-six-mile drive up Bathurst Street, and Dad would buy the same cheap flowers, and Mom would sort Grandpa's mail into piles of what was important and what she could throw away. But on Friday, Dad's rust-bitten Corolla was waiting for me after school. Dad never picked me up. As I approached the car he made the usual hamster faces, balling his hands at his cheeks as though he was cleaning his whiskers, but I could tell that something was wrong. Bony the Bug Eyes slipped into the passenger seat. The whole interior reeked of gasoline and Dad's egg salad sandwiches.

"Where's Mom?"

He told me she was shopping. Then he said that Grandpa had slipped in his apartment and broken his hip. "He's at Branson Hospital. He's resting now and Florence wants us to wait, let him get better, then all go together on Monday. That means that I'll have to miss my meeting. We're going to his place now to get him some of his things."

At Grandpa's building, Dad parked the car under the usual willow tree. "This will be boring for you, going up there, because I also arranged to talk to the super." He cleared his throat. "About turning off the heat while he's not there. Because heat's expensive. So go to the store and buy yourself some treats and just walk around for a while. I'll get things done." He handed me a dryer-faded five-dollar bill and then checked his watch. "I want you to meet me back here in exactly one hour." He had forgotten Mom's rule that I wasn't allowed out on my own for more than half an hour.

When we reached the main door, I told him I could just go up with him. "It's too cold to walk around." Dad's face looked small peeking out from his massive fur hood. "You have a scarf, though. It'll be okay." Then he turned and disappeared into the building.

I checked the time — 4:44 — as I made my way toward the variety store in the lobby of the building next door. 4:44, maybe he'd be back by 5:00. The bell chimed as I opened the door. I ducked immediately into the first aisle, trailing my finger along the dust-coated peanut butter jars, the boxes of Jell-O pudding, the pretty little tins of cat food. Halfway up the aisle I lifted a jar of jam from the shelf and read the label a few times. *Smucker's 100% Blueberry Jam.* Every time the worries got into my head, I had to stop reading and start again from the beginning. *100% real fruit and no added sugar,* but I hadn't seen Lulu all day and who would take responsibility? Terrible things could happen. *No added sugar or preservatives. Blueberry and* what if Grandpa –

"What are you looking for?" It was the woman at the counter. She had glanced up from her tiny television.

"It's okay," I said. I put the jam jar back on the shelf. "Everything's okay."

Outside the door of Grandpa's building, I checked my watch again. 5:01. It was still too early, but I was too cold. My knapsack was heavy as I went into the little vestibule and dialled Grandpa's extension. Once Dad buzzed me in, I would sit on the crushed velvet couch in the lobby and wait for him. But the phone kept ringing. I leaned my back against the marble wall and let my body slide down until I was sitting on the wet floor with my knees pressed up to my chest. I untied my shoelaces and tied them again. I cradled my elbows in my hands to stop them from shaking. Then I remembered the lipstick in my knapsack. I took the tube out and unrolled its pinkness two inches. I brought the lipstick to my nose and breathed in its dry pencil shavings smell, only slightly sweeter. I felt the tip dabbing my skin, but I didn't care. I put the lipstick on, first a single coat, then a second and a third, and I kept applying it until a woman carrying bags of groceries walked into the vestibule and buzzed herself in. I got up and held the door open for her. Then I followed her inside and sat on the couch to wait. I was restless, though, because I was worried about Dad. Maybe Dad wasn't answering the phone because something terrible had happened. Maybe he'd been throwing away the old carnations and spilled some water on the floor and slipped, so he was now lying all broken and calling my name, only I couldn't hear him. I took the elevator up to Grandpa's apartment. When I got to the end of the hall the door was unlocked, so I went in.

Music. The first thing I heard was music. Oldies, the kind Dad played in his car. Dad's parka was on the floor, spread out like a hunted animal. In the kitchen, I saw the outline of limp flowers on the table. A curtain of sweet perfume closed in front of me. I took the jar and put it into the sink. Then I went down the hall and stood at the darkened doorway of the living room.

That's when I saw Dad.

He was slow-dancing with a woman, and their bodies were swaying back and forth like two boats kissing. The woman's head peered up from above Dad's shoulder, but her eyes were closed and she was smiling. It was Crashing Wave.

I turned around, went out through the door, and ran to the elevators. In the lobby I used my sleeve to rub my mouth until I felt I was going to pull off my lips. I could feel the lipstick smeared across my face. I ripped a page out from one of the magazines on the coffee table, spat on it, and rubbed it against my lips until the elevator doors opened and Dad was standing there in his parka.

I could tell that he'd noticed my mouth. I closed my fingers around the page and crumpled it. I didn't want him to see it.

"What the hell did you put on your mouth? Is that what you bought with the money I gave you?"

I couldn't look at him at all. I nodded.

"Lucy," he said, "you're not the kind of girl that wears makeup. Give it to me. Give it to me now, Lucy."

"No," I said. I felt the lipstick digging into my pocket. "Where's Grandpa's things?"

Dad shook his head. "You know what? I completely forgot."

On the way home, we stopped to buy TV dinners at Loblaws. We didn't talk at all. I kept seeing Dad and Crashing Wave, their bodies locked in a dancing pose. There was a handwritten note from Mom on the kitchen table: I'M SLEEPING. KEEP IT DOWN. Beside the note was the folded classifieds section stabbed with pen marks. The heat had been turned off and the whole house was frigid, the rooms filled with the vaporous smell of frost. Dad dumped the two TV dinners onto the table.

"My foresight leads me," he said. "Zap these things for four minutes apiece. I have to be alone for a few minutes. Upstairs, in my study." Underneath his parka, his cardigan had been buttoned up wrong.

I wanted to ask him if Crashing Wave was more important to him than us, but I couldn't make myself say those words. So I said, "Is Grandpa going to be okay?"

"Grandpa lied to himself," Dad said. "Because no man is an island. Remember, Lucy, it's better to be weak than to be lonely."

As he left the kitchen, I thought, Maybe you can be both.

▶

On Saturday night, after Mom went to bed early, Dad said it was time to clear out the tomatoes. Out on the deck Dad stood in front of me, the yellow glow of the floodlights catching the white stripes on his windbreaker – what he wore when he was being "physical" – and the strands of white in the short hairs on either side of his head. A sweet metallic scent that made me think of pineapple from an expired can rose off his clothes.

It was cold, and the basil plants were turning inward, stiffening with early frost. The parsley was wilted and soft, stinking up the whole patch around it.

"We should have done this a month ago," I said. "We're always late at doing the most basic things." People like us, I wanted to tell him, aren't fit to keep a garden. We aren't fit to keep a house. People like us, I wanted to point out, probably wouldn't even be friends if we met each other at school. Not even if we met each other at a deserted bus station at three in the morning. Even if we were hungry, and the other person had food to share, we wouldn't be able to ask for a scrap of it. Not because we were proud, but because we wouldn't be able to find the words. We'd become a family of empty gestures. Flowers for fathers who don't love their sons. Hands covering ears that have already heard more than they wanted to. Fights taken upstairs but fought behind open doors.

Dad said, "Let's get to work, okay?"

The entire front section of the lawn was covered in rotten and mashed tomatoes and giant tuberous cucumbers, inbred and sallow with that waxy shade of yellow that promises nothing but bitterness and seeds. Dad went down into the yard and I followed him. There was only one hoe so I stooped and began rolling the tomatoes into a pile. It was cold, even for November, and I could smell winter coming. There were hundreds of tomatoes and this work would probably take all night.

"Well," Dad said, stooping to pick up the hoe. "I have some news." His fingers curled around the hoe's neck, and I noticed the blood-edged beds of his nails. His habit of picking his nails had got worse. "I've finalized everything now, Lucy. I don't want you to worry anymore. No more fighting in front of you. No more."

Some of the tomatoes were fat and unblemished, perfectly green. Still I rolled them into the pile. On hands and knees, I dug my nails into the squirting flesh of the tomatoes, rolling them anywhere, just away from me. Each time I pushed away a tomato, I'd try to push away that image of Dad and Crashing Wave dancing but barely moving.

"I'm going to leave her," Dad said. "At this point, it's only a question of getting the ball rolling."

If ALF from Melmac were here, I thought, he'd take his furry hand and cover Dad's mouth and tell him gently, but firmly: "Stop talking. I am 193 years old and far wiser than you. Just stop. She knows it all anyway. Just shut up now." I took up the shovel from where Dad had left it and started plunging it into the hard green tomatoes so the frosty outer skin broke, releasing juice. My pile quickly became a pool of pulp. That was taking responsibility.

Then Dad, who had been holding a sliver of nail up into the moonlight, grabbed the hoe from me. "Why so rough? This is an art and you've got to use your brain. We could have made pickles out of those."

"Tomatoes are biodegradable," I said. "The patch will be better for it next year."

His grit teeth glowed in the dark as he began making piles again. "I don't see myself being here next year. So next year's lawn is really —" he sighed and knocked at a tomato plant through its cage so it rattled in the wind. "Irrelevant to me."

There was no safe place here, outside in this rotting yard. No place to find the right footing, no telephone line to Melmac, no words of objection.

Bony the Bug Eyes said, "I guess you should tell Mom soon."

➤

Visiting hours at Branson Hospital were after six, so on Monday, Mom, Dad, and I drove twenty-six miles north, making one stop at Sue's Flowers. While Dad went in to buy the bouquet, Mom pulled down the visor mirror and ran a finger along her bare lips.

"Your skin is clearing up," she said.

"I don't care," I mumbled. "If I have pimples all my life at least I'll know that people like me for my brain."

When Dad handed me the bouquet wrapped in silver foil, I just tossed it onto the seat beside me. I thought his bouquets were stupid now. I played with my shoelaces, wrapping them around my fingers tightly so they bulged like sausages and burned from the lack of blood. When they started to turn blue, I let go of the laces and waited a minute. Then I started again.

"I bought daisies today," Dad said as we passed the dreary video arcade, its big clown-head sign stained with bird shit. The pot-smoking kids were gone now, probably because they were out somewhere slow-dancing.

"Yeah?" I said.

"Yeah. I thought it was time for a change."

I could tell they'd stuck Grandpa in a room that was meant for new mothers because the wallpaper was climbing with yellow duckies. Two tubes ran down his arm and another tube, with a little timer hanging off it, was stuck inside his nostril. The air smelled like cleaning solution. Dad bent over the bed, so his face was a few inches away from Grandpa's, and just stared at him. Then Dad reached his hand out to touch Grandpa's cheek. Grandpa wasn't wearing his false teeth so his face looked deflated.

"You know, he's here," Dad said. "But not here. It's hard to understand."

Mom didn't say anything. Usually, she said her *Mosby's Medical Encyclopedia* was better than any MD, but now she just picked at some flaking leather on the strap of her purse.

When the nurse came into the room, she told us that Grandpa was doing all right, but the doctor had given him some sedatives. "Because he was having bad nightmares. When he woke up he wouldn't talk about them. All he wants to do is sleep and eat."

Dad scowled. "Isn't that what a hospital is for?"

Mom interrupted. She always had to when Dad was being short with people. "What he means is, will Sol be able to live alone?"

The nurse blushed, but I figured she probably handled these situations all the time: families at each other's throats even though there was a sick person in the room.

"He'll have to walk with a cane," she said. "He's going to need a lot of care."

▶

They fought constantly for the next few weeks: first behind their bedroom door, which they now remembered to close, and then their problems spread throughout the house. When I was in my room, I'd sometimes hear Mom's voice from downstairs, rising above Dad's, the sounds of cupboards slamming shut. I heard the word *she* in a hissing tone and I knew they were talking about Crashing Wave. On Monday nights, Mom continued to go to her cake-decorating class at the community centre, and Dad still went to his meeting. But now they left me at home by myself. I tried to watch *ALF*, but I was restless. Every few minutes I got up and looked through the window for their cars. I fed Charlie Sheen oversized hunks of cheese and Lulu full cans of tuna. When the tuna juice spilled on the floor, I didn't even clean it up. I wanted Dad to come home and complain about the stink. Then he would have to fight with me instead of with Mom.

I was relieved when everything quieted down. Mom came home with her own newspaper and I thought she might be looking for a vacation so she could finally "go places" with Dad. Dad went back to his normal routines. He swept the kitchen after dinner and cleaned the counter with his J-cloth. Maybe terrible things wouldn't happen.

Tuesday morning was sunny but cold. I sat still and silent as oldies tinkled out of the radio, clashing with the sound of Dad's plastic AA tags slapping against one another as we drove. The bronze medallion meant eight years. Still, we were all taking it one day at a time. I looked at my reflection in the mirror and fluffed my bangs so they wouldn't look so greasy.

"When you're smart, looks matter very little," Dad said.

"Thanks," I said, but I didn't buy it because his eyes clung to the butt of every blonde we passed.

"Next year, if you get into The Elms School, you'll like it more, I promise. You'll meet other little spelling bee champs like you. If I'd gone to an advanced school, I probably would've been something more than a travel agent. I'd be a photographer for the *New York Times* or something."

His dreamy tone annoyed me, but it also made me sad. "You can still take photos," I said. "No one's asking you to feel like a travel agent inside."

"You're a smart girl," Dad said. "That's just what you are. I need you to be a good girl now. When you get home tonight clean that hamster's cage. It smells like a Dickens era slum. And try brushing Lulu once in a while. Because if you look at her back it's this colony of dandruff and I don't think she appreciates it very much. Then I want you to be nice to your mother until I get home." I had the feeling he was giving me directions not just for tonight but for the rest of my life.

"Okay."

Dad pulled into the usual spot across the street from my school. "Every morning I see you counting tiles, on your hands and knees. Why?"

I could see Estelle Pomper and her friends gathered around the air vent near the gates. Their skirts were ballooning like tropical mushrooms, and they were all laughing. The only things that mattered to them were getting the crease right in their khaki skirts or finding out how to do highlights at home without getting that brassy tone. But I couldn't stop thinking about how terrible things could happen. I would come home and find Lulu run away, Charlie Sheen crammed into the dairy compartment of the fridge, his body stiff like old Gouda. Mom would be holding a single knee-high stocking to her eyes to catch her tears. Dad would never come home at all.

"Why?" Dad said. "Why are you always checking things?"

"Because –" I stared at the girls, tugging at one another's sleeves

"Because what?" Dad leaned over me and unlocked the passenger door.

I wanted to say, "Because I'm scared," but the only thing I could say was, "I don't know."

I stood outside the car on the sidewalk and we stared at each other through the window. Dad smiled like nothing had happened. As usual, he brought his hands to his cheeks, making his famous hamster imitation. Cleaning the whiskers, clearing the air. He rolled down his window. "Tonight, the three of us are going to talk. For your sake as much as for our own. And Lucy" – he dropped his hands into his lap – "I love you very much."

That day at lunch, I sat with Hyman in the corner of the lunchroom, shredding my sandwich into bingo chips and dreaming about the day when Dad would get his ten-year key tag, the gold one, and he wouldn't have to go to meetings anymore. After ten years, Dad said he could stop taking it one day at a time. By then, he'd have learned how to live life on its own terms. He'd have taken an inventory of all the people he'd hurt and gone back and corrected the things he could and accepted the things he couldn't. After ten years he would have the wisdom to know the difference.

I was wearing my favourite ALF T-shirt and I was feeling hopeful. I was starting to get this feeling that when I got home from school, I would find a big top set up in the backyard, a parade of donkeys and ponies circling it, and a clown who made balloons in the shape of racecars and sausage dogs. Mom and Dad would suddenly slip out from behind one of the hedges, their fingers laced together, holding a giant balloon. "Good job," they'd say. "You took responsibility. We never could do that. All your hard work paid off. We're not perfect, but we're sticking together."

I heard the sound of chair legs scraping against the floor all around me and when I looked up, Hyman was stuffing a half-eaten cheese-string into his knapsack. "The bell rang," he said. "You looked so tired I thought I'd let you keep snoring."

I collected my empty juice box, my plastic sandwich container.

Hyman blew a spit bubble. "Why do you have to wear that ALF shirt all the time?" he said. "The show hasn't been on for years."

I felt my face flushing. "It's on every Monday night. I missed it once because I had to go with Dad to –" Don't mention the meeting.

"*ALF* was cancelled, like, three years ago," Hyman said. "Maybe you were watching a rerun."

"A rerun?"

"Yeah, you never heard of a rerun?"

I shook my head. "What about ALF, though?" I said. "The *real* ALF."

"You mean Gordon Shumway?"

"Who?"

"That's ALF's real name. The Tanner family names him ALF. On Melmac his name was Gordon Shumway." Hyman pulled a double-sided box of Nerds from his pocket and snuffled some up. "I thought you knew everything about that show. You're wearing the T-shirt." He narrowed his eyes. "That's pretty sick."

How can someone be your hero if you don't even know his real name? I walked home that afternoon, the name Gordon Shumway rushing through my head like a swear word, piercing my ears with its hard sounds. How can you trust someone who never even told you his real name? Surely I was to blame. I was the one who'd never seen the first episode.

There was a suitcase just inside the front door when I got home. I took a deep breath and dropped my knapsack onto the fake marble tiles, all unsafe now, and made my way toward the backyard, where surely a big-top tent would be rising up from the ground. Mom and Dad were sitting at the table on the deck, but there was nothing in the yard but dead leaves under a thin coating of snow. I opened the screen door and walked outside. Where was the sound of the organ grinder, the incessant call of the ape, the aroma of caramel corn?

"Lucy," Dad said, "sit down so we can all talk."

The third chair was missing. I suddenly remembered that it had a broken leg and then I saw it at the corner of the deck, upside down among a pile of broken clay pots and rusting tools. I was the one who broke it, a week after my birthday, when I was trying to count some leaves on a branch that hung over the flower boxes. If I didn't count them all, I'd been thinking, terrible things might happen. Then the chair had fallen out from under me.

"I'll stand," I said. "I prefer to stand."

"Okay. Well," Dad said, "you probably saw the suitcase in the hall. That's your grandfather's. He's going to be moving in with us."

"You're staying together," I said. I looked excitedly at Mom's chin and waited for it to nod.

"That's what we need to talk about. Your mother and I, well, we've decided that it's a good idea if we give ourselves a little break. You know, like a time-out. Like in sports."

"I'm looking for an apartment – somewhere nice," Mom said. "That way, Dad can look after Grandpa here. So you won't have to give up your room. When we move, you'll have your own room and I'll have my own room too. We're going to go places. It will be a kind of adventure."

"We shouldn't go. You don't even like driving at night," I said. "You'll be scared. I'll give up my room."

No one said anything. I waited for Mom to say she was kidding. That this was one of her stories, even if it wasn't funny.

"It's okay," Mom said. "I've been checking the papers every day for an apartment where we'll be really happy."

I imagined Grandpa asleep in their bedroom upstairs, Dad curled up on the couch, their snores the only sounds in the house. I began tapping my shoe on the wood of the deck.

"Well," Dad said, "I'm glad you're taking this so well. You're a smart girl and that's what you are."

Mom and Dad began to get up. This was my last chance.

"Wait," I said. "Have you ever heard of Gordon Shumway?"

"Who?"

"Gordon Shumway," I repeated. "The hero."

"No," Dad said, shaking his head. "Never have."

"Mom?"

"Yes, the name is familiar." Mom squinted like she was seeing something in her mind that was far away. "But you said his name wrong. Amway. Gordon from Amway. He was that crazy guy who used to come around selling those useless plastic containers. He had a big spiel that went along with it. Safe for the microwave. Can withstand heat up to three hundred degrees centigrade. Frank, do you remember him?"

It was the first time they'd spoken to each other in their normal voices in a long time.

"Yeah, I do. He was covered in sores, like he had a plague or something. I never opened the door for him."

"I pitied him," Mom said. "Because I once knew a guy who was very handsome and then woke up one morning with leprosy. Anyway, Gordon would drag this box around filled with plastic containers. He claimed he was selling them for Amway, but I don't think he had anything to do with them. If you bought one of these containers, Gordon said he was going to enrol you in a program where you were supposed to get new kitchenware every month. But after I paid him, I never saw him again. The container melted in the microwave about a week later."

"A pyramid scheme," Dad said.

"A scam artist, is all," Mom added.

We went into the kitchen and stood there for what I was sure would be the last time, the three of us fitting together like jigsaw pieces.

"Why are you asking about him?" Mom said. "You were too young to remember that. You were just this little thing sitting in your crib, sucking on your big thumb. Remember how quiet she was, Frank? You never cried. You were so peaceful. Your eyes were bluer than the sky after a storm."

4

In early December Mom packed half of my clothes into an orange Samsonite suitcase and moved us four miles south, into a furnished two-bedroom rental at Tivoli Towers. The lobby floor was covered in small soggy mats that Mom said were there to protect the marble, but in between the mats I could see the cracked linoleum floor. Near the elevators was a square couch like one I'd seen on *The Mary Tyler Moore Show*. There was a security guard too. His name was Seville, and his job was to admire himself in the mirrored walls and use spit to slick down his eyebrows. Riding up in the elevator, Mom pretended that our moving here was the most exciting event of our lives. But when we got to our door, she said she wished she had a bottle of water, because in Bulgaria throwing water into strange doorways brought you good luck.

My bedroom had shaggy blue carpeting and a cot that pulled out of the wall. "That's called a Murphy bed," Mom said, yanking the squeaking bed down. From the colour of the mattress, grey with a few round yellow stains, I figured that no one had slept on it for about fifty years. "It used to be a fashionable, New York thing. All the actresses used Murphy beds in the 1950s." And when I couldn't think of anything to say back, except "What are those stains from?" Mom licked her lips and sat on the bed herself and tried to bounce on it, but it was too hard for bouncing. I wouldn't have minded if she cried or screamed – anything but trying to bounce on my bed. Instead, she talked as if I was the one who needed comforting. "I can buy you a new bed. If this isn't good for you. Or if you're scared, you can sleep in my bed with me. On the days you're not at Dad's."

It made me almost wince to see her trying so hard. I told her not to worry, that I wouldn't be at Dad's too much.

"*I'm* not worried. I just don't want you to worry about me. Especially when we're apart. Your dad and I agreed that you could stay with him on Thursdays and Fridays, if you want. It's your choice."

That night, after we'd unpacked our suitcases and set up our toothbrushes by the green scalloped sink, Mom said she was too tired to buy groceries so I should order us Chinese takeout. As I waited for the food to arrive, I tried to imagine what Lulu was doing – maybe putting curlers in her hair, or pulling stockings up her calico legs. Dad had probably forgotten to feed her, and I could picture Charlie Sheen lying depressed in his woodchip pile, living off the food he stored in his cheeks. When Mom first told me that Tivoli Towers had a no-pets policy, I wasn't sure I wanted to go with her.

"You'd choose a cat and a hamster over me?" Mom had said. "When's the last time Charlie Sheen bought you groceries?"

We ate our supper straight from the white foam boxes: chow mein with shrimp and cashews and lemon chicken with igloos of rice. I was impressed that Mom could use the wooden chopsticks that came with our food. "Since when do you know how to use chopsticks?" I said. "Are you hiding any other special skills?"

Mom smiled a little. "I can knit. And I can make potpourri sachets out of old underwear."

"Come on, tell me something I don't know. Tell me something you did when you were my age. An exciting thing."

"Okay," Mom said. "When I was about sixteen, I was in love with a bus driver who looked like Omar Sharif. You know, Yuri in *Doctor Zhivago*. I would ride the bus three, four times a day, right to the end of the route, then get off, and get back on. Just to be around him." I couldn't imagine Mom doing this: Mom, who was afraid of driving at night, making left turns, spiders, and men who wore ripped jeans.

"One day I asked him on a date, in front of all the passengers. I thought, Well, I have nothing to lose. If he rejects me, I'll walk for the next month, by then he will have forgotten me." Mom nodded to her chow mein. "But he said yes."

"What happened?"

"We went to a café. He looked good, but like a gigolo, with a shirt open to the navel. He talked about how he was going to open up a hotel on the Baltic with his cousin. I asked him why. There were a million of them already. He said for money. No passion in his voice at all. I didn't like that. I'd already decided my dream man would have a passion. Your dad had bad ideas, but at least he was passionate about them."

"So you turned him down?"

"I told him our relationship had to stay above the neck. That closed it for him. But I still saw him on the bus. When I reached to drop my coins into the fare box, he would cover the opening with his hand and smile."

After Mom had gone to bed, I didn't know what to do with myself. So I paced in front of the glass doors that led out to the balcony and put on a phony British accent. "*Hello*, everyone, this is Robin Leach and welcome to Lifestyles of the Not-so Rich and Famous. Today I take you inside the sad case of Tivoli Towers —"I plopped down on the rattan couch and held a chopstick to my mouth like it was a microphone. "Look, Robin," I said, dropping the accent, "let me cut it to you straight. This place gives me the creeps. The Murphy bed's stained and —"

"Lucy, who are you talking to?" Mom's half-asleep voice called from the bedroom.

"It's just the TV," I yelled back.

I unlocked the sliding door and stepped out onto the balcony, wearing only my socks and pyjamas. Already it was cold, the kind of cold that makes even your hair smell of winter. I wrapped my arms around myself and went to stand by the railing. We were on the eleventh floor. I could see the CN Tower with its ruby necklace of lights, and hundreds of illuminated office building windows, narrow as winking eyes. I thought about how easy it would be to fall off this balcony and tumble, like a piece of laundry, onto the lawn below. Now that Mom and I were on our own, I didn't know who would drive us places at night, or lift the lid off the toilet when too much paper got stuck and it wouldn't flush. It worried me to think of Mom all alone. She was never even alone at work. I tried to imagine Mom in her empty classroom. But nothing came to me. From the balcony the city looked huge, a fall without a net, deep as a canyon.

When I came back inside, I could hear soft snores coming out of Mom's bedroom. In my room, I snapped open my suitcase and lifted out the three animals-with-jobs colour lithographs that I'd secretly taken from our living room at home. Mom had found them in a cardboard box outside a veterinarian clinic during her lunch break.

There was a smoke-coloured cat sexily lacing its leg around a microphone, a dachshund holding a gavel, and a rat dentist standing in front of a wall of diplomas. I loved them because I had fantasies that Lulu was actually a showgirl trapped inside a calico's body. Then I knelt and pulled the ALF shoelaces out of the holes of my sneakers and laid them out on my pillow. I dove onto the Murphy bed and, like a cat, rubbed my cheek against the laces, letting the plastic tips scratch lightly at my nose. Even though I'd stopped watching the show, I whispered, "Earth to ALF, earth to ALF, over and out." The shoelaces just stank of rubber. They didn't help. I tossed. I turned. I saw Crashing Wave's face peering up at me from the plastic-covered page of the Glamour Shots album. "Lucy," she said, her body leaning backward and then forward as she laughed, "I wore a crown of laurels on my head when I met your dad. It was true love. Want a cookie? Want a book? Want this lipstick?"

I squeezed my eyes shut, but I couldn't stop thinking.

In the taxi to Tivoli Towers Mom had said, "You're not a kid anymore. So I think you should know the truth. Your dad has met someone else. A woman from his meetings, someone he's known for three months. Three months with her and he throws out sixteen years with me. This is how I know the whole thing is unstable. But what the future is I don't know." Then to get off the subject of Dad, Mom asked the taxi driver if he did more business in the snow or the rain.

In the backseat I had stared at my ALF shoelaces, but his friendly eyes had turned mean on me. They were calling me a liar for not telling Mom what I already knew: Dad had known Crashing Wave for more than three months. But I wasn't going to say anything that might make things worse. I needed us to go home again very soon.

▸

Mom had found our apartment at Tivoli Towers through an acquaintance at school whose sister, a divorcee named Merle Gaddick, had been living in the building for years and "loving it." I'd never known Mom to be social – her idea of a hot night was staying in and watching CNN – but the strangeness of living at Tivoli Towers, with its hotel-like loneliness, probably sped up the process of her calling Merle Gaddick. I didn't have a good feeling about Merle. Her name made me think of the woman I'd seen in the elevator who'd worn a dead little fox around her neck with the eyes all bugged out.

"No, she's not mean," Mom said. It was our sixth morning at Tivoli Towers and we were in the kitchen, which was narrow like a ticket booth at a carnival. "You're just thinking of Merle Norman, the cosmetics place in the mall. You were nine, probably you blocked it out. I paid ten dollars to have your ears pierced and then you chickened out and went to have diarrhea in the bathroom. They wouldn't give me my money back."

"That was you," I said. "Why do you always pretend that things that happened to you happened to me?"

Mom ignored me. "Merle is nice, you know, one of these artistic women who like to go to galleries. So don't go talking about the Salvation Army to her. Or to Diana. That's the daughter. She's the same age as you. Very shy like a little nut, so try to bring her out of herself –"

Merle and Diana stopped by our apartment later that morning. Mom was right, Merle was not the dead fox lady at all. She reminded me of a powdered art teacher, with her red hair cut in big chunky bangs, her three-tiered peasant skirt, and her brown lace-up boots, the kind that belong to an 1800s lady who's wild about horses. Diana had thick, red wavy hair and an upturned little kitten nose with nostrils the size of Tic Tacs. Mom gave me a "be hospitable" look so I took Diana to my room. I'd folded the Murphy bed back up that morning, but now I had to pull it down again so we'd have somewhere to sit. Diana plunked herself on it, crossing her curvy legs.

"Oooh, this is one of those lousy cots, isn't it? They come with the cheapo units. Feels like a slab of burnt toast."

"It's not a cot," I said, "it's a Murphy bed. All the actresses used them in the Fifties. It was kind of a fashionable thing."

"That's a crock of shit. They're for poor people without any space." Her blue eyes swivelled around my room, taking its pathetic grey walls in. I could already tell she thought she was the boss of me. She pointed her French-manicured fingernail to the only shelf in my room. "You should get a plant in here. I have a Venus flytrap in my room and if you squint, you know what it looks like?"

I shook my head.

"A vagina. And you know what else? You're supposed to feed it twice a day, but I put mine on a diet to see if it closes up or what."

When we went back out into the living room, Merle was standing against the sliding glass doors; the light was shining through her red hair, making the lighter pieces glow like little sticks on fire. "I love Rothko. His canvases represent such *fin-de-siècle* madness, real urban grit. What about you, Joy? Who do you like?"

Mom ran her finger over her lips, which were a bright orange colour that reminded me of spreadable cheese; she'd put lipstick on before Merle had arrived, so I knew she was trying hard. "I like Norman Rockwell," she finally said. "I like his animal stuff."

I heard Diana snicker behind me, but Merle didn't say anything. The silence reminded me of being in class when you've given a crazy wrong answer and the teacher lets you hang there for a while. I loved Mom's ugly lipstick at that moment. But I had a feeling that if we were going to fit in at Tivoli Towers, we'd have to stop being ourselves.

▶

Mom and I gradually settled into a kind of routine at Tivoli Towers. Florence called at least three times a week and although we had only one phone, the apartment was so small I could hear Mom's end of the conversation no matter where I was. I could always tell when she was on the phone with Florence because Mom tried to sound cheerful by using this high-pitched voice I called her "telephone" voice. It was the same fake-sounding happy voice she'd started using around Merle. "Oh, you know, we're so busy here discovering new things," Mom would say, dodging Florence's questions about how we were doing. It was only when Grandpa called that Mom sounded like her old self again. Grandpa's call always came on Monday nights, after Dad had left for his meeting and when the only thing on television was the newscast from Buffalo, which Grandpa found aggravating because it was all crime and animals up for adoption. I figured he wanted to come live with us, because Mom would say things like "We're up too high, Sol, your ears would pop" and "Who says I make good boiled chicken? I've never heard that from you before. You're just trying to butter me up."

After Mom got off the phone with Grandpa, she and Merle shopped for meat at Sumo's, the gourmet store in the concourse. All chicken breasts were half-price after eight, and they would take their three pounds each upstairs and freeze them into giant tinfoil blobs. "I like having a friend in the building, but if she didn't know a good bargain, we'd have nothing in common," Mom said. "Zero."

Diana and I were an even bigger flop. Every time Mom went over to Merle's apartment, she'd make me go with her. In her room, Diana would lay her skirt and pant sets out on the bed in the shape of bodies, and tell me about how she was going to be a model as soon as she got her growth spurt. The only way I could get through these visits was to tell myself that we'd be moving home in a few weeks. I always asked Diana to keep her bedroom door open, so I could overhear Mom and Merle talking. Merle liked to talk about men, and I hoped Mom would start talking about Dad but she didn't. Merle went on and on about how Diana's dad was a celebrity dentist who'd invented a compound to bleach teeth as white as new snow. After he'd made all his money, Merle said he'd left her for a younger woman "with no self-esteem."

"It's unfair how men get to age and we don't," Merle said.

"Even if I were twenty-five, Frank and I still wouldn't have any chemistry," Mom said.

Back in our apartment, I asked Mom if we had to spend so much time with the Gaddicks. I was worried that Merle was a bad influence on Mom. I was afraid she'd make Mom never want to move home.

"Tell me the truth, does she make you feel cool?" I asked her.

Mom made a face like she'd sucked a lemon. "What do you want me to do? You want me to grow old looking at four walls?"

But I could tell that Mom's friendship with Merle was already having an impact. Mom wore lipstick all the time now, even to go to Sumo's, a new deep red colour that reminded me of old brick houses. She'd started putting walnuts and canned tangerine segments in our salads. She'd also bought new high-tech deodorant so the white stuff wouldn't show up on her clothes. "There is a difference between antiperspirant and deodorant, do you realize that?" she said, pulling a stick of "invisible solid" out of her Sumo's shopping bag. "I mean, they're the same price, but they have different purposes." She looked triumphant standing in our kitchen, as if this was the small but important secret that had been holding her back. It made me wonder why she hadn't tried this hard when we were still living at home.

I spent every Thursday and Friday night with Dad. On Thursday afternoon, Mom was still at work, so I let myself in and went to my room to pack my orange Samsonite suitcase. I didn't really need to pack anything since I had clothes at home, but I felt very adult carrying the suitcase out with me, swinging it as I walked through the apartment the way I imagined Mary Tyler Moore did in the 1970s. Then the intercom would buzz and it would be Dad waiting for me downstairs. When I came out of the elevator that afternoon, he was standing on one of the soggy little mats making hamster faces at me, his cheeks wet like he'd been crying but of course it was only snow. Instead of his parka, he was wearing an old leather jacket with cracks at the elbows.

Dad was different now that he was living only with Grandpa. He talked more and he talked fast, like his mouth was running out of time. That evening, for the whole ride back to our house, he went on about a new car that he wanted to buy: a vanilla-coloured Maserati that he'd seen on a used car lot on his way to Sun and Waves.

"Do you know what a Maserati looks like?"

"It sounds like a kind of cheese," I said. "What's wrong with this car anyways?"

Dad's shoulders fell. "Lucy, do I block your dreams?"

We ate supper on the living room floor while Grandpa snored on the couch. Dad showed me some photographs he'd taken in the last week with his old Kodak Brownie camera. "That's a little Italian place on Baldwin Street," Dad said. "When Grandpa first moved here, he worked for a furrier on Baldwin Street. But now it's a pretty hip neighbourhood."

I wanted Dad to ask me about Mom, but I was pretty sure he wasn't even thinking about her. I could smell his new cologne. He even smelled different now. He was changing, just like Mom was.

"Are you happier?"

"No," Dad said. "I'm just happy."

"Are you happy because you're seeing her?"

"Mom and I decided to be open with you, so I can go ahead and tell you. I didn't do a good thing by going out with another woman.

But it's done and we have to make the best of it. I'm forty-six years old, Lucy. I want to experience life."

Later, Dad went out to the garage to wash his car and listen to Roy Orbison, what used to be his morning ritual. Without Mom and me here, his schedule was all jumbled. Grandpa was awake now, so I sat with him in front of the TV and tried to get him to talk about Crashing Wave.

"The woman with the blonde hair," I said. "What does she do when she's here?"

Grandpa used his long pinky fingernail to dig caraway seeds out of his bread. "She's not Joy. Not even Betty. She don't even make the cakes."

He was going senile. It was obvious. Especially after dinner, when the pill drama would begin. Grandpa kept a plastic case of pills on top of the television, a case so old that the days-of-the-week labels on each compartment had rubbed off, which made it hard for him to tell if he'd taken his post-supper pill or not. "Who saw me take my pill?" he'd say as if he were addressing a packed concert hall, and not just me. "Who? You?" I'd take the pill case to the kitchen table, spill out all the capsules, and count them against the week, and his drug regime, to figure out if there was an extra one in there. There never was. By the time I came back to the living room he'd be asleep on the couch, his hearing aid lying on the coffee table like a lost seashell.

I went upstairs and opened my night-table drawer and took out Crashing Wave's lipstick. I unrolled the lipstick and sniffed it, but I wouldn't let myself put it on. I couldn't. Just looking at it gave me a queasy feeling in my gut, so I put the lipstick away.

The house felt strange without Mom in it. It felt like a hot-air balloon without the balloon. As I walked through the house, I couldn't stop myself from thinking about Crashing Wave's plastic blue heels walking where Mom used to. I saw Crashing Wave on the couch, reaching her red-nailed fingers to grab the TV remote control. I saw her in the laundry room, examining the pencil marks on the door frame that year by year had measured how tall I was getting. In the bathroom she was smiling as she combed her hair, leaning into the mirror as if it were water to wash her face in. And when I stood by the kitchen windows, I saw her in the space between the man and the woman mannequin, throwing her head back and laughing.

If she had been anyone else, I would have been glad to know her as Alicia. I would have loved her to be Alicia at the bakery, handing me a cookie. Or an Alicia at the pet store at the mall, selling twisty-tube hamster cages. I would have listened to my teacher Alicia. But she was the reason Mom and Dad weren't living together now. As long as she was the one standing between them, I couldn't think of her as a regular woman. She had to remain Crashing Wave.

►

At the end of January, Merle Gaddick hosted her own birthday party, and Mom and I attended with our out-of-the-box potato latkes. The Gaddicks' apartment had a sunken living room that reminded me of a drained kiddie pool, and milling around it were women I recognized from the elevators. Most of them had big, dry curly hair, like the men in heavy-metal music videos. I didn't know whether Mom looked right or wrong in comparison. She'd worn her only "suit" for the occasion, a green seersucker that made me think of a safari guide.

"There's Diana," Mom said. "Who's that man she's talking to?"

I spotted Diana across the room, leaning against the buffet and talking to Seville, the doorman, who'd come up with two bags of ice.

"That's Seville. You probably don't recognize him out of his uniform, but you pay him to admire his hair in the lobby mirrors."

Mom didn't laugh at my joke. She kept looking around the room as little pearls of sweat popped up above her lip and near her temples, where her reddish hair dye had worn off to reveal the grey. Nobody else in the room had greying hair except Mom. But I was proud of the way she stood out. She was the only diamond in the room. I grabbed her elbow and tried to pull her toward the food table, but she resisted.

"Never eat as soon as you walk into a party," she whispered, "it's gauche." I figured this was a Merle Gaddick word because I didn't know what it meant. "You're supposed to mingle and only go to the food table if there is *absolutely nobody* to talk to. That's what Emily Post says."

"What's the point of being at a party if you don't eat?"

"Shhhh, you're making a scene."

Beside us, a woman with liquid eyeliner running off her eyelids in a swoosh that reminded me of the Nike logo was talking about a new dating service. The Millionaire Match dealt only with men "in possession of two boats and a three-car garage minimum." I could tell Mom was getting more anxious by the way she kept angling her nose into her armpit to check for perspiration. Then the woman wearing a pearl-studded headband, who'd been bragging about her twenty-eight-foot-yacht boyfriend, asked Mom if she was seeing anyone. Mom sipped at her seltzer water and said, "I'm not jumping into anything like that. Friendship is fine, but understand that I've just emerged from a shit storm."

Once, to annoy Estelle Pomper, I'd told her that when I grew up I wanted to buy a run-down old bank and convert it into a cat petting zoo and vintage movie theatre. Pearl-head was now looking at her friend in the same condemning way Estelle Pomper had looked at Missy Lakakis. Merle's party, I realized, was like being in a school-yard except the dirt and grass here were hardwood floors and Persian rugs, and the climbers and slides were big blobby paintings and a couch that looked like two hard cubes. But it was the same old thing: I'm popular and you're not. I'll talk to you and I won't talk to you. Pearl-head extricated herself from Mom's shit storm and came over to me.

"Hi there," she said sweetly, "do you have any more of those wraps?"

The only rapper I knew was M.C. Hammer, but I didn't have his tape. Before I could say anything, Mom cut in. "That's not a waiter. That's my daughter, Lucy."

Pearl-head covered her mouth and cringed. "Oh, oh. I thought because of the black pants and white shirt she was working –"

That's when Mom grabbed my hand and dragged me to the food table, where she stood looking around in the same hopeful way I imagined I'd stand at dances for the rest of my life. Merle found us, put her arm around Mom all chummy, and pointed to the opposite end of the room. Standing at the window, beside the fake plum tree, was a man. He'd tied his suit jacket around his waist, which I'd never seen a grown man do before. Merle leaned into Mom's ear and whispered, but it was that kind of drunk whisper that adults do, which is actually closer to loud talking.

"That's Robbie Roth, and I need to tell you –" She giggled, then hiccupped. "Joy, when you walked in the room he said to me, 'Who is that zaftig woman?' I said, 'That's Joy. And she *is* that and more." She broke out laughing now. She was the kind of person who could really get excited about puns. "He's a very eligible man," she continued. "A hothead businessman. A developer of real estate. But lonely. Lonely as hell. So lonely he sleeps in the fetal position."

I spent the rest of the evening eating mini egg rolls and sneaking looks at Robbie Roth. He looked older than Dad, and had an old-fashioned hangdog face with deep folds on either side of his mouth. His eyes were pale as cocktail onions. He wore a tight black dress shirt and a tie printed with piano keys, and he ate grapes like a little horse, scooping them out of his own palm.

Mom had been looking at him too. In the elevator, she said that he looked interesting in a wounded kind of way. To me this was a bad sign, to say the words *interesting* and *wounded* in the same breath.

"None of this transition is easy on me," Mom said. "You need to be supportive."

"I am supportive," I said. "But what is Robbie Roth doing living at Tivoli Towers if he's such a hot-shot real estate developer?"

Mom didn't talk to me as we walked down the hall to our apartment. I felt as if I'd won something, but I didn't know exactly what. But then, as soon as she closed the door behind us, she burst into low sobs. "I hate parties," she cried. "I am a one-on-one kind of person!" Then she went to her bedroom. A few minutes later, Julio's soothing voice slipped out from under her closed door.

So I started swallowing my words. When I came home from Dad's the following week, and Mom's hair was freshly dyed bright cherry red and cut in a new style — short at the back with permed, gift ribbon bangs — I didn't say anything, at least not at first. I just watched her in the bathroom mirror as she squinted and smoothed down her flyaways. She looked pensive, as if she were on the edge of a diving board.

"Lucy, if you squint, do I look forty?"

I cocked my head to the side, squinted, and took a few shaky steps toward her. "Is that you, Mom? Or is that you, Merle Gaddick?"

Mom froze. "That's mean. You're making fun of me."

But I wasn't trying to. A few months ago, she would've found that funny.

Later that night Mom went out for coffee with Robbie Roth. I wasn't sure if he'd asked her out before or after the new hairdo, and in a way I didn't even want to know. I was happy to have a break from her. Just seeing her reading Merle's etiquette books or fumbling with one of her new lipsticks irritated me. When we were still living with Dad, she had gone to the ten-dollar hairdresser and told him to do whatever he wanted. She had never gone for colour. With Dad, she'd never cared about makeup or looking forty. It made me think she'd been saving up her best self for people she didn't even know. That bugged me. It had been two months since we'd moved to Tivoli Towers and we should have been home by now.

After Mom left, I called Diana and asked her if I could come over. Merle answered the door wearing a black and red mask, and sitting around the sunken living room were a group of women and men wearing the same mask. It was Kabuki divorce redramatization, and I kept my eyes on the rug as I made my way to Diana's room. I got along a little better with her now because she let me read her *Seventeen* magazines and try on her least favourite shoes. I was a tourist in her world. When I opened her bedroom door, she was standing by her Venus flytrap, pressing a pencil tip to one of its closed traps. Its purplish flesh had turned a wormy grey colour in the week since I'd seen it. I asked her if she was going to feed it and she asked me where Mom was.

"Question for a question," she cooed, flipping her hair. She knew I was jealous of how it resembled five foxtails sewn together.

"She's out with Robbie Roth," I said, sitting down on her couch – I'd never met anyone else who had a couch in her bedroom. "She says he's a nice guy. She wants some companionship."

"Companionship," Diana snorted. "Merle helped set it up. Good luck to you. He's the cat man of the building. He tells girls he has this cat that's about to pop out kittens and then you go up to his apartment and there's no cat, zilch, just this stuffed cat sitting on his couch with a bowl of tuna beside it. But if you play with the cat, like pull its legs and arms, he gives you five dollars." She smiled, revealing her bright white teeth.

I'm so glad I'm not going to know you for much longer, I thought. In a month, when Mom and I moved home, Diana would be as forgettable as an old sticker in my album. For now, I just wanted to get off the subject of Robbie.

"Diana," I said, "I really like your shirt."

It was one of those mint green polo shirts with a small horse logo above the breast pocket. Diana flopped down beside me and grabbed the collar of her shirt. "You *always* say that. You know what girls are gonna think if you compliment them so much? They'll think you're some big lesbo. Unless you are a big lesbo and then you should say to me now, if you're a big lesbo, 'Touch my tots.'" She grabbed at my chest, which really hurt. "Take off your shirt," she said.

I pushed her away. "You're nuts."

"Show me yours," she said. "Here, I'll go first."

She took off her polo shirt and her beige bra with the little tennis rackets appliqué between the cups, and then dared me to touch her breasts. Her breasts were different sizes and I didn't know which one to touch. So I chose the smaller one, because I figured she resented it. I just pet it, the way you pet a cat you hardly know. My hand made little circles on her breast, feeling the curve of her top rib, soft yet hard at the same time, like a piece of celery.

"You're a big lesbo," Diana said, her voice gentle but firm. "You're getting so turned on right now. Like, if you were a man, you'd come all over the place."

When she said "man" I thought of Mom laughing with Robbie Roth, his piano-key tie twinkling, and Dad laughing with Crashing Wave. I'd never felt so sad. I took off my shirt and Diana looked at me, her blue eyes all narrowed, and said that I was okay the way the school dentist did after a thirty-second poke around my mouth. Then she told me to put my shirt back on. It was an ugly shirt from the Salvation Army, with a granny drawstring at the neck.

She didn't put her shirt back on, though. That was the thing about Diana. She thought she was so beautiful that she had the power to boss everyone else around. I thought of taking my shirt off again, just to show her up. But my breasts were non-existent compared to hers, and I didn't want her looking at them anymore.

"We're totally different," Diana said. "We have nothing in common, do we?"

"We're both stuck at Tivoli Towers."

"Yes," Diana said solemnly, covering her breasts with her hands. "And we're both in love with no one."

The next Monday night, after the meat had been mummified in tinfoil, I overheard Merle telling Mom that Robbie Roth was cultured, and that he knew about such things as symphonies and art.

"If you want to know more," Merle said, "you can go to the library."

Then Mom said, "I'm a teacher, Merle. I know all about the library. Please don't treat me like some kind of project."

Finally. I thought this would be the beginning of Mom's return to her old self.

But two days later, she started signing out paintings from the public library. On the second floor of the Yorkville branch was a wooden box of "fine art reproductions" – actually posters glued to slabs of plywood – that you could borrow for up to three weeks. I guess the city was full of people trying as hard as Mom was. She began signing out new art all the time: paintings of water lilies, ballerinas bent over double, and one week, the Mona Lisa with her searching eyes. One afternoon Mom came home with a really horrible painting: little men in tight pants scurrying around on a background of spoilt egg yellow. Merle had lent her a hammer and nails and Mom proceeded to bang an illegal nail into the living room wall.

"It's Brueghel," she said when she'd finished hanging the picture. "He's Flemish. This painting is called *Young Folk at Play*. Do you see the nice kids dancing?" She pointed to a few little midgets wearing hot pants. "All those kids are having a good time. You know why? Because it's good for them."

"You can see those guys' dicks," I said. "You'd better take it down."

When Robbie Roth stopped by later that night, he was wearing the same silk piano-key tie. He stood in our apartment doorway and held out his gift to Mom – a tray of chocolate balls with red licorice sticking out of the ends of them. "Choco-mice," Robbie said. "I'm two left feet in the kitchen except when it comes to baking. I like how the oven does half the work for me."

Mom laughed, like this was supposed to be a joke. Then I remembered what Diana had told me about how adults make jokes to cut the sexual tension, which is why most of their jokes didn't make sense.

When we sat down in the living room, Robbie said he'd brought me a present because he'd heard from a little bird that I liked to read. He gave me a pile of yellowed *Life* magazines that I leafed through to be polite.

"You had a good day at school today?" Robbie said.

"It was pretty good –" I started to say, before I realized he was talking to Mom.

"It was okay," Mom said, looking at her hands. "Not too exciting." Usually, she could talk for an hour about incidents at school that bugged her: a teacher who was changing the desk formations too much or how the microwave in the staff room was always spattered with cheese. Her silence made me dislike Robbie Roth even more. Crushes on the wrong person were like bad sore throats, I decided: they made you lose your voice.

"It's just that I've never known a teacher, so it's exciting to me," Robbie said. "The only teacher I knew used a ruler to rap me on the –" I was glad he didn't finish his sentence. I didn't want to think about his butt. "So I'm interested in what else teachers spend their time doing."

Blushing, Mom said, "Well, I just teach new Canadians. They really like to learn about practical things. So today we did post-office etiquette." She was getting pink in the cheeks, and the colour made her look younger and happier. "I taught them how to ask for single stamps rather than the whole booklet. And how to ask for the economy rate when sending a parcel. That kind of thing, nothing important."

For a flash of a second, Robbie put his hand on Mom's orange nylon knee. "No, that *is* important," he said. "It's these little things that make the quality of life."

Spare me, I thought.

For the next twenty minutes I sat on the arm of our rental armchair, trying to figure out what was going on between Mom and Robbie Roth. They sat beside each other on the rattan couch, below the new gold-framed mirror that Mom had probably bought at Merle's suggestion, and clearly not from a junk store. Neither of them touched the coffee or the choco-mice on the table. Handel's *Water Music*, which Mom had bought specially for the occasion, tinkled in the background. Diana said that people who are into each other give off a kind of animal scent that's related to, but not exactly, skunky. I sniffed the air. All I smelled was the strong Turkish coffee.

Then Robbie turned to me. "Tell me, Lucy, do you like the building? Joy told me that you had to leave a cat named Lulu at home, right? Cats are wonderful, I have a few myself. And one of them is about to become a mother to some little kittens." I nodded. Even though I didn't believe what Diana had said about Robbie Roth, to me this was a bad sign, a grown man talking so much about his cat.

Mom cleared her throat and looked at me. "Robbie's in real estate. You know, like in Monopoly." She turned to Robbie as she poured him another cup of coffee. "Tell her about your renovations. Lucy loves makeover stories."

"Basically I buy a house that's so run down no one else will. A real haunted house. Places that have crazy words written on the walls and little china dolls from 1900 buried in the foundations. Then I get my guys to come in and fix it up. I rip out the hardware, the floors, then the fixtures, whatever it takes. I go to great lengths to improve the look of the place. After I put in everything new, I divide the house up into units and I sell or I rent. Depending on if it's a buyer's or a seller's market."

He looked at me once he'd finished, like I was supposed to hand him a prize.

"So basically you're a slumlord," I said.

Mom forced out a sharp laugh that was the sound of popcorn popping when it's been in the microwave for too long. Then she smoothed down her new bangs and inhaled. "Robbie says he has some gorgeous Victorians in Parkdale that he's working on right now. And maybe we'll even move there, if he has something very nice for us. So you can have a backyard. And get Lulu back. Wouldn't you like to get her back?"

By the middle of March, Mom was going out for coffee with Robbie Roth at least three times a week. She blow-dried her hair every day now. She wore lip-liner, too, though sometimes she forgot the lipstick and I wouldn't tell her. A mean, secret part of me hoped that Robbie would have a problem with this and break up with her suddenly.

"Are you keeping it above the neck?" I asked her.

"We're friends now," Mom answered. "And we're going to see what happens," which was a totally unsatisfying answer.

It was bad enough that Mom and Dad weren't talking, but now I felt shut out of her life too. Mom and Robbie Roth had been seeing each other for a month and a half and I still had no clue what was going on. The picture of Mom and Dad I held in my head kept scattering, as unstable as a sand painting. Diana became my main source of information, which was pathetic, because I just wanted to hear it from Mom. Diana told me that the women in Tivoli Towers envied Mom for having landed a catch like Robbie Roth. Even Merle, which I thought was strange. Merle had dated Robbie but dumped him because she'd decided he was too old.

"It was a guilt match," Diana told me. "Merle felt guilty for dumping Robbie so she threw your mother all over him."

I didn't like to admit it, but Mom seemed less cynical and happier with Robbie Roth around. "I feel safe around Robbie," Mom said, "I feel like someone is finally listening to what I am trying to say."

The next time Robbie came over, I watched how Robbie behaved while Mom was talking. He spread his hands on his lap, palms up, and leaned his head closer to Mom's mouth, like he was scared to miss a thing. And he nodded a lot, breathing as serenely as the monk I'd once seen on TV, who taught meditation at five in the morning after the TV switched over from the coloured bars. He was attentive in a way that Dad wasn't. He listened to her. I needed to tell Dad about Robbie. I needed to do something because I wasn't so sure anymore that we were ever going home.

A couple of days later Diana and I were lying on the deck of the indoor pool. I was in an old one-piece with a frumpy skirt. Diana, with her shiny waxed legs, wore mini shorts and a floral bandeau with sequins on the petals. She was lying on her stomach, reading *Madame Victoria*, a sexy novel she'd stolen from Merle. When she turned to me, her breasts mashed into a line.

"Oooh, do you think it would be fun to be a hooker?" Diana said.

I was beginning to feel that the world tolerated Diana because she was just so cute. Her nose was prettily fluted, her eyes wide, stuck in that goggle-eyed expression of perpetual amazement. If I showed her a picture of a zebra in my science book, she said, "Oooh." If I told her Grandpa was trying to get on to *The Price Is Right*, against doctor's orders, or that Mom couldn't pay the rent now, and the bills were piling up on our microwave, she said, "Oooh." The only time I'd seen her upset was last week, when her stereo ate her Ace of Base tape.

"A hooker?"

Diana put down her book and sat up against the sweaty pillar, so her chubby stomach collected into a little bowl above the line of her shorts. "Think about it," she said. "In *Madame Victoria*, she's rich, and all she has to do is lie in this canopy bed while the men flock to her. When it's done they leave the money in the chamber-pot, so her mother won't find out."

"Classy. But wouldn't the money get mixed with all the —"

"Tell me the truth, do you hear it through the wall all the time now?" Diana sat up and cupped her chin in her hands. "When Robbie did it to Merle, it was a groany sound like mmmmppph! mmmmppph! which is what it sounds like when it's going through the back."

The back? No. "Robbie and Merle did that?"

"Sure," Diana said. "He was her *real estate* agent too."

I stood up so fast that the blood rushing to my head made me feel as if I was going to fall down. "You're nasty, Diana. If you want to be nasty, you can just stay here." I tried to think of something else to say, something mean, and sexual, but nothing came to me. "Are you swimming with me or not?"

She waved her hand. "See, that's what I mean about you. I just dissed you and now you're asking me into the pool. You're desperate. But I'm plugged up anyway so go ahead." Diana never went into the water. She thought she could get a tan from the slats of faint sunlight that came through the glass atrium above us.

Underwater, I scissor-kicked down to the corner of the deep end, nine feet down, where I lay my back against the slimy tiled wall. I thought about Diana and her nasty book full of prodding members, her expensive bikini. I thought about Mom and Robbie Roth making out in our bankruptcy suite. I'd looked at her pay stub one night, and I didn't think we could last much longer here. I thought about Dad and Crashing Wave at our house. Only maybe Crashing Wave had already taken over. Maybe she'd taken back her lipstick from my dresser drawer and thrown out Mom's things. Maybe she was stroking Lulu's ears in the way only I knew how to do. My hair loosed around me like dark seaweed. Then Seville plopped into my mind like a frog. He was on all fours but still wearing his blue uniform and gold nametag. "Fuck me," he said. "I'll pay you." I came up out of the deep, gasping.

Diana was still reading when I lay down on my towel and stared up at cracks in the glass ceiling. My eyes followed the beads of rain running down the glass block, the corners foggy like someone had breathed on them. March was a depressing month, I decided. It didn't know if it was winter or spring.

"My parents are getting back together," I said. "You need to know that. So why is my mom dating Robbie anyway if they're just taking things slowly and being companions?"

"She's a woman. She has pubic needs."

"You're brainwashed."

"Even Merle says so." Diana put down her book. "She says she's glad your mother found someone to take care of her."

I could tell there was something more she wanted to say. "What? Say it."

"I just think you ought to be more supportive of your mother. That's all. My mo – Merle said –"

"Tell your mother that my parents are getting back together, before she develops some other cockeyed idea. To go with her fugly horse boots. To go with her stupid fugly masks and her bitch-head."

"Oooh, bitch-head?" Diana giggled. Then she started reading aloud. "*At first Madame Victoria was wary of the advances from the young simpleton, whose horsehair shirt confirmed a past criminal status.*" She paused. "What's horsehair shirt?"

"Luxury probably. Keep reading." I wanted to get far away from the topic of Mom and Robbie Roth.

"*However, when the time of rueful kisses gave way to nether region fires, she understood that this was no financial transaction –*"

She closed the book. "This happens in real life. Merle told me that last month Robbie Roth bought your mom a gold-framed mirror from Pier One Imports and that now he'd lending her money so that she can pay her rent."

All at once I felt as if I was in a photo being crumpled in some-one's hand.

"So you're saying my mom's a hooker?"

"No, no," Diana said. "All I said was that she had a boyfriend."

When I let myself into the apartment, I went over to the phone in the kitchen and stared at it. I knew it was time to call Dad. I'd been too patient, waiting for Mom to stop seeing Robbie Roth. If Dad knew what was going on, he'd realize that he was about to lose her.

Mom was at the *Phantom of the Opera* with Robbie, and her

bedroom door hung open like a laughing mouth. I imagined Mom in a dark room with Robbie, sucking on a purple olive, raking a chopstick over a raw fish head – twenty bucks she couldn't afford, worse if he was paying for her – then Mom kicking off her Lady Shoes, forgetting about Dad. Dad was going to worry when I told him about Robbie Roth. He was going to worry that he'd missed his chance.

The phone rang six times before Dad answered. When I heard his voice he sounded so far away that I wanted to be closer to him. I told him I wanted him to pick me up.

"Tuesday's your mom's night," he said. "So I can't just kidnap you like that. Why don't you watch some television? Or eat a banana."

He wasn't listening to me. "Dad, I don't feel good. Mom's at the *Phantom of the Opera*. I just want to come home."

His voice was as tinny as a robot's. "I'll see you on Thursday, sweetie."

Sweetie. A fizzy feeling in my chest, a feeling that made me think of boxed candies, Nerds, melting everywhere inside me. He never called me that. He wasn't even paying attention. He never paid attention to me anymore.

"Is she there with you? Whose voice is that?"

He said there was no one there.

"Dad, I can hear a girl talking."

"That's you. It's an echo. Your mom always buys cheap phones."

"Mom's spending all her money," I said. "Did you know?"

He told me that it was her life.

"We can't afford this place. And I don't like the people here. They're weird. There's a man here, he's the cat man of –"

"You're too critical. She can get an extra teaching job if she wants. If she wants to live the life, she'll have to learn the hard way. And you need to quit putting the magnifying glass down on other people's lives."

"But, Dad. She –"

"I know, Lucy. She has a boyfriend. Florence told me. You don't need to worry so much."

"You're a liar, Dad."

But I knew he was telling the truth, and the truth was he didn't care that she had a boyfriend. He wasn't coming over to tell Mom that he'd made a huge mistake. I sank into my shoe. I felt my eyes sliding down my leg into my shoe, followed by my mouth, my ribs, my ears.

Dad sighed. "Where's my old Lucy? She used to love cats and hamsters. She used to ask about her Lulu. You know what Lulu's doing right now?"

He was treating me like I was an idiot. "Bye, Dad."

Then I hung up the phone and went to my room. My ALF shoe-laces were under my pillow. I lay them out on one of the yellow halo stains on my bed and pressed my cheek against them – Earth to ALF, ALF to Tivoli Towers – but they did nothing. So I squirmed under the blanket and pressed my hand onto the private of my jeans. I rubbed myself. I squeezed my eyes shut and pictured a pond with an empty field around it while I rubbed myself. Starting with the pond I put fish in it, plop, plop, plop, goldfish, swordfish, scaleless and whiskered fish that sucked the bottom, then geckos, frogs, and toads. I squeezed my knees together and brought them up to my chest, rubbing. I squished my eyes shut tighter to focus on the animals. First a family of deer with soft, brown backs spotted Bambi white. They grazed by the tree I was growing, long trunked and wide. On its branches I hung some hairy red gibbons and some Dodo birds. Behind the tree I put elephants and Bengal tigers, lions and two rhinoceros plodding downhill into the water. The warm churning feeling was starting to turn like a top in my private so I kept rubbing. The gibbon was swinging ten feet at a time, his brown eyes sparkling almost red. The gibbon was sighing. I painted in flamingos and six storks dipping their beaks into the pond. A pressure in my private. My eyes felt shaky and hot. I began subtracting the animals. They wanted to stay. They were begging me. The private of my jeans was making a scratching sound, so hot. I sucked the fish out of the pond and I wouldn't listen to their screaming. I plucked out the wild cats, the monkeys, everything, and then I chopped down the tree. It didn't want to fall, I didn't want to let it fall, but it had to. It fell. The gushing feeling of a tree falling. I took my hand away.

▶

A month later, Robbie drove us to one of his investment properties, the place Mom said we might move to. He said it was cheaper than our place at Tivoli Towers and had a "lot of character," so I figured it would be ugly.

I sat in the backseat as he drove us five miles west in his blue Town car, with its maroon, potato-chip-smelling velvet interior that reminded me of his 1970s suit jacket. Rain was sliding against the windshield. I could see tiny purple crocuses pushing up out of the soil on the lawns we passed.

Robbie turned onto a street dense with rundown-looking houses that slanted to the left, all of them painted brown with other shades of brown showing through the chipped parts. He pulled up in front of a house with five doorbells under the porch light.

Mom and I got out of the car and stood on the sidewalk. The air reeked of soil and manure, and Mom made a big show of sniffing, and sighing, as if she was suddenly a person who was into nature. All I smelled was garbage. Beside me, piled on the edge of the lawn, was a La-Z-Boy chair with all its stuffing coming out in foamy, yellow clots, a fridge with the doors ripped off, and bags of junk spilling out boxes of instant pudding and potatoes, the cardboard crinkled from the rain.

Robbie marched around on the lawn with his arms crossed on his chest, smiling. He walked proudly, pretending he wasn't aware of how his legs had to keep stepping around garbage.

"Robbie wants to show me around." Mom handed me a five-dollar bill. "There's a big dollar store two minutes down on Queen Street. So walk straight down this street and don't talk to anyone. When you pass the hospital I want you to keep your eyes on the ground. It's full of nutcases."

I walked south two blocks until I hit the No Frills supermarket behind a crumbly old hotel with a sign of flying Canada geese, their wings flared out like boomerangs. People were crowded into the supermarket parking lot, near the shopping cart shelter. There was a man selling all kinds of things on outspread children's blankets: crinkled vinyl raincoats, baby-blue snow suits with built-in booties, and toys – mechanized cats and puppies, rattles and Glow Worms, and so many teddy bears they had their own blanket. The peddler was dressed in a ringmaster's tight red suit. He waved his hand at me and then pointed to his toys. "*To-ys!* It will make her *happy!*" he sang. "*To-ys!* Au-to-ma-tic puppies. Cats with real tongue and feeling too."

I felt emptied but rattled. A pop can with the tab pushed in. I had the five dollars in my pocket so I bought a bright blue Smurf from the man and started walking along Queen Street. I didn't see any hospital, just a big park with enormous rain-coated poplar trees. I sat down on a bench as a homeless man was parking his piled-high shopping cart a few feet away, by the garbage can. He was Dad's age, and he had a coffee-coloured beard and pants that were just shredded rings around his skinny red legs. He walked over to my bench and sat down on.

"This city. *This city.*" He was wailing.

I moved my hand across the bench and tapped him on the shoulder. I wanted him to do something crazy to me – to yank my hair, to punch me to the ground, to hurt me, anything – so this could all be over, this time of Tivoli Towers. But he didn't do anything. He just sat there like he couldn't even feel my hand.

"It's okay," I whispered. "I'm not scared of you."

When I got back to the house with the muddy lawn, Mom was standing outside alone. She was staring at the ground and pulling on the ends of her curly bangs. In the afternoon light, I could see that her red hair had faded to that yellowy colour of leaves at the end of fall.

We took a taxi back to Tivoli Towers, neither of us saying a word. Once we were in the apartment, Mom threw her leather gloves on the floor and went to sit on the rattan couch. I didn't know what to do, so I went to kitchen and mixed a glass of orange juice and soda, her favourite. When I gave it to her she was shaking her head.

"So that's what he thinks of me, the slumlord. He showed me a little cave in the basement, talked it up like it was a bargain, like I should be so lucky to live there. Like he could look down on me from high." She took off her glasses and spit on the lenses, then used the hem of her skirt to clean them. "Millipedes coming out of the drain and in the kitchen two feet of sawdust. You can imagine what's in the walls. And he keeps saying what a good deal it is 'on a teacher's salary.' Like I have no options. I don't know what Merle sees in him, but maybe she should take him back."

Mom put her glass on the floor. Then she got up, went over to the Brueghel on the wall, and took it down. "This perm," she said, staring at the painting, as if the men in hot pants were just this puff of dyed red curls, "it's so ridiculous, and God knows how long it will take to grow out. Probably they put in some chemicals that seeped down into my brain."

For two months, I'd wished that Mom's "romantic companionship" with Robbie Roth would blow up like a tab of Alka-Seltzer in a glass of fizzy water. Now it had. But I didn't feel any better.

Mom was staring at a spot on the wall where the Brueghel had hung. "I need to get some filler for this hole," she said.

▶

In the middle of April, I got a letter from The Elms School. Mom and I were sitting at the table with a plate of feta pastries and a bowl of speared cucumbers between us. I opened the letter and read the white page.

"Do you they want you?" Mom said.

I pushed the letter across the table. "Yeah."

Mom smiled and clicked her teeth affirmatively. Robbie Roth was history, but she'd picked up this habit from him. "I'm happy for you," she said. "We'll buy you some new clothes. Turn the new leaf."

Later that night, Mom came into my room and sat on the edge of my Murphy bed, crossing her legs, so I could see the inflated toe of her Big Ugly Shoe glowing in the dark. I was listening to the *Sunday Night Sex Show* on the radio, and Sue Johanson's voice said, very seriously, *You may feel like you're losing your mind, but rest assured it is all completely natural.* I lowered the volume.

Mom tried to bounce a little on my bed, but it still didn't work. "You've probably noticed that I've been talking to Florence a lot more lately. Well, she's been talking to Dad too."

I wished my pillow was a well so I could dive into it. I was scared she was going to tell me that we were staying here for good.

"Dad's decided not to be with that woman anymore, that fly-by-night. And for the last two weeks, we've been talking with a marriage counsellor. His name is Myron. He's helping me to come to terms with your dad's screw-up. You know what he helped us figure out? We don't want to be alone."

"What about Dad?"

"He's sorry," Mom said, though she sounded like she was the one apologizing. "He's like a kid. He acted on a whim. But I feel okay enough now to forgive him."

I was smiling, but the room was too dark for me to see Mom's face. Before we moved to Tivoli Towers, I could read the tone of her voice the way a thermometer measures the temperature down to the half-degree. But now I couldn't tell from her voice alone if she was really okay.

She was quiet for a long time. I knew she wanted me to say something, to tell her if she was making a mistake. But I didn't care if it was the right choice or not. I just wanted us to be a family again. Even if it meant going back to the way things used to be.

Two weeks later we moved home.

5

There was a ride at the CNE called the Tilt-A-Whirl, and in scariness it was three notches up from the giant Ferris wheel, and two down from the Ghoster Coaster. You sat in a spinning car attached to a platform, which revolved up and down, and made you feel like a flying pinball, your breath catching in chokes in your throat. Afterwards, the ground underneath your feet would feel wobbly and the scenery would blur. That's how it felt to be at home the summer Mom and I moved back from Tivoli Towers: the ride had ended, but I was still spinning.

The night Mom sat on the edge of my Murphy bed, she'd seemed set on starting again. So I didn't understand why Mom wasn't trying harder to get along with Dad. She'd thrown out all of her lipsticks and eyeliners and let her roots grow in. When Dad asked her out to the Chinese buffet on Wednesday nights, which were half-price, Mom would say, "I like Mr. Noodles more," her eyes fixed on Larry King, who was her new weeknight date.

I could still picture Dad and Crashing Wave sitting at our kitchen table. Maybe despite Dad's offers to take her to the buffet, or to a movie, or on "drives to the country," Mom could still picture them too.

I figured all she wanted was for Dad to ask her how her day was. Robbie Roth had at least got that part right. "Ask her about her students," I told Dad. "Make her feel interesting."

Dad shook his head. "I don't bring my work home. That's dull. I just want things to be sweet again." But the mood in the house was sour.

Then in July it got worse. I found Charlie Sheen in his cage one morning, belly up, his pink paws curled on his chest as though he'd been beating it Tarzan-style at the moment he passed away. When school started in September, I was glad to have somewhere else to go, where I wouldn't think about Charlie Sheen or Mom and Dad.

From the outside The Elms School looked like an L-shaped jail with a smokestack and a raggedy fence around the perimeter of the yard. In homeroom, I sat in the first desk in the row closest to the door, in front of Petra, who had small furry animals hanging off her knapsack; a boy named Kim, who sang quietly to himself in Korean; and a girl named Suha, who played with small paper dolls she hid in her pencil case whenever a popular girl walked by. Beside me, in the next row, was Tommy.

Tommy was my one friend.

Everybody at The Elms knew Tommy. He wore a fedora tipped to the side, a blue leather jacket with a phoenix he'd painted on the back, and cigarette-leg blue jeans with gold stitching up the legs. His leather jacket was so old that when he tapped his elbows, dust puffed out like smoke. Mrs. Grace, our homeroom teacher, liked Tommy because his clothes reminded her of the 1950s. But most of the boys weren't impressed by Tommy's style.

"Hey, Tommy, why are you wearing girly pants?" This kid named Joey Klein would say the same thing every time.

Tommy would shrug. "I just like them."

I admired Tommy's clothes. Our mothers shopped at the same thrift stores, except Tommy's mother had an edgier fashion sense than Mom did. She bought him clothes that made him look like James Dean, except shorter and without the sideburns and the motorcycle.

At lunchtime, Tommy and I hung out in the art room instead of the basement cafeteria, which smelled like burning gravy. There were lots of things to do in the art room. Out of grey clay, we made little figurines of our teachers and made them swear and ask each other out on dates. We listened to Nirvana and the Smashing Pumpkins, who I liked but Tommy said were "too mainstream."

We traced each other lying down on huge pieces of paper, and then filled ourselves in like maps with pictures we cut out of magazines. I glued a picture of a cat to my brain and an ice cream sundae to my hand. Tommy cut pictures of Elvis and Little Richard out of the library copy of the *Encyclopedia Britannica*, but then the librarian caught him and banned him for a month. He said he couldn't finish his map until he got some old pictures. So one night, while Dad was still at work, I searched his study for his Elizabeth Taylor photo, but I couldn't find it. The next best thing was the Glamour Shots album, but I didn't want to open that ever again. Now that Crashing Wave and Dad were finished, there was no reason to think about her anymore. Then I remembered the three *Life* magazines still packed in my orange Samsonite suitcase. The next day I took them with me to the art room, as a surprise for Tommy. I could tell he liked the magazines by the way he held them up to his nose, closed his eyes, and inhaled.

"I love the smell of old newsprint. Where did you find these?"

"My mom dated this guy Robbie Roth a while ago. She thought he was her dream guy, but he turned out to be a slumlord. Anyway, he gave them to me."

"But a man answered the phone when I called you," Tommy said. "That's Robbie?"

I told Tommy that my parents had got back together, thanks to their telephone marriage counsellor Myron. But I didn't want to get all heavy, so I said that Mom had found Myron's name on the corkboard at the No Frills and gone with him since he'd been cheaper than the in-person alternative. Then I took out the bag of candies I'd bought that morning at 7-Eleven.

"Adults can be dumb," Tommy said, biting into a jelly frog. "At least your parents leave you alone. My mom still leaves my soccer cleats by the door. Whenever I watch an old movie, she says, 'Shouldn't you be doing something outside?'"

"Yeah, nature's overrated. I can barely get my cat to go outside these days. That's why Lulu's getting *tuhh*–bee."

Around other boys, I was always holding my neck at painful angles so they wouldn't see me in profile because Diana Gaddick had once said that, from the side, my nose looked even bigger than it actually was. All that thinking about my nose gave me a big headache. But when I was with Tommy I never felt self-conscious. I said whatever came into my head, even if it was, "Why is the crossing guard such an a–hole whenever we cross on yellow?" With Tommy, I was 100 per cent myself.

At the end of October, I came home from school one day to find Florence sitting with Mom at the kitchen table. The smell in the room was white and dark, feta cheese and coffee. I assumed they were talking about Grandpa being a stud at his retirement home because there were photographs on the table. Grandpa was always taking pictures of himself with the knitting circle, the craft club, and the current events roundtable, the only male member at each group.

Florence patted the chair beside her. "Come here, Lucy," she said. "I want to show you something."

"Lucy," Mom said. "Sit."

I figured I was in some deep shit because they both used my name. But when I saw Florence's red leather bag on the extra chair, I thought she was just going to show me some phony love quiz in one of her women's magazines. She called them "the ten pounds in her bag" – her fashion bibles, maps to dieting and fitness, and palm-sized star guides to love. Or worse. As I sat down, I suddenly wondered if the "thing" Florence wanted to show me was a tampon.

"Lucy," Florence said, "I hope this question doesn't embarrass you –"

"I know where the stuff is. Under the sink."

"No, not Kotex," Florence said. "I wanted to know if you were – if you were interested in meeting someone. There's a boy who mowed my lawn over the summer. His name is Michael Forrest. He's thirteen. A lover of animals. I think you two would hit it off."

I waited for Mom to say, "Florence, she's twelve years old!" but Mom just smiled as if she was smelling the summer breeze.

"He's going to shovel my driveway at the first snowfall. I'll invite you over. Then the chemistry will take over." Florence tapped the table. "See, I rhymed. It's already working."

"I saw his picture," Mom said. Her smile had an urgency that belonged in a toothpaste commercial. "He is handsome."

I pictured the kind of man Mom found handsome: a thirty-five-year-old who drove a top-down car and had hairy arms like Julio. But I had only one prerequisite.

"Is he into cats?"

Florence sighed. "How into cats are we talking?"

"He crosses the street for cats. He's going to a party and he risks being late by walking up an alley filled with tin cans and old needles because once he saw this calico there and her tail was swishing around all bitchy –"

"Okay," Mom said, "we get it. Show her the picture."

Florence had taken the photo of Michael Forrest through her living room window but with the curtain in the way, so he was a two-inch stickman caught beneath blowing cotton. I wondered how many hours she'd waited for the photo op.

"Nice, isn't he?" said Florence. "You see that leg hair?"

"Yeah, hot stuff," I said. "I bet if you blew this up and put it up at Inglewood, Grandpa would lose all his girlfriends."

Mom grabbed the picture. "She can't see him here. Where's the other one?"

Michael Forrest looked about six feet tall. He had a tan the colour of a five-cent caramel and he was wearing a Chicago Bulls nylon jersey, his shoulders indented with muscles. I could see a single silver hoop hanging from his ear. He didn't look thirteen to me. He looked like one of those "I-do-sports-plus-I'm-sensitive" guys who never looked at me unless I was at the front of the class doing a presentation. He was a Diana Gaddick boy, some nice trophy she'd bring home to show Merle.

I passed the photo back across the table. "I don't think I'm his type."

"You *are* his type," Mom said. "If you like him, you can go for him." "Go for him" was definitely from Florence's magazines.

"No," I insisted, "you can't just go for anyone. Maybe it was like that in the Fifties. But now there are different levels. If he's a jock, I can't go for him. I mean, I wouldn't even *want* to go for him."

"You're complicating things, Lucy," Mom said. "Florence is doing a nice thing. So you should thank her and go on one little date. It's not good to get so caught up in your insecurities." She turned to Florence. "It will be cute, won't it?"

It occurred to me that maybe Mom hadn't been depressed lately after all. Maybe she was just tired out from putting together my From Bulgaria With Love trousseau fifteen years in advance. I could almost see it: the carved black-pepper smelling box filled with embroidered towels, wooden canisters of rosewater, and an American hand-blender.

Florence drummed one long nail on the other. "Now this is awkward," she finally said. "Because I already showed him your photo. He said, 'That girl's face has got a lot of character.'"

Coming from a thirteen-year-old boy, I knew having "character" was probably a euphemism for having a big nose or too many freckles. But on the off-chance it wasn't, I said, "Did he say anything else?"

"I told him that you and Joy had been living at Tivoli Towers. He told me he goes to the same school as a girl who lives there."

"Small world," Mom said, getting up from the table, which I knew was her way of changing the subject. Since we moved back home, she never wanted to talk about Tivoli Towers. And whenever she inadvertently got on the subject, or I raised it, she used her "I'm-feeling-really-great" voice, a strained sound that made me think of a plastic rose stem twisted into knots.

"What's the name of the girl he knows?"

Florence got up and started collecting the magazines from the kitchen table. "Oh, I don't know now. Deanne something. Maddox."

"Diana Gaddick?"

"I really don't remember, Lucy. I see teeth, I memorize muscles, I feel when Mercury is in retrograde. But I don't remember names. These are really not the most important things."

"Let Florence set you up," Mom said. "Where else will you meet a nice boy? At school you're too shy."

I had made a point of not telling Mom about Tommy. I knew she'd want him to come over to our house so she could ask him about his grades and what he wanted to do when he grew up. Then once he'd left she'd say his jeans were too tight and why was he wearing a "Sol hat"? I wouldn't know what to tell her. Maybe I'd quote one of Florence's women's magazines. I'd stand very solemnly and say, "The heart has no roadmaps, Mom. We make them for ourselves."

When Florence left, I went to my room and called Diana Gaddick.

"Diana, do you know someone called Michael Forrest?"

"Michael Forrest?" It was the first time I'd heard her voice soften. It was the sound of a maple tree dissolving into syrup. "How do you know that name?"

"My aunt knows him. He cut her grass in the summer. She thinks we would hit it off."

Diana didn't say anything for a second. Then, "Yeah, I know him. He plays basketball and he's built. He's basically, no offence, the last guy I'd ever picture you with."

"Why? Because's he's popular?"

"He's on my level," Diana said coolly.

"Do you think I'd like him?"

"You like touching my boobs. And harassing every cat that walks in front of you. Asking me what so-and-so's cat does for a living. So how should I know?"

This was only the second time I'd talked to Diana since Mom and I left Tivoli Towers, and now I remembered why.

"I know cats don't work," I said. "It's a joke."

"Look, I'm just surprised," Diana said. "I mean, on the hierarchy of things, he's way better than that Tommy guy you've been hanging out with." I'd made the mistake of telling her about Tommy, who she decided was a loser because he spent his lunch hour with me. And when she said "hierarchy" like "hi archie," I thought of how in an Archie comic book there were only ever two kinds of girls. Florence was like Veronica. She was popular and flashy, and dumped her boyfriends when they got "too serious." But Mom wasn't like Betty at all. She didn't care about going on dates or trying to make herself all sweet and chirpy. Was I going to grow up to be like that too?

"I should go now," I said. I tried to make my voice as cool as Diana's. "Mom's taking me shopping. For my date with Michael Forrest."

Later that night Dad offered to drive Mom and me to the Zellers at the Galleria Mall. Since Mom and I had moved home, Dad had made an effort to be a better husband, which meant sprinkling blue crystals into the toilet every Saturday morning and driving us three miles to the Galleria Mall since it was on his way to his meeting. And it meant no longer going to Crashing Wave's meeting. Now he went to one on Tuesday nights, where, he complained, he didn't know a soul.

After Dad let us out of the car, Mom suddenly turned back and knocked on the passenger window. Dad looked exasperated as he reached over to roll the window halfway down.

"I want you to bring me back a pamphlet. From your meeting."

"I don't want to steal literature. Those pamphlets are for new-comers."

"I don't care what you bring back," Mom sighed. "Just so I know you were there."

I was tired of hearing them argue. They thought they were being considerate by keeping their voices down, when they were as relent-less as a washing machine always grumbling in the background.

The parking lot was a city of orphaned carts, and as I walked away from the car and toward the pop machine, a seagull landed, ran forward a few steps, and then grabbed a blue hamburger wrapper that was skittering across the pavement. I was beginning to wonder if this was maybe what strength was all about: not being the first, or the tallest, or the prettiest. Being strong, I decided, was about catching the bright things that blow by every day, and knowing when to let the garbage drift away. Tommy was strong. He didn't let anything get to him.

Mom found us a shopping cart by the doors, which made her happy because it earned us a quarter. Inside the store, the luncheon counter was open, but I didn't ask if we could stop. A year ago the waitresses' pink frilly uniforms and the swivel stools had seemed magical. Now the waitresses looked tired and the backlit menu mounted on the wall was half-burnt out.

"Did I tell you I'm thinking of quitting Myron?" Mom said as she rolled us into foods and soft drinks. I knew Mom couldn't stand the way Myron was always asking her to "open up," but I figured that was because she saved all her words for her coffee sessions with Florence.

"Tell me again why you can't stand him?"

"Because he's always asking questions. If I wanted more questions I'd sit alone in the dark in my room."

"Last time, when I walked by your room I heard you talking about your dream man."

"My Dream Man? I don't even remember who my dream man is."

"No, you did have a dream man. That bus driver who looked like Omar Sharif."

"No, that was just my teenage thing. Anyway, I can only tell you what my dream man's not. When we have guests over he doesn't start washing the dishes when we're still sitting there eating. And he doesn't go do something stupid and expect me to be sweet again." She went to rummage through the bins of knee-highs and stockings. When she didn't wear her knee-highs, I could tell she was getting older: thin blue veins squiggled around on her calves like unravelling seahorses. "You know who would never do any of these things? Someone like Michael Forrest."

"Come on, you don't even know him."

"I had a good feeling about that boy as soon as Florence showed me his picture. He looks solid. The type of person who would go into engineering. In ten years, someone like that will be giving dinner parties with wine. He'll take you on vacations to resorts. When you came home from work, he'll ask you how your day was. That's the kind of person I'd like to see you with."

I didn't want to talk about Michael Forrest. Thinking about meeting him confused me: I couldn't tell if I liked him, and if I did, if it was because he was tall and handsome, or because Mom, Florence, and Diana Gaddick liked him because he was tall and handsome. The two things were getting mashed up in my mind. My own opinion was the kernel that had turned into a fluffy piece of popcorn.

"Anyway," I said. "I thought you liked businessmen." I was trying to change the subject so I could draw Mom's attention to the bras, even though it was probably hopeless. She had the bizarre idea that I could wear her old bras – very Bulgarian bras with panels of itchy lace on the cups – even though she was a D cup and I was an optimistic A. In Mom's world, bras were as durable as cast-iron pots, good for twenty-five years.

"No. Those guys are always on the phone," Mom said. "And when they snore it sounds like an empty call centre. Filled with dial tones."

When we were lined up at the cash, Mom pulled a tiny piece of plastic out of her pocket and shook her head. "This is the corner of the milk bag I cut this morning. I cut the corner and then I put it in my pocket. This is where my head is now. Ever since we moved home –"

"You cut corners," I said. I was trying to keep things light. Lately, the only time I wanted to hear about Mom and Dad's problems was when I eavesdropped on their conversations with Myron. That way, when I'd had enough, I could just hang up and walk away.

"Yes, it's true," Mom said, lowering her voice. "The one airplane I ever got on took me halfway around the world so I could try to make a life for myself. I had dreams, you know. I thought I might be a fashion designer or start my own business. Then I thought, I like to talk, so maybe law. I could get into arguing, even in that heavy robe. But then . . . well, I decided teaching was more stable. Instead of living out my dreams, I gave up and married the first man who gave me a flower."

I didn't want to hear about her problems anymore. Listening to her was Dad's job, but I was beginning to feel like he'd passed that responsibility onto me.

▶

The first snow fell on a Wednesday morning three weeks later. Florence called me to say that all "the ducks were in order" and that she'd pick me up after school to drive me to her house. Michael Forrest would already be there. She'd strategically asked him to start shovelling at five.

"I'll make the hot chocolate," Florence said, "and you'll bring it to him. It's how I'll begin my speech at your wedding."

All day I felt like I was back on the Tilt-A-Whirl. The thought of meeting Michael Forrest filled me with dread and hope and confusion. At lunchtime, I drew hearts on the window and then crossed them out while Tommy painted sparkles over a picture of Frank Zappa he'd cut out of a music magazine. I felt I should at least tell him about Michael Forrest, but I didn't know why I thought he would care. I walked from the window to the seat beside him and hovered. I stared at my shoes, then at my knees, then my hips. My jeans were tighter, probably from all the candy I'd been pigging out on with Tommy.

"I'm going on a date later, Tommy." Then I waited, hoping to hear the sound of his paintbrush hitting the floor. Nothing. "My aunt is setting me up. The guy is pretty hot. She took photos."

"That's intense." Tommy turned and raised his eyebrows. "Is she in the CIA?"

"Yeah," I said. "Probably."

Tommy put his brush in the cup of water and stirred it. The water looked white-grey as the snow Michael Nobody Forrest would be shovelling in five hours, but not as white as the marshmallows in the hot chocolate Lucy Phony Bloom would be carrying to him in five hours and fifteen minutes. Tommy got up and took something out of his knapsack. It was a photograph of a beautiful woman with flowing red hair and wearing a ruffled Flamenco dress.

"Remember I told you that Lulu looked like a famous actress? That's her. That's Rita Hayworth." Tommy looked at his hands. "I don't know, maybe it's stupid. But they both have orange in their hair so I just thought – "

"Tommy, this is great. Thank you."

"So if anyone ever asks what Lulu's job is, you can say she started out doing Spanish classical dancing. But then she moved to Hollywood."

"What about Dino?" Dino was Tommy's cat, an old orange tom. "What does he do? Is he in show biz too?"

"No. He works in a cafeteria. But he recently got fired for stealing a jar of olives –"

My nervousness had floated away. "Yeah, and I bet the olives were industrial-sized. Dino probably thought he could make a necklace out of them. Like, string them on a piece of wire."

"Yeah, he's clueless like that," Tommy said. "He tries, though."

When I got home, there was a bottle of shampoo waiting for me on the bathroom counter, a brand name that Mom never bought because it cost three dollars more than our regular shampoo. As I made bubbles on my head under the hot spray, I imagined a long lineup of girls snaking through the ages, from Cro-Magnon to me, all of us washing our hair for our dates with boys. I couldn't decide if this was a stupid or wonderful ritual. Mom wanted to blow-dry my hair straight, but I told her Michael Forrest would have to take me with curly hair or not take me at all. My compromise was to put on the fake pearl studs that she wanted me to wear, and a red pleated skirt with a small poodle at the hem, which I pointed out Michael Forrest would never see since I'd be wearing my parka. Still, Mom insisted, hovering around me like a light-hungry firefly. Even after I locked her out of the bathroom, she kept talking to me through the closed door.

"Maybe you'll go for a walk with him," she said. "The day I met your dad, we had coffee and then he met me later for a walk. He walked too fast, though. He thought I was lagging behind to look at his bum. I should have taken that as a sign. But a walk is good for young people. But don't go too far. Or go so fast your heart rate goes up a lot. And if you get the sense he'll want to hold your hand, take off your mitten. Otherwise it gets awkward. It could get fumbling and then he'll lose his nerve."

"Maybe he won't even be there," I said. "Maybe the snow melted."

"Are you parting your hair down the middle? It makes your neck look longer. And put on the lip gloss."

I felt like a doll being dressed for a tea party. Only the tea party had strict rules. Michael Forrest couldn't see my nose in profile. My hand, when near his, had to ditch its mitten. I jogged on the spot and made arm circles. I did ten jumping jacks and watched my cheeks turn pink in the mirror.

"What's happening in there?" Mom called.

The bathroom mirror was fogged up and I drew my initials on the surface: LB. Beside them I added MF. Then, TR. For Tommy.

"Nothing," I called back. "I'm getting into my character."

"Just be yourself," Mom said. "You know, your best self."

At 4:45, Florence picked me up in her white Grand Am, silver-plated on the hubcaps. It was a Veronica car, bold, flashy, and purring. She smoked as we drove, dangling her fingers out the window and using her thumb to chop the ash. I held her red leather bag on my lap, resting my chin on the rough ledge of magazines that extended out of it.

"I feel kind of weird about all this," I said. "You're sure he saw my photo?"

We slowed toward a red light, which gave Florence time to give me her pep talk. "Lucy, there's a thing called the law of attractions. If you put out that you're lonely, or plain, you meet people who'll make you lonelier, or you won't meet anyone at all. You put out that you're popular and people see that, they gravitate."

"Well, what if I like loneliness? What if I think it's really beautiful?"

Florence sighed. "Look, your mom was unhappy without your dad. I get her back with her husband. She's unhappy. Do you hear what I'm telling you?"

I wanted to tell her that maybe matchmaking was a lost art for a good reason, but I didn't. I waited for the right moment to tell her to let me out of her car, but by the time I was ready to spill it, we'd already turned onto her street, with its wide lawns and low bunga-lows as placid as sleeping turtles.

I waited in the kitchen while Florence made hot chocolate for

Michael Forrest. I heard the spoon tinging the side of the mug as I watched him push the shovel across the backyard. Florence had asked Michael Forrest to start there, so my grand reveal would be more dramatic than her pulling the car into the driveway and me hopping out. I was beginning to understand that romance was all about planning, which didn't seem very romantic at all. Florence sprinkled mini marshmallows over the froth.

"See how thorough he's being?" she said. "That shows focus and attention, and we ladies want that in a man." She put the hot mug into my hand. "Now go outside and give this to him. And smile. Be confident. Be fun."

I went outside and stood on the deck.

Michael Forrest was wearing a quilted black parka and headphones blaring scratchy music. I wanted to gulp down the hot chocolate myself and go back in with the empty mug, but Florence was probably watching me through the lens of her camera, ready to snap the second installment of her documentary. I couldn't move. I was sure that he didn't know I existed. I was sure in the same way I was sure the phenomenon of my being invisible to the Michael Forrests of the world would repeat itself after today. I felt that as clearly as I did the snowflakes falling onto my cheeks. And I had a feeling I could live with that.

I walked down the steps of the deck and called his name. But he still couldn't hear me. This was too much. "Hi," I said, this time louder.

I had to practically stand in front of his shovel before he finally noticed me. He pulled off his headphones and smiled with all of his teeth, as white and straight as Florence had promised they would be.

"Hey, you're Florence's niece." He leaned the shovel up against the deck and sniffled. His nostrils were red and wet. "She mentioned you. She, uh, said you like cats."

"Yeah. You like cats too?"

"I used to have one called Cosmic. I'd dress him up like a little cop. I had a mini NYPD T-shirt that fit him."

"So he was a police officer?"

Michael Forrest shook his head. "No. I just dressed him up as one."

Our breath made clouds in the air between us, filling in the silence. He drank the rest of his hot chocolate and handed back the mug as if he was giving me a gift.

"Can I ask you a weird question?" Michael Forrest finally said. "You don't mind?"

I recognized this moment from the movies, from Florence's magazines. It was the moment of the single stars of the matchmaking galaxy meeting, creating the kind of miraculous energy that can move rivers, push blossoms out of closed buds. But I was embarrassed. I didn't feel anything for Michael Forrest.

"No, go ahead." I was holding his mug in my hand. I couldn't tell if it was half empty or half full.

"Your friend Diana. Do you think you could introduce us?"

In the branches above us, a blackbird was waving its wing at me.

When I let myself into the house, I heard Mom in the kitchen, talking to Myron on the phone. She always sounded sorry and serious when she spoke to him, as though he was her worst student and she was flunking him. I pictured Dad upstairs in his study, sighing and dispensing a word here and there but only when Myron asked him to. I went straight to my room, where Lulu was waiting for me on my bed. I lay down beside her and ate chocolate-covered almonds from my night table drawer until I felt sick. Then I picked up the phone.

"And how does Frank's adultery make you feel, Joy?" Myron said.

"It makes me want to throttle him," Mom said. "He goes and does his romancing and all this time I feel like some kind of fool. How would it make you feel, Byron?"

"Well, Joy, it wouldn't make me feel too good. But my name is Myron and let's keep the conversation on you now, okay? Let's focus on what you're feeling now."

"I feel less cheated-on than cheated," and then she began to sniffle. "Hold on, I need to get a tissue." I heard the phone clatter down – a hard clank, and then a sigh from Dad's end.

"Frank?"

"I'm here. But I'm frustrated. I've apologized. I just want things to be sweet again."

Mom picked up the phone again. "It's just a dust allergy. Anyway, I don't remember where I was so maybe we should just call it –"

"You were saying you felt cheated," Myron said.

"I feel cheated because I realize –" Mom sighed. "I realize that I didn't pursue my dream man –"

Very gently, I put down the phone.

Mom came into my room ten minutes later. She stood in the doorway and pulled down the sleeves of her housecoat instead of sitting down on the edge of my bed the way she usually did when she wanted to talk. I could tell she was agitated. Her silence sprouted spikes all around my room.

"Well, how was the date?" she said.

I wanted to tell Mom that the "date" had been an embarrassing waste of time. I might have been twelve and a half, but I wasn't some doll she and Florence could play with: just because things weren't going well with Dad didn't mean I was bait for their version of *The Dating Game*.

Then I saw how her eyes were a little wider than usual, as if they were waiting to fill up with good news. She was smiling with her teeth and I hadn't seen her hold a smile like that in a long time. Mom wanted a 1950s story about a boy and girl in a winter wonderland. That's what she wanted for herself. Suddenly I wanted it for her too. I couldn't tell her the truth.

"Well, he was handsome," I began, "you know, like . . ." I tried to picture Michael Forrest's face, but all I could see were his giant cushioned headphones and his dripping nose. I tried to imagine what kind of boy Mom would find attractive. I settled on a child version of Julio mixed with somebody from *Dallas* with chest hair popping out of his shirt. "He had a tan and chest hair," I blurted. No, that was crazy. He was thirteen and wearing a parka zippered up to his chin. "I mean, he had chest*nut* hair."

Mom waved her hand. "You're nervous. Just slow down and start from the beginning. Tell me what he was wearing and how you felt. I want to hear everything."

"Sure . . . Okay. I walked outside with the hot chocolate. I think he was wearing . . . a blue coat." I needed to tell her how I felt. The coat was irrelevant. "I was petrified. I watched him from the deck. Then I went down the steps and said hi to him. And as soon as I started . . . I mean, as soon as he started talking . . ." All at once I thought of Tommy. I remembered being with him in the art room and talking about Lulu and Dino, how easy it was – "Mom, I can't describe it . . . I just felt comfortable."

"Go on," Mom said.

I told her that Michael Forrest and I strolled through Florence's neighbourhood, our boots making twin tracks in the snow, our mittens side by side. We played twenty questions and at first our questions were kind of boring, like "What's your favourite movie?" and "Did you ever cheat on a test?" But then we got into serious ones, like "Who would you rather sing like, Elvis or Michael Jackson?" and "What's your guilty pleasure?"

"And?"

"I said eating three Jos. Louis in a row."

"And what did he say?"

"Zoos."

Mom's laugh was a deep, wonderful sound that filled my room like an ocean. "That's so clever. A brain and a heart. You never see the two together now."

That's where my story for Mom ended, with her feeling satisfied, and me having just told a whopping lie. I realized we were still on the seesaw. Except now it didn't matter if I was down. But when she was down, I had to go on a date with someone who was supposed to be my dream boy when he was really hers. I had to make up stories she wanted to hear, just so she wouldn't be disappointed.

Our seesaw was broken. Maybe it was time for me to get off.

Two

6

Every day after school, I saw the same couples kissing against the raggedy fence in the yard, their bodies pressed together like soft slices of white bread. They were in grade eight, like me, but I felt like we were on different planets. The girls wore lipstick that twinkled as brightly as rock candies, and their hair was shampoo-commercial smooth. Although I told myself not to look, I always did. I was pretty sure they wouldn't see me. After all, unkissable girls were invisible. But I didn't want to be an invisible girl. I didn't want to be one of those girls who lingered by the Valentine's Crush-O-Gram table at lunch, glancing at the packaged cinnamon hearts, waiting for someone to send them a cello-packed version of love.

I couldn't tell Tommy in words that I liked him, so I made him a mixed tape with songs by Nirvana, the Smashing Pumpkins, the Doors, and all the top-twenty angst I could cram onto one ninety-minute Maxell cassette. But when I listened to the finished tape, I began to wonder if Jim Morrison singing "Light My Fire" was a bold enough sign for Tommy. I started again. This time, I recorded velvety songs from Dad's Roy Orbison cassette. I dubbed soft rock off the radio, singers I'd never heard of but who said ooooh and ahhhh a lot. For some reason, I trusted that pop stars who sold 20 million records would be able to express my feelings better than I could.

"So, what did you think of the mix?" I said.

"I listened to both sides," Tommy said. "It's blank. Did you hold down record and play at the same time?"

I gave up on mixed tapes and decided to be more obvious, like the girls who kissed against the raggedy fence. They knew what they were doing. They wore shimmering blue eyeshadow and heavy lipstick that made them pout. I was blasting my lips with ChapStick every day and hoping for miracles. So a week before Valentine's Day, I went into the Save-On Drugstore after school, lured by the "Free Makeover" sign in the window. I'd planned on asking the cosmetics girl to help me find a cheap but spectacular lipstick, but when I got to the counter she was glued to the phone and gave me a bored I-can't-make-a-sale-on-you kind of look, which I took as a sign that I was on my own. I walked down the aisle until I found myself standing in front of a massive wall of makeup. There were hundreds of lipsticks standing at attention like little soldiers, protected in their shiny uniform shells. I wanted to find the right Scarlett red lipstick for our *Gone with the Wind* video night. Tommy and I had been planning it for weeks as a cooler and more exclusive alternative to the grade eight dance on Valentine's Day night.

Already I could picture the scene: Tommy, as Rhett Butler, would be bold. Lucy, as Scarlett O'Hara, would be the belle of the ball. We'd kiss and keep holding hands, even if they got kind of sweaty.

I tried on a cola-can red lipstick first, painting it on bowlike. Then I outlined my eyes in black pencil like Elizabeth Taylor's in *Cleopatra*. When Tommy and I watched it last week, he'd said that she was the most beautiful woman he'd ever seen. I'd spent the rest of the night wondering which of her features he liked the most, hoping it was the brown hair, the only feature I shared with Liz. Since last summer, Tommy came over every Friday night with classic movies he rented on video. We watched two or three movies a night while pigging out on Nibs and Jiffy Pop. We'd scream at the corny lines and admire the dresses, the green silk like mermaid skin on Esther Williams, the plunging necklines on Jayne Mansfield's unlaced bodice.

"Study her breasts," I said, pointing my finger onto the screen so static popped at my skin. "I would ride in James Dean's Porsche for boobs like that."

When we watched *Doctor Zhivago*, I put my hand on the cushion border between us, where it waited for the entire journey from Moscow to Siberia and back again. As the credits rolled, Tommy sighed.

"What?" I said. I thought that if he liked romantic movies, maybe he could be romantic about me too.

"Next time, no movies over three hours," he said. "My leg's asleep."

I put on another layer of red lipstick, but I still didn't feel I was done-up enough. I found a tester of orange crème blush and dabbed some on my fingers, smiled at the mirror, and painted the apples of my cheeks the way Diana Gaddick had once shown me how to do. I looked in the mirror: better now.

I'd been browsing for about twenty minutes, my wrist covered with slashes of lipstick, when I heard a thump. The cosmetics girl had put down her phone.

"You need some help?"

Every time I met a pretty girl over the age of fourteen I'd start imagining her love life and all the ways she and her boyfriend did it. Did he loom over her, a plank with arms doing pushups, the way it looked in the sex-ed diagrams? Or was it just weird, how the people in Diana's lousy romance novels did it? Or maybe the cosmetics girl didn't have a boyfriend, maybe she touched herself, so her fingers smelled like saltwater and Ivory soap afterwards.

"Oh, it's okay," I said.

The cosmetics girl came out from behind the diamond island. I could hear the thighs of her pants rubbing. She was a little fat, I guess. Fat girls always had the most incredible hair.

"You can't just test the makeup for free," she said. "It has to end in a purchase."

"I know," I said, shrugging. "I guess it has to lead somewhere."

I left the drugstore and clomped through the snow, which looked brighter than usual. I wanted to sing. *I felt pretty!* I didn't know if it was the lipstick, the eyeliner, the blush, or what, but I loved how beautiful the makeup made me feel inside: I could smell the talc on my cheeks, and if I ran my tongue over my lips, I could taste the apricot-dusty flavour of the lipstick. Usually people never noticed me, but now heads were turning to take a second glance. Out of nowhere, I remembered how Crashing Wave had walked so tall, knowing people were watching her. I smiled at an old woman wearing a rain bonnet, but she must have been shy because she quickly looked away. I smiled at a man driving a van and he smiled back, showing both his top and bottom teeth. I passed the window of Coffee Time and caught my reflection in the glass. My eyeliner had run, but there was no time to fix it. Tommy would be getting out of band practice soon.

When I walked up to the school Tommy was just coming out the doors behind a group of boys carrying black instrument cases.

"Tommy!"

He stopped in front of me. He was wearing a red toque and his hair fell out from under it in straight, streaky pieces, down to the top of his neck. He looked at my mouth, my eyes, my cheeks. I figured he wasn't used to me looking this good, and that's why he was clamming up.

"I thought you went home," he finally said.

"Nope," I said. "I wanted to surprise you." I smiled at him with my lips closed so he could get a really good look at the lipstick.

Tommy bit his lip. "You look different."

When he said "different" I had to fight the frown off my face. People used that word when they were trying to say something else.

"I got a makeover. At the drugstore. Do you like it?"

Tommy shrugged. "I don't know. It doesn't look like you."

Neither of us said another word until we got on the streetcar and I asked Tommy if he'd reserved a copy of *Gone with the Wind* for Valentine's Day night. That broke some of the weird tension. We were talking about which scenes we were going to act out when two high school boys got on the streetcar at Avenue Road and sat down across from us. They had sideburns and they swore a lot. Underneath their unzipped parkas I could see their blazers and their rumpled shirts. They looked like angry men trapped in schoolboy uniforms.

The boy with the shaved flat-top haircut whispered something to his friend, who had a mole on his cheek. Then they both looked at me and grinned. I wasn't used to guys looking at me so I figured it was because I was wearing makeup. High school boys were admiring me. High school boys knew more than junior high boys, that's why Tommy hadn't complimented me.

"I still need to find my Rhett suit," Tommy said. "I think in the movie it's silk —"

Flat Head suddenly jabbed Mole. "You hear that? Pretty Boy needs to find his wet suit. In case he wets his pants."

They laughed, loud nose laughs that sounded as if they were pushing rocks out of their nostrils. That's when I realized they hadn't been looking at me in a good way.

Tommy was pretending not to notice the laughing. "I was thinking we could go to a thrift store. We could go to Queen Street maybe —"

Flat Head slapped his knee. "Pretty Boy, aren't you going to answer?"

I kicked Tommy's shoe to signal that I wanted to change seats, but he didn't notice.

Mole looked at Flat Head and smirked. "Leave him alone, man. He's like ten. He's probably got his house key under his shirt on a string." .

Flat Head shook his head. "No, he's not ten, he's sitting with his girlfriend and look at her, she looks like a —"

Tommy jumped up out of his seat. "She's beautiful! Don't say anything about her."

My face was on fire. I needed to get off the streetcar, to disappear. All of a sudden I was too visible. I made myself think about Lulu so I wouldn't start to cry.

In the subway station, Tommy acted as though nothing had happened, but I was wobbly and raw. Every inch of my skin prickled. Each time a person passed by us, I was convinced they were looking at me and thinking I looked like a —

Tommy touched my sleeve. "Hey, did I tell you that Dino lost his job at the cafeteria? His boss finally found out he was stealing olives. Remember, Lucy, for the necklaces?" He pulled a package of Swedish berries out of his pocket. I took a couple, just to give my hands something to do.

I knew this was my cue to start talking about Lulu. On any other day I'd tell Tommy that she was getting all dolled up for a job as a stand-in on a biopic about Rita Hayworth, which meant sticking feathers into her hair and learning how to walk in three-inch heels. But I didn't feel like joking around now. I was turning into a jellyfish with all of my nerves exposed.

"I need to get home, Tommy. I'll just see you tomorrow."

When I walked into the house that afternoon, I smelled the fake food buffet. Mom had started burning food-scented oils with names like "farm fresh" and "country style," which Dad resented because they gave him the false hope that Mom had a roast chicken and an apple pie in the oven. Lately we'd been eating nothing but chicken cutlets out of boxes and Minute Rice. I knew it was time for dinner when I heard the microwave beeping three times.

I dropped my bag by the door and walked toward the living room. "Mom? I need to talk to –"

"Good, you're home." Mom was on the couch, trying to hold Lulu down on her lap. "See this? I just found this sweater and I want you to help me get Lulu into it. It's cold and I worry about her. Wandering around in the ravine and who knows where." Mom shook the tiny pink cardigan. "You wore this when you were eleven pounds. Now guess how much Lucy weighs. I mean Lulu."

For the first time in months, Mom hadn't changed into her pyjamas straight after work. She was wearing her felt vest and Bermuda pants, and even her cheeks were that rosy winter colour. Her good moods were like soap bubbles, ready to pop from the instant they formed. I didn't want to spoil the moment.

I sat down on the couch. "I don't know. Eleven pounds?"

"Thirteen. I weighed myself today holding her and then not holding her. That's the trick. First I tried just with her. But half her body kept running off the scale."

That's when Mom actually looked at me. She had a way of staring that made my skin feel hot, as if she were running a scanner over it. "You're wearing so much makeup. What happened to you?"

"I like trying new things, okay? You don't have to give me a hard time."

"Well, you shouldn't draw outside of your lip lines like that. It's a cheap look." She went back to fussing with Lulu, who was giving me SOS eyes. "You've got big lips as is. That's all I'm going to say."

That night, I lay in bed with Lulu, trying not to think about what had happened on the streetcar. It kept charging into my head, though. I saw the treads on Flat Head's boots, the way his lips had been dry and whitish, how Mole's earphones had flicked against his neck when he laughed. I was also thinking about what Tommy said. If he'd said that to me at any other time, I would have been thrilled. But what if he'd only said it to defend me?

Then the phone rang.

"Can you talk?" Tommy said.

"Yeah." I was trying to sound casual. I didn't want him to know how much I hurt. "What are you doing?"

"Nothing. Staring at Dino. How about you?"

Maybe he was feeling guilty. The whole insult on the streetcar had started with Flat Head and Mole noticing him, not me. Nobody had ever made fun of me when I was on my own because I was invisible. Being with Tommy had made me visible, but in the worst kind of way.

"Nothing now," I said. "But I got roped into selling Crush-O-Grams tomorrow. I've got to wear my nasty red gym pants, you know, to show school spirit. So I need to get my fugly uniform ready."

"That sucks. I can't stand wearing the same clothes as everyone else. It makes me feel like I'm invisible."

"Yeah," I said. "I know what you mean."

In the morning I felt better about the whole streetcar incident. I'd decided that I'd probably overreacted. Maybe Flat Head and Mole were going to say, *She looks like that girl on television.* They probably flirted with lots of girls on the streetcar by teasing them. Just because Tommy hadn't said anything about my makeup didn't mean he didn't like it. After all, he did say I was beautiful. On my way to school, I played this game with the cracks in the sidewalk. I'd count to ten, and if on ten I didn't step on a crack, it meant he liked me. If I did step on a crack, it meant he didn't.

When I got to school, the sidewalk said he did like me.

I had to sit at the Crush-O-Gram table with Suha until the first bell, and it was clear we weren't going to make any sales. The hallways were dead. The student council girls always gave invisible girls the early shifts because the cute guys only came around at lunch and they wanted to be there when that happened. To kill time, Suha and I assembled the Crush-O-Grams. The girls who got them meowed as excitably as women in diamond commercials, even though they were just baggies filled with cinnamon hearts and tied with a red curly ribbon. Still, I wanted Tommy to send me one.

When the bell rang, Suha passed me two construction paper figures, their hands these little, red interlocked paws. "I think you two are very good together," she said.

"Who am I good with?"

"You and Tommy." I could tell it gave Suha hope to believe that a fellow invisible girl could get a boyfriend.

At lunchtime, I brought the paper dolls with me to the art room and showed them to Tommy. "People think you're my boyfriend," I said, dropping the dolls onto the table. "Suha gave these to me this morning."

I waited for him to say maybe that wasn't such a crazy idea, but he didn't say anything. He just picked up the dolls and turned them around in his hands. I was determined to get a reaction from him. "Don't you think that's ridiculous? That we could be a couple? Like those kissy people on the side of the school?"

I wanted him to say that Suha was right; that she'd expressed with her dolls what he hadn't been able to with words. That's what I was hoping for.

"It *is* crazy," Tommy said. "All we do is watch movies."

It was time to be bold. "I bought you a Crush-O-Gram today, Tommy."

He kept turning the dolls around in his hand, looking down at the table. "I thought you said they were stupid. That's what you always say. So I didn't buy you one."

"It's okay." I turned to the window because I was afraid my mouth was trembling. Mouths always gave you away.

There was a long silence. Then Tommy said, "Don't worry, I'll make it up to you on our *Gone with the Wind* night."

All afternoon I replayed his promise in my head. I imagined us sitting on my orange flowered blanket eating cinnamon heart cupcakes. He would admire me in my Scarlett costume . . . Then the kiss – warm. Closed lips. I didn't know if I could handle a tongue yet.

I was still in la-la-land in last period when Mrs. Grace distributed the first annual Love Quest2000 Test. We were given thirty questions on love and dating, and a scan card. On Valentine's Day, everyone would have to line up in the front hallway after school to buy their "love match" printouts for a dollar before the dance. I knew the test was a fraud because most of us were thirteen and had just started taking the subway alone, but the questions were written as if we were thirty-year-old globetrotters.

Your dream date is:

a) A walk on the beach.
b) Dinner in Paris.
c) A night at the opera.
d) New Year's Eve in Times Square.

I glanced over at Tommy so I could roll my eyes at him, but he was looking down at his scan card. At the top of the question page was a disclaimer. *Please note: This test is for entertainment purposes only.*

Mom was cleaning out the closet in her bedroom when I got home. She'd been doing bursts of physical chores lately, and then abandoning the whole job when she came across something that made her sad. Now Mom sat cross-legged on the floor with her old clothes around her, these piles of the past. There were skirts and gowns that I recognized from her photos, including the gold dress that she'd worn at the Miss Sophia West Pageant. It made my heart twist to see it lying there, bunched up and as forgettable as a dusting rag.

"I need to get rid of this stuff," Mom said. "I have way too much stuff. The clutter of it is making me feel overwhelmed."

I'd never heard her use that word before: *overwhelmed.* Her natural state was overwhelmed, but it was strange to hear her acknowledge it. It was like a giraffe going out of its way to say, "I'm tall."

I sat down beside her and lifted up the dress: it felt coarse, as if over time it had aged like skin. The peacock feathers were drooping.

"What are these?" I picked up a pair of brown pants with a crotch down to the knees, gold coins sewn into the cuffs and the waistline. "I thought you said you wore a smock made out of a camel's ass." I was trying to make her smile.

"Those are called harem pants. They were popular in the 1970s. Florence convinced me to buy them. Along with the fake fur coat. And I never had a chance to wear the suede vest with the beads . . ."

Mom covered her face with her hands, and then her shoulders started to shake. At first I thought she was laughing, but then I wasn't sure.

"Mom, are you feeling okay?"

When she took her hand away from her eyes, there were finger smudges on her glasses. "I feel stressed out. But also, I feel bored. You're thinking I'm a mess, right? If you do, I understand."

"You're okay, Mom. Don't worry."

"But do you think I'm weak? For not staying alone? Because I thought we could. Just the two of us. But I wasn't happy. What does somebody do when they're unhappy?"

I felt the heaviness of her question, as if it were something she'd been carrying around inside for a long time. But the truth was I didn't understand why she couldn't *try* harder to be happy. She'd turned down Dad's offers to take her out so many times he finally stopped asking. She never even registered for the level II cake decorating class at the community centre, like she said she would. I wanted her to be happy, but there was nothing I could say.

Lulu swished into the room and started clawing at the pile of clothes, meowing and kneading.

"She wants her wet food," Mom said. She pointed to the heap of clothes. "You can have whatever you want. Just put them back in the box and take them to your room. The rest you can just throw away."

I carried the box to my room, sat on the floor, and looked at every dress, pair of shoes, and scarf. There was a long dress with a lacy collar, two suede skirts with snaps at the front, the Mary Quant dress, and two rayon blouses, in bright blue and pink. They were colours I'd never seen Mom wear.

Just before the last bell, two Crush-O-Gram delivery girls showed up in the doorway of our classroom. "Is there a Petra here?" It was probably from her boyfriend so nobody was going to call the press. "Is there a Joey Klein here?" Joey still gave Tommy a hard time about his "girly jeans," but Joey wore a Maple Leafs jersey every day, so who was he to talk about fashion?

"And Tommy? Looks like you have a lady friend."

"More like his boyfriend," Joey muttered.

He was such an ass I wanted to kick him in the leg. But it was Valentine's Day and I was almost Scarlett O'Hara. So I just smiled and hoped the cinnamon hearts would rot Joey's teeth.

That night, I dressed up in a white blouse and a red suede skirt I'd found in Mom's box of discards. Mom and Dad sat in the kitchen with Grandpa, eating pinky smoked meat warmed up in the microwave. I could smell the meat from the living room. All afternoon Mom and Dad had fought over what to serve. It was a symptom of a strained intergenerational encounter. It was a symptom of them.

"He wants a whitefish," Dad had said. "And that's all. Keep it simple."

"Well, I bought smoked meat," Mom said. "Are you keeping me off that too?"

Now I could hear Grandpa yelling with his mouth full, the thud of his knotted finger hitting on the table. "A man . . . who takes his . . . meat . . . lean is a meshugener."

"Just drop it," Dad said. "Drop the whole thing."

I went into the kitchen to get a glass of milk. Dad was picking at his nails again. "We're going to take Grandpa to a movie. You okay to stay home alone?"

"Of course. Anyway, Tommy's coming over. And we're doing a *Gone with the Wind* re-enactment. We have to be our characters for the whole evening. Then we're going to watch the movie."

"Well, just don't turn on the stove," Dad said. "I left you a plate in the fridge."

After they left, I waited for Tommy in front of the windows. I paced the short distance from curtain to curtain, letting the itchy material fall over my face like a veil. I imagined how Tommy was going to "make it up to me." Maybe he'd show up with a rose, a fat one with dew drops on the petals. Outside, the empty street glinted hints of ice. The reflection of the streetlamps on the snow looked like enormous yellow traffic lights. Slow-down lights. I ran my tongue over my lips, tasting the slightly bitter, creamy taste of "Cherries in the Snow."

I was disappointed when Tommy showed up without his costume on. I'd pictured him in a suit or at least a blazer. Anything but a plaid shirt with snap buttons. I hung up his coat and took him to the kitchen.

"Okay, close your eyes," he said.

He smelled like snow and fabric softener. I could hear him opening the black shopping bag he'd brought with him. There was too much rustling going on for it to be a rose.

"Okay, you can open your eyes now."

Tommy had unscrewed the lid to a Mason jar filled with a thick brown liquid that reminded me of molasses. "Remember I promised a surprise?"

When I brought my nose to the mouth of the jar, I smelled rubbing alcohol mixed with Drano. I hoped he had something else in the bag.

Tommy pulled the jar back. "It's vodka, peach schnapps, rum, and red wine. If I took a lot of one thing, my parents would notice, so I had to take a little of each."

I got two glasses from the cupboard and I watched the sludgy liquid rise to the halfway point as Tommy filled them up. I was disappointed, but I figured it wasn't worth getting hung up on as long as we started the game.

"Why, good evenin' Mr. Butler! It's delightful that you should think of stoppin' by." I stretched out my syllables as if they were strands of honey.

Tommy passed me my glass. "It's awfully frigid out there, Ms. O'Hara. I brought this especially for you."

I didn't want to drink it, but Tommy dared me to, so I gulped it down like it was a glass of milk. It was a burning torch in my throat. My ears popped. Prickly hot water sluiced in front of my eyes. Tommy refilled our glasses and I drank slower this time.

"I dare you to drink two in a row," I giggled.

We leaned against the wall for a while like we were waiting at a bus stop. And I could feel my elbow and my knees starting to get soft and springy.

Finally, I said, "Does the liquor warm you, Mr. Butler?"

"It makes me feel silly." Tommy shook his head and laughed. "I mean, that red looks good on you, Ms. O'Hara."

I didn't want him to feel silly. I wanted him to play our game so we could have our movie-style kiss. "Mr. Butler, maybe you could put on your evening wear? You can change in my room . . ."

As I climbed the stairs, the floor became an elevator, dipping and rising, and I had to hold on to the wall to keep myself from tripping. When we got into my room, Tommy threw his bag onto my bed and pulled off his T-shirt. I'd never seen a boy without his shirt on in person except at the swimming pool, and that didn't really count. I tried not to stare at him, but I wanted to know things: if he had any armpit hair and what his chest looked like under his clothes.

"The spot on your chest," I said. "I used to think that's where the heart was."

He pointed to the small hollow in the centre of his chest. "This?"

"Yeah. I thought the heart was right under there."

"It's a muscle," Tommy said, "it can't be in a place where there's an indent."

Tommy had one arm in the sleeve of his white shirt when he saw the box of Mom's clothes beside my bed.

"Are those peacock feathers?" He pointed to Mom's gold dress. It was hanging out of the box, so I grabbed it and held it up to my body. I felt Tommy's Mason jar sludge rush through my arms and my legs, making me say stupid stuff.

"Do I look like the belle of the south, Mr. Butler? Tell the truth."

"You do," Tommy grinned. "I dare you to put it on for real."

I looked at Tommy and then at the dress. I knew I wouldn't fit into it. The breast part would probably sag. "I dare *you* to put it on," I said.

We were both laughing now, big laughs like chokes, and I could imagine our bright red faces and our eyes bulging out. We pushed our heads into the clothes the way dogs do with laundry, and tackled each other, grabbed each other's armpits and squealed no, no, *please no*, and then Tommy nearly screamed because I'd pinned him down by the ankle and was tickling the bottom of his foot. *Come on, I'll scream and your neighbours will think you're murdering me.* Then I stopped tickling him. I reached over and brushed some of the streaky blond hair away from his forehead.

"You still dare me?" he said.

He didn't give me a chance to answer. He left my room carrying Mom's dress over his arm. I sat on the pile of clothes, wondering if he was still joking. Then I heard the bathroom door close. When

Tommy came back, he was wearing the dress. He laughed at himself in the mirror, and I laughed too because I had to admit that he filled the dress out better than I would have. He had big shoulders for a thirteen-year-old.

We went downstairs, finished off the rest of the sludge from the Mason jar, and sat on the couch. We'd decided in advance what our first lines would be; then we'd improvise. But my brain suddenly felt cloudy. "What's my first line?" I whispered.

"It's 'Are you afraid to sit with me like this?'" Tommy said. "Then, 'What if perchance my boyfriend came by?'"

"Okay. Are you afraid to sit with me like this? What if my boyfriend came by?"

Tommy leaned in closer to me. "Do you really have a boyfriend, Miss O'Hara?"

"No. He doesn't write back. Perhaps he was killed at Shiloh, Mr. . . ."

"You can just call me Scarlett . . . if you think there's room for the two of us." Suddenly I wished I'd hadn't dared him to put on Mom's old dress. I wished he was in his suit. This wasn't the way I'd planned how the night would go, but there was nothing to do about it now.

"Sure there's room for the two of us," I said. "I like the advice of a woman. An honest woman. Tell me, Scarlett, would you want to kiss me? If you were a man?"

"Yeah, I would," Tommy said.

"You ought to then," I said. "Just to prove it."

He kissed me then. His lips tasted sweet and metallic. It wasn't the taste I'd imagined. But his head felt so warm, as if golden thoughts were rushing around inside. I closed my eyes and I kissed him. I kissed him until I needed some air. Then I opened my eyes. That's when I saw the gold strap of Mom's dress sliding down Tommy's shoulder. I thought suddenly of the girls at the dance wearing beautiful dresses that their mothers had bought them, and their dates in shirts and ties leaning in to see if they could steal kisses when the teachers were turned away. They were all dancing . . . I looked down at Mom's shabby old skirt.

"You shouldn't be wearing that dress," I said quietly.

Tommy flicked at a peacock feather. "Come on, you dared me. I thought we were just . . . playing around."

I couldn't stop thinking about the kissing girls on the side of the school and how certain and beautiful their kisses were. I was sure I'd screwed up my first kiss. I got up off the couch. "We weren't supposed to kiss like this. Rhett Butler would never wear a dress like that. Why do you have to make things so screwy?"

"Wait, wait. I just need . . . to sit here for a minute." He stretched out his legs and rested his head on a pillow. I waited for him to say something. I knew there wasn't a big difference between a dress and a pair of pants, they were just pieces of cloth. But I felt like I'd just failed at the most straightforward thing in the world: ask a boy over to your house and kiss him. He's wearing pants and you're wearing a dress. It was probably happening all over the world a thousand times a day. What would Diana Gaddick say?

"Tommy, I don't feel too good."

Tommy closed his eyes. "I'm just going to sleep for a sec . . . we can watch the movie."

The house was whistling like an empty seashell. "No," I said. "I think you should just go home now."

I woke up sick the next day. As I leaned over the toilet, retching up air, I remembered the Mason jar sludge, the gold strap on Tommy's bare shoulder, the kiss. Suddenly, I hated *Gone with the Wind*.

Tommy had steel band practice at lunchtime, so I didn't see him until afternoon break. I met him in the hall and told him that I needed to talk to him about what had happened last night. I wanted him to know how confused I felt, and I wanted to know if he felt confused too. We agreed to meet after school so we could walk to our usual spot by the fence and talk.

We were halfway across the snowy yard when Joey and two of his friends ran up and made a circle around us. Joey's eyes were blood-shot, like he'd been playing video games all night, and behind him were two shorter guys in black toques who didn't go to our school. One of them was chewing really hard on a white lollipop stick. I tried to keep walking but Joey was standing in Tommy's way.

"What do you want, Joey?" Tommy said. "Why are you block-ing us?"

I thought Tommy should be quiet and just look at the snow, like I was looking at the snow. It was clean and white and it reminded me of Flat Head's dry lips, the way they'd looked when he told me that *I looked like a —*

"Tommy, let's go," I said. "Please."

Joey was huffing. He pulled a scrunched ball of paper out of his pocket and whipped it at the ground. When he finally spoke he sounded furious.

"What the hell did you do, Pretty Boy? Did you copy my answers or something?"

"What are you talking about?" Tommy said.

Joey was two inches shorter than Tommy and as squat and blocky as a refrigerator. He was wearing huge ski gloves and he brought them up to his face. "Your name's at the top of my fuckin' love test." He grabbed Tommy by the collar. "You're a fuckin' fag."

Joey gave Tommy a hard shove, and Tommy stumbled backward. Then one of the shorter guys shoved him again. This time Tommy fell onto his back into the snow.

I wanted to scream at Joey, I wanted to push him into the snow and kick him, but I couldn't move.

Tommy started laughing. "What do you want from me?" he yelled. "You want me to kiss your ass because some computer scrambled our names? It's funny!" He tried to get up off the ground, but the guy with the lollipop stick pushed down on Tommy's shoulder with his boot so he slumped back into the snow.

Joey kicked snow into Tommy's face. "You want me to smack you? You want that? You want that, little Pretty Boy?"

Tommy shook his head. "Shut up!"

The boy with the lollipop grinned. "You know what we should make Pretty Boy do? We should make him do some snow angels."

Tommy turned to me. "Lucy –"

Joey blared, "Make me a snow angel!"

"Go, Lucy," Tommy said, his voice more serious than I'd ever heard it.

I didn't know what to do. He wanted me to go. He didn't want me to see him on the ground being humiliated, making stupid angels like kids do. I didn't want to leave him, but I was afraid they'd turn on me. Joey and his friends would push me into the snow, call me stupid, and ugly, and say no one would ever want to kiss me. I'd crack into a hundred bits of ice. Tommy was stronger than me. I watched him move his arms up and down, his legs opening and closing, so the snow all around him became wings. His eyes were closed.

"Lucy, just go!"

I turned and ran across the yard, through the gate and out into the street. I ran up the slushy street and I wasn't even trying to run, my feet were running without me. He'd told me to go. There wasn't anything I could do. They would've turned on me next. He told me to go.

The snow was falling fast now. I ran past the Save-On Drugstore, past the streetcar stop. The snow blurred around me, and I imagined a small door opening inside me. I put Joey and Flat Head behind the door. I put Mom and her gold dress there too. Forget Tommy, put him behind the door.

I was so tired. Why did everything have to be so hard? Maybe I'd let myself feel too much, and what was the point of that?

I'd tried too hard. I wouldn't make that mistake again.

Snowflakes ran down from my eyes. I stopped running. I closed the door.

7

"Sorry about cancelling movie night last week," Tommy said. "I couldn't help it."

It was the first night of summer, and Tommy and I were lying in the damp grass, on our backs. In the house, Mom was watching an infomercial on vacuum cleaners, so we had to kill fifteen minutes before we could use the TV.

"It's okay," I said. "I mean, I cancelled the week before."

"What was that? The dentist?"

"No." I rolled over and opened my mouth chimpanzee-wide to show him my teeth. But then I felt ridiculous so I closed my mouth and rolled onto my back again. "My dad wanted help out here. He needed his tomatoes planted by the fifteenth of June or all hell would've broke loose."

I waited for Tommy to say something, or at least give me a cheap laugh. But he didn't even roll his eyes at me. So I just stared up at the sky, which was pearlescent grey, like the underside of a shell. I could hear crickets buzzing and smell the topsoil Dad had lay down that afternoon. I listened to Tommy's breathing. Out of the corner of my eye, I could see the plastic VHS case on his stomach rising and falling with each breath, and the bottle of pop by his side.

When we went inside, I put four Jos. Louis on a plate for us while Tommy opened his bottle of pop. I guess it had been shaking around in his bag all the way from his house, because a fountain of Coke exploded out of the top, sloshed along the countertop, and spilled onto the floor. Four months ago, this Coke fountain would've had us cracking up. Now, I felt like Little Orphan Annie scrubbing at the orphanage – serious as hell. Things hadn't been the same since the snow angels. I'd thought about telling him I was sorry, but we never talked about what happened. We didn't talk about anything now.

Tommy had rented *Pillow Talk*, even though we'd already watched it together three times. It was a kitschy Doris Day–Rock Hudson romantic comedy where the two main characters trade one-liners for two hours straight – pretending not to be totally in love – and then, in the last five minutes, they smooch and sing a duet. I loved it the first three times, but it seemed so phony now.

We sat on the couch for half an hour in silence, neither of us saying anything. I was about to suggest we watch *Taxi Driver* instead when Tommy turned to me and said, "What's wrong with Lulu?"

I hadn't even noticed she was in the room. "Nothing. She's fine."

Tommy paused the movie. "No, look. She's in the corner and staring at the wall. You don't see that?"

"She's probably watching a fly or something. Forget it." Lately he always made a big deal out of nothing, as if our lives had to be more thrilling than the movies.

"Hold on, I'll turn on the light so you can check."

Lulu was as still as one of those ceramic cat statues I sometimes saw in dusty laundromat windows. I went to her and rubbed the coarse hairs on the tops of her ears. There was no fly on the wall.

"She looks really skinny too," Tommy said.

"No, she's the same. You just haven't seen her in three weeks." I hated having to prove things to him. "Look, I'll bring her to the couch and you'll see." I reached my hands under Lulu's belly to lift her, and that's when she let out the hiss, so seething that spit flew out of her closed mouth and clung in beads to her whiskers. She'd never hissed at me before.

"Lucy, you should take her to the vet. The same thing happened to Dino's Mom right before she —"

"Lulu is fine," I said. "Why do you always have to ruin stuff?"

"Ruin what? I'm just telling you the truth."

▶

Over the next few weeks, Lulu began to change. Lying low to the floor so her elbows stuck up as sharply as fins, she pulled her tail into her body like a measuring tape suddenly released from its lock and then crept around near the baseboards as if we couldn't see her there. By the beginning of July, her fur had thinned out to reveal scales, rows of black, orange, and white, in the same calico pattern I knew so well from fourteen years of devotion (55 per cent black, 35 white, 10 orange). I sat on the couch and stroked her. Soft purrs radiated from her body. I wished she would tell me what she was thinking. That's the worst thing about cats: they never tell you. Then one day her mouth started to open and close rhythmically, as if she were trying to tell me something, but I was deaf. She wouldn't let me hold her.

Then one morning she hopped up onto my bed, gasping.

It was seven-thirty in the morning. Dad had already left for Sun and Waves. Mom told me to get Lulu's travel carrier and to put an old sweater in it so Lulu would smell me and not feel scared.

"Our vet won't be open yet, so we'll have to take her to the emergency clinic," Mom said. "It's probably nothing, but just to make sure. Don't just stand there, Lucy. Go get the cage."

The funny thing about Mom was that in a crisis, she converted her frayed nerves into a vital confidence. I was the one who was scared. My palms started to sweat as I got the pet carrier from the basement. When Lulu saw me coming up the stairs with it, she cowered into the corner of the living room, her tail puffed up like a feather duster. I had to shove her into the carrier by pushing her on the bum. I didn't like how easily I overpowered her. It was a bad sign.

"Mom, is she going to be okay?" I said in the car.

"Shhhhh," Mom said. "I have to make this left turn."

In the waiting area I set Lulu's carrier down on the plastic-covered chair beside me. I was trying not to take things too seriously – she had a breathing problem, no big one. Lulu stared at me through the bars, her pupils so dilated her eyes looked black instead of green and suddenly, guiltily, I wished I had a blanket to cover the cage with so I could pretend she wasn't suffering. It was only 8:00 A.M., but the waiting room was already full. Across from me, a woman had a basset hound on her lap and she was lovingly rolling his ear up like a tortilla. I heard someone say "chemo." Then a young, fat vet in scuffed Reeboks came out and told us to follow him into the back.

In the examination room, the vet pulled Lulu out of her carrier by the scruff of her neck and set her down on the cold-looking metal table. When he stuck a thermometer in her behind, I closed my eyes. When I opened them, he was listening to Lulu's breathing; her mouth was opening and closing really fast now.

"Uh huh, well, we're gonna run the tests," he said to Mom, moving his stethoscope around Lulu's back. He reminded me of a mechanic – all quick hands and potent declarations. "You can wait outside for the results." I wanted to ask him what kind of tests, but he was looking at Mom in that adult-to-adult way that I knew meant my opinion didn't count. After Mom paid the receptionist, she went to talk to the woman with the basset hound. Then she moved along to a guy with a Chihuahua in a green mesh carrier. She didn't even like dogs. When she was nervous, Mom couldn't sit still. I counted all the women in the room, then all the men, the boys, all the people wearing running shoes, the bare ankles and ankle socks . . .

A technician opened the yellow swinging door. "You can come into the back," she said.

Mom said, "You go, Lucy."

I didn't want go in alone. But then I decided it was better if I were the one to see Lulu if she was sick. Mom would just cry and that wouldn't help anyone.

The technician held Lulu's head with both of her hands as the vet stuck a fine needle into Lulu's chest and drained out a bottle of Pepto-Bismol-like liquid, pink and thick as syrup. My jaw turned stiff, as if all the tears I wanted to cry were getting trapped in there and hardening. Afterwards, Lulu sat in the newspaper-lined cage staring up at me, her eyes peculiarly human, as if the real human in her was at that moment on the edge of pushing out. But then she meowed and was a cat again.

I couldn't let her sense that I was worried. "Lulu, I know the letters in *cat* rearranged spell *act*. You joker. You just faked all of this to get of the house, didn't you?"

Back in the waiting room, I sat down beside Mom, who raised her hands to her ears when I tried to tell her what they were doing to Lulu. "Don't tell me. I can't know." She clutched an old lipstick-stained tissue to her mouth and spit up a yellowy liquid. She'd had a cold for two months straight and wouldn't go see a doctor, but the second she saw Lulu gasping, she was on the phone to the vet. When I mentioned this to Mom, she said, "Why should I see a doctor? I can open up *Mosby's Medical Encyclopedia* and find out what's wrong myself."

When the vet came out a few minutes later, his arms were crossed on his chest. "Well, she was fractious," he said.

"What's fractious?" I said. Our regular vet never used words that I couldn't understand. He had pictures of orange cats in tutus on the walls and two canisters on the reception desk, one labelled "Cat Treats" and the other labelled "Human Treats."

Mom said, "It means Lulu was mad."

"She was fractious," the vet repeated. He said that Lulu had a respiratory problem that was filling her lungs up with fluid, making it hard for her to breathe. "We've drained the lung. She'll likely do the fish-mouthing periodically. I want you to just watch her. If she stops eating or starts gasping, bring her in."

On the way home, I stuck my fingers through the bars of Lulu's carrier. Lulu stared back at me, her pupils dark. She looked at me this way the whole ride home.

▶

Mondays became Wednesdays and Saturdays became Tuesdays and I didn't care when Mom said the summer was halfway over and why was I still as white as Casper the Ghost. All I cared about was Lulu. No one was going to keep me from being with Lulu.

As soon as I woke up every morning, I warmed up a bowl of wet food in the microwave and delivered it to her like it was a pizza.

Lulu usually cowered in the same corner where Tommy had found her at the beginning of summer, facing the wall. I picked up tiny balls of wet food and pressed them into her mouth, not giving up until she got at least a few morsels down. But she sometimes panted after I fed her, so I couldn't be sure if I was really helping her.

"I made you a sandwich," Mom called, banging a cupboard shut in the kitchen.

"Put it on the table. I'm with Lulu." As long as Lulu wasn't hungry, I wasn't hungry either.

Tommy phoned while I was feeding Lulu. When I told Mom I was too busy to talk to him, she said it wasn't right to forget about my friends, even if I was worried about Lulu. "If you ignore your friends, they're going to disappear. Do you want to be forty years old and talking to a bunch of cats?"

When I called Tommy back, he asked if I wanted to go to High Park with him. "We could check out the paddock. I heard that two peacocks just graduated from police academy. They're having a huge party that we could crash."

"I can't," I said. "I wish I could, but I need to be here with Lulu."

"I'm sorry," Tommy said. "I figured something was wrong. I mean, you don't call me back. Even right now you sound weird."

He was the one who sounded weird. His voice was cracking, not mine. He was the one who thought peacocks were policemen.

"Lulu's changing. I don't know if you get that."

"Lucy," Tommy said. "She's dying."

I hung up the phone before he had a chance to say anything else.

The room was hot, and so bright I could see dust flowing through the air. But I was cold. The sandwich Mom had left for me on the kitchen table looked grey and sad. I took a tiny bite, then another, feeling worse each time I swallowed.

▶

When I was a little kid, I thought that people turned into animals when they passed away. It started the winter my grandma died, when I was six. I didn't understand how a person could just suddenly *not be there*, if their shoes were still in the closet, and everybody still remembered them. I asked Mom and Dad where Grandma was and when they said they didn't know, I felt they were lying. They were adults, so they were supposed to know everything.

On our way home from sitting shivah, I saw a red robin sitting on a branch. My grandma's hair was also red and suddenly I was sure the bird *was* Grandma. After she had died, she snuck out of the hospital and went to the park and traded bodies with a robin. Now I understood why her casket had been closed at the funeral. It wasn't because closed caskets were a Jewish tradition, like Mom said. It was because the casket was empty. My grandma wasn't dead, she was just a robin.

Fish-mouthing. That's what the vet had said. Lulu was fish-mouthing.

I imagined my grandma the robin sitting in a tree.

Then I imagined Lulu the catfish floating on her back in a sun-streaming pool.

"Catfish. Catfish," I whispered, stroking her whiskers. "Come on, little catfish. Breathe." Even as I said it I didn't believe it. Every time her mouth would close, I'd think she was going to be okay again. Then it would hang open once more.

Before the future, before the change was complete, I wanted to make a list of all the things I wanted to remember about Lulu.

Lulu's sense of humour. How as a kitten she'd initiate games of hide-and-go-seek. When I found her asleep in my dresser drawer she'd beep and raise her ears like a pair of receiving antennae. And when I dangled my ALF shoelaces in front of her, she'd get up on her hind legs and dance.

Her sense of entitlement. The way she pulled a chair out for herself when she smelled salmon baking in the oven.

Her ability to turn door handles.

Her independence. When she sat with Dad while he watched the evening news, she'd allow only her front legs to rest on his knees. Her hind legs she kept on the couch, neutral territory. Sometimes she'd disappear into the ravine for hours at a time, then come home smelling of dirt and wagging a dead grass snake in her mouth.

Her arrogance. She slept in my closet on a shelf, nestled on an old gym bag. If you turned on the light she'd look aggravated, like you were some overstepping maid.

Her stubbornness. She always searched for hard, sharp things to expressively splay herself out on – a bench covered in clothes pegs, a pile of old shoes, a scrunched paper, or keys – as if to say, Don't take me for a regular cat because I can do without those creature comforts.

Her resilience. When she was two she got caught in raccoon trap, lured by the scent of sardines. She continued to lick the can even as the animal control man used a saw to get her out.

Her modesty. I never once saw her admire herself in the mirror although she had plenty of reason to. She found the sound of her own voice uninspiring – she preferred birdcalls, can-opener calls, the song of Pounce treats shaking in their shaker – which is why she was usually quiet, a rare thing these days.

Lulu knew that she was becoming a catfish. That's why she was scared. When she meowed, a trapped sound came out from deep inside her guts. When she slept she trembled, as if she was preparing to pounce on an enemy. She wanted to fight the change, even if fighting wouldn't stop it.

I knew that was the confusing thing about change, how it *will* happen, even without your permission. It's like being strapped into a roller coaster and suddenly you're sure the track is screwed up or the operator is drunk. All you want to do is make a scene, scream, anything to get them to stop the ride so you can get off. But I wasn't that kind of person. I never made a fuss. I didn't make a fuss when Dad told me how happy Crashing Wave made him feel. I didn't make a fuss when Mom started dating Robbie Roth.

So I told Lulu to stop fighting the change because it was making her weak.

I told her to think about the sea, to imagine all the free tuna. "I know you feel bad now, I get it. But you just have to believe that in the end it will all be worth it."

Lulu was sitting beside me, but I could've been talking to myself. I was changing too. Layers of pudge had crept onto my thighs and the tops of my arms over the past six months, filling my body out, but in all the wrong ways. My stomach was puffed out, but my breasts were still in hiding. So I understood how Lulu could feel that her body was letting her down. But I told myself that once I got to high school, my body would even out, in the same way that Lulu's would when she finished her transformation.

I didn't tell her any of this. I just told her how, as a catfish, she'd be able to go down to the bottom of the sea and feel the softness of water on skin all the time. I tried to soothe her by rubbing her ears gently, the way I'd been doing since we were both young.

▶

In the middle of August, Lulu collapsed on the kitchen floor. As I picked her up, her limbs felt boneless and didn't kick back. They just folded under her as I slipped her into the carrier, locking her in.

This time Dad drove us to the emergency clinic, and the same fat vet in the scuffed Reeboks came out to take Lulu into the back for tests.

We waited for a long time. I counted all the women in the room, then the running shoes, then the boys . . . I thought about Tommy, and how we'd drifted apart. In two weeks, we'd be at different schools. He would make new friends and so would I. Everything was about to change.

The vet came out and told us to follow him into the back. Mom led, with Dad lagging behind me. In the hallway I could hear a dog whining from every direction.

The backroom was silent. Lulu was sitting in a cage and she had a plastic bubble around her head. The vet explained it was connected to an oxygen tank to help her to breathe, but I didn't think it was really working. The inside of the plastic bubble was sprinkled with spit. Lulu's tongue was hanging out of her mouth as if it had suddenly become too heavy to hold in. She tried to shuffle to the end of the cage, to get closer to me, but the plastic tube running to the oxygen tank held her back.

"Why's there so much spit on the bubble?" I said.

"She's totally stoned," the vet answered. He said it like she'd been getting stoned all her life, like she was this girl with patchouli-scented hair and pockets stuffed full of Zig-Zag rolling papers, lounging on the bike racks outside the video arcade.

"What's her outlook?" Dad said. He picked at his nails and studied a plastic chart on dog breeds taped to the white-painted cinderblock wall.

"To be honest, she's a mess."

As usual, Mom looked for a miracle. "Could there be a sudden recovery?"

"I'm not God," the vet said. "But I really don't see that happening. We've drained the liquid from her lungs, but every time she takes a breath they fill up again with a little more liquid. Without oxygen she'll be dead in a couple of hours."

"Will it be painful?" Mom said.

"It will feel like drowning," the vet said. "Not nice."

I held Lulu on my lap. She was trying to get away from me, flipping around in a way that reminded of the time I once went fishing for pickerel. When one landed in the boat, it stared at me very intensely, with a look that said, *I trust you, don't kill me.*

Lulu fought the technician as she fastened the IV to her wrist sloppily, as if it was a twenty-five-cent friendship bracelet. Then Lulu went slack suddenly, draping herself across my lap, her head rolling off my knee. The technician removed the plastic bubble. The fish breathing had stopped. Lulu looked like herself again, only hungry.

"Pet her," the vet said.

Lying across my knee, Lulu didn't look like a fish. She looked like a calico cat receiving an overdose. The vet pushed the needle into her IV and I pet Lulu's neck, the soft white fur, but I was miles away. I started to think of dead celebrities, the famous overdoses of Jimi Hendrix, Jim Morrison, and Janis Joplin. Shannon Hoon from Blind Melon and Marilyn Monroe, Elvis and River Phoenix. John Belushi. Keith Moon. Then I felt the weight of her vanish as the vet lifted Lulu off my lap. Dad walked out of the room.

Mom began to sob. "Why did we do this? Now she's gone."

On the way home from the vet, I waited for Mom or Dad to say something. But Mom just dabbed at her eyes with a tissue. At every stop sign, Dad idled as if we were parked. Tiny raindrops hit the windows. The world had suddenly slowed down. Mom started sobbing again, and without actually touching my ears, I blocked her out. I blocked out everything but Lulu. I pictured her swimming underwater, this tricoloured regal flash across Dad's windshield, whiskers fine as embroidery needles. Her eyes were shining as luminously as two emerald insets. She was an ocean queen, a furry drama, and smart enough to stay away from hooks, this Rita Hayworth of the deep.

Dad's windshield wipers flew across my dream.

I worried that Lulu wasn't ready to become a fish. Or maybe it had happened in the wrong way. Maybe Lulu would have preferred to change at home, in the backyard, alone . . . the way a caterpillar does it, in its cocoon, or a snake, unlacing itself from old skin.

When we got home, Dad went upstairs to his study and I heard Roy Orbison begin to sing. I heard Mom closing her bedroom door. I'd never been in the house without Lulu before. Everything felt different. I needed to talk to somebody. I picked up the phone and started dialling. That's when I realized that I was calling Tommy. His line rang and rang, but nobody was home.

I'd spent the whole summer caring for Lulu and now I didn't know what to do. My stomach had little knots in it, so I thought maybe I was hungry. I went to the fridge and took out all the things I needed to make a sandwich and carried them to the counter. I pulled two slices of bread out of the bag and spread mustard across them. I peeled salami slices from their packaging and layered them on top of the mustard. I closed the sandwich with my palm and held it there. The warmth of the bread entered my hand and travelled up my arm like I was touching laundry fresh out of the dryer. It felt good. I carried my sandwich to the table and looked out the window.

Outside, on the sundeck, I saw a flash of red, but what I thought was a robin was just a geranium that had fallen from the flowerbox onto the lawn.

I peeled the crusts off my sandwich. I made fingerprints in the bread. But I wasn't hungry anymore.

8

Lucy Bloom was a brain, not a body. This was a fact I learned early on, in elementary school, when our grade four class had lined up in the baseball cage so that the two best athletes could pick teams. I'd waited so long against the chain-link fencing that my skin was imprinted with red diamond patterns: I was always picked second to last, just before the Saudi newcomer everyone avoided because three times a day he had to go into a stairwell and pray. But I knew at least half of the elements on the periodic table as well as the sea green, amber, and roast nut brown shades that had made up Lulu's spectacular irises. I wasn't a body but a brain, and I accepted this. I used to think this meant I'd never have to be like those confused plain girls, in their big glasses and stirrup pants, who did everything imaginable to try to look like the popular girls they followed around at lunchtime. That was the best part of my unlucky deal. I thought I'd never have to play at being a body. I was a brain and that was all.

►

Two weeks after Lulu died, I started high school at Central-West Secondary. On the first day, I wore the outfit Mom had picked out for me, a woolly navy blue vest with gold buttons embossed with sailing ships, a white shirt, and a pleated skirt with a giant kilt pin stuck through it. Dad went through an entire roll of film as I sweated beside the tomato plants. Between the sound of the shutter whizzing open and closed, I heard Mom say, "Frank, doesn't she look like a woman now?" and I wilted a little more. I drew my arms to my chest and stared over Dad's shoulder, the sun burning into the part in my hair.

As I packed up my knapsack the phone rang. It was Tommy calling to ask if I wanted to meet up in the subway after school.

"I can't. I'm hanging out with some girls. You'd be bored." I had no clue what girls I was talking about. I figured I'd make some friends in the gym, where everyone had to go to pick up our schedules. Maybe I'd see a girl wearing nice shoes and compliment her on them. Then she'd tell me that she was thinking the same thing about my shoes, and we'd laugh. Then she'd introduce me to a few of her friends and after school we'd all go out to Harvey's for hamburgers.

"How about tomorrow?"

"No," I said. "I don't think I can."

Afterwards, breakfast passed strangely: I watched Mom energetically slit open mini croissants and implant their insides with squares of cream cheese and spoonfuls of strawberry jam. The jam ran onto her fingers, sticking to the beds of her nails. I was too nervous to eat. Instead, I put my fingers on either side of my yellow Pyrex plate and rotated it like it was a clock. At seven-forty, I'd leave for Central-West, which was a streetcar, subway, and bus ride away from home. At eight-thirty, I'd pick up my schedule in the gym and meet my new girlfriends. Then we'd all go to the washroom and comb our hair to get rid of the frizz. Good Teenagers on TV shows never had frizzy hair. It was illegal. Same with falling in love with people who had pimples. Or with short guys.

I moved my plate back to its starting position. At seven-forty, Tommy would be leaving his house too. We were going in different directions, and I was okay with that.

During the quiet of the last two weeks, I'd thought about the kind of person I wanted to become in high school. I decided I wasn't going to be shy. Being shy, I'd realized, only worked if you were gorgeous, because that made you mysterious. But if you were a brain, you had to fly out there and meet the world head on. People would know me; I'd talk to everyone. I'd join the debating team, even though I didn't like speaking in front of more than two people at a time. I'd volunteer to do costumes for the drama productions and cart in Mom's old clothes. I wouldn't be like the high school girl who lived next door to Hyman, who, he said, smelled like burnt wires and was always nodding off from the drugs she smoked. I saw her once. Her hair was a knotted pile of purple snakes and her skinny body seemed to float in her man's suit jacket and baggy pin-stripe pants, cool Marlene Dietrich clothes I'd never seen on a real-life girl. I felt uneasy watching her. She looked lonely and I knew that in high school you could suffer for that. I wouldn't let myself be like her. I would not be friendless.

"Let me pack your toast," Mom said. "You can eat on your way."

When I got on the subway, there was a girl sitting across from me wearing a tight pink T-shirt with Hot-to-Trot written in puffy letters across the chest. I smiled at her, but she just sighed and checked her pink plastic watch. Another girl got on the subway wearing a stonewashed skirt and a Sweet Baby T-shirt. She sat down beside Hot-to-Trot and flicked one leg over the other, lightly as toothpicks. I looked down at my thighs. My skirt suddenly felt too tight. When the subway train left St. Clair station, I shimmied my skirt around so I could roll down the waist to read the label. "Made in France, Size 36." It was a European size, and I didn't know what it meant. Was I wearing a plus size? Or maybe I was wearing clothes meant for someone twenty-two years older than me? I stretched my leg out in front of me and noticed how sprouts of hair, like barbed wire bits, stuck through the nylon. How my calf jiggled as the train passed Davisville station. In the darkness of the tunnel, I thought about the advice Mrs. Grace had given our grade eight class about essay writing: what you leave out is just as important as what you put in. Maybe I'd put too much into my brain and not enough into my body. Maybe that's why I wasn't Hot-to-Trot. When the subway pulled into my station, I followed Hot-to-Trot and Sweet Baby up the escalator.

At school we were all herded into the gym, where I waited in line for my schedule behind two girls wearing T-shirts that said Hottie and Cherry. I looked at their shoes to see if they were pretty enough to compliment. Hottie was wearing sandals and her toenails were painted ice blue. Cherry wore white tennis shoes. They didn't respond when I said hello, so I inhaled the sticky air and pretended to be busy looking around. A boy marching around in a football jacket waved at Cherry and she waved back by wiggling her fingers only. At my side, I practised Cherry's finger wave. I felt like I was typing.

When we were almost at the front of the line I unbuttoned my vest and draped it over my arm. Hottie turned to look at me before turning back to her friend. "Yeah, it's her," I heard Hottie say. "I can see the sweat at her pits."

On my way up to homeroom I saw a debating team sign taped to the stairwell wall and I ripped it down. Still thinking of Hottie and Cherry, I stuffed it into my knapsack and walked on. I didn't like how my morning had started. I was going to rewind the tape now. I just needed a few minutes alone.

In the washroom, I locked myself in a stall. Messages written in black magic marker were scrawled all over the walls and the door. Who fucked whom and how. What boy had no pubic hair or orange pubic hair, who had a fat ass and who stayed at home for two weeks after she got her abortion. Who was a druggie and who was a fat nerd bitch.

When I came out of the stall, I wanted to smooth my hair before class so I stood behind two girls applying lipstick in front of the mirror, but their hair was blocking my view. Then one of the girls turned abruptly: it was Estelle Pomper. *Oh shit.*

In two years, she'd developed more than I had, and in all the right ways. Her breasts looked solid, as if she was stashing giant cupcakes under her blouse. Her skin radiated like it was being lit from within. I pretended not to notice her by ripping a square of paper towel from the dispenser. When I turned around, Estelle was standing behind me.

"Excuse me," she said.

If she called me Bony to my face, I was going to tell her we weren't eleven years old anymore. Then, maybe, that I liked her shoes.

"You're blocking the paper towel."

Maybe she didn't recognize me. Or maybe she was pretending not to know me. I didn't know which was worse. My stomach began to ache.

In homeroom, I felt so full during "O Canada!" so disgustingly full. While the teacher took attendance, I undid the inside button of my skirt and loosened it by half an inch. Then I looked around to see if any of the girls at the back had noticed. Probably not, since most of them were grooming. They held tweezers lightly and pulled hard at their eyebrows. They passed their tweezers around. They passed tubes of lip gloss and hairbrushes and notes on lined paper folded into squares the size of chicklets. Everything they wore was a colour that could be found in a fruit salad. No one was wearing a second-hand private school uniform, trying to be classy. No one had a shiny swath of blue ribbon fastened to her head like a best-in-show cow. I looked at the two chunky girls who sat together in front of me, drawing words out of search puzzles, while the grooming girls ignored them. Beside me, a boy with freckles and a crest of red hair riding his head was reading the *New York Times*. The smell of old farts and luncheon meat was coming from either his body or his knapsack. He lowered his newspaper enough so I could see his braces twinkling. "Hi," he said. He had a friendly smile, but it was obvious that he was a nerd. If I became friends with him I'd be a nerd for the next four years. So I said hi back, and then I turned to say hello to Hottie in the next row. She was the girl from the gym, but I had rewound the tape and now we could start again. Her binder was covered with shiny heart stickers. There was no paper inside. I stared at her open, laughing mouth, shadowy as a beautiful drain.

Between classes, the hallways surged with laughing girls in skirts of single ruffles, their legs tanned and as shiny as the hoods of waxed cars, and everyone so thin. In comparison, my legs were bowling pins. In my second period class, the redhead boy sat next to me again. He asked me if I wanted to go with him to the debating club meeting at lunch. "No, thanks. I need to go out and buy my lunch today." He offered to share his lunch with me. I couldn't shake this guy. "I'm meeting some friends," I said, "so I can't."

At lunch I found a grassy knoll on the side of the school, where I could gaze at Estelle, Missy, and the other groomed girls whose names I didn't know. It was against the rules for people to smoke on school grounds, so Estelle and her crew stood four feet off school property, facing the south doors, and puffed long, white pen-shaped cigarettes, as though they could smoke out words. I thought about what I would say to them. Maybe I would compliment one of them, tell her how nice her T-shirt was and ask her where she had bought it. While I thought about how I might approach them, I tore my sandwich into strips and rolled them into pinwheels. Then I stuffed them into the bottom of my lunch bag. I dug a hole in the ground with a stick and buried my grape drink, peanut bar, and boxed raisins. I ate my pear and watched Estelle and her girls.

I knew that some girls were good at having many friends at the same time. I saw these girls in the subway, by the tiled kiosks, sharing large foil bags of dill pickle chips as they watched the private school boys in their blue-striped ties — the Flat Heads and Moles of the world — fly down the escalator. These girls were quick, radiant, and light, a storm of butterflies careening out of a net. I was slow and focused, like a steam locomotive moving up a hill. I wasn't invisible. I was impossible to miss, but in the worst way. Maybe I was no different than Hyman's next-door neighbour. At any second, Estelle and her crew would turn around and see straight through me. They'd think I was weak. And just thinking of that made me want to hide.

The next day, I started wearing a loose rain jacket to school and felt less exposed. From the grassy knoll, my lookout hill, I imagined that my jacket was a tent and I was nothing but a tiny, fallen branch caught inside of it. *Blow me away wind, melt me away sun, blow away the old me, and bring me a better one.* I sat on my lookout hill, digging graves for the salami sandwiches that Dad woke up fifteen minutes early to make for me every morning. I watched the girls.

▶

By the third week of school, strange noises had begun to crawl up from my stomach. They reminded me of the sound wind-up toy cars make when you lift them up – their little wheels still spinning – and they came out of my mouth in powerful buzzing burps. I sat on my lookout hill at lunchtime and chewed hard tooth-shaped pieces of gum to get rid of the taste of these rotten egg burps. At first it was hard eating only one pear for lunch, but by the fourth week of school, I felt lighter, as if the soles of my shoes were balancing on confetti of solid air.

In homeroom, the word-search girls were elected student council reps. Each time they made an announcement about events or activities happening at school, I felt superior to them and their little world of crafting clubs and dance committee meetings. I knew that, like me, they would end up going to the dance alone, but at least I wasn't trying as hard as they were. Miles, the literary redhead, became chair of the debating club. He still asked me to come out to their meetings, but I couldn't stand his luncheon meat smell, and I was ashamed of the way he ate lunch every day, slumped in front of his locker so that the rugby guys could walk by and kick him in the shins by accident. The rugby guys had smooth hair and wore wraparound sunglasses and matching jackets with red leather sleeves. After school, I sometimes saw them driving home, four to a car, the engine gunning the sounds of war. I decided that I wanted a boyfriend who made a lot of noise, a strong blond guy who travelled in a pack, like an animal.

During the fifth week of school, I began to feel cold all the time. At lunch, I sat outside wearing two sweaters underneath my raincoat and rolled my soft white bread sandwiches into balls. On my lookout hill, I took half an hour to peel a navel orange, another twenty minutes to remove the roughage from its squirting flesh. I began to feel a little silly, but I didn't care. I imagined what kind of personality the garbage can would have: it would be quiet probably, always trying to talk, but instead just getting its mouth stuffed with food. What about the lamp post? It was frustrated and stiff-necked from always hanging around and never doing anything. The mailbox on the corner was emptied twice per day, so clearly she would never feel full. I kept on watching Estelle and her girls. Sometimes, I made little *o* shapes with my mouth, imitating how they smoked and blew kisses across the cement out front of the south smoking doors. When I saw the girls laughing, I tried laughing too.

Hahahahahaha.

Between periods, I idled on the pencil-scented stairwell and watched the girls drift upward and downward, luxuriously, their elbows and shoulders these bobbypin-thin right angles. The image of perfect shoulders fixed itself in my mind, and nothing I did could remove it. On the way home, I stared at my own reflection in the darkened subway windows and imagined the soft curves of my shoulders and the C-shape of my hips dissolving, the way sugar cubes do in hot water. I wanted to be all straight, uncomplicated lines, like fresh September notebooks. It was okay for eyelashes and breasts to be plentiful, but that was about all.

When I saw Mom on the couch as I marched up to my room, my back molars ground against one another and swear words punched my lips from the inside, struggling to get out. The less I ate, the more I noticed how she ate her food, always on a yellow glass plate, balanced on her lap, as she slumped in front of the TV. I noticed the slice of vanilla cake, its icing thick as toothpaste, suspended in a highway of a moment between her fingers and her mouth. How her coffee was a sewer of sugar. The mini croissants that she baked for future use and stuffed in the egg compartment of the fridge brought sour acid up my throat. I slammed up the stairs and lay in bed, smoothing my hand over my stomach, over the border of my pelvis and the hard ridges of bone there. Tracing my bones made me feel calm and happy and excited about the future.

One night Mom came into my room without knocking. She was wearing her robe and pink shower cap, the lobes of her ears sticking out from under the vinyl like flesh-coloured pearls. "What's the matter with you?" she said. "You never want to eat with us."

I couldn't look at her. I couldn't stand how the old silk of her robe strained at her hips. How her fingers looked flushed and fleshy spread out on the tops of her thighs. Every time I looked at her now, I was sure that just being near her was screwing me up. She was the reason why I had looked like a best-in-show cow on my first day of school. Her lifetime achievement of worrying about everything in front of her face had made me a gutless person. I wanted to scream, *You. What's wrong with me is you.*

But instead I said, "Don't you know you're supposed to knock before barging into someone's room?"

I'd stopped returning Tommy's calls during the first week of school, and soon he stopped calling me. Then, during mid-terms, I ran into him on the streetcar platform at St. Clair station on my way home. He was with a group of people and I was embarrassed to have him see me on my own, so I went to stand behind the phone booth, where I could watch them without being seen. The girls had beautiful skin and were wearing vintage T-shirts underneath cropped leather jackets while Tommy and the other boys wore high-tops and hooded sweatshirts and headphones. They were a walking GAP ad for second-hand clothing. I pulled the belt of my raincoat tighter. Tommy had punked out his hair. It was shaved on the sides, long on the top, and spiked up into a Mohawk. He was smiling.

I wasn't going to let him make me hide. He wasn't some movie I was going to watch like an invisible girl. I came out from behind the phone booth and walked back to the escalator, then made my way toward the platform again so he'd think I'd just come up from the subway. He smiled when he saw me, only now with his teeth. Why was he smiling? He hadn't called me in three weeks. Obviously that was no big deal to him.

I went up to him and his friends drifted away as though I was a big rain cloud. "Hi," I said.

"I haven't heard from you in ages," Tommy said. He was eating french fries from a greasy bag, bending them into his mouth and manoeuvring them with his tongue. His lips were stained with salt. I had kissed those lips. Then I'd run away from him. But I couldn't run away now. So I just watched his mouth open and close, then open so wide again that I could see the mash of pale brown french fries inside and his too prominent epiglottis, which was soft pink and reminded me of a small dog's erection.

He made the awkwardness worse by asking me if I was all right, as if there was something wrong.

"I'm fine," I said. "Why are you asking?"

When the streetcar pulled in, I told Tommy that I was waiting for someone and that he should go ahead. I watched him climb on through the back doors with all his new friends. I really didn't care that he didn't turn around and wave goodbye to me.

The next streetcar arrived a minute later. I couldn't stop my lips from trembling. I thought it would help if I talked to someone. The old woman sitting beside me had a little dog on her lap. "Who's that you have there? Is that a cocker spaniel?"

"That's Danny," the woman said. "He's a Yorkshire. Do you like Yorkshires?"

I asked her if Danny had a job.

The woman frowned. Her lips were as thin as the crust of a Melba toast. "Danny is a dog, dear. His job is to keep me company."

Sometimes, on my way home from school, I imagined Estelle and her crew flitting around in their thin dresses like butterflies. Sometimes they appeared eating dripping cheeseburgers, which I didn't appreciate. I wanted them to eat only air, so I could too. To get rid of the image of cheeseburgers, I stopped on the sidewalk, leaned against a pole, and pushed two fingers into each of my temples. I was starting to notice how soft my skull was. How squishy my brain felt underneath the thin shell of bone. When I started to get headaches, a stabbing pain at my temples, I thought of Frankenstein's monster and the two bolts struck through his head – painful but necessary for keeping his brain together.

At home, I watched TV talk shows and drank diet soda so my stomach would stop aching and sucked on lemon wedges to stop it from making those spinning-wheel noises. When Mom sat beside me I moved as far away from her as possible, onto the arm of the couch, where Lulu used to sit. If I looked closely, I could still see Lulu's hairs on the pillows, these thin white strands. I felt so alone without her.

I made excuses not to eat dinner with Mom and Dad: I'd eaten a late after-school snack. My cramps were killing me. Homework calls! I had a pressing errand like buying Bristol board at the drugstore. I spent a lot of time at the drugstore, standing in front of the wall of diet snack bars and fasting drinks. I loved wandering down the aisle of hair colour products and staring at the photos of women with their shiny helmets and heaps of hair. Beautiful women with their hair combed back or flying forward, like Crashing Wave's – laughing, confident hair. You-all-want-me hair. If I was feeling good, the hair colour women stared back at me encouragingly. But if I was really hungry, their faces would animate into frowns as if to say, *Do more* and I'd feel like knocking them off the shelf. On the way home from the drugstore, I let myself buy one jelly foot candy from the convenience store, on the condition that I made it last for the entire walk home. If I felt ambitious, I ate only the toe and threw the rest down a hole in a sewer lid. At school, not eating was less of a problem. I found that the more I watched the girls, the less hungry I was. I bounced through the halls with an airy step.

When it started to snow at the end of November, I bought a watermelon-coloured jersey dress with a pony logo on the breast pocket to reward myself for losing thirteen pounds. One of Estelle's girls had the same one, but I wore mine with jeans underneath and a cardigan over top. It looked kind of rocker-ish that way. It was the first new item I'd ever bought for myself and I felt like a diva when I wore it. I ripped the shoulder pads out of a blazer Mom never wore and stuffed them into my blue shell cup bra, to fake the appearance of breasts. The nubs I had were gone now. Then I found an old white purse in the basement and placed a pencil case and one notebook inside. It couldn't fit anything more. When the teachers asked where my textbooks were, I shrugged decisively while turning to watch the girls. I waited for one of them to admire my dress. I opened my cardigan and pretended to adjust my top to help them along.

After five minutes, I got tired of waiting. They obviously had no taste. They were sheep on leashes. Their mothers probably did their shopping for them. I pressed my fingers against the ridge of my hip bone. I continued to watch the girls.

Yet for all the pleasure it gave me, I worried about my habit of watching the girls. So one day I decided to do an experiment in class. Estelle sat at the back of the room, still wearing her Liesel costume from the dress rehearsal for the school's production of *The Sound of Music*. For the experiment, I imagined Estelle's clothes melting away, the way ice cream does in August, so that all at once she would be sitting there in homeroom with her perfect body exposed. Yet hard as I tried, I could only see Estelle's nude body as a collection of ice creams, her breasts two generous scoops of vanilla, her torso an expanse of maple, but the pale, sugar-free kind, her crotch a swirl of strawberry sprinkled with Oreo crumbs. The eyes were the only interesting part, tiny gumball-shaped scoops of pistachio that looked nearly edible. But I didn't feel excited in a down-there kind of way. It felt more like a science, watching Estelle, and watching others watch Estelle.

By the middle of December I had stopped eating the orange segments and made a rule to only eat the roughage, which had the taste and texture of hangnails. My ribs ached. When I combed my hair, the part seemed wider, as if my scalp was bossing its way through. My pimples were so hard I couldn't pop them. I tried anyway, and tears gushed out of my eyes. I couldn't keep my thoughts straight. My brain felt as scrambled as TV snow on the channels only rich people got.

So when Estelle in her just-fresh-from-stage lederhosen and a group of her girls surrounded me, demanding to know why I was always staring at them, following them around at lunch and in the halls, I thought she had some nerve. I was about to say so when I suddenly lost the words. I could almost see my brain liquefying and pooling at their feet. Even though it was winter, Estelle and her friends wore open-toed sandals in school and changed into boots when they left the building. Their sandals were a mark of their difference, their excellence. Estelle wore candy-red sandals with yellow buckles and chunky wooden heels, and her toenails were painted the in-colour, shiny midnight blue. Her friends wore similar, less expensive sandals made of fake leather, and their toenails were painted orange creamsicle, baby pink, apple red, snowflake blue, and the bright silver of scissors flashing forward –

When I opened my eyes they were gone. I leaned back on my locker and looked at the floor as usual. That's when I saw the brown gerbil near my shoe. Or maybe it wasn't a gerbil. It was too large, a plump ball of fur. Maybe a degus, that South American rodent with the name that made me think of the painter of ballerinas. No, not a degus. My hand flew up to touch the back of my head. I'd worn my hair in two buns that day, in imitation of Louisa, the younger and clearly less pretty sister in *The Sound of Music*. Now I felt only a rough stump where my right bun had been. They had cut my hair. My hair was now lying on the ground, next to my shoe. I felt something sour rising up my throat.

After I looked up and down the hallway to make sure that no one was there, I removed the elastic from my remaining bun and combed what was left of my hair to the other side. It would have to do. I picked my bun up off the floor and shoved it into the front pocket of my knapsack. Then I grabbed my coat and ran down the hall, down the stairs. Where was I going to go? I checked my watch but the numbers were too blurry. I took the back exit, through the caretaking office, a room with pictures of half-naked girls stuck to its greasy walls, where tattooed guys repaired old chairs and desks by banging on them. When I got outside, the air smelled of gasoline and the sky looked strange, too grey to be so warm, shot through with chopsticks of light. I walked across the prickled dead grass of the football field, thinking how I would miss French, the conjugation quiz on *étre* and *avôir*, and then biology. Our class was slated to meet our fetal pigs and take them apart like cars.

I felt trapped just standing and waiting at the bus stop, so I started to walk. The people passing me on the sidewalk looked crooked and frightening. It was hard to keep my balance: I was rocking up and down like a boat. I walked close to the storefronts, trailing my fingers along the doors and front windows, so that if I fell, I'd fall against them instead of straight down. But then the outcoming people bumped into me and scowled. Their faces seemed huge, their bodies sticklike. They were a people of lollipops, flavourless and composed of a simple compound. What was sugar? One part carbon, two parts hydrogen, one part oxygen. I imagined my body dissolving or caramelizing right there in the street. Did I have a temperature? Hot skin connected with a wet hand. I wondered what would happen if I lay down on the sidewalk and pretended that my body was safe, nothing but a little pea zipped in a crispy green pod jacket. I thought about crazy textbook words like *symbiotic, biological,* and *tyranny* and then tried to use them in the same sentence, speaking aloud as I walked. "The organs and tissues of the human body work symbiotically," I began, before pausing as I passed a dazzlingly lit ice cream store, "unless they are deprived or overworked."

My heart tightened in my chest, and I pictured it shrivelling like an apricot abandoned in a paper lunch bag. I saw hideous businesspeople lined up like oxen at a McDonald's take-out window. "Lastly, the brain will eat itself, a phenomenon that is nothing short of biological tyranny."

I stopped at the mall entrance that led to the subway and tried to open the door, but it was too heavy. I had to wait until a man opened it from the inside. I slipped underneath his arm, imagining that I was thinner, like sexy cigarette vapours. While I waited on the subway platform, I pulled two failed math tests from my white purse and threw them into the garbage. The questions had been unfair; the bar raised too high.

On the subway ride home I imagined a pair of tiny teeth making its way around the circumference of an apple, leaving just a spindly core. Then I remembered the cow brain I'd bought in grade five from the Italian butcher for my project on the nervous system, the brain being its central organ. I'd handled its slimy grey matter with bare hands, then stuffed it into a pickling jar filled with rubbing alcohol. After my presentation, the teacher had given me an *excellent!* and put the jar on a shelf. There it had stayed, the water clouding after a few weeks until you could no longer see the brain.

I snapped open my coat and smoothed my watermelon dress proudly over my body. I could feel every one of my ribs, the ridges, the strength hidden in the hollows. I thought about Estelle and her crew and decided they were just jealous. They knew they couldn't touch me. I was stronger than all of them. The train chugged through the darkened tunnel, and with each squealing corner turned, I felt the smile on my face grow and grow until tears of pride filled my eyes. My brain could sit on a shelf for a while, growing cloudy, awaiting my return.

9

At the end of grade nine, Estelle Pomper started a rumour at school that I collected cats, tens of them, and jammed them into my room the way those square stale candies are jammed chock-a-block into a Pez dispenser. At this point, I weighed about ninety-three pounds – and when I'm delirious I'm the least defensive person in the world. So when Estelle called me the Imelda Marcos of cats to my face in class, I decided to play along. Instead of clawing back with my calcium-deficient nails, I threw back my head and tossed my hair – the way Whitney Houston does in *The Bodyguard*, in the scene when she's triumphant and looks really thin in the leather bustier – and that, for some reason, closed down the joke pretty fast for Estelle. She just stared at me, though she stayed planted in her seat beside me.

"Can I ask you something, Lucy? For real, I mean."

I couldn't believe I was even listening to her. Six months ago, she'd come at me with scissors and chopped off my hair. I could still see my bun on the ground, wearing its frizzled silver hair elastic.

"The diet you're on," Estelle said. "What's the name of it?"

I never admitted to anyone I was on a diet. I didn't even think of it as a diet. It was a rule, a *should*, strong as pliers around my heart.

"I'm not on a diet," I said. "Why do you think I am?" If she was going to buzz around me as persistently as a fly, the least she could do was tell me I was skinny.

"Well, you were really skinny in elementary school," Estelle began, "but then you got a little heavier after. No offence, I mean, we all did. At the beginning of the year you were thin, but now you're, like, *skin*ny. And your butt is really small. Your arms too. I was just wondering how you did that."

"Why?" I said. I wanted her to try harder, like I had.

Estelle looked around, to see if anyone was listening to us. Then she leaned closer to me, so close I could see the tiny light brown hairs growing outside of the perfect arcs of her eyebrows. "Sometimes I try to make stuff come up. But I just start choking usually. And it's hard not to eat, because I get dizzy. I mean, don't you ever get dizzy?"

It made me laugh inside to think I'd spent so many years straining for her approval. Now she had nothing on me. "Estelle," I said. "I want to read my book now."

I could tell she was pissed then because her eyes crossed slightly in a way that I knew boys found attractive. Then she got up and went over to some girls who were talking about their summer cottages. I went back to reading *The Catcher in the Rye*.

For the last two weeks, Mr. Hardaway had been talking about the symbolism in the book, how the field of rye was not a *real* field of rye but a symbol for peace of mind. Some of the people in class, including Estelle, were pretty convinced that Mr. Hardaway was a loser and the field of rye was real. When they got to the chapter where Holden dreams of the field, they got negative about the whole novel, as though the title was a lie. I loved that the field wasn't real. If a place actually existed, like Estelle's cottage, or the resorts Dad sent his customers to, then anyone could find it and go there. But if you dreamed up a place in your head, the way Holden did, that place was safe and nothing and nobody could take it away from you. I had a place like that in my head where I went to whenever I hadn't had anything to eat. When I closed my eyes, it sounded as calm as a beach at night. Every time I inhaled I would feel as if I were stopping time.

I tried to focus back on the page. I was at the scene where Holden is in New York City and holes up in this sleazy hotel where he doesn't know anybody and tries to pick girls up in bars. The girls aren't interested one bit, but they tolerate him because his wallet's buying them drinks —

But I couldn't concentrate. I was so hungry that the type was swimming in front of my eyes, smudging into blots of bluriness. This happened all the time. It would start with the commas. They'd sway like sneakers being dangled by their laces from an overpass, and then bang, they'd tumble off the page. Then went the apostrophes, these westward fledgling sparrows that my eyes craned to catch but missed. The regular letters made up words I had to squint to follow. Lately, reading a book was as deadly as watching a train derail. I'd miss one word, then a line, and then the whole page would crash.

I closed my book.

I could hear Estelle talking about her summer vacation plans. "Mine's a two-piece," she said. "I don't like one-pieces because they wreck my tan."

I was going to spend the summer working with Dad at Sun and Waves. I couldn't imagine Holden Caulfield ever working at a travel agency. But then it was also hard to picture Dad working in one. He'd probably take his time to help some blonde book a cruise, but more likely he'd just thrust a couple of airline tickets at an old lady with blue hair and tell her, "Here. You can go now."

Sun and Waves was located at the far end of the Lawrence Plaza, one of those concrete bottomless squares that Dad said was built in the 1960s, when no one cared if buildings were ugly. At the south end of the plaza was a bus stop and a shoe repair shack that always smelled like horse shit, but Dad said that was actually the boot cleaner the shoe guy had to use for police shoes. On one side of Sun and Waves was a nails supply place, and on the other was a store that was completely empty except for some old chewing gum racks.

Dad worked with only one other person at Sun and Waves, and that person was his boss. Dad's boss was a man, but his name was Marg Nutter. I think that's why he was always in a bad mood, because he had a woman's name.

Marg Nutter sat at the front of the store so he could greet his customers as soon as they walked in. But I think that's another reason why Marg Nutter was always in a bad mood, because nobody ever came into the store. The customers were mostly phone-ins, old people who wanted to go to Boca Raton, Fort Lauderdale, Palm Springs, or, if they were looking for something more exotic, Varadero, Negril, or Guadalajara. Sometimes the old people got mixed and instead of "Guadalajara" they'd say "Guantanamo," and then Dad would have to explain that it wasn't that kind of resort.

Marg Nutter had offered to pay me less than minimum wage to deliver flyers to the high-rise apartment buildings surrounding the plaza. The only part of the job I was looking forward to was the exercise I'd get, because I'd read in one of Florence's women's magazines that power walking burnt 567 calories per hour. I was also in charge of folding the promotional flyers Marg Nutter photocopied on a machine so low on toner that the leaves of the palm trees were almost invisible. They just looked like these long stalks, more like middle fingers than leaves, and when I folded the flyers I'd sometimes think, Yeah, Fuck you! Go to Florida!

"Lucy? What's so funny?" Dad was talking to me from the front room.

I had started to laugh out loud at tiny jokes I told myself in my head. Once I started laughing it was hard to stop. I figured this was how smoking pot made you feel: your head all airy, as if your brain had dissolved into dancing dandelion spores. I also noticed that I laughed more on the days I'd eaten almost nothing. For instance, if I had two saltines for breakfast and drank two cups of coffee with two Sweet'N Lows, I'd be laughing at the swearing palm trees by about ten in the morning. But if I ate more than the top of a muffin or a piece of plain toast, the trees weren't so funny – they were actually kind of depressing – and Marg Nutter's voice, which sounded as if it was strangling through too small a space, became even more unbearable. Whenever I ate more than I'd planned to – sometimes Mom offered me a sandwich at a moment when I was feeling weak – I felt myself leaving my field of rye and the heaviness of the food spread through my body the way a bee sting on your hand can travel up the entire length of your arm, throbbing. Food didn't give me energy, it sucked all my strength away. I didn't know if the draining feeling meant "eat more" or "stop eating," so I usually just stopped eating.

I covered my mouth to stifle the laughing. "Nothing, Dad."

Around the middle of July I decided I would deliver only half of the flyers. Marg Nutter was paying me less than a chocolate bar an hour, so I felt justified throwing out the rest. I'd walk halfway across Lawrence Avenue, hitting up the two aquamarine apartment buildings where mostly pensioners lived, people who stood on the wavy concrete path talking to their dogs in creaky amazed voices. I liked walking on that path because there were no trees and the sun hit me in a totally absorbing way. I felt like a creature dipped in honey. That's where I ditched the remaining flyers.

I'd just stepped off the path when a red car slowed beside me. I kept on walking tall in my shoes, which I'd bought for fifty cents at the Salvation Army. They were beige and made out of a dry leather-like material as stiff as a chewed-up dog toy, but they were my only heels and I thought they made my legs look skinnier. The car was crawling along the shoulder beside me. The passenger window rolled down in intervals, as if the person inside had a weak arm or was still deciding whether I was worth talking to. When I saw his face my first thought was that he was famous. It was Archie from the comic books, with the ski jump nose and five freckles on each of his cheeks so uniformly round they could've been drawn in with a ballpoint pen.

"Hey, honey, do you know where Bathurst Street is?"

Then I remembered that Archie was a cartoon character, not a real man.

"Next major intersection, six blocks," I said. "I'm walking there."

Archie grinned. "That's far. We're lazy asses. We don't walk anywhere. You want us to give you a ride?"

He was flirting. I forced out a laugh, rocking forward on my heels. I imagined Mom's face right now, her tortoiseshell glasses superimposed on the bright clouds, her mouth yelling, "No! He does drugs! It's not safe!"

I decided that taking the ride wouldn't do any harm. I opened the back door and slid into the seat. The driver was a guy with blond hair cut into the shape of a police cap. Archie started asking me questions about where the nearest Taco Bell was, but I wanted to make sure Police Cap was driving toward Bathurst before I answered. Only when I saw that he was did I start listening to Archie, who was going on about how he'd just quit his job at a computer factory in Ottawa because they'd been "busting his balls" by not paying him overtime, even though he worked on Christmas and Boxing Day. "Two fucking years in a row!" He thumped his thigh and the Burger King cup between him and Police Cap spilled coins onto the hollow area where I figured the radio used to be. Archie turned around and smiled at me over the backrest of his seat before turning around again, so I knew he was checking me out. I crossed my legs and pulled my jean skirt down my thigh a bit. Diana Gaddick used to say that showing a little leg was good, but not so much that guys got the wrong idea. Archie turned around again.

"Say," he said, "do you have rickets?"

"What?" I said.

"Hey, don't take it wrong. You look cool. I just never seen someone as thin as you." He turned to Police Cap. "You?"

"Nah-uh."

"This is pathetic," I said, "picking a girl up and then asking her if she has some kind of outdated disease. What kind of pickup is this?"

Archie looked embarrassed. "We were just giving you a ride," he said. "Why did ya have to go make it all uncomfortable now?"

When they dropped me off outside of the Lawrence Plaza, I felt insulted. They didn't want me. They hadn't come on to me. If I looked sexy, I didn't understand why they hadn't tried to come on to me. Was I not pretty? As I weaved in between the parked cars in the parking lot, I studied my arms, how the veins popped, how the bone of my inner thigh jutted out through my skirt. I walked through the door of Sun and Waves, not even stopping to say hi to Dad or Marg Nutter, and went straight into the bathroom.

I stared at myself in the mirror.

My face had become long and thin, my nose as gaunt as my cheeks. I didn't understand why I didn't look like the ultra-thin models in the Ralph Lauren perfume ads, their ribs delicately visible through cotton sundresses. They were New England girls, I decided, whose grandmothers had names like Portia and Rosaline, and who always knew which fork to pick up when the salad came around. These were the girls who starved and flourished, their big eyes made bigger, their tiny noses made tinier, by the absence of food in their stomachs.

When a Jewish girl starves, I thought, something entirely different happens. Her cheeks recede and her nose grows – and so does her guilt. She thinks about her mother constantly: the ways she will make it up to her mother in the future when this eating "thing" settles down, compensate her for the hours spent staring into the pantry, wondering what kinds of carbohydrate combinations – rice and farfel, bowties and kasha, potatoes and rice – she can, by some nurturing magic, sneak into the glass of Lipton's chicken bouillon that is now the extent of her daughter's dinner.

I got on my knees and put my finger down my throat, feeling the smooth skin that reminded me of a raw scallop, slippery out of the grocery bag. But I wasn't good at turning my insides out. Nothing came out. Then Marg Nutter knocked on the door and told me to take it outside, his customers shouldn't have to hear me coughing up a lung. So now he was hallucinating a lineup of customers snaking out the door.

We were similar in a way, Marg Nutter and I: we both looked at what we had, what we were, and told ourselves stories to make the truth a little softer. Marg Nutter told himself he had a successful travel agency that was just going through a temporary slump. I told myself that if I weighed a little less, when I looked in the mirror I would finally see the girl I had always wanted to be staring back. Instead, I saw a line of hard pimples blazing across my forehead like a Las Vegas sign. Only this sign said, *Move along, folks. Nothing to see here.*

On the last day of July, I walked into Sun and Waves and saw a pile of flyers on Marg Nutter's desk. They wouldn't have been remarkable except they were stained with a purple liquid that looked like Grape Crush soda. Marg Nutter came out of the backroom and told me that one of his clients had found hundreds of them in the garbage. The old man had been throwing out some dog shit in the courtyard of his building.

Marg Nutter didn't yell when he fired me. He spoke quietly, putting on the regretful tone of a teacher who's just found pot in his star student's locker. "You may think what you did was a joke, and not a big deal. But there's something about honour that you have to learn, Lucy. If you say you'll deliver, you have to deliver." The pun was unintentional, and I felt bubbles of laughter – the I've-eaten-nothing-today kind of laughter – building up in my throat. Then I saw Dad sitting at his desk, looking grey and ashamed.

"We're sorry to have to let you go, Lucy," Marg Nutter continued. "But we're a business. And in a business we can't tolerate these kinds of antics." Each time Marg Nutter said the word *we*, a nerve in Dad's face twitched. I couldn't tell if the twitch and his look of disappointment were because of what I'd done or because he hated thinking of himself as part of the *we* that was Marg Nutter and Sun and Waves.

After I walked out of Sun and Waves, I turned around to take one last look at the place. I had a feeling that I would never go back. Dad was standing in the store's tropical-island-themed window with his hands in his pockets, and I could see the downward slope of his shoulders, the way his beige and orange plaid shirt looked old-fashioned but not on purpose. They were the clothes of somebody who doesn't care anymore; someone who lives in the past, when his hair was still thick and the dreams in his head were bouncy and too quick, like those rubber balls you can buy for a quarter in the front of grocery stores but that always end up getting lost.

In the weeks that followed my ejection from Sun and Waves, Dad kept his distance from me. He stopped popping his head into the living room on Tuesday nights to say he was going to his AA meeting. Instead, he'd just close the front door behind him, this soft thud, not even bothering to lock it from the outside, which is what he always did. He'd always been so paranoid about "hoodlums" breaking in, and the change in this small gesture, the not locking up, made me feel like he was sending me a message, that now I was on my own.

We didn't say much to each other until the morning we got up early to go to the CNE. It was our annual end-of-summer tradition; Dad and I had been going to the fair together since I was six. Neither of us really wanted to go this year, but Mom insisted, even though she never came with us. She couldn't stand the crowds and her feet would start to hurt as soon as she'd bought two silk fans and a family of bonsai miniature men from the "international" pavilion. I tried to picture the amusement midway, the clowns reeking softly of pot underneath the hint of mouthwash, the choked ponies wearing tassels, and the measly-chested bears with upside-down smiles, starved to fit into their small cages.

Mom was baking banana-nut muffins and the buttery aroma was testing me, but I was stronger than that. I had to tell myself disgusting things to keep from yanking the burning tin out of the oven. I wanted to devour the whole tray. "Those muffins are filled with pigeon shit. Those muffins are filled with fingers."

Mom opened the fridge, took out a couple of juice boxes, and handed them to Dad along with two soft bosc pears in a crumby diet bread bag.

"Lucy, I want you to eat a muffin before you go," she urged. She looked isolated, her greying hair tufted in chaotic fluffs.

My head shook itself no.

"Frank. Tell her you won't take her until she eats a muffin."

Dad said, "Lucy, are you hungry?"

Mom stamped her foot. "She's *never* hungry." She tried to grab my hand, but I pulled away and shoved both hands under my armpits. It felt cold there. Mom watched me. "Well, you have to take your hands out of there sometime." But I didn't. I just held them there as I turned around and walked all the way out the door.

Dad and I took the crowded streetcar down Bathurst Street, standing in the articulated middle section that from the outside looks like an accordion. It curved when we made turns, and I had to hold on to the steel bar to steady myself. When the streetcar straightened out again, I took my hand off the bar and brought it to my nose. It smelled of metal. Then it hit me that I hadn't had my period in three months.

Dad asked me if any of my friends were going to the CNE, but he sounded kind of sad as he said it, like I should've been going with them instead.

"Not even Tommy?"

I shook my head. "I don't talk to him anymore."

"Why? You don't like those old movies now?"

I kicked a gum wrapper, but it didn't go anywhere. "We just don't talk anymore. I don't know. Are you friends with everyone you met when you were twelve?"

Behind us, three kids were eating candy necklaces and arguing about whether a donkey was the same thing as a mule. Their silliness made a warm hammock for my brain to lie in.

"The mule mom is a donkey and the dad's a horse, I *know.*"

"Well you know what a donkey's called on a farm?"

"A donk." Soft giggles like rice sliding in a tin.

"No no, I know. A fonk."

"No. An ASS!"

The sound of candy cracking in their teeth reminded me of how Dad and I used to take coins from the Mason jar in the front hall closet and walk to the convenience store 679 steps away to buy me Sweet Tarts and sour balls. "We're going to Candy Land," I would say and Dad would wiggle his nose at me like a hamster. "Where's that?" he'd say. "I've never been to Candy Land before." So I would take him by the hand and lead the way.

Dad and I got off the streetcar at the Exhibition Loop and walked along the teeming platform. I smelled suntan lotion as people rushed by us, their faces gleaming like olives, their hair slicked back from the heat. Every small detail pierced me: how the humidity made curls at the temples of the beautiful Italian women, and the soil-scented teenaged boys swaggered and mopped their faces with bandanas. Elbows jostled into my ribs and I struggled to keep up with Dad. He was walking with a postman's purposeful stride, his arms pumping speed.

In the midway, the air was a combination of candy-corn sweet and diesel exhaust. Stalls were selling hot dogs, popcorn, and cotton candy, and the coloured flags strung up between electricity poles were blowing softly, inhaling and exhaling, like wind-filled clothes on a laundry line. The Conklin man logo was everywhere, the clown face with its curly hair and exclamation-mark nose, the mouth a half-interested lipsticked leer. We passed a man outside a small, outhouse-shaped booth. He wore a sign that said – *Lucy*.

No.

It said, *Lucky People Line Up Here.*

We were waiting in line for the Cosmic Spinner when I felt a wormy stripe of pain, a yellow ache, moving through my chest and choking me.

"Dad," I said, "I need to sit down."

We found a bench and we ate our pears, the juice running down our chins. Tattooed men with neon pink tans and big-armed wives passed by, children straggling behind noisily like tin cans. I panted. I watched the line for Cosmic Spinner lengthen, loop around the side of the ride.

"You look very white," Dad said. His hand floated up to my forehead. "It's so hot out here that I can't even tell."

But I was cold. I brought my arms in close to me and tried to concentrate on the green wool of my cardigan, but I couldn't hold my attention on it. I kept looking down. The pavement shone as if it had been freshly tarred. The bench rocked like a Ferris wheel gondola.

"I'm okay."

Dad pointed somewhere. "There's the food building. I'm going to get my Billie Bee honey and buy you a drink. What kind do you want? Sprite?"

Forward and then an inch back, I pressed the sole of my shoe against the ground to steady myself. "A fizzy water. Please."

Dad went to buy my drink and his one-dollar honey in a plastic squeeze bottle in the shape of a bear. I told him I'd wait in front of the Tiny Tom Donuts kiosk if I didn't stay on the bench. As soon as he left, I drew myself up and walked the thirty feet to the donut stand. Hypnotically, the wet and squishy mini donuts rolled along a metal belt before dropping into a sea of boiling oil. I kept repeating this sentence to myself, as if it were my compass: "Dad is in the Food Building." I stood in front of the kiosk for a long time, watching the passersby, their big teeth, the brims of their straw sunhats. I listened to the call of the barkers getting louder and shriller, the slinky spinning sound of the roulette wheel. A new feeling was going through me. It wasn't so much wobbliness, or a head sickness, or nausea, but a desire to reach out *and kiss someone,* to hold on to them. I didn't care if I looked crazy, all I wanted was for someone to hold me; their arms would slow everything down. But I didn't move. I couldn't. I just kept watching those happy teeth and sunhat brims and swollen knuckles and red fingernails and cartons of caramel corn, the insides of the kernels dark like dirty molars – and then I was on the ground.

When I woke up, I was lying on something hard: I thought it was the ground, but there were four mint green walls around me. I rolled onto my side and pushed myself up. A woman in a blue safari shirt was sitting in the chair beside me, reading a novel with gold letters on the cover. I could taste wood in my mouth. Did I choke on a stick? Then I remembered the Tiny Tom Donuts van and arms, two sets of them, pulling me up – one person on each side of me – and my first thought had been, *Am I that heavy?* The woman in the blue safari shirt got up from her chair and, as if the floor were made of eggshells, walked over to me very slowly. She was wearing a walkie-talkie strapped to her shoulder and a baseball cap with the initials of the Emergency Medical Services stencilled across the front. Her nametag said, Denise.

"You're in the medical trailer," she said. "Your father is waiting outside. Do you want a glass of water? Or some crackers?"

I sat up and pulled my knees to my chest. My head felt sunburned and raw, but the tops of my legs were covered in goosebumps. I didn't know what was happening. I just wanted to get out of there. I heard the sound of water gushing out of the tap.

"How long have I been here?"

"You fainted about twenty minutes ago." She handed me a clear plastic cup of water. "Have you ever fainted before?"

The bubbles in the water were trembling, and so was my hand. "No," I said.

"When was the last time you had something to eat?"

I drank the water. It tasted as funky as a metal watch. "I'd like to go now please."

"You should lie here for a few more minutes. And eat some crackers."

"No. It's okay. I'll just go now." I wobbled a few steps toward the door, then turned around. "Thank you," I said. "I mean, thanks for —" I was about to say "helping" but that would have sounded like I actually needed the help. "Thanks for the water."

I saw the toes of Dad's socks first, peeking out from his sandals. On the grass beside him was a see-through bag with a drawing of a giant yellow bumblebee on it. Inside the bag was the fizzy water I'd asked him to buy.

"You don't need to tell Mom about this," I said quietly.

"The woman already talked to me. I need to tell Mom." Dad paused, as if he was searching for the why, and I knew that whatever answer he gave would have more to do with his own life than mine.

"Lucy, you have to understand," he said. "I don't have secrets from her anymore."

10

"Do you have enough underwear? Are you cold back there? Do you want me to close my window?" Mom kept turning around from the front passenger seat to ask me polite questions.

I am me, I wanted to shout. *Talk to me like I am still me.*

It was the first day of school: I should've been starting grade ten. Instead I was on my way to a "facility" for the criminally thin. I repeated those words to myself: *criminally thin.*

Gilroy Guesthouse wasn't near a town, a shopping mall, or a movieplex, not even a gas station. Nothing but fields surrounded Gilroy, rolling bright humps that reminded me of the opening scene of *The Sound of Music.* From what I could tell, the only thing nearby was Crystal Beach, an ex-resort-spot turned ghost town six miles down the highway. All that was left of it now was an enormous billboard for a hotel, with a flaking illustration of a man in swimming trunks tossing a beach ball, a sand-coloured dog holding a stick, girls with long sunny hair, and the nonsense slogan – VERY CRYSTAL BEACH! The hotel was nowhere in sight and had probably been razed to rubble years ago.

I held my knees to stop them from trembling. I hadn't eaten today, so at least I still had that.

We stopped at a McDonald's on the side of the highway and Mom pulled egg salad sandwiches from home out of her bag. Kids were screaming in Play Land, popping out of the pee-smelling plastic balls.

"Lucy," Mom said. She held the Wonder Bread crusts out to me, so soft they took on her fingerprints. I took a crust and broke it in two, then brought it up to my mouth. *Open your mouth. Open it. She's watching you.* I bit off a tiny piece and chewed. It tasted like her Jergens hand cream.

Dad went to ask for ice water and came back with a sour look on his face. "Five cents for one goddamn cup."

Mom widened her eyes at him, as if to say, *Not now.* Dad chewed his ice and started picking at his nails. Mom just smiled at me and patted my hand. I saw their next six weeks without me stretched out in front of them, shaded in boredom, punctuated by big fights in the kitchen over little things.

Gilroy Guesthouse was a two-storey stone farmhouse with a pink siding addition on either side. The door was cherry lozenge red, with a tiny stained-glass window at its centre. When I clutched the knotted brass knocker, the veins in my hand stuck out from the strain of lifting it up.

The woman who opened the door was wearing about ten gold

necklaces and jeans that were tight on the hips because she had big ones. "I'm Cora, I'm one of the aides here. You must be Lucy." She had a Caribbean accent, but I didn't know from where.

"That's Lucy," Mom said, as if I couldn't talk.

Cora took my suitcase and stepped back into the doorway. She wasn't quite blocking it, but the gesture made it clear Mom and Dad weren't allowed to come inside with me.

"If you don't like it here, you can call me —" Mom took a step up into the doorway.

Dad interrupted. "Be a good girl, Lucy." As if I had been bad.

For the first time in my life, I didn't feel trapped between them. Even though they were wrong, they had finally agreed on something: they thought I was sick.

Cora carried my suitcase upstairs and into a room with bunk beds on each side, eight beds total. Attached to the frame of each bed was a painted wooden cutout of a type of food: a flaming pink slice of ham, a head of bok choy, a cluster of grapes.

Cora put my suitcase down on the closest bottom bunk. "You're Bananas," she said, pointing to the yellow cutout glued to the frame of my bed. "So every day, when you go to the rec room, you gonna check the activity chart for Bananas." Cora told me there were a lot of activities I could do at Gilroy, like sports salon, writing club, arts and crafts, and current events. She scratched her neck and one of her gold necklaces shifted, so I could see the damp skin underneath. I wondered if she was the only fat person here. "Every day at nine, you gonna go to group. Everyone does group. Then you do a chore. Check Bananas to see which one. Then you gonna be free for the rest of the day." Cora showed me the bathroom and the fire escape. Then she asked me if I wanted to unpack first or go and meet the other girls in the recreation room, only she called it the Sun Spot.

I pictured Mom and Dad driving back down the highway. I wanted to be in the car with them. I would go to McDonald's now and eat all the soft bread crusts Mom gave me, even if they tasted of her hand cream. "I guess now," I said.

Cora grinned. "You a brave one. After lunch is a wild time."

The funny thing about the Sun Spot was it wasn't sunny at all. Except for the far back wall with the one window cut into it, the rest of the room had walls that looked as though they were stuffed with cotton batting.

"I'll introduce you to some people," Cora said.

"It's okay," I told her. But Cora insisted on taking me by the arm as if I was some rickety elderly person. The first girl she took me to was using a blow dryer as a dumbbell. She stopped when she saw Cora coming and pretended she was doing her hair, even though the cord was unplugged and dangling around her arm. She was the tiniest girl I'd ever seen. She looked about twelve, and her skin had a fine sheen over it that wasn't oil but something closer to dew.

"Jen, this is Lucy Bloom," Cora said.

"Howdy," Jen said. "So are you Bananas or the new Ham?"

"Tessa's still here," Cora interjected. "She just sleeping elsewhere right now."

Jen rolled her eyes. "Okay, whatever you say. But maybe next time I feel like getting a private room, I'll just down some Ipecac and go fetal in my bed." She winked at me, but I didn't smile back at her. I wasn't like her, so I couldn't get her jokes. I knew that Ipecac made you throw up, but I'd never tried it. I had nothing in my stomach to get rid of anyway.

Next, Cora introduced me to Clarice Sinclair. Later I learned that nobody ever called her anything but Clarice Sinclair, as if she was too insubstantial to go without both names. She had a cleft palate that had been corrected, but her upper lip still jutted up a little toward her left nostril. She was sitting on the carpet and using a plastic ruler to slice a lipstick into tiny red discs. I felt bad for her because I figured the cleft palate was the reason she was slicing lipstick instead of wearing it. Cora bent down and grabbed the lipstick in the same resigned way people grabbed chewed shoes away from their dogs.

"What you doing now?" Cora snapped. "Messin' everything up again?"

"No," Clarice Sinclair said. But she didn't fight it.

The only girl at Gilroy who wasn't skinny was Roz. She had big arms that spread out like sails and a thick brown ponytail tied with a Minnie Mouse scrunchie. She sat on the rag rug in front of the television using wood glue to fit two pieces of maple together. She said she was building a box. Cora patted her shoulder. "That's a good girl," she said. I figured Cora was nice to Roz because they were the only fat people at Gilroy.

Then Cora took me over to a big chart taped to the wall and ran her finger along the Monday column. "These are the chores, you see? You're doing bathrooms tomorrow, you see the bananas? Bok Choy is Alice and she's in charge of the plants today. Alice, you watered the plants or you gonna let them die?"

"I watered them," a voice said. It was coming from a girl wearing a raincoat buttoned up to the neck.

"That's Alice," Cora said. "Beside her is Sarah. Ladies, this is Lucy."

Sarah ignored me. "Cora, I want to show you my painting, come."

Cora touched my elbow. "Why don't you look around? I'm right here."

I didn't want to. But Cora was watching me, so just to show that I wasn't helpless, I went back toward Roz. She was still gluing her box together, her fat arms flushed with little red bumps. I wandered toward the back of the room. There was a girl standing by the window with the sheer curtain draped over her head like it was a wedding veil. I didn't appreciate the way she was staring, as if there was something wrong with me. She was the one wearing a pink macramé dress like we were about to sing "Kumbaya."

"Ooh, look at what the cat dragged in."

It was Diana Gaddick. I barely recognized her. Her face was so gaunt that every feature – her tiny nose, her bow lips – had knit closer together the way buttons do on a shrunken sweater. It was her hair, though, that shocked me the most. Her hair, her incredible red hair was so thin now, just this red string scraggling down her shoulder. It made me think of something you'd use to catch a fish with.

"There's been some kind of mistake. I'm not staying." I wanted to call Mom. I needed to go home.

Diana began to laugh. "Your tits are gone," she sang, clutching her stomach. "Your tiny tits are gone!"

▶

When I was younger, Mom used to take me to the Christie Pits public pool. I loved being there in the morning, when it was all mine. I'd float on my back in the deep end and gaze up at the sky drifting by as steadily as a slow blue movie. Sometimes I'd watch these boys cannonball off the diving board, because one of them looked just like the real Charlie Sheen in *Hot Shots*, with muscles that made me ache but in a good way. But when the pool was extra busy it was a different story. I couldn't float around because people got all showy and jumped in at crazy angles, so I never knew if I was going to get clobbered. The deck felt as wild as a jungle and the whistle was always blowing. To get away from all the noise, I'd swim down to the bottom of the deep end, where it was dark and warm and quiet. There, I made myself into a tiny ball and blew bubbles. I would challenge myself to stay down there for ten more seconds, then another ten . . . but then I'd have to come back up to the surface. My first two weeks at Gilroy felt like coming up, again and again, into the noise, when all I wanted was to go back down to my quiet place. I wanted to stay down there as long as I could.

In my banana bunk, I tossed and turned, dug my face deep into my pillow. I heard every sound in the room as if it was amplified, and I was sitting inside the noise itself. I heard Roz on the bunk above me, her snores like water crashing onto a rock. I could hear the crackling sounds of Jen, across from me, listening to Nirvana on her Walkman. I pushed my face deeper into my pillow. I tried to imagine Holden Caulfield in his field of rye, but there was too much food in my stomach and my brain was moving so fast. In my head I heard Cora repeat, in her lilting accent, what she'd said to me after supper on my first night: "You're lucky that you're here just in time. Your heart is a little mouse nearly run out of breath." Then I remembered the plastic anatomical model sitting on Dr. Burchill's desk. You could pull out any old piece – the kidneys, the navy blue liver like a tiny purse, the butterfly-wing lungs – turn it around in your fingers, then pop it back in again. I loved how it made the body seem so simple, your fingers an expert surgeon. I recognized each organ from my grade nine biology book, especially the heart, a strawberry split open, filled with blue and dark pink squiggly lines. Dr. Burchill had picked out the heart and said, "When a person doesn't eat for a long time, the heart muscle shrinks."

My fingers felt cold. I brought my knees up to my chest and tucked my fingers into the crooks of them. I floated, thinking of the CNE, lying on the ground underneath the counter of the Tiny Tom Donuts kiosk, staring up at this picture of Tiny Tom spray-painted to the corrugated metal. A speech bubble erupted from his mouth: "Have a sweet day!!!"

At Gilroy Guesthouse, even if you looked like a cadaver, you couldn't just lie in bed like one. Three a day was the rule: three meals, three activities. Every morning, I had to check the activity board to see what Bananas had scheduled, so I knew where I had to be and at what time. I didn't have much incentive to break the rules – we were in Nowheresville and I didn't smoke – but girls broke the rules all the time.

On my fifth day, Cora was running around looking for Alice and Sarah because they were both supposed to be in current events. "You seen them?" Cora asked me, rushing by. Bananas was in charge of cleaning the second-floor bathroom that day. While I was tossing cleaning powder into the sink, I had seen Sarah and Alice through the window, sitting in the backyard, a few feet down the sloping hill. They were sharing a cigarette, their shoulders touching.

"No, I haven't seen them," I said. I thought Cora was nice, but I wasn't going to help her. I had more in common with Sarah and Alice than I did with her.

Current events was the club where you cut articles out of the *Toronto Star* using scissors one of the aides gave you out of the locked cupboard. Then you made collages of thin women from advertisements that had nothing to do with current events. Sports salon was a fancy name for the badminton net on the lawn and the table tennis game in the Sun Spot. That was the most popular activity because you could move around, which burnt calories. There was also a writing club, which I liked because it was the one activity where I didn't have to socialize. Diana Gaddick hated going to the writing club. "It's a bunch of wussies who've never been kissed writing poems about their mothers and all the boys who never liked them. Not for me. *No thanks.*"

The facilitator of the writing club was a graduate student named Shawna. She had blonde hair pinned behind her ears with silver barrettes and really big lips. Shawna was doing a psychology degree at the University of Toronto.

"So that's like Freud, right?"

She changed the subject really fast, as if I'd said something wrong. That sort of made me think that Shawna thought I was a weirdo she couldn't speak to about personal things. I wanted her to know that I wasn't like the other girls. I knew what psychology was. I wasn't just some patient.

Shawna gave us these assignments called Free Writes. She'd hand out pieces of plain lined paper and then she'd say a word, just one random word: it could be *pickle,* or *fear,* or *ostrich, love, decision,* or *photo* – I never saw a pattern in the words she gave us. Shawna said there was no such thing as important words. It's what you felt about the word and what you could express out of it that was really important. I wasn't sure I believed this. I always thought of words as having a kind of currency, all the words in the world arranged on a ledger, in their own word hierarchy. Hate words like *bitch* and *loser* had a low value, but love words like *kisser* and *bejewelled* were worth a lot.

One afternoon Shawna brought in what appeared to a cake box wrapped in a big plastic bag from the Bay. I think Jen thought it was a cake box too because she looked really happy and sad at the same time. But then Shawna opened the bag and it was actually a stack of books. I could tell from the covers they were children's books.

"Today we're going do an exercise called adaptation," Shawna said. "You're going to read your book and then change around the story, *modify* it, so it's personal to you. You can change names and details, whatever you like, but use the story as a starting point. Everyone follow me?"

Diana raised her hand. "But isn't that plagiarizing?" When she wasn't being annoying by trying to be gorgeous all the time, Diana actually had some original ideas.

Shawna picked up the book on the top of her pile. It was *Peter Pan* by J.M Barrie. "Okay, good question. Everyone knows Peter Pan, right? Well, nobody here is really a Tinkerbell or a Peter Pan.

So really, this story has nothing to do with your experience in a direct way. But for this assignment, you go ahead and make it your own. Okay?"

Shawna needed someone to throw her a lifeline.

"Okay," I said. "That sounds good."

Diana pinched my knee. "Teacher's flat-tit pet."

My book was called *Where the Wild Things Are*. It was about a boy in a wolf costume who wouldn't eat his supper, even though his mother kept bugging him to. He dreamt up a wild forest and escaped to it, only he was lonely there. When the boy returned to his bedroom at the end, though, his supper was waiting on the table and it was still hot. It wasn't such a sad story.

For the first time in months, the page wasn't swarming with orphan commas and my head didn't hurt. I picked up my pen and started writing.

Clarice Sinclair read her story first. Hers was an adaptation of *Peter Pan*, but it didn't make a lot of sense. It was about her favourite aunt, who collected Hagen-Renaker miniatures – I guess Tinkerbell was the association – and then died in a car accident a few years ago. Clarice Sinclair's hands shook as she read and her neck broke out in a reddish rash. I looked away, feeling embarrassed for her. I was glad that my story wasn't a diary of my bleeding heart.

Diana sighed. "Can I use the washroom, please?"

Shawna shook her head. "In fifteen minutes, when we're done."

I wasn't expecting Shawna to ask me to read, because she never asked me anything. "I don't really write stories."

"We're all beginners here," Shawna said. "Go ahead."

"We could all turn around if that makes it easier," Jen said.

"I want to hear your story," Diana said. "Come on."

I didn't want to read my story out loud, but now that Diana was basically daring me to, I had no choice.

"Once upon a time, I was like the kid in the wolf suit. Only mine was a suit of bones. I wore it everywhere and it was heavy as hell and noisy. Most people don't realize how noisy wearing bones on the outside can be. If they ask me, I tell them, 'It's like wearing twenty wooden bracelets on each of your arms. You're a percussionist with no musical training.' I went to the movies. People forgot all about the talkers and the loud popcorn chewers, they were so furious at me. Clank, clankity, clank." And here I heard Jen drum her fingers against her book. "That was the sound of my kneecaps adjusting when I squished my legs to the side, so a latecomer could slip by. The latecomers liked me because my bones glowed in the dark. I was brighter than the usher's flashlight. But again, that's another reason people couldn't stand me in the theatre. The end."

When I finished, Diana clapped a few times, very slowly. "That's, like, better than John Grisham," she said. Shawna nodded. She was probably disappointed that I hadn't cried a river. I figured she needed tons of those for her thesis. Finally she shuffled her papers and said, "Lucy, were you taking the assignment seriously?"

Jen cleared her throat loudly. It was incredible that such a loud sound could come from such a tiny throat. "Hey, to me that sounds like a true story." Then she turned to Shawna. "Have you ever worn a bone suit? If not, I don't think you can say what's true and what's not."

At Gilroy Guesthouse, nighttime conversations revolved around two topics: food and sex. We exaggerated our craving for boys – in football uniforms, naked, at the movies, on their knees – and downplayed our hunger for food. Alice, who almost never spoke, told us she used to work at a bakery in Owen Sound, where she decorated wedding cakes with royal icing and roll fondant roses, so many of them the cake looked more beautiful than a botanical garden.

"The boss was always mad at me," Alice said softly. "He said that if I decorated one cake so much, he'd have to do all of them like that and then he'd lose money."

"If your boss wanted money, he should have just been a pimp." Diana sounded totally serious. "Anyway, can we quit talking about cakes? You're giving me a cavity and my dad said there's no decent dentist near this shithole."

"Well there's no one to have sex with either and you're still always talking about it," I said. "How do you explain that?"

Diana just took that as a cue to start talking about her favourite subject. "I've been with four guys," she said, "and each had a bigger cock than the last." I heard the grin on her face, and could picture the corners of her mouth widening, which what they did when she lied. "Not that bigger is better. Because the first cock looked like an E.T. finger and still, it was a good one for me. I felt like Casanova."

Diana's voice was as frantic as knocking castanets. She talked about her love life in the same way she'd read me passages from *Madame Victoria,* authoritatively, and proudly, as if she was the author *and* the heroine of her tales, which I suspected she was since I was sure they were all made up. Still, like the other girls, I listened silently to her stories. They had life, flesh, zigzags of colour that made my hands tremble like I'd had too much coffee, the outlawed drink at Gilroy. Above me, I could hear Roz's breathing slow in anticipation, a whirring sound like a low-speed fan.

Across the room, I could just make out Clarice Sinclair sitting up in bed and grinning. Her cleft palate made people look away when she talked, but in the dark she was a little more vocal. "Who was the guy, Diana? Was he cute?"

Diana giggled. "Clarice, I have a better idea. Why don't you tell us about the first guy you ever kissed?"

I was so tired of the way Diana picked on people. She was

calculating and mean. She was a vulture who knew where to find your weak spot and then picked at it.

"Hey, Casanova," I said. "You know, that's the word for a male lover.'

"Fine, then what would you call a *wo*man lover then?" Diana shot back.

"I don't call her anything," I said. "It's just whatever her name is. Whenever you talk about guys, or sex, it's always like you're playing a part in some cheesy porno. You sound so anxious it's like your head's gonna blow off."

As soon as I'd said it, I knew I had found her weak spot. Diana was silent. The longer she stayed that way, the more I wondered if she was feeling the kind of embarrassment she inflicted on all of us.

Finally, Diana filled in the gap. "How about you? Tell us about the best lay you've ever had." She was back to her sarcastic self.

I shot up in bed. "Me? Oh, there's just too many, I don't even think I could count." I never told stories about boys who stared at me lustily in the halls, or boys who wanted me at the swimming pool. The material just wasn't there. Instead, I told wild stories that made skinny bodies giggle and mattresses creak in the dark.

"Of course my favourites were the times without protection, skin on skin, that's when you really get to know someone, don't you think? You girls get loose with just about anyone after your period stopped? Uh huh, that's what I figured. No chance of pregnancy there. Too bad I got sent to Gilroy after this hunk tried to do me at the CNE under a Tiny Tom Donuts van. Anyone feel like they're being punished?"

The girls giggled. They knew my routine.

"But really. The best kiss was —"

"Ooh, who would ever want to kiss you?" Diana said. "That's a punishment."

But I could get personal too. "The best time was this guy named Michael Forrest. He mowed my aunt's lawn, and well, he was pretty cute but I just wasn't ready for the kind of long-term relationship he wanted from me. He was just so needy. So I told him –"

Diana screeched. "That's bullshit, everyone! Michael liked me and –"

If we were being too loud, Cora would come in and tell us to be quiet. "Hush time," she'd say. "Hush to sleep." When she left, the spell was broken.

I don't think any of us had ever seen a naked boy in person. At Gilroy Guesthouse girls lied. Girls cut stars into our arms. Girls wrote letters to their mothers pretending they were their boyfriends. Girls ate itty-bitty lettuce. Girls sighed in the dark, touching themselves to climaxes two seconds long, the most real event of our days.

During my stay at Gilroy I had to get weighed three times a week at the nurse's station. The nurse kept my paper gown in a filing cabinet, tucked into a manila folder marked LUCY B.

"I'll be back in a minute," she would say. Along with letting me close the office door halfway when I called home twice a week, the nurse leaving the room so I could change was one of those meaningless gestures that was supposed to make me feel as though I still had a private life in here.

I had to remove my watch, my ring, my bracelet, and put them in a kidney-shaped plastic dish. I had to strip down to my underwear. I even had to let my hair down. Clarice Sinclair had been caught with a rock stuffed into the bun of her hair, to weigh her down, so we called the hair down rule the Clarice Sinclair rule. It made her feel sort of special.

After my first three weeks at Gilroy I'd gained eleven pounds. I could no longer see my ribs, and it made me anxious. I was sure that as more fat crept onto my body, the more ordinary I would look, until the day I reached my target weight, and I was just this plain Jane, this Bony-the-Bug-Eyes Deluxe.

I stepped up onto the scale and I stared at my feet, listening to the ticking sound of the nurse sliding the weights into place. I could stay down at the bottom of the pool, where it was dark and safe and quiet. I could just as easily stay down here forever –

I ran into Jen in the hallway after my weigh-in. She wasn't wearing any shoes or socks. I was surprised to see her because she was supposed to be in sports salon.

"We're all going swimming now," she said, grinning.

The staff had filled three plastic kiddie pools in the backyard, round shallow things decorated with pictures of Disney creatures. It was the last week in September and the sky was cloudy, the wind starting to blow. I stripped off my socks and Jen and I sat on the grass, with our legs bent and our feet wading in the water. Alice and Sarah were sharing a pool, and across from us, Roz, still in her jogging pants and a sweater, had the last pool all to herself. Clarice Sinclair sat on the grass beside Shawna, who was reading a thick book called *Cognitive Mapping Skills*. I'd stopped asking Shawna questions because she obviously thought she was smarter than all of us. Diana sat on a crappy green deck chair that looked like it was about to snap. She was rubbing suntan oil on her blue-veined arms and wearing sunglasses even though the sun was just this tiny orange blip in the sky. I wiggled my toes and felt the blood rushing through them. I watched the clouds in the huge blue sky above me drift, twirl, and then dissolve.

"I wish we could soak our feet like this forever," Jen said. "Don't you?"

"Yeah, kind of," I said. But I didn't want to go on like this. Inside I was thinking that in two weeks, I would walk away from Gilroy Guesthouse and go on with my life. I'd never see any of these girls again. I hoped they would be okay, even if they decided to stay down at the bottom of the pool. But it was time for me to come back up.

In early October, while most of us were getting ready to go home in a week or two, Diana and Jen had their terms extended. Jen said she didn't care. But Diana was furious.

"They don't under*stand*. Models have to be thin."

Then she started bragging about how she'd modelled – she'd done runway shows and appeared in print ads, including a campaign for a Japanese beer called Pinga.

"I've never heard of that beer before," I said. "Hey, waiter, give us a round of Pinga!"

"You're a zit farm," Diana said. "You wouldn't know the first thing about the industry. I know I look good. Two years ago, did an agent who represents models in Paris come up to you at a skating rink and give you his card? Did he?"

I just rolled my eyes at Jen. Then Diana pulled from her monogrammed suitcase a magazine page preserved in plastic and told us to feast on the evidence. "Just look, stupids," she said, passing the page to Clarice Sinclair, "and don't get it rumpled. I know you all know Gitano jeans so don't play dumb. That is me, I swear to you, one year ago."

In the ad, Diana was wearing a lizard green bikini and was trapped inside a water tank, the kind Houdini was famous for breaking out of. Her hair was floating around her face and curling around her neck as if they might strangle her. It was the Diana I remembered.

Diana was silent as we sat in a circle and passed the magazine page around. She sat on her haunches, her nostrils flaring, and craned her neck forward so she could check our reactions to her photo. Finally, she pulled her bone-cap knees to her chest and said, "Do you think I look better or worse now?"

The girl in the Gitano jeans ad was guitar-shaped with lioness hair – a pinup that an old-time sailor would get tattooed on his bicep, a cross between Bettie Page and Olive Oyl. Now Diana's body looked like danger and her hair was falling out. When I cleaned the bathrooms after breakfast I found the red clumps of hair, and she was the only redhead here.

"Do you think I look better or worse now?" she repeated.

We were all too embarrassed to answer her. Clarice Sinclair pretended to be looking at a freckle on her arm and even Jen frowned and glanced away. Diana was staring right at me. Her lips were quivering and she was wringing her hands. I saw through Diana's shield. For all her arrogance, her bullying, and her bragging about how special she was, she was the most insecure person in the room. She was so desperate for me to tell her that she was okay, as if she couldn't imagine being anything more than that. She was going to spend the rest of her life waiting for people to tell her the same thing. Her need felt so strong it was a current of electricity running from her body to mine. I'd answer her just this once.

"You look okay," I said.

That night I dreamt of the same things I'd been dreaming for weeks: silver horses stomping donuts, and a vending machine at North Central that spat out little bones instead of colas, thin pliable bones that I assembled on the lunchroom floor into the shape of an arched-back cat. I kept apologizing to the blue-shirted janitor, who leaned against his broom smoking a wand of Diana's red hair.

I woke myself up at dawn saying, "Lulu does good journalism." When I opened my eyes, Diana was standing over me, a toothbrush hanging out of her mouth, asking me who the fuck Lulu was.

"My cat." But as soon as I said it I remembered how Lulu's face had looked in her carrier, her huge afraid eyes. I didn't ever want to be weak around Diana, so I back-pedalled into a joke. "She's the online feline fact-checker at the *Sun*, but in the end she just lets all the errors through. She spends most of her time comparing herself to the photos girls send in to try out for the page three Sunshine Girl."

Diana made an icky face at me. She'd slipped back behind her shield. "When you leave here you're going to need the shrink Gilroy forces on you," she said. "Because you're still screwed. And your cheeks. They look puffy."

I went to the bathroom and looked at myself in the mirror. It was true, my cheeks looked full again; the hard pimples on my chin were clearing up. I locked myself in a stall, lifted up my shirt, and pressed a finger to my stomach to check how much fat was there now: more than before. On the back of the door, someone had written in bubble letter Magic Marker, *You can't stay on the edge forever, Laydeez.*

When Mom and Dad picked me up, they looked heavy and pale, like they'd been eating takeout food for six weeks. We drove home, past the place where the VERY CRYSTAL BEACH! billboard had stood. Sometime during the past six weeks it had been dismantled and now all that was left was a big pile of sand.

"Well," Dad said, "in a nutshell, how are things?"

"Shhhh," Mom said. "We don't need to talk about that now."

I figured Dad wanted the comic-strip version of Gilroy or a snapshot of the menu. Mom was probably imagining all the TV movies she had ever seen where people wore pyjamas all day and muttered to themselves. I had a feeling that it would be hard for us to talk about me being at Gilroy unless we disguised the story in a story about someone else's daughter, someone else's life.

I looked out at the bright blue morning sky passing by me.

▶

A few weeks after I got out of Gilroy Guesthouse, Clarice Sinclair called me. "Diana downed a whole bottle of Ativan with a whole bottle of Grey Goose. She's dead. I couldn't believe it. Can you believe it?"

I could.

During our group sessions at Gilroy Guesthouse, the facilitator had always said that 10 per cent of us would die within ten years. I'd looked around the room and thought, One of you – or me.

I curled up on my bed. My room was a car on the Tilt-A-Whirl, lurching up and down.

Clarice Sinclair cleared her throat. "The funeral's tomorrow. Do you have a pen? I'll give you the information."

As I got up to get a pen, pictures of Diana flashed through my head. I saw Diana shoving a pencil into the mouth of her Venus flytrap. The way her stomach had made a little bowl above the line of her tropical bikini bottoms at the Tivoli Towers pool. Her brilliant red hair the colour of carrots soaked in cherry juice. I tried not to think about the clumps on the bathroom floor.

When I picked up the phone again, Clarice Sinclair was laughing hysterically. Then Diana's voice came on the line: "Oh my god, we got you bad. Are you mad? I got out two days ago and Clarice and I are eating nachos and Ding Dongs. We got the club pack, and there's like –" I heard her asking Clarice Sinclair how many Ding Dongs there were in the box.

"Hello, are you still there?" Diana said. "What? Did you actually think I would die?"

11

W hen I came home from Gilroy Guesthouse, I wasn't expecting a welcome home party with our family and donkeys and clowns – Mom wasn't big on "hanging her dirty laundry" on a line. But I wanted to start sharing things with Mom again, so I waited for her to ask me questions. They'd be tame ones, the kind people ask when there's a "very sensitive" person in the room.

"So, how *was* that institution?"

"Any Jews?"

"Were the sheets always clean?"

But when a week passed and Mom still hadn't said a word about Gilroy I didn't push it. Maybe it was easier for her to pretend that Gilroy was a summer camp that I'd been left at for an extra month and a half. Or that I was sitting with her on the couch every day after school, eating pretzels out of a plastic bowl, and watching reruns of *Laverne & Shirley* because I needed a break from my busy social life.

One day Mom sighed during the commercial break. "I love this show. I wish we could watch this show all the time together."

"Maybe you should make us monogrammed sweaters," I said. "Then we can be like a Jewish Laverne and Shirley."

I thought the joke was obvious. But I guess spending six weeks alone with Dad had been tough on Mom's sense of humour. The next day, she came home with a plastic bag from Kepper Wools and pulled out three balls of red acrylic, alphabet stencils, and a swatch of black felt. For the next several days, she stayed up late knitting and I didn't know how to stop her. Since coming home from Gilroy, I was as good as a radio that's not plugged in: there was a voice inside me ready to work; I just didn't have the power.

When Mom finished my sweater, she wrapped it in blue paper even though I'd seen it just an hour earlier, on her lap, as she finished the last row. I already knew I was never going to wear it. It reminded me of something Burt from *Sesame Street* would wear if he'd been allowed to change his clothes. The neck was a perfect pie-crust edge and the sleeves were so puffy they could have been hiding shoulder pads. The black "L" appliqué on the chest looked like a boomerang.

"Well, don't keep yourself in suspense," Mom said. "Open it."

It felt even worse on. The wool itched against my skin and it had a strong musty smell of a basement filled with wet vinyl suitcases.

"I know, the knit is loose because I'm new at this," Mom said. "So wear a camisole or else you can see the nipples."

I pulled at the neck. "I don't know, you don't think it's kind of . . . not *me*?"

Mom shook her head. "It's *exactly* like you. You look like a good girl again."

For Mom, a Good Girl was fifteen years old in body but seven and a half at heart. She had proud Jewish curls, her untamed frizz a sign of *her wholesome character*. A Good Girl always came home right after school and watched *Larry King Live* with her mother and ate sloppy food that came ready-made in boxes. She didn't go away to some backwoods place for people who hated eating.

"You look too good. That's why I don't want you out gallivanting."

The only places I went were to school, my appointments with Dr. Costa, and then home. My life was as exciting as a maze for two year olds. "You don't need to worry," I said. "I'm almost sixteen. I just want to take a walk. Go to the park. Nothing crazy."

Mom shook her head again. "You went and fainted in front of a donut truck. How will I not worry about you for the rest of my life?"

I was happy to have left Gilroy behind: the plastic "safety" knives at dinner with their smooth spatula edges that gave me ideas where there had been none before; my whole day's schedule written on the wall, for everybody to see – all of this had made me feel I was a prisoner. At home, the knives were actually sharp enough to cut food, there was no schedule, and no goals to meet on a checklist. But every day I had to face Mom and her sweater. I felt Mom wanted me to be perfect now, to make up for all the ways I'd disappointed her. That's what the red sweater was all about. It was the uniform of a Good Girl, a Little Red Riding Hood girl. Though I hated the sweater, I wore it around the house out of guilt, knowing I had let her down. I wasn't a Good Girl anymore. I was the one who ate the wolf.

▶

When I wasn't at school or at home being Laverne to Mom's Shirley, I was at my appointments with Dr. Costa, the therapist I had to see for a year in order to "graduate" from the Gilroy Guesthouse

Program. Dr. Costa showed me photos of food laminated onto flashcards and asked me to rate how the photos made me feel on a scale of one to ten. Then she'd ask me to draw a picture of myself eating. If I drew myself with a zucchini and high cheekbones, Dr. Costa would say, "Can you tell me why you drew yourself like that, Lucy?" If I drew myself with an ice cream cone and a saggy diaper bum, she'd say the same thing. Once I told her that if she wanted to know what I looked like when I was eating I could just bring her a photo, but she said that wasn't the point. The point was getting in touch with my feelings and not using humour as my shield.

"Why can't I use humour as my shield?" I said. "Is it better to use it as a weapon?"

I liked Dr. Costa a lot. But I thought she should stick to her flash-cards and quit trying to analyze my life. I didn't need flashcards to know what my feelings were. I already knew I was uncomfortable about how my body was thickening with fat like a polar bear in March. My shrinking jeans, the way I could gauge my weight gain by how deeply the seams indented the skin on my legs, made me feel as though I was losing something. But I knew that talking about food for fifty minutes with a stranger was not going to help me find it. With every picture Dr. Costa showed me, I would feel myself drifting up, up, and away from the office, until I was on the roof, looking down and pitying us, especially Dr. Costa. I was probably boring her to hell.

Still, I kept going back to her. Aside from Mom, she was my only friend.

As soon as I went back to school in the middle of October, I started going to the library at lunchtime, because it was the one place in the school where I didn't feel like a loser for being alone. Plus, there was a turtle that lived in an aquarium on the sign-out desk and I felt like we had a connection. The turtle was pretty miserable. Whenever I would tap on the glass, he would look at me with his disappointed slit eyes. He was way too big for his aquarium and when he backed up, he had to manoeuvre himself like Grandpa in his old Cadillac, inch by inch, always checking behind him. One day I told the librarian, Mrs. Venetti, that she should maybe think of getting Slider a bigger aquarium.

"He feels totally stuck," I said. "He's probably supposed to be bigger, even. If he had a bigger aquarium, he'd probably grow to his full size."

"Oh, he's fine," Mrs. Venetti said. She was sorting cards and not even looking at me. "Anyway, what would I do with a giant turtle? He already outgrew the science lab and none of the kids wanted to take him home. That's why he's here. So I don't want him getting any bigger."

"But he's not some plastic plant," I mumbled.

Mrs. Venetti came out from behind her desk and told me to follow her over to the computer station. "Say, did you know that we just got the *Internet*?" She pointed to the burping grey computer. It had a Toronto School Board screensaver on it and already it looked boring. "Do you know how to use the Internet? Or do you need me to show you how to do a search?"

I had no clue what the Internet was, but I was still pissed off about the turtle. "I'm okay," I said. "I know how to use it."

I guess Mrs. Venetti got the message because she turned her attention to the girl at the computer beside mine. It was hard not to give this girl your attention. Her hair was pixie short and bleached blonde, parted in a zigzag down her scalp. Behind her ear was a yellowed silk flower that looked as though she ripped it off an old wedding dress. She had two rings on every finger, the bright kind you get in grocery store machines, and her fingernails were cherry red. She looked cool, but kind of intimidating, the kind of girl I imagined walking her pitbull on Queen Street.

Mrs. Venetti leaned over the girl's shoulder and peered at her screen. On it was a painting of a woman with a really long neck by someone named Modigliani. "Is that school related, Erin?" Mrs. Venetti said.

The Modigliani girl shrugged. "It's school work. Kind of. Well, it *should* be."

Mrs. Venetti sat down on her haunches. "Well, I know you have a geography assignment coming up, so why don't we look for some research on that, okay?"

I couldn't play *Wheel of Fortune* now that Mrs. Venetti was hovering around, so I just got up and walked back across the library. The turtle was still freaking out. His shell was bumping against the glass now and his eyes looked desperate. I reached my hand into the aquarium. The water was warm. It probably smelled of turtle poop. I swished my fingers around and the turtle turned, sensing the current, and swam over to me. I pet the turtle's shell. His green legs flutter-kicked softly.

"You never wanted to be a librarian, did you?" I whispered. The turtle kicked its legs harder. "You're just this little turtle hanging around the muck, trying to make your way in the world, aren't you?"

Mrs. Venetti was back behind her desk and staring at me. I really needed to get a life.

Two weeks later, the Modigliani girl from the library transferred into my home-ec class. She walked in with a swish, rocking her hips up and down proudly as if she'd made them from scratch. Pinned to her bleached porcupine hair was a new white bow that looked like a folded seagull wing. Her black bra straps were showing on the edges of her pale shoulders. She strode past the sewing machines, past the three kitchenettes, and stopped in front of the table where I was sitting alone. Then she looked at me straight in the eyes and smiled. "I know you," she said.

The experience of having somebody besides a teacher purposely walk up to me was new, so I instinctively looked down at my hands, which suddenly felt sweaty.

"Um, well, I go to the library sometimes . . . I mean, at lunch-time . . ."

"No, I mean last year," she said, dropping into the seat beside me. She made a lot of noise as she rooted through her knapsack, not seeming to care that Mrs. Alvarez was talking. "I mean, I used to see you around. You were always dropping bread crusts in the hall. I called you Gretel because I didn't know your name. I'm Erin."

"I'm Lucy."

"You look better now," Erin said. "Do you feel better?"

Her question was so direct but soft that I just opened up. "Yeah," I said.

At the front of the classroom, Mrs. Alvarez was demonstrating how to use the countertop griddle. "You want it hot, hot, hot, ladies," she crooned.

"Oh, fuck," Erin whispered. "I feel like we're back in 1954." She put her chin in her hands and leaned her head against the table. "So tell me, Lucy, why are you taking this class?"

"Oh, well, my mom, she thinks cooking . . . well, it's a good skill to have."

Erin smiled. "Yeah, mothers always think cooking will save us."

While our banana bread was in the oven, we sat at the dropleaf table in our kitchenette and Erin told me about how she'd started the year in art class. "Okay, so, in the course description it says *figure drawing*. Well, when you draw the human figure, it's the naked body. Not people wearing snow boots and cardigans, right?"

"No," I said. "I guess not."

"This boy, I don't even know his name, offered to model for me after school. I thought Ms. Flavelle had gone home . . . well, anyway, they were threatening suspension. Instead, they transferred me into cake land."

Then she yawned energetically, the way a cat does, opening her mouth so wide even her back molars showed. "Hey, the oven's buzzing," she said. "Does that mean we get a prize?"

Before it got winter cold, Erin and I ate lunch on the bleachers above the football field so she could smoke. I was just glad to have somewhere to go besides the library. Plus, I had never sat on the bleachers before: I thought they were reserved for football jocks and their groupies. That was the kind of statement Erin hated.

"No, it's all public space," Erin said, ashing her cigarette against the metal bench. "Same for the south smoking doors. Estelle Pomper doesn't own it."

Before I met Erin, I still listened to the same bands I'd idolized in grade eight. But Erin was always listening to music I'd never heard of, and at lunchtime she'd stick one of her Walkman ear buds into my ear so I could listen to the Ramones, Television, Patti Smith, and Richard Hell. Her music sounded raw, but like poetry.

"Do you like Roy Orbison?" I said. I thought I could bring her Dad's tape.

Erin blew a smoke ring. "I guess. More than Elvis. When Roy sings, I actually buy his vulnerability. With Elvis, I feel like he's just acting."

Most people talk about their dreams with shaky voices because they're afraid someone's going to chop them down, but Erin had certainty. Erin announced her future plans as if she was just an inch away from achieving them. She was going to be a famous painter. I asked her which artists she admired most, and she said her goal was to become a combination of Amedeo Modogliani and Jean-Michel Basquiat. The only artists I knew were Norman Rockwell and Brueghel. And I knew about Andy Warhol for his paintings of Marilyn Monroe and soup cans.

"Yeah, but I wonder about Andy Warhol," Erin said, lighting a fresh cigarette. "I mean, he's *respected*, but let's say a woman had painted soup cans before he had. Do you think they still would have been a hit? Or just cans from a lady's kitchen?"

After we finished our lunch, Erin and I would walk along the perimeter of the football field and tell each other stories about our lives, like they were tiny seashells we were holding up to each other's ears. With every story I told, I took another step farther away from Gilroy. At first we told each other tame stories that didn't reveal much about ourselves. Erin told me about breaking her leg when she was nine, and then she rolled up her ripped jean legs to show me how one of her calves was a little thinner than the other. I told her about how Dad was still afraid I'd burn the house down. Then one day, I told Erin how when I was younger, I used to think people became birds and fish when they died.

"My grandmother's sick," Erin said, pressing a finger of her Kit Kat bar into my hand. "But I don't think she's becoming a bird. She's got diabetes bad. That's why my mother's gone most of the time. She goes to Kingston to take care of her. She rents a chair in a salon so she makes a little money at least."

Erin had a part-time job as a cosmetician at the Save-On Drugstore. I thought that was the most glamorous job in the world for an almost-sixteen-year-old. "You have all those colours," I would say. "You get to transform people."

"In the end, it's just sales," she'd say. "It's just like selling paint or bricks. Makeup won't change your insides."

I wouldn't let up on the glamour. "But you wouldn't rather sell tires, would you?"

"I help my mother with the rent," Erin said. "For me, it's just a job."

One day in the hallway, Erin took my hand. "You walk too close to the lockers," she said. "You don't have to do that, Lucy. Take up some space." I shook my head. I still felt too vulnerable walking down the middle of the hall, adrift like a buoy in sea of people. Erin pulled my hand. It was a gentle pull, more a squeeze as she drew me closer to her, into the deep centre of the hall. "See?" she said. "No big deal."

I felt my world growing. My weekends with Erin were filled with patchouli oil, kebabs, and henna, and as kaleidoscopic as twirling, falling leaves. We went to Kensington Market and Erin took me into musty shops that sold pipes and posters of Ganesha and Bob Dylan. The guys behind the counters would give her free chocolate rolling papers just for coming in to say hi to them. Men stared at Erin with soft looks in their eyes, like they were reading an old book they really loved. I was the period of the sentence that Erin's swishing hips wrote.

We went into vintage clothing stores and Erin picked items off the rack she thought would look good on me. Sometimes she'd get exasperated when I followed her around instead of looking at clothes myself. "You need to know what you like before you can trust what I like for you," she said. She pulled two sweaters off a rack. One was a peachy cardigan with pearl buttons, a Good Girl sweater to the extreme. The other was macramé, a plant holder. "Which one do you like more?"

"Neither," I said. I searched through another rack and picked out a T-shirt with a picture of David Bowie on it, a thunder bolt down his face. "This is cool. I like this."

"So, how was the library?" Mom said. "Did you get a lot of work done?"

Through all of it, I lied to Mom. Every weekend, I told her I was going to the library to do non-existent projects. I was sure it would be a bad idea to introduce Erin to Mom. She would take one look at Erin's fishnet stockings and her bleached hair and decide that she was a neo-Nazi. Case closed. And that was just Erin walking through the door. A horrible fantasy ran through my head sometimes, of Erin and Mom having dinner together. Erin would talk about sketching naked boys and then excuse herself to have a smoke. Mom's foot kicking mine under the table would feel like a panicking woodpecker.

"Oh, the library was great," I said, unpacking my books. "I got a lot done."

➤

After the Christmas holidays, Erin and I got our final home-ec assignment on a water-stained brown recipe card: we had to bake a Lady Baltimore Cake from scratch. *No help. No instant cake mixes. No excuses.* It was a take-home.

Mrs. Alvarez took Erin and me aside in class.

"I know you're friends and you like to work together, but you've burned almost every assignment this term," she said. "You might want to pick different partners for this one and, you know, branch out a little."

I was sure the real reason she was taking us aside had nothing to do with our marks. Like all my first-term teachers, Mrs. Alvarez knew I'd been at Gilroy, but to make matters worse she also knew Mom. They'd taught at the same school back when polyester was the new technology. So her talking to me was a half-personal and half-professional obligation.

I didn't wait for Erin to speak up. "We want to work together," I said.

At lunchtime, Erin and I went to the library and searched for a picture of a Lady Baltimore Cake on the Internet. It looked fancy, more like a lace hat than a cake. It was the kind of cake you see in society wedding stories in the *New York Times.*

"Okay, don't panic," Erin said. "Read me what it says."

"This is a decadent white three-layer cake filled with dried fruits, pecans, and walnuts. Once the icing is boiled, it is then whipped into peaks . . ." I skipped ahead. It already sounded impossible. "For the experienced baker, the average preparation time is an hour and a half to two hours."

"Okay, we're screwed."

I shook my head. "I'll show it to my mom. Maybe she knows a shortcut."

But after she'd scanned the recipe card, Mom handed it back to me and shrugged. "It's an elitist cake. To me, any cake with more than six ingredients should be paying me for the trouble of baking it." I couldn't tell if she meant it or if she was being cool because I hadn't worn her red sweater in more than two weeks.

On our way from the subway station to her apartment, Erin warned me that her neighbourhood was the pits. "It used to be gorgeous a hundred years ago. But then landlords divided every house up into, like, ten sardine-can units and let it fall apart."

I thought of Robbie Roth strutting around on his lawn, the king of the downtown shit-heap. "Yeah," I said. "I used to know someone like that."

Even though Erin's neighbourhood was kind of seedy, it was new and unfamiliar and that energized me. My eyes were tiny pencils taking notes on whatever I saw. Most of the stores had bars across their doors. There were guys hanging around phone booths who Erin said were drug dealers and storefronts that had pictures of money and the word LOANS spray-painted on the windows. We walked over a rusted CN rail bridge. On one of the bridge girders, someone had spray-painted a picture of a six-foot-high orang-utan with a speech bubble over its head that said, "Fuck Bananas!!!"

"Hey, Andy Warhol," I whistled. "Looks like you've got competition."

Erin stuck out her tongue to catch snowflakes.

We stopped at a variety store so Erin could buy her cake ingredients. There was a hand-written sign on the door that said, One Kid at a Time Only above a picture of two kids in a circle with a diagonal line running through it, so I waited outside. In my mind, I heard Mom's voice telling me to *Come home!* Mom thought I was staying late at school to bake the cake with my group, my hundredth lie of the season. When we started walking again, Erin linked her arm through mine. It took me a few seconds to let my arm relax. Erin jostled it. I jostled her arm back. Then we laughed.

I felt so happy. Everything I looked at seemed extra bright, as if the sun was shining straight over it. The green stove in Erin's kitchen was the colour of kiwis. The yellow curtains shone like wet sand. While we mixed the cake batter, Erin turned on the radio so loud the teacups on the top of her stove rattled. Milo, Erin's cat, jumped on the counter and started pawing at the walnuts, shooting them onto the floor. Erin grabbed my hand and danced us around the kitchen. "Mrs. Alvarez should see us now!"

While our cake was baking, we went into Erin's living room. Instead of a couch Erin had two folding seats from a movie theatre propped up on cinderblocks. There was a record player with a lot of records strewn around it. Erin picked up a record and passed it to me. It was Patti Smith's *Horses*. We lay on the floor and listened to it. I held the record cover up in the air above me. I loved how Patti looked so beautiful on the cover and she wasn't even wearing any makeup.

"When I listen to Patti Smith I burst into flames inside," Erin said. "You?"

I put the record down beside me. "No. I feel more like I'm on this roller coaster, and it goes up and down, and it spins, but I know I'm going to land in one piece. Like, it's this wild ride that I trust a hundred per cent."

Erin reached over and spread her fingers open on my knee, making a spider. "I'll make you a tape."

Erin's room was the smallest of the two bedrooms and it smelled of old papers and clay. It was so messy that she took my hand and led me through the piles of clothes, magazines, and empty coffee tins spilling paintbrushes, so she could show me her easel, in the corner beside the window. The painting was of a girl in a white dress holding a white rabbit, except the rabbit's tail was a parking meter that said, Expired. When I asked Erin what it meant, she shrugged.

"I paint at night. When I'm tired, my conscious mind's shut off."

I could imagine Mom looking at the painting and saying, "Well, then maybe she should paint with her conscious mind instead." But I loved it.

I sat down on Erin's bed and bounced on it. Erin opened her dresser drawer and pulled out a white birthday candle and stuck it into her mouth.

"Is that for the cake?"

Erin stood up straighter and pursed her lips. "Class, we baked well today," she crooned, imitating Mrs. Alvarez, "so now I invite you all to get baked. Please pull out your matches." Erin held up a matchbook and pulled one match, as if she was demonstrating how to light it. "You want it hot, hot, hot, ladies!"

The windows in Erin's bedroom didn't open more than two inches, so we went to the bathroom and huddled on the edge of the claw-foot tub. The smoke hit the back of my throat, and then disappeared somewhere up on a shelf in my brain. I imagined a Pink Pearl eraser sweeping clean across an entire year. The year of Gretel and Little Red Riding Hood.

"No, you're not inhaling, Erin said. "Let me show you."

I got up and shivered a little. My mouth tasted skunky, but the bathroom had begun to look as pretty as a tiny dollhouse room. On the side of the sink, Erin's rings shone with the sheer glow of blue, yellow, pink, and green Life Savers. I started laughing. I thought of Mom and what she would say if she saw me like this. "What are you *doing*?" Nothing, I would say. I walked to the toilet to ash the joint. Above the toilet was a sequined picture of Morrissey with sweat drops flying off his face. I smiled at that and then at the creamy foot of Erin's claw-foot tub. "We should give your claw-foot a pedicure."

Erin handed me a bottle of red nail polish. I pointed to the claw-foot. "Maybe she should go to beauty school and start contributing to your household," I said. "All she does is stand around all day."

Erin giggled. "I know! But she says she's too old. Maybe you should try convincing her. Her name's Agnes."

I kicked the claw leg of the tub. "Hey, Agnes," I said. "I'm going to paint your nails now so hold still." I painted a red toenail onto the claw-foot, then another, and another.

"I want to do it too," Erin said. "Save me one."

I felt so relieved and happy that it was nine at night and I wasn't at home with Mom watching *Larry King Live*. I didn't want to pretend to be a Good Girl anymore. I wanted to be myself again, and I wanted be Erin's best friend. It was the one thing I was certain of.

That's when I smelled something burning.

When Erin and I didn't have a cake to show her the next day, Mrs. Alvarez raised her eyebrows and stalked off to the office. I only figured out that last part when I got home from school and Mom was waiting for me in the kitchen. I knew I was in deep shit as soon as I saw her coffee mug: it was full. Usually she gulped it down as soon as she got home from school. I was standing in the doorway of the kitchen, but I might as well have been standing on the edge of a black hole.

"You've been lying to me," Mom said. "This whole time."

"I didn't lie, I just didn't —"

Mom came around to the other side of the table. She told me she knew I had failed my last home-ec assignment. She knew about my "new friend." Mrs. Alvarez had told her all about Erin's late entry into our class. I couldn't tell which Mom thought was worst: another teacher calling her to say I was failing or that I was hanging out with a girl who had almost been suspended. "I don't know what's happening to you," Mom yelled. "All I know is that before you went to Gilroy you were a good girl. Now I don't know who you are, and you're hanging around someone who is sticking spikes into your jacket and *ruining you*!"

They're studs, not spikes, I wanted to say. And Erin isn't ruining me. She's helping me break out of my shell. But I didn't say that because I was beginning to realize that Mom lived in a shell of her own, and I knew she wouldn't understand why I'd been so uncomfortable in mine.

"We ruined a cake, Mom. It's not a life, it's a cake."

"You're grounded. One month."

"I barely go anywhere! How can I be grounded?"

"You lied to me. How many times?"

I couldn't keep my anger inside anymore. I didn't even want to. "You — You're always trying to keep me at home with you — I need more friends than just my mother!" I yelled. "You have to get that. I'm not Hyman, I'm not going to go to math camp and become a fucking computer programmer just because you want me to. I'm not your little doll anymore."

The kitchen felt dead as soon as I said it. I heard the sound of a thousand plugs being pulled from their sockets. I waited for her to say something. But she turned out of the kitchen and went upstairs.

"She's trying to control my life," I told Erin at lunch the next day. We were sitting in the library, in the carpeted reading pit. I wanted Erin to suggest that we run away together. Last night, I'd fantasized about going to the Greyhound station on Bay Street and buying tickets for as far as our money would take us. I wanted to go to the bars where Patti Smith went, and sit in movie theatres with Erin and share warm jelly beans out of her hand. I wanted to be free. "She wants me at home. She grounded me. I can't go anywhere."

Erin made a spider on my knee. "Maybe it's not so bad. I mean, we can still see each other at school. And we can talk on the phone. I know it sucks, but at least you know she cares. At least you have someone around to ground you."

I thought she was joking. But she just bit her lips and stared back at me.

A week into being grounded, I got tired of staying in my room. Besides, I didn't want to give Mom the satisfaction of thinking I was feeling guilty by hiding in my room. So one night I went downstairs and sat on the arm of the couch as far away from Mom as possible. I held a book in front of my face, just so Mom would know I wasn't interested in watching *Larry King Live* with her. I refused to look at the screen. It was a matter of principle: I wouldn't be the one to break the silence first.

"How many pairs of suspenders do you think Larry King has?" Mom finally said. "Do you think he has a whole closet full of them?"

I knew this was her olive branch, but it wasn't good enough for me. I wanted Mom to say she was wrong about Erin and shouldn't have grounded me in the first place. But she was never going to do that.

"He probably has a whole closet," I said. I kept my eyes on my book.

"Hmm," Mom said. A few minutes later, she muted the TV during the commercial break. "So I guess you're going to start hanging out with the druggie again pretty soon." There wasn't any edge to her tone. She just sounded a little sad. Like she was going to miss me moping around the house.

A few weeks later, I was in the kitchen doing my final makeup assignment for Mrs. Alvarez on the history of pancakes when the doorbell rang. Dad was coming down the stairs with a newspaper folded up in his hand. "Tell whoever it is I'm not buying anything," he said.

The sound of the doorbell ringing on a snowy night always filled me with a sense of hope. When I was younger I used to imagine a Jewish version of Santa Claus arriving with all the gifts I'd missed while we hunkered down with our dreidel and takeout pizza. By the time I stepped into the hallway, the doorway was filled with light. Mom had already opened the door.

It was Erin, her face sparkling with snow. She was wearing an old faux-fur coat and scuffed suede boots embroidered with flowers. Her hair stuck up in blonde quills that I figured Mom would see as a sign of Erin's waywardness. Erin extended her hand. "Hi, I just had to drop something off for Lucy. I'm one of Lucy's friends. I'm Erin."

At first, Mom didn't take Erin's hand and I imagined the worst: Mom would tell her to get off her porch. Mom would tell her she'd been a bad influence on me and to never come to our house again. Worse, Mom would invite her in and grill her in the living room. "And where do you buy your pot?" Mom would say, giving her the evil eye.

But Mom just shook Erin's hand. "Oh, I've heard a lot about you." Then Mom said something I never expected. "Would you like to stay for dinner?"

I waited for something to go wrong at dinner. We were eating spaghetti and Erin tucked her napkin into her collar, which Mom probably liked because it was practical. When I blinked I imagined bongs and cigarettes falling out of Erin's pockets. I imagined her swearing. Dad didn't say much at first. I knew he was trying to figure out if Erin was a natural blonde. Dad hoped all blondes were natural in the same way kids hoped that Santa and his reindeer were real.

"I love your mannequins," Erin said, turning to the window. "Are the clothes they're wearing vintage?"

"Oh, those are mine, do you like them?" Mom said. Then she told Erin about how she'd worked in the Petites section of the Eaton's Department Store when she first came to Canada. Erin cupped her chin in her hands and held on to every word of Mom's descriptions of fringed vests and floor-length polyester dresses.

"I once thought of going into fashion design," Mom said. "Is that what you want to do?"

Oh no, I thought. Here's where it will all fall apart.

"I'm going to be an artist," Erin said. "A painter."

"That's nice. But what will you do for a job?"

Dad straightened up in his chair and pulled himself closer to the table. I'd almost forgotten that he was still there. "She said she's going to be a painter, Joy." He turned to Erin. "Who are your favourite painters?"

While Erin told Dad about the problem with Andy Warhol's soup cans, I turned to Mom to try to catch her reaction to Erin. I was worried that she'd be staring at me with that "look." The one she gives me when we walk by a man on the street with lots of tattoos. The "I'm not into this" look. But Mom wasn't even paying attention to me. She was holding her fork in mid-air and watching Erin speak. Now I wanted to catch her eye so she could give me the nod. The nod wouldn't just be a nod. It would be a sign and if the sign had a sound it would be the squeak of a birdcage door opening. But I couldn't catch Mom's eye. Then I realized that I didn't need to.

▶

When the winter ended, Erin and I started to go to all-ages concerts at Lee's Palace. We swayed and sweated with the crowds at the foot of the stage and I felt I was finally part of something larger than myself. One night, a hand groped at my breast and Erin slapped it away. At first I was disappointed because I didn't know when someone would try to do that to me again. But I understood that Erin was just looking out for me.

When we left the club, the sky was purple, ruffled like wet velvet combed backward. Erin said she was hungry so we went into a 24-hour grocery store. We didn't speak a word, but somehow I knew what to do next. I went to look for walnuts, pecans, and eggs, and we met up at the express cash. On our walk to Erin's apartment, the air was misty, the way it gets at the end of April, when bluebells sneak out of the ground.

It was easy to follow the directions on Mrs. Alvarez's brown recipe card now that we didn't have to. Our Lady Baltimore cake wasn't exactly beautiful. It looked like a football iced with shaving cream, oozing cherries and walnuts. I stuck my finger into the centre of the cake, pulled it out, and licked the cream off it lollipop-style. Erin broke off a hunk of cake.

"Lucy."

I turned and she smeared the cake onto my face.

I was laughing so hard it hurt. Erin was laughing too. Her cheeks were bright red, and tears were collecting in the corners of her eyes. She took a few steps backward and held up her hands. "Truce, okay truce," she said. "I swear, I won't do it again. But your face was right there and . . ." She started laughing all over again.

I grabbed a handful of cake and it felt warm and squishy between my fingers. "I'm going to get you with this whipped cream, straight in your ear," I said.

"No, let's just eat it," Erin said.

It was delicious. Seriously the best piece of cake I'd ever had.

I thought about drawing this moment for Dr. Costa to add to my funky collection in her filing cabinet, but I wanted to keep it all for myself. Then as I licked my lips, I pictured the whole summer stretched out in front of us, and I could see Erin and me following the sun on our bikes through the streets, staying up all night and feeling so free.

Three

12

At the end of summer, I got a part-time job at Moby's, the giant discount superstore. To me it was just a job with a uniform, but Erin told me I was making a political statement by working at the last non-multinational bargain store in the city. Secretly, I thought Erin's artistic side admired the window displays at Moby's, which were famous in the neighbourhood for their dramatic animal scenes: dozens of grey Velcro sneakers hung above a mannequin dressed and posed to look like Tippi Hedren in *The Birds;* a male mannequin in a dead-stock polo shirt watched multiple ceramic Dalmatians feast on cans of tuna and the other weekly specials. I was grateful to have a job, but I didn't like the monotony of standing in a basement for eight hours every Saturday. When it got slow, I would sneak away from my cash desk so I could read Anne Sexton behind the humming salami fridge — until the manager walked by and made a gesture at me like he was slitting his own neck. This meant "Get back to work."

Erin would meet me in the parking lot after my shifts so we could walk back to her apartment. I loved walking west at dusk, especially when the sun burned the colour of watermelon. I'd tell her about the eccentric customers that came into Moby's — including the flirt who carried two Pomeranians in his messenger bag — and Erin would tell me what she'd drawn that day, and then sometimes we'd play the question game.

"Berlin or Paris?"

"Hmm, that's hard. I guess Berlin if we could pull a Bowie and Iggy Pop. Your hair's long enough. But in Paris we could eat baguettes in the Louvre. See a Modigliani in the flesh. I guess Paris. Okay, my turn. Would you rather sing like Bryan Adams or sing and play the drums like Phil Collins?"

"Oh, that's a tough one. But . . . Eighties love songs and his leather jacket just make me warm and gooey inside. Yeah . . . so Bryan Adams."

"So you'd give up two talents for one? What if Bryan Adams never made it as a singer? Then all he'd be left with was a little apartment and a voice. You're saying people don't need a plan B?"

"We're too young to have plan B. I don't even know what my plan A is."

The door to Erin's apartment always stuck, so she would pretend to be a cop by smashing her shoe against the jam, and when the door flew open she'd yell, "Stick em up!" Then we'd hustle into her doorway and her cat, Milo, would lift his striped orange face from his food bowl and look at us as though he thought we were hopeless as humans.

Mom thought sleeping in my own bed somehow correlated to my getting high marks, so I limited staying at Erin's to just two nights a week. It was my olive branch. We always shared Erin's bed, our heads against the angel-face headboard Erin had found for ten dollars at a second-hand store on Queen Street. Sitting up with my messy bun smashed into the mouth of the angel, I did my homework while Erin, in her long men's dress shirts, tried to tidy up, her face scrunched up in the same expression she wore when she was sifting Milo's litter. No matter how much time Erin spent cleaning, her apartment always looked as if a bullet train had run through it. The only area of her bedroom that was tidy was around her easel by the window. Beside it, Erin had a cleared a space for the giant clay chess piece we'd found sitting on the curb outside a bankrupt theatre. Erin had insisted we carry it back to her apartment because she didn't want it to be an orphan.

"Well, don't worry, it's got lots of company now," I'd said. Scattered around the chess piece was always a week's worth of underwear, each lacy pair curled up as delicately as a fallen tropical leaf, pink, mint green, and cantaloupe.

I especially loved how Erin's room was messiest whenever she was working on a new project. Strewn all around were avalanches of papers, some of them covered with sketches, others blank but crumpled, and silver paint tubes, brushes, and cans filled with murky water. Pinned to her walls were rough sketches of cityscapes, bright dripping colours, a flying streetcar that reminded me of a sideways flame. It made me wonder if all artists lived in chaos because they were always in a state of production, their work spaces assembly lines emptied out onto the floor.

"From far, far away," she'd say, "a beaver dam looks like a huge mess, but it's actually one of the most organized structures around. If you ask any beaver, she'll tell you that branches sticking out everywhere are necessary for the construction as a whole."

"Thank you, Dr. Doolittle."

She'd crack a big smile. "No problem, Bloomer. Anytime."

▶

I had passed grade ten home-ec on the strength of my B- paper on the history of pancakes. But Erin hadn't done hers, or any of the written work Mrs. Alvarez had asked her to do to make up for the first nine weeks of term she'd missed, so she had to retake the course. Now every time she went to Mrs. Alvarez's class, she wore a frosty pink lipstick that she called Florida cruise liner special and "made like Betty Crocker," which meant asking at least five questions per period. "You know, 'Do all donuts have yeast?' 'Can flourless chocolate cake really be called a cake?' That kind of thing. It helps her feel I'm engaged."

I guess all of Erin's questions got her noticed, because in March, the only boy in her home-ec class asked her on a date. I was surprised that Erin said yes. When Chuck Klaas said hello to you he looked at your sneakers, and when he smiled his lips bunched up like a broken zipper from trying not to show his teeth. He wore plaid shirts with stiff cardboard collars and his face was as white and soft-looking as melted-down marshmallows. While most guys pasted pictures of Pamela Anderson to the insides of their lockers, Chuck had three colour pictures of his Abyssinian cats. For me, this was his sexiest feature.

I was even more surprised when Erin agreed to go out with him on a second date. I'd always imagined Erin dating an older guy in a leather jacket and rolled-up jeans, a bent cigarette between his teeth. But if I had the poster for *Grease* stuck in my head, Erin had *Happy Days* stuck in hers. She said she was curious about Chuck because he reminded her of someone from that show, but a minor character they never gave any lines to because he was too sweet to incite any drama. When Erin told me about how he'd brought out his Ouija board, on their third date, I began to feel sorry for him. I knew that in a week or two, Erin would get tired of his nervous smiles and quiet mumbles and then she'd tell him they could stay friends – but only if he agreed to make eye contact. In a few weeks, Chuck would be history.

After they'd been dating for two weeks, Erin made her big announcement. We were standing outside the south smoking doors, and she was holding her cigarette like a joint, letting it burn down to the quick. "I like him for real, I figured it out today," Erin said. "We were walking inside and he held the door for me, and I looked at him, and there was this *moment*."

"Come on, are you joking?" I said.

"No. I felt this tingling in my heart. It was like a seatbelt clicking in. I felt . . . Well, I felt stable."

Stable. It was a word I'd never heard her use before.

"This is how stable he is. Hold up your arm." I didn't like how the whole conversation was beginning to turn a little surreal, but I held up my arm anyway. "See how the hairs stick up in different directions?" Erin tugged at the hairs on my arm to demonstrate. "Well, Chuck's hairs are always combed the same way. It's a symbol for how stable he is. His nostrils are even the exact same shape. What do you think about that?"

"Maybe he got a nose job," I said.

But she didn't laugh. She just looked at me and rolled her eyes.

Once school was over at the end of June, I picked up extra shifts at Moby's. Erin met me after work twice a week. The rest of the time she spent with Chuck.

Whenever Erin described the long drives they took together, she'd emphasize every detail as if we were in an endless driver's education video, and I wouldn't know which details were the important ones. She told me about how Chuck would take his right hand off the steering wheel and place it on her knee, the way his hand moved up her thigh before coming to rest on the calm edge of her underwear. She'd go on from there, but I'd get distracted thinking about how I didn't even know what kind of underwear she wore anymore. She used to alternate between the lace rainbow and the 99-cent Moby's specials, the ones with *Don't Forget Me* written on the front. Now, for Chuck's sake, she was probably wearing something crisp, white, and shaped like a sailboat. He seemed the kind of person who would find colourful underwear a big turn-off.

On the hot summer days when Erin did meet me in the parking lot of Moby's, we'd sit on overturned milk crates and smoke. Erin used to smoke 95 per cent of her cigarette and I would take the butt, but now I was smoking half, she a quarter, and we were stamping out the rest. We suddenly had awkward silences, and I would look up at the sky and wonder, How had it become so hard to talk to her?

"You're so quiet," Erin said. "Hey, why don't you ask me something about Chuck?" She always wanted me to ask her about Chuck. I figured this was her way of keeping me from feeling left out.

"Have you done it with him?" I hadn't done it with anyone, so I was still caught on the ten-million-dollar question of whether it changed your life or not.

"We haven't. We're still on tongue kissing. But I know that when we do, he's going to be considerate. Ask me how I know?"

"How?"

"Because when he brings me flowers from his backyard, he always wraps up the stems in a plastic bag so I won't get dirt on my skirt."

What do you say to that?

People on TV were always acting out how love changes you, and usually for the better. The oil tycoon rescues the receptionist from her life of canned dinners on a hot plate; a leggy redhead shows a stockbroker that square dancing is better than stock trading. I had seen *Pretty Woman* ten times with Mom back in my red sweater days. But I didn't see why capital-L love needed to be alchemy. Even though they'd been dating for only two and a half months, I noticed how Erin's clothes were dowdier, these shapeless sack-coloured skirts and pallid blouses with embroidery on the collars. They were the kind of clothes Mom would love.

"I never thought of it this way, but Chuck says women look good in less showy clothes. Suggestion is sexier than anything. Don't you think?"

Maybe Chuck should write a book, I thought. I was still in the phase of believing that if you had it, you should flaunt it. I didn't have it exactly, so I relied on other people to flaunt theirs for me. "But what happened to your old clothes? The white cowboys boots and the ripped jeans. Your outfit today is . . . is so . . . Gloria Vanderbilt."

Erin put her hand on her hips. "I'm experimenting, what's wrong with that?" Her colourful rings were gone, the two or three rings to each finger, along with the way they made her hand smell as green and coppery as rain.

Later that night, we were lying in Erin's bed and the only sounds were the streetcar wheels on Queen Street, metal combing water, and her seashell mobile gently clacking above us. I pressed my nose against the back of Erin's neck, which smelled warm and sticky, a mixture of hot milk and honey. At least she still smelled the same.

"You can ask me anything about him," said Erin. "Because I'm not leaving you out or anything. I want you to be totally involved."

I wished I could tell her which tracks on the new Manic Street Preachers album were my favourite or that I'd figured out how to avoid getting caught reading at work by hiding in the women's washroom. Talking about Chuck was dead boring.

"Did you have a nice drive in the country on the weekend?"

Erin flipped around to face me, the whites of her eyes sparkling, or trembling, I couldn't tell which. "Wouldn't you rather know something juicier? Like if his penis is splotchy or curves to one side?"

I didn't want to know that at all. Yet for Erin's sake I said yes, I wanted to know about Chuck's penis. And the more Erin talked, the more she described, the more I felt a shape near my stomach hollowing, collapsing into my guts, so that by the time she finished and turned away, instead of a stomach there was just this empty thing inside me, shaped like a giant, cleaned-out clam shell.

It's not that I minded her and Chuck spending time together, or their being in love and driving out of the city on roads that curled along Burger King and Winners strip malls into wire fence and sheep country. It was more the thought of another person in Erin's life commanding that kind of attention, taking up space in her heart that I imagined was limited.

I was afraid of losing my best friend.

➤

When I wasn't with Erin, I was either working at Moby's or at home reading books my English teacher, Mr. Hardaway, had lent me for the summer. It was quiet at home now. Dad was working long hours at Sun and Waves, and when Mom wasn't teaching her summer course, she was in her pyjamas, lying on the couch, denouncing the egg rolls at the $3.99 buffet near her school, which she said had given her an ulcer. Once, after she'd been talking about her stomach for ten minutes, I suggested she go to the doctor.

"Maybe it's not a stomachache," she said mysteriously. "Maybe it's a Y2K bug."

"I think that only affects computers, Mom."

"A Y2K bug," Mom said, ignoring me, "is a virus that aliens are spreading. I saw two experts talking about it on TV today. They're spreading it so when they get down here on New Year's Day 2000 they can take us without a fight."

I knew she wasn't serious, but it was good to see her making jokes again. "Well, if aliens do arrive, I'll call you the Pyjama Prophet."

The books Mr. Hardaway lent me were Penguin paperback novels with thin yellow pages he'd read when he was my age. I was flattered that a teacher would lend me personal books, and I liked reading each page knowing that he had read it too.

Erin thought my friendship with Mr. Hardaway was "weird and unnecessary." She didn't understand why picking up crabapples in my yard or going on the Internet to look at cat ads while she spent all her time with Chuck wasn't enough for me.

"I mean, I understand liking your teacher because he teaches Ginsberg and knows jazz. He's cool, I get it," she said. "But hanging out in the summer is really pushing it. You could probably get him fired even."

"I'm not hanging out with him. I'm just returning his books." Then I felt stupid for defending myself. It wasn't as if I'd ever called Chuck "weird and unnecessary" or asked her what she saw in him even though I wanted to so many times.

Erin was getting ready for her date with Chuck, who was taking her out for their four-month anniversary. While she stood in front of her bathroom mirror, crushing pale green and pink powder balls with the translucent handle of her brush, I stood behind her, feeling as useless as an accessory head, swallowing my words like spit. I looked around her room. It was as organized as a hotel room now: papers stacked, paintbrushes and underwear gone from the floor, a Glade Plug-In in the wall dispersing its fake cherry scent. Her easel was still in the corner, but her jean jacket was draped over it. There were no paintings anywhere. Now, Erin's radio was always tuned to classical, and when I gave her a dubbed cassette of the Buzzcocks' first album, she thanked me and quietly put it into a wicker box under her bed that was filled with needles and thread.

Erin turned around. "Do I look okay?"

Her uncertainty made me that much more sure that her relationship with Chuck was screwing her up big time. Whenever the old Erin talked about her clothes, it was to show me how she'd sewed a silk flower onto a dress or made gloves out of old fishnet stockings. The old Erin had never wondered if she looked okay. Now she was wearing a plaid blouse tucked into a pleated skirt. It was the most conventional outfit I'd ever seen her in, yet she was acting as if she was taking a major risk.

"Erin, you used to be a vixen," I said. "You always said you'd rather die than wear plaid. You wanted to be the next Jean-Michel Basquiat. Now you don't even paint anymore. You're too busy driving around in Chuck's car."

"I wasn't a vixen, Lucy. I was just this fucked-up girl living by herself. Have you ever thought that this is what I'm supposed to be?"

The next day, I was turning my bike onto a clear sunny street when Erin's words floated back into my ears. *I was just this fucked-up girl.* I still couldn't believe that she'd said that about herself. And worse, *This is what I'm supposed to be?* It was as if she had forgotten who she really was.

I locked my bike against a pole outside of the bakery where I was supposed to meet Mr. Hardaway to return his books. I always wanted our meetings to last longer, because he never asked me questions about my classes or my aspirations, or went in for any of that adult-to-teenager talk that could have come out of a script. When he came up the street, I waved and he waved back. He was wearing jeans and penny loafers, and carrying a canvas bag with lettuce sticking out of the top of it. After he put his books into his grocery bag, he told me he was going to get a hamburger and did I want one too.

"You can't ride all the way home on an empty tank," he said. "My treat."

We ended up at a little hamburger place with red plastic chairs and pictures of Niagara Falls on the walls. I had never been to a restaurant before with an adult who wasn't Mom or Dad, so it felt special. In the back of my mind I kept wondering if the waitress thought I was his daughter, or what.

We talked about my job at Moby's for a while, and he told me that when he was my age, he'd had an even worse job stacking six hundred chairs every night at a convention centre. "I thought that working at a convention centre sounded glamorous," he said.

"I always thought being a cosmetician sounded glamorous, but Erin said it's not. So I guess it's hard to tell."

Then, when our cheeseburgers hit the table, I suddenly blurted out how Erin and I were drifting apart. "I can't stop thinking about what she's doing, and the more I think about it, the more I feel like I'm losing her."

Mr. Hardaway just nodded.

"You know, at first I thought I was maybe in love with her. But I don't want to marry her, it's not like that. But I love her. Now that she's with someone else all the time, I feel like whatever we had together is disappearing."

Mr. Hardaway didn't flinch or look away or do any of the things adults did when they wanted you to stop talking. He smiled, then squirted some ketchup onto the side of his plate. "It reminds me of something from *The End of the Affair*. The protagonist, Maurice Bendrix, falls in love with Sarah Miles, only she's married and eventually, after promises, obsession, it falls apart and Bendrix, well . . ." Mr. Hardaway made a sound that was a cross between a sigh and a whistle. "He finds himself consumed."

"He kills himself?"

"No, no. Not at all. It's subtler than that. He lives with the obsession, but it multiplies. He is jealous of her shoes. The buckle of her shoes. Her stockings. Even the pins that hold her hair." Mr. Hardaway bit his french fry in half, a careful, definite movement. "What I mean to say is that he loves her so much he becomes fixed even on the tiniest things. And all of these tiny things become a way for him to re-establish his connection to her. It's his way of not giving up."

It felt hot in the restaurant all of a sudden. "I don't get that," I said.

"Well," said Mr. Hardaway, setting down his glass. "That's all right."

"But I want to get it."

Mr. Hardaway smiled. "Don't worry. One day you will."

▶

A few days later, I sat on an overturned milk crate in the parking lot, reading and looking up every fifteen lines to watch for Erin's approaching figure. After about ten minutes, Callum came out through the back doors holding a headless mannequin. He was one of the three guys in charge of the window displays, who I'd see smoking pot on their breaks. He was about a year older than me.

"Suntanning?" he called out. He set the mannequin against the wall and walked over to me. Except for this thin, beige scar on his cheek, he had the kind of exquisite skin that some guys have without trying at all. He was beautiful, in the vein of an entertainment talk show host, but I wasn't that attracted to him.

I put down my book. "I'm just waiting for someone." He didn't move so I added, "What are you doing with that mannequin?"

"Throwing it out. We got a bunch of new ones. Fuller figured. Different colours, a more multicultural set. What are you reading?"

I showed him by Anne Sexton book. "Depressing stuff," he said.

After Callum went back inside, I waited for another forty-five minutes, but Erin didn't show.

Erin called me the next day to apologize for not showing up. She said that she'd mixed up the days, thought it was Monday instead of Tuesday. When she realized her mistake she'd ridden her bike to Moby's, but I had already left.

"I met this guy in the parking lot. Callum. He said he works with you." Her voice was cream soda, pink and bubbly. "He asked me if you had a boyfriend. I think he's interested in you. Plus, he's really cute."

"Do you think so?" I tried to make my voice sound pink and bubbly, but it came out flat.

"Totally," Erin said. "You should go for it."

Then, suddenly, Erin and I weren't talking much at all.

Even Mom and Dad had noticed that I was hardly going out after work or on the weekends.

"You need to get active," Mom said. "Mow the lawn. Or draw a picture."

"You've put all your eggs in one basket," Dad said. "You need to branch out by joining some clubs."

"I called you," Erin would say. "Did you get my message?"

By now I'd got into the habit of going to the Bay after work and walking around in my Moby's uniform, which Erin would have called a political statement two months ago. I tried out lipsticks and sprayed myself with the most unaffordable perfumes. In the fifth-floor restaurant, where pre-made plates of baked sole dressed with buttons of butter and parsley sat waiting in self-serve fridges, I drank cups of coffee filled halfway with cream and watched the women who were three times my age eating lunch in little clusters.

"I was out," I'd say, trying to sound busy, like I didn't care.

The lunching women at the Bay were in their forties, fifties, and sixties, and they had careful hair, short styles of peachy and vanilla blonde, hairsprayed into little waves. They had weekly hair appointments, I figured, and they'd known their hairdressers for twenty-five years. For them friendship was rich and contained, but not too meaningful, like the single-serving 10 per cent cream they poured delicately into their coffees. I envied these women, who I imagined were never confused. Their lives seemed beautiful and totally made. It was hard to believe they had once been seventeen.

"Oh," Erin would say, "I was out, too."

➤

In the middle of August, Erin gave me the key to her apartment because she needed someone to look in on Milo while she was on holiday with Chuck. I hadn't even known she was going away.

"Chuck's cousin invited us to his cottage. I've never been to one, so I just said okay." She pushed her house key across the table.

"I didn't know you canoed," I said.

Erin got up and went to the window, smoothing the pleats of her starchy white tennis skirt. "You sound so disgusted," she said finally, not looking at me. "For no reason. You should hear the way you sound. You're always so negative about the things I do now. Why?"

I picked her house key up off the table. "Who are you?"

Erin turned. "What?"

I had nothing left to lose. I had this horrible fantasy that she would go away with Chuck and never come back.

"I don't know who you are anymore. You don't paint. You don't ride your bike. I can't even make you laugh anymore. I try to start a conversation and you always bring it back to Chuck."

"You're jealous," Erin said. "You're jealous that I have a boyfriend."

"I am not jealous. If Chuck makes you happy, then that's great. No, I'm upset at you. Because ever since you met him, you've turned into a phony. The way you walk, how you dress, the things you talk about, it's not you."

"Why are you attacking me? I've never attacked you."

"If I was pulling what you are, you would. Or at least the old Erin would've. I have no idea what you'd do anymore."

"You think I've changed? You're the one who doesn't answer her phone. Who's never home. I try to talk to you. I told you about the cute guy at Moby's who seemed into you and you just ignored me. And when I talk to you about Chuck, you look like you're sleeping. I'm happy. Why can't you just be happy for me?"

"Because you're not being yourself."

"This is stupid," Erin said. "You just want people to stay the same. Well, they can't. That's not the way life works. Don't you get that?"

"No," I said. "I guess I don't."

Two days after Erin left with Chuck for the cottage, I was in the backyard with Dad, picking crabapples off the lawn. It was the first Saturday in months Dad had been home. He didn't seem relaxed, though. He kept bending over and saying "Goddamn it" at all the gopher holes in the grass. When I laughed and said they were cute, he said, "You'll feel differently when you own a lawn and vermin are tunnelling through it."

I threw some apples into my bag. "Why are you in such a bad mood?"

"It's nothing," Dad said. But he didn't move away from me.

"Is it something with work? Is that why you've been working so much?"

Dad nodded. He put down his bag of crabapples. "Sun and Waves missed the boat. It doesn't have a website and all our competitors have websites. I didn't know what a website was until last week."

"What about your regulars?"

"Last year at this time we'd already sold two hundred and thirty tickets to Florida. This year we've only sold twenty-five."

It was only August, and the snowbirds didn't leave until mid-October, so I figured he was overreacting. "Maybe Mom can give you some ideas? Or put up signs at her school?"

"No, she's so tired lately I don't even want to mention it. Let's keep going here. I need to leave for my meeting at eight."

Later, in my bedroom, hunched on my bed like a ladybug, I called Erin at the distant cottage. I had no idea what I wanted to say. Even as the phone rang I could see it: pea green and wall-mounted, in a kitchen of sunflower curtains, rugs, tea kettles, everything made less serious by the sun; the phone ringing infinitely, the sound waves rattling the lake loons, the algae, the eggs in the fridge in a cloth-bedded wire basket, *all the eggs in one basket*. The phone kept ringing. I hung up and dialled Mr. Hardaway. He'd given me his number a while ago, and told me to use it if I ever needed someone to talk to.

A woman picked up and I could hear opera in the background, and soft sounds, lettuce whirling in a salad spinner.

"Is Mr. Hardaway there?"

She laughed lightly, generously.

"Phil's just gone out to get veggies, but I'll let him know that you called."

During my next shift, Callum came up to my cash counter and asked me to help him hang eight feet of blue gauze for the beach scene in the northwest window. I didn't want to screw up and give the manager any more reasons to slit his neck at me, so I told Callum I wasn't artistic.

"You hold it, I'll pin it," Callum grinned. "It's easy, don't worry."

The window was cramped, six feet long but only two feet deep: it was like being in a fish tank with a high ceiling. When we stood side by side, our elbows were almost touching.

"We're making the sky, so it should look kind of ruffled," Callum said. "Yeah, that's good. Keep holding it up like that and I'll pin it."

I was transfixed by how quickly his fingers moved, slipping the silver pins through the fabric, fixing it into place. The way he was holding the pins in his mouth made him seem kind of sexy.

"Aren't you afraid you're going to swallow those pins?"

When he smiled, cute laugh lines crinkled at the corners of his eyes. "Don't. Make. Me. Laugh," he said through his teeth. Then he closed his hand around mine and squeezed.

Through the glass window, I could see people on the street taking slow summer strolls. Behind me the tiny white door leading to the store was shut, and in front of me there was no exit. For the first time in many months I felt calm. I was tired of waiting around for my summer to begin. But I didn't have to wait anymore. I closed my fingers around Callum's hand and squeezed back.

Callum was leaving for university in a couple of weeks, but after seeing what a relationship had done to Erin, I was fine with NSA — no strings attached. We went out for pizza after work a few times, and then he asked me if I wanted to go to a movie. I did, but I had to feed Milo. "You can come with me," I said.

My shirt was slicked to my shoulders as I stepped into the heat of Erin's apartment and the smell of overripe oranges. Milo was in the kitchen and his tail quivered as I poured kibble into his food dish. Callum wandered around the room. Except for Tommy I'd never brought a boy back to my house, let alone someone else's. But I wanted to get to the next stage, where I had my own life instead of always waiting around, watching Erin's. By staying at Erin's side forever, I'd always be the one listening to stories about how other girls kissed boys, let boys touch their legs, and felt the warmth flowing in their chests when they knew that a boy wanted them. I wanted to be able to tell these stories too. I needed to take the first step forward. I undid the top two buttons of my shirt. I was going to start flaunting it.

"It's cool that you live alone," Callum said.

I didn't correct him; I liked imagining myself living alone in this apartment. "Do you want a drink or anything?"

In the bathroom I peeled off my Moby's shirt and uniform pants. I found a razor in the soap dish of the tub. Stuck in between the twin blades were light hairs, Erin's light hairs. I sat in the claw-foot tub and shaved my legs and my armpits, and then washed between my legs with two wafers of soap stuck together, the cold water pushing up goosebumps on my inner thighs. I got out and stuck my legs through the holes of Erin's bathing suit. It was one of the old Erin's fashion statements, and it was wild, with gold tiger stripes and cut so low it exposed half of my chest. I opened the mirrored medicine cabinet and took out a pair of tweezers and plucked my eyebrows. The hairs fell into the sink. He will love me. He will love me not. He will love my body. He will love my body not. Then I stopped myself. I wasn't doing it for him. I wasn't going to be the kind of person who waited for people to tell her that she was okay.

"You are pretty," I said to the mirror.

Callum was in the kitchen, looking at postcards on Erin's fridge, the pre-Chuck postcards: the bookshops of Saint-Germaine-des-Prés, the cathedral with stained-glass panels of cherries and golden apples, the cemetery Père Lachaise and the ivy-covered tomb of Modigliani. The sun streaming into the kitchen lit up every falling mote of dust.

"You look amazing," Callum said. He snapped the strap. "Do you usually invite boys back to your place so you can model your bathing suit?"

The window in Erin's bedroom had been left open and the gentle smell of laundry detergent was drifting in. I sat on the bed below the clacking seashells. On Erin's easel was the same painting she had been working on since April, the unfinished city scene, the red streetcar wild like a long flame. Callum stood beside Erin's desk and played with her typewriter. Even though he was only a year older than me, he had downy hair on his arms and that made him look older.

"Callum?"

"Yeah?"

"How many girls have you slept with?"

He laughed. "Oh, I'm not sure, maybe about –"

"No, don't tell me," I said. "Forget it."

Callum switched on the typewriter, which buzzed with a warm and productive sound, then clattered out a sentence, and folded the sheet into a tiny square. Then he sat down beside me and pushed the note under the strap of my bathing suit with a shy smile. I felt dumb all of a sudden, wearing Erin's bathing suit while he was still wearing his pants, T-shirt, and high-tops. I pulled the note out from under my strap: TAKE IT OFF.

I moved the straps down, so they made big loops around the tops of my arms. "Wait," Callum said. "Can I take a picture of you?" He pointed to Erin's camera on the desk.

I didn't know if this was normal, but a boy had never asked to take my picture. "Okay . . ."

In the corner of Erin's bedroom was the three-foot-high chess piece Erin and I had carried back to her apartment. Callum dragged the Queen to the centre of the room and then hung Erin's camera around his neck. He arranged Erin's blanket on the floor and I got off the bed and lay down on it. Girls in magazines always stuck out their boobs while making baby eyes at the camera, so I just did that for a few shots.

"Now wrap your legs around the Queen," Callum said.

I lay on my back, arching it, and lifted one leg off the floor, balletic and trembling. All of a sudden I had an image of Dad telling Crashing Wave to do this exact pose twenty years ago at Glamour Shots.

"This is actually hurting my butt." I sat up and pushed the Queen away. "Let's do something else."

We moved to Erin's bed. Callum pulled my bathing suit down to my stomach and bent slightly to take my nipple in his mouth. I waited for the special feeling to begin. I closed my eyes and tried to imagine loving him, how that would make this feel different. But when I opened my eyes I didn't love him.

"Be flirty," he said.

I told him to take off his shirt. His stomach was flat and hairy, the stomach of someone who did a lot of situps. The tops of his arms were round with rubber ball muscles. Then I asked him what we should do next. He flipped onto his back and crossed his arms behind his head. Then, when I didn't do anything, he sat up and wrapped his arms around my shoulders and pulled me down onto the bed beside him.

"Hi," he whispered.

While it happened, I thought about soap. Callum's hands stringing Soap-on-a-Rope across a clothesline in the Moby's window. His face was incomplete, a jaw with no mouth or eyes. His hand urged me closer. A closet full of soap. A chess piece carved out of Ivory soap. He straddled me, his walnut-shell knees knocking into mine. The aisles of discount bathroom accessories at Moby's, the toilet cleaners and soaps and the pyramid of GIV soap beneath the blistering banner of Breck Gold Formula Hair Crème. He bit my ear. My neck filled his cupped hands. I was thinking of a song in my head, okay, okay, okay, and the words arranged themselves on a staff of music, O and K and A and Y, waving up and down the lines, and I concentrated on the letters until I heard him groaning, the sound of fur if it could talk.

After, Callum looked at the sheets. "You bled," he said.

"I must have got my period." He looked confused. So I said, "What, do you think I was a virgin?"

We laughed a little. That was the best part.

Once we were dressed, Callum asked me if I wanted to get some pizza, but I told him I needed to wash my hair. I knew it was a pathetic excuse, but he nodded like he was accepting a code.

After he left, I wandered into Erin's kitchen. While I drank a glass of orange pop, I picked a strip of photos off her fridge. They were photos Erin and I had taken in a photo booth back in the pre-Chuck days. Erin had arranged the orange and blue backdrop curtains so they met halfway, then we combed each other's hair with our fingers, like two cats grooming, and positioned ourselves carefully in front of the camera so that neither of us would be cut off. We pursed our lips in the black reflection of the screen in front of us. The flash went off four times, with four seconds between each shot. Three minutes later the strip of black and white photos slipped out of the machine as curly as a yawning cat tongue, only stinking of a chemical.

I didn't say anything, but I was disappointed by the photos. There was a big difference between how I imagined we looked and the way we actually did. In our shabby vintage clothes, we were two young women dressed as spinsters. The beads on my collar looked home sewn and crooked, and the feathers in Erin's hair weren't artistic, but messy, like she'd been rolling with peacocks. In the first photo Erin was pretending to bite off my ear, in the second my nose, and in the third we were facing each other like a couple in a silent film, coy as if we're hiding a lion in the dresser drawer. The fourth photo was overexposed, our faces peony white with hourglass shadows around our noses, as if we'd eaten each other up.

I took the film out of Erin's camera and tossed it into the garbage.

The next time I worked at Moby's, Callum and I didn't get a chance to talk until the end of the shift, when we were waiting for the manager to search our bags to make sure we weren't stealing. Callum stopped me just outside the door.

"Can I come over tonight?" he said.

It had been fun, but I couldn't see us going any further than this moment.

"Maybe some other time."

▶

The day Erin came back from the cottage, she called and asked me to come over to her place right away. Her voice sounded urgent and I could hear music playing in the background. I was convinced she was going to show me a ring and tell me she was the new stepmother to Chuck's Abyssinians.

But when I got there, Erin opened the door wearing a long white men's shirt splattered with paint. Music poured out of her room as she took me down her hall and told me she had broken up with Chuck. The reasons she gave were vague. When she parted her hair in the middle, he had told her she reminded him of a teacher, but not a sweet one. He had commented on her hairy knee, then asked her if it was a feminist statement. I knew she wasn't giving me the whole story, but I didn't push.

"He seemed so wholesome," Erin said, flopping down on her bed. "I wanted to know what that was like. To be with that kind of guy. I wanted to know what *I* would be like with that kind of guy." She was wearing her old rings again, all of them the colours of the rainbow and heavy with the smell of rain. "I'm sorry, I know I acted like a total loser. I got caught up in myself. Or out of myself. You have every right to be mad at me, okay? But I never meant to hurt you, I think I was just . . . I don't know what I was doing. Are you mad at me?"

There were clothes strewn all over the floor, and on her desk were a jumble of silver paint tubes. "No," I said. "Just don't act like a phony again. And pinky swear that the next time you wear the grain-sack dress, it'll be on Halloween."

"What about floral? At least let me keep the floral," Erin moaned.

I didn't tell her about Callum that night. He was already part of another summer. In the end, maybe Erin and I had both spent the summer trying to be something we weren't. I preferred being with Erin in her room, our heads against the angel headboard. It was comfortable and easy like this. I didn't have to try at all.

In the corner, I could see the streetcar painting resting on her easel. She'd finished it that morning, right after she'd returned from Chuck's cottage. Over top of the gritty grey buildings and the streetcar, she'd painted branches hanging velvety green and yellow leaves. It looked like the two sides of her summer overlapping.

When I got home from Erin's later that night, I thought Mom might be watching TV – the Pyjama Prophet making more of her Y2K predictions – but Dad was there instead. He was listening to Roy Orbison and sitting cross-legged on the floor, detangling a long string of paper pineapples. I recognized the pineapples right away. I'd hung them up in the front window of Sun and Waves two summers ago. I remembered seeing my reflection in the glass, my hipbones jutting out through my denim skirt, and thinking I looked really hot. On a plate by Dad's foot were the corner of an onion bun, the stems of a few hot peppers, and an apple core that was already turning brown.

"Dad," I said, "I don't think Mom's going to be so into those if you hang them up in here. Maybe you should hang them in your car instead."

Dad's voice was as calm as tap water. "Sun and Waves went bankrupt. The landlord came this afternoon and changed the locks. I saved what I could. I filled cardboard boxes. The rest of the stuff's in the car." He tried to make a joke. "Maybe you could put in a good word for me at Moby's."

I sat down beside him. "Did you tell Mom?"

"I told her. She's upset. She's upstairs listening to Julio." He looked down at the pineapples on his lap and fiddled with the strings, then dropped them. "What do you think Grandpa's going to say about this? My second failed business venture."

I knew Dad never liked his job. I remembered how he'd flinched when Marg Nutter called Sun and Waves a "we," as if he wanted no personal association with it. Now it occurred to me that just because you don't like something doesn't mean you won't miss it when it goes away.

13

"Ⅰf I don't help him, who will?"

Mom swivelled her computer chair around and gave me one of her *I'm on my own here* kind of looks, and this time I couldn't really dispute it. In the three weeks since Sun and Waves had folded, she'd drawn on her emergency store of energy to snip ads out of the *Toronto Star* and navigate the maze of Internet job sites with the verve of a high-scoring Pac-Man player at the 7-Eleven. But the late nights were exhausting her: she'd taken three sick days since the school year had started. Now sweat glistened at the collar of her nightgown. It was Saturday morning, and I couldn't tell if she'd woken up early or stayed up all night.

What I really wanted to say was *You look tired, Mom. Maybe you should take a rest.* Instead I said, "I know you're trying to help. But if Dad wants to go door to door handing out his resumés, you should just let him."

Mom shook her head furiously. "No, he's just being stubborn. Who goes door to door now? Impostors with chocolate cookies. People who have nothing to offer. That's all." Mom swivelled back around to the computer. "What do you think of this one?"

Onscreen was a photo of an airplane with the words *1000 Travel Agents Needed Now For $$$ Opportunitie*s set in party invitation font, sprigs of confetti jetting out of it. The single qualification listed was "enthusiasm."

"They'll probably ask him to a job interview. Then try to sell *him* a vacation."

"You need to show Dad how to use email," Mom said, ignoring me. "It's almost the year 2000. Everyone's doing email. People in prison. Children. Even Grandpa is sending me forwards."

I heard the dishwasher squeaking open and then dishes clattering into piles. Mom tipped her head toward the kitchen and mouthed *Go*.

Dad was bent over the cutlery rack, pulling out forks and knives and tossing them onto the counter. He picked up a mug and held it out to me. "If you put away a mug without drying it you know what's going to happen?"

"What?" These were the extent of our exchanges now.

"It's going to stink up the whole cupboard."

Mom strode into the kitchen and picked the newspaper up off the counter. "Hmm, I need some peace and quiet in here," she said, eyeing me, then Dad. "Why don't you and Lucy go into the living room?"

Over the next half hour I set up a Yahoo email account for Dad and got him to practise logging in and out. Before the blinking monitor, Dad shifted in his seat beside me, picked at his belt, took off his glasses, and then put them on again.

"You know, this whole email thing is useless," Dad said. "Because if I'm at the job centre I won't even be able to open this mailbox." He touched the mailbox graphic on the screen. "Won't all my mail be stuck in this computer?"

"It's on the Internet, that's the point," I said.

Mom must have heard us slamming against a wall, because she strode into the living room just then, holding a fistful of newsprint. "I have some leads," she said, dropping a newspaper cutout onto the keyboard: it was for a job at a call centre. The woman in the ad was wearing a low-cut T-shirt, as if calling strangers for minimum wage and getting hung up on was sexy. "I just phoned. They're having a group interview on Monday."

Dad picked up the ad and stared at it for a few seconds, then slipped it underneath the mouse pad. "I'm not going to some cattle call. What else?"

Mom dropped another ad onto the keyboard. "This one is sales. Brooches and fabric wholesale."

"No. I can't stand brooches. Or fabric. Do I look like my father? I would do better with something technical."

When I looked up at Mom, she shook her head, which meant *Keep your mouth shut*. At Sun and Waves, Dad had often faxed pages backward so his clients received an itinerary of nothing.

"Read me another one."

"Okay, this is good. One-hour photo attendant. At the mall."

"That's lousy. Too much of a step down." Then Dad got up abruptly. "I wish you would listen to me for once, Joy. I told you that I don't want to sell anything that I can hold in my hand. Photos, no. Tickets, no. Luxury cars, yes. Machinery, yes."

"Fine," Mom said. "I'll keep looking."

When we were alone again, Dad whispered, "You know, she worries too much. In a few weeks, I'm going to have a real job. Not some Joe job, but something that is actually me. And she's going to see that Sun and Waves going under was the best thing that ever happened to us."

For his sake, I hoped he was right.

━

Twice a week, Erin and I took the streetcar across Queen Street to a collective studio for young painters called the Feather Factory. While Erin prepared her fine arts portfolio, I sat in the café next door and laboured over my university application essays. Just thinking about going away to university with Erin exhausted my brain with utopian visions: we would live in a third-floor walk-up and cover our floors with overlapping antique rugs; we'd listen to music all night, invite boys over "for tea," and have three cats named Milo, Bowie, and Iggy. Erin and I would pack beat-up leather suitcases and ride trains to places for no reason other than we liked the names of them.

I bought a coffee and sat by the window. I tried to concentrate on the fan of typed pages in front of me, but I kept looking up at the people walking on the street. I knew Dad was at that moment walking deep into the city, trying to mine something of value from offices, receptionists, and the job centre corkboards that fluttered with old notices. After five weeks, he still hadn't had one interview and I was worried about him. His unemployment was the black hole we circled in every conversation at home, even when we were supposedly talking about me.

"*General* arts?" Mom had sounded incredulous when I'd told her what program I was applying to. "This is not good, Lucy. When I was in school, you went into a stream. Teacher stream.

Engineer stream. Doctor stream. I mean, what profession does that connect to?"

"She wants to explore," Dad said. "That's what she ought to do right now." I loved Dad even more than usual when he stuck up for me – for us – like that, and risked having Mom shoot him with her *you're unemployed* look. We could both see the larger world in front of us, we just weren't sure how we were going to get there.

"No, people need to get a profession when they're young. They can do their exploring later. By going on a cruise. Or doing aerobics," Mom said, sealing the conversation like it was one of her student's report cards.

It was too noisy in the café to work, so I packed up my things and walked out into the snowy street. The neighbourhood was a half-dusty and half-shiny strip where the past and present crashed into each other like tectonic plates, pushing up between them mismatched blocks of the rich and the poor. A block away from The Feather Factory, there was already garbage under my feet: a chocolate bar wrapper, a dented lighter, and bits of plastic too gross to even contemplate. At the curb was a discarded stroller, the legs bent backward like a dead insect's, and stacked outside a house with boards nailed across the door was a set of dresser drawers covered in *Little Mermaid* stickers. I passed a row of washing machine repair shops, and gathered outside of the last one were men with coarse silver hair smoking, and talking in Vietnamese. I stopped and stared at the poodle painted on the window of a laundromat.

Suddenly I remembered looking up at the poodle, my tiny fingers tugging at Dad's hand to make him stop so I could gaze at it. "A doggy!" I yelled. And then Dad was singing, "How much is that doggy in the –" We were on our way to Grandpa's tailor shop. His shop was somewhere on this block.

Grandpa closed his dry cleaning business when I was six, after Grandma died. That was eleven years ago. I took my time walking down the rest of the block, looking into each storefront, waiting for another tug of déjà vu. But nothing looked familiar. The neighbourhood had changed so much and my own memories of the shop were hazy: the storefront sign of a needle and a blue spool of thread, the upholstered yellow chair in the window that faded a little every year, like an old photograph. When I reached the end of the block there was no tailor shop. Just a quick-cash loan store and a guy yelling into a payphone.

I headed back toward The Feather Factory, which was on the new block. Here, history was being renovated away. The buildings were restored, the new window panes iridescent as rainbows, the sidewalks clean. There were art galleries one after the other, and cafés with ironic one-word names like Jest and Zero. Almost every woman I passed was holding a disposable cup of coffee stained dark at the rim with lipstick and blowing cigarette smoke out in aggravated little puffs. I saw a group of kids my age leaning up against the front window of a café. The girls were wearing red lipstick and white boots with western-style fringes. The boys had sparse sideburns and hipster moustaches that looked glued onto their baby faces. They glanced at me in the same disinterested way that I looked at the guys who blasted techno music out of their cars in the parking lot after school. Even though I didn't care, I felt invisible to the world on this block.

I wondered if this was how Dad felt when he threw himself against the world every day. Maybe when he walked the city, vertically and horizontally as if it were a giant Scrabble board, he had the feeling he was losing the game. Maybe he had to duck around people with computer skills, people just strolling around aimlessly, people who could lay down words like POT and CAT and feel satisfied. Dad was aiming for the double- and triple-score squares. Everything else was just a waste of time.

"Anything new, Frank?" Mom asked at dinner.

"I saw a woman in a park who wrapped herself in a blanket coated with bread crusts so the pigeons would cover her completely," Dad said.

Whenever I went to the park, all I saw were golden retrievers slobbering over sticks and guys smoking weed behind the equipment shed. I thought that Dad was lucky to have caught such a beautiful sight; to him it was just another wasted day.

When I got home that night, Mom was sitting in front of the computer as usual, white pages spurting out of her printer. The sound of Roy Orbison was sliding down the stairs. I knocked on the door of Dad's study, and when he didn't answer I just pushed it open. At first I thought the room was empty. But then I saw Dad, sitting on the floor, cleaning his old Kodak Brownie camera with a rag. I'd seen him with the camera in the last few weeks, but never on the floor before. This wasn't good.

I told him that I'd been on Queen Street and remembered Grandpa's dry cleaning shop when I passed the old laundromat window. "Dad, remember the poodle?"

He didn't look up. "I don't know what you're talking about." He spat on the rag, wiped the eye of the camera.

People are like switches. When they're on, the currents of life are flowing through them: they're funny, they sing you a bar of a stupid song without caring about how they sound, and they talk before they have a chance to think about what they want to say. I was like that with Erin. Dad used to be like that with me, in his own blunt way. Now he shut everyone down. Now he'd shut himself down.

"Grandpa's old dry cleaning shop, Dad. I walked around looking for it, but I couldn't find it anywhere. Do you remember the address?"

He didn't skip a beat. "I can't remember that." He didn't even give himself time to think of it. He didn't want to. "You know how long it's been, Lucy? I wasted enough time there when I was a kid."

By now the camera was clean, but he kept rubbing it. Like it was a magic lamp and a middle-manager genie was about to pop out with an opening in sales and a starting salary of fifty grand. The Roy Orbison tape had ended, but the wheels of the cassette were still turning. I knew I should leave him alone. He didn't care about Grandpa's shop – Grandpa thought he was a meshugener for having failed at a second business – and I didn't care about the shop now either. I missed him, and I wanted him to talk to me.

"Well, do you remember what Grandpa's shop looked like?"

Dad put his camera down on the floor. "It was two-storey red brick covered with pigeon shit. There was an apartment on top. A picture of a needle in the window. A yellow chair by the door." He sighed. "Lucy, why all the questions?"

He picked up his camera and started cleaning it again. Just like that, the switch went off. His study was a time machine, and yet he wouldn't talk about the past. He was cleaning the camera industriously, as if it were 1975 and he was back in his studio and preparing for his next photo session – the phones are ringing behind him; his two assistants are setting up the lights; his secretary is leaning over his shoulder to ask him to sign something. That's what he wanted his life to be like. A big success. Only here we were. I was bothering him with questions and he was cleaning a camera that probably didn't even work.

"It doesn't matter," I said. "I was just wondering."

By November, Dad barely talked to us at all, except to say hello and goodbye when he left for and came home from the employment centre every day. In the morning. I'd see him irritably pulling on his toque, a one-size-fits-all thing that was so tight on his head it made me think of a bottlecap holding in an explosion. Mom's own bubbles of activity had settled like carbonation gone flat. She still surfed the

Internet, but her focus and fervour were gone. Now it was all about browsing online for household appliances, including machines that chopped vegetables into stars and mega-voltage coils that removed hair permanently, even though she never shaved her armpits. "I just want to see what's out there," Mom would say. "Not for me because I don't need anything. But it's interesting to see what *other* people need." She smiled mischievously. "And these windows that pop-up. Today one was trying to sell me a pill." She lowered her voice. "It was Viagra."

So I was surprised when she ordered Hack Boyer's Complete Jewellery Kit.

"This is going to be very special, this kit," Mom said, peeling off the bubble wrap, "so don't laugh. Or be cynical. While you and your dad are out gallivanting, I need to have some fun too. And who knows? Maybe this will become a lucrative business."

Mom snapped the chest open and her smile was so luminescent, I wondered if we were seeing the same contents in the tiny compartments: metal charms in the shape of apples, peace signs, teddy bears, kittens, crosses, and hearts, along with hooks and clasps, some of them dark green, the shade of a mood ring after you wear it out in the rain.

"Not bad for twenty dollars," Mom said.

Hack Boyer's jewellery reminded me of the kinds of things you find on the floor of a parking garage or in the schoolyard and feel really excited about but would never pay for. For Mom's sake, I tried to keep a smile on my face. "It *could* be creative," I said. "Maybe social too. You could invite Florence over to make some earrings together."

"I know what you're thinking," Mom said. "You're thinking I should return it. But you haven't seen the video yet." Hack Boyer, a blond man with the face of a digitally aged lost child, popped up on the TV screen, demonstrating how to make a pair of a "designer style" chandelier-drop earrings. "Listen," Mom said, turning up the volume. "He's not just some salesman. This man actually has interesting things to say. Lucy, don't roll your eyes."

From that point on, whenever I walked by the living room, I would hear Hack Boyer's faintly Southern drawl. "When you break into the jewellery business, you see beautiful life on a tiny scale," he'd say, or "Quit trying to make things perfect. Nobody knows the difference between a garnet and a red cubic zirconium anyways." I thought the video was a bizarre cross between a TV sermon and a Saturday-morning children's show, but Mom seemed to enjoy Hack Boyer's philosophy of giving new life to dead-stock consumer goods. She tried to get Florence to come over a couple of times to make necklaces with her, but Florence was into yoga and said it wasn't good for her sacrum to be sitting on a couch for more than fifteen minutes at a time.

"This kit is lucky," Mom said. "Just wait."

At the end of November, Mom claimed that Hack Boyer's good luck kit had something to do with Dad getting his first job interview. To me that was like saying that brushing your cat every day would get you a boyfriend, but I kept my mouth shut. I could tell Dad was happy, though he tried to contain it with logic and planning. "It's a position at a car wash, filling the needs of the client base," Dad said. "I'm going to buy new shoes for the interview."

"You should wear brown," Mom said. "Men look good in brown."

Hack Boyer wore a brown polyester suit. I bit my fork.

"No, Joy." Dad's voice had gained confidence since the call. "You don't know about men's fashions. Brown is for snake oil salesmen. I'm going to go make an investment in this one. I have a good feeling."

The day before his interview, he got a haircut from the Portuguese barber on College Street, a brush cut that made the dome of his head shine from all the pomade. He had his teeth professionally cleaned. He bought new shoes, green fake-crocodile loafers with two tassels on each shoe that reminded me of unripened raspberries. As he was getting ready to leave for the interview, the crunching noise of him removing his shoes from the brown paper they had come wrapped in sounded almost like applause. I thought, *Please let him get this job. If he gets this job, I won't have to worry about Mom sitting on the couch alone and Dad will finally talk to us again.*

Dad slipped his argyle sock feet into the new shoes. "These are going to be lucky, I can feel it." It was the last thing he said before he walked out the door.

When he came home two hours later, his parka bobbed straight past me and into the kitchen. Dad told Mom that when he'd arrived at the car wash, the manager hadn't even been expecting him.

"Oh no. He forgot?" Mom sounded crushed. Then she gathered her usual indignation. "What kind of jerk is that? Was he on drugs?"

"It wasn't even an office," Dad said. "It was a storage room. There were all these bottles of windshield fluid. Old hoses –"

I felt his disappointment in my gut. Nothing had changed. Dad didn't have a job. He had a new pair of green shoes. I stared at the open pages of my history book. I knew I wasn't going to get any more work done tonight.

"The ad was total BS," Dad said. "The 'filling client needs,' that was filling the soap tanks in the goddamn car wash. Pouring the soap into the top of the machine. That's it."

There was just silence from Mom and then the kettle began to whistle. "Maybe I could call Inglewood and see if they have something available. It's a nice place and you know people there already."

"Inglewood? Can you imagine what my dad would say if I schlepped a mop at his retirement home? No. That's horrible. Just give me some more time. By January I know I'll have something. Things always pick up in the new year."

"Well, what if they don't? What if you don't find anything? Do we stop paying bills? Do you just keep walking around the city handing out resumés?"

"What's so bad about that?"

"Well, if you're going to walk around the city, you might as well get a paper route." The legs of her chair squeaked against the floor. "Frank. I don't mean that at all."

Dad was already thumping up the stairs.

We never mentioned the fiasco with the car wash again, but it had clearly put a dent in Dad's optimism. He left before breakfast with his plastic folder of resumés and he stayed out all day. Then his green shoes, ruined from the snow, blocked the doorway at night while his oldies slid down the stairs.

I wasn't home a lot and I didn't really want to be. I hated the cold, empty smell of the house. How objects stayed in the same place for days like pieces in a museum. Mom's pillbox sat untouched on the kitchen table. An orange ripened and shrivelled on the counter. The fridge looked emptier than it ever had.

I picked up an extra Thursday-night shift at Moby's. My savings account wasn't in terrible shape, but I knew I'd need a lot more money if I wanted to leave the city for university. After I deposited each paycheque, I'd update my bankbook, watching the pale blue numbers spill downward like Rapunzel's braid, only I didn't know if I was the princess in the tower or the prince climbing up to rescue her. All I knew was that I needed to get out. I imagined the braid of numbers getting longer and longer. Yet sometimes all it took to ruin the fantasy was imagining Mom and Dad in our house without me.

▶

At the beginning of January, Dad came home from his daily search and told us he had found a job.

"It's a good position," he said, sinking into the couch, flecks of snow still stuck in his moustache. "Doing outside sales. For a market research company. I'll be moving around a lot." His voice trailed off. "It'll be long hours, Joy. I'm going to be moving all over the building learning different tasks. There's a lot I'll need to pick up."

"All this moving around sounds complicated," Mom said, sitting down beside him. It was the first time I'd seen them sitting on the couch together in months. "I didn't even know you had an interview. You didn't even tell me." I could tell she was hurt by the way she was fiddling with her pliers, opening and closing them as if she was trying to hold on to something.

"I just saw a sign in a window."

"Of an office building?" Mom said. "Are you a seagull?"

For the first few weeks of Dad's new job, Mom waited up for him. She slumped on the couch so her stomach made a bubble shape and watched Hack Boyer's tanned hands assemble a pearl necklace he claimed could be "re-gifted" for twenty dollars, although we hawked similar ones at Moby's for two. Mom's hands were less steady with the pliers now. She would try to attach a lobster clasp to the end of a necklace but miss the ring, so the beads went tumbling across the carpet. "I don't get it," she'd say. "In the commercial it looked so easy. I have no one to blame but my fingers. Do they seem bigger to you? Since when do people gain weight *in the fingers?*" She paused as though she were about to finish with a joke. But then she just went back to her necklace, periodically looking up to stare out the window at the road. The way Mom poured her energy into making jewellery that she didn't even wear kind of worried me. Her hands were busy, but her mind was so distracted.

When I'd ask her a question it would sometimes take her a full minute before she turned around and said, "What?"

The next time I talked to Erin, I mentioned that Mom seemed kind of down and might feel better if she had someone else around for company besides me and Hack Boyer. "Want to come over and make some jewellery?"

Mom tolerated Erin now, even though she didn't approve of her lack of a career path. She thought going to university to do fine arts was like going to a buffet and eating green salad. But as I flipped channels, I could tell that Mom was happy to have the company. She needed people to listen to her outside of the classroom.

Erin pointed to the screen. "Who's that Romeo, Joy?"

Mom scooted forward in her seat. "That's Hack Boyer. He was penniless until he started his costume jewellery business when he was only seventeen. In the Fifties. He's totally self-made. A man with initiative."

Upstairs in my room, Erin flopped on my bed and rolled her eyes. "You know, I think if your mom could break Hack Boyer out of the TV and marry him, she would."

She was right. The two men in Mom's life were unavailable to her in completely different ways: Dad was real but never home. Hack Boyer was an illusion but always there when she needed him.

If I was studying in the kitchen late at night, I would hear Dad coming in at midnight, and sometimes close to one in the morning. He always went straight upstairs to take a shower, and if he was hungry, he'd come into the kitchen wearing his paisley pyjama set to make himself a sandwich. I didn't know what kind of outside sales job required people to stay at work for sixteen hours a day, but Dad said the training process was intensive and he wanted to make a good impression.

"I'm competing," he said, slicing a pickle down the middle and adding it to his onion bun. "I'm competing against new hires in their twenties and thirties. The boss is going to favour them unless I make an impression. And that means staying late. So enjoy your youth." He laid discs of hot salami on the open face of the bun, then hot peppers, cheese, lettuce, pickles, and tomatoes. He made his sandwiches so carefully, I knew this must be the best part of his day.

He looked exhausted. Brown shadows had appeared under his eyes, and the skin around them was a weird purple colour. I knew it wasn't the best time to tell him the truth, but I had to. "Mom is lonely. Isn't there any way you could come home earlier? Or at least call her sometimes? You can't just work all the time."

Dad shook his head at the cutting board. "You don't understand, Lucy. I'm moving around every second. It's on-the-job training, so the pressure's on. I have to learn an ordering system, how to use their computers. People are asking me for things –" He sighed. "This will settle down in a few weeks. It'll be smooth sailing then. You'll see."

▶

It was seven-thirty on a Thursday night and already Moby's was dead. I kept peering up over the roof of my book, expecting to see my manager slitting his neck at me. But the only other person in the basement was the glamorous elderly lady with the Paris kerchief wrapped around her head who was turning the personalized pens carousel. She came in every Thursday, browsed for two hours, and bought nothing but two Mars bars. She always made me enter the barcode manually because she thought the scanners infected food. Now she was turning the rack of jewellery round and round, like a broken dreidel. Last month, for Chanukah, I'd bought Mom a pair of earrings off that rack as a gag gift. On the card I'd written, *From my deluxe line, Love, Hack*. Mom had said, "Thank you," without even getting the joke.

It was just after nine and snowing when I left Moby's, and I didn't feel like going home yet. Mom would still be awake, in her waiting pose, the fuzzy plaid blanket pulled up over her stomach. I'd have to tell her all about my day, when all I wanted to do was go upstairs, phone Erin, and work on my history essay. I walked in the opposite direction of the subway, toward the park, and I took off my hat and felt the flakes melting against my hair. I stopped in front of the frosted windows of a café I'd never been into before. I loved being in a café at night, especially if it was almost empty. Between school, Moby's, and home, it was my only chance to be in quiet place alone. It was 9:30. I wanted to give myself half an hour not to think about Mom or Dad, university, or if my grades were going to be high enough for me to even go. I'd give myself thirty minutes and a hot chocolate and then I'd go home. I pushed open the door.

The café was as long and narrow as a train car, and there were no customers inside, just a guy standing behind the counter with his back to me. He was listening to his Walkman, his yellow headphones snaking from his back pocket around the side of his body. He was chopping potatoes and dancing on the spot at the same time. I knew how precious it was to get ten minutes of alone time on a long shift, so I just waited, standing against the counter and watching his shoulders sway. Then he reached beside him to grab another potato –

It was Tommy.

My first thought was, Leave now. Just turn around, fast, so the only thing he'll see is your jacket. Lots of girls wear wool plaid jackets. Your ponytail is one in a million. But I didn't move. I didn't want to be the kind of person who was always running away.

"Tommy," I said. Then, a little louder, "Hey, Tommy."

He took off his headphones and came right up to the counter. His smile lit up his entire face. "Lucy. Wow. Hi. Hey, sit down. Can I get you something? A coffee? A hot chocolate?"

"A hot chocolate would be great. I'm not interrupting you, am I?"

"No, not at all. You look different," he said, smiling. His face was soft and relaxed. He was tying knots in the strings of his apron, not waiting for an explanation. The last time we'd seen each other I was fourteen and living on two hundred calories a day.

"Thanks," I said. He looked different too. His shoulders were broader and he had blond sideburns. I traced my finger in some spilled sugar on the counter. I wasn't used to noticing how boys changed into men. "How long have you been working here?"

"About a year. I did a grade eleven co-op in culinary arts. It's a cool job. I get to listen to music. And name dishes. Last week we had this sandwich special, avocado and brie on a croissant. I called it the Otis Redding. And today . . . well, you can see it on the chalkboard."

I scanned the foamy drinks, the teas, the sandwiches, the desserts – Dino chocolate pie. It took me a second to remember that Dino was the name of Tommy's cat. "Dino! How old is he now? Like a hundred and twenty?"

"Seventeen. He still climbs the curtains. And he barfs up leaves every day. "

"Is he still working?" I fell back into our old joke without thinking.

"Oh yeah. I don't think I told you. He's doing animation now. He landed a job with Disney in their Mickey Mouse department and he's moving up. Drooling on the page, but apart from that . . ."

A customer came in and ordered a latte. Tommy snapped into worker mode as I stayed at the counter drinking my hot chocolate and watched his quick hands. We were so far away from grade eight – and the snow angels. But I couldn't stop thinking of them. When we were alone again, we talked about school for a while. I told Tommy about Erin and I applying to universities together. He said he was thinking of going to chef school.

"Tommy, can I say something? What happened at the end of grade eight. In the yard. The snow angels. You were in trouble and I ran away —"

He shook his head. "Lucy, I told you to go."

"But I wish I'd stayed. I should have stayed. I'm sorry. I wanted to help you. I was just so scared."

Tommy looked straight into my eyes. "I know you wanted to stay. But it's okay. You don't have to apologize."

"I know. But I've thought about it a lot. I want to. It's important."

The next time I checked the clock on the wall it was 10:15. I didn't want to leave, but I knew that Mom would start leaving messages on the Moby's answering machine if I didn't show up in twenty minutes.

"Maybe you could visit me at work sometime," I said.

"Sure. I could make us some Dino sandwiches. Is there a place we could eat them?"

"Yeah. There's the basement storeroom. It's full of old rain boots from, like, 1970, and kid's pianos that sound like hyenas. It's pretty cool."

Tommy grinned. "Okay, it's a deal.

On Valentine's Day night I invited Tommy and Erin to come over so we could all make dinner together. I didn't want Mom to be home alone, and I thought the company and the food would cheer her up. I knew she'd enjoy seeing Tommy again, but I didn't want to risk leaving her alone with him in case there was a chance she'd say something embarrassing, like "You're the only boy Lucy ever brings home!"

While we ate, Erin kept getting up to change the tracks of the CD. "What do you think of the Ramones?" Erin passed Mom the CD cover and danced back to her chair. "Hot or not?"

"They look too skinny," Mom said. "Probably they would look better if they gained some weight and cut their hair. You cut your hair, didn't you, Tommy? It looks good. But I miss that old hat you used to wear."

Tommy grinned. "Okay, next time I'll wear it for you, Joy."

When the phone rang halfway through dinner, Mom practically dropped her plate onto the floor as she jumped off the couch and jogged into the kitchen. I hadn't seen her move that fast in months.

"Your dad?" Erin said.

I nodded. Dad had no phone number at work where Mom could reach him, so she waited for his calls every night. When she came back into the room, Mom's shoulders were dropped and she was shuffling in her pink slippers.

After Erin and Tommy left, I sat on the couch with Mom and tried to find something cheerful on TV for us to watch, but every channel seemed to be a reality show, with someone screaming and swinging on a vine. Hack Boyer's Complete Jewellery Kit still took up most of the coffee table, but nothing had moved for a week.

"So what do you think of Tommy, Mom?"

"I've always liked Tommy. Even more now that he's tall and filled out. But what's the catch? He cooks. He's polite. He has a mind for business." Tommy had told Mom that his dream was to open a diner after he finished chef school.

I picked up the remote control and muted the TV.

"Was that Dad who called?"

"Yes . . . He was having a hard day. I could tell. So much noise in the background it sounded like a hippo was groaning. He said some shelves fell and that's why he had to go so fast . . ." Her voice trailed off. "But he sounded okay."

"We never see him. That's not okay."

"I know. I don't understand why he can't talk for longer." Mom picked up a strawberry charm and rolled it between her fingers, kneading it like a tiny stress ball. "Have you ever heard of job train-ing that takes two months? What kind of office job has people working sixteen hours a day?"

I didn't know what to say. But I didn't want to go jumping to con-clusions with her. I didn't want to get caught in the middle again.

A few nights later I was studying at the kitchen table, and it was past midnight when I heard Dad's key in the door. It had been days since I'd seen him for more than three minutes at a time, so I closed my notebook and went into the hall to meet him

"Hey," I said. "Long time no see."

Dad took a step back when he saw me. "What are you doing up?"

"I'm studying. Mid-terms are coming up." As he began to unzip his parka, I noticed how exhausted he looked. His skin was the colour of an egg shell. He had raccoon rings around his eyes. I imag-ined him hunched over a tiny desk in an office without any windows and buzzing with machines, staring at the carpeted dividers that people stuck pictures of their dogs and their wives to —

Dad threw his parka over the side of the banister. That's when the smell hit me. He reeked of beer and chicken wings.

The pictures of his office disappeared. I saw him hunched over a table in some bar, hamming it up with his new work friends while Mom was home alone, waiting for his call.

"Where the hell have you been?"

"Lucy, I've been working." Dad fumbled around in the closet for a wire hanger. "There's a lot of new stuff to learn."

"You stink. Why do you smell like you've been swimming around in beer?"

"A few of us went to a restaurant after work."

"Mom was waiting up for you. Don't you know she waits up for you?"

"You've never worked a real job, Lucy. You don't understand

the social aspect of work. You have to go out with people you just spent twelve hours with, just to seem polite."

Dad stared down at his green shoes. They were ruined. The tassels were unravelled strings of leather, the toes splotched with islands of grease. He couldn't even look at me. "Please go to bed, Lucy."

"No. Tell me what's going on, Dad."

He didn't say anything. He just walked right past me and up the stairs.

Dad continued to come home late, but Mom stopped waiting up for him.

I had started to shut down too.

When I tried to do my homework, my brain felt like a crushed pop can trying to wiggle itself back into shape. So I wasn't surprised when Mr. Hardaway stopped me on my way out of his writer's craft class at the beginning of March. I hadn't even opened the last two Penguin paperbacks he'd lent me. So I felt extra guilty for not having handed in my last assignment. He was my favourite teacher and I knew I was letting him down.

"No story today, Lucy?" Mr. Hardaway said, sitting on the edge of his desk. "I don't want to hound you, but it's three weeks late. How about you sit down and we talk about it."

If "it" was the story I didn't want to talk about it. I hadn't started the thing. I sat down at a desk. On top of it, some idiot had drawn a girl with really big boobs and a lid on her head like she was a jar. I licked my finger and rubbed at it, but I couldn't get it out. "I'm sorry. I just don't know what to write."

"Well, how's it going so far?"

"I keep starting. Then I stop." Whenever I gazed down at the blank page, I'd think, Nobody cares. Nobody cares about the stories that you would know how to write. Then I would put my pen down and stare at the page until it gave me a headache. "I don't know," I said. "I'm sorry."

Mr. Hardaway didn't say anything for a minute. He didn't mind the silence as much as I did, but I was the one on the spot, feeling like a pig roasting on a spit.

"Well, if you're having trouble writing, you might not be writing the right story."

This was useless. I didn't want to get philosophical. I wanted him to give me a outline the way he did when he assigned us an essay so I could just be done with it.

"Do you follow me?" he said.

I shook my head.

"I think about it sometimes," he said. "How we know when we're beginning the right story. And I guess it's that moment that scares you, that might even hurt because it's so true. But you continue. That's the right story."

▬►

I was mixing chocolate chip cookie batter and I could hear the canned laughter streaming from the living room. Mom and Dad were watching *Cheers*, typical Sunday-afternoon programming. Dad and I had barely spoken since the night he'd walked away from me, but I was relieved that he was finally making time for Mom.

I was shaping a cookie between my fingers when the phone rang.

"Lucy, can you get that?" Mom called.

"I can't. My hands are a mess. Can you?"

Dad came into the kitchen and answered the phone, turning his back to the stove so the yellow wire stretched as far as it could go.

Like I would eavesdrop.

He made some grumbling sounds and then put the receiver back into the cradle. He padded back into the living room.

I was thinking about what Tommy would say about his cookies when I heard Mom yelling.

"This is crazy! Call them back and tell them you can't! Or let me call them back. I'll give them a piece of my mind, making you work like a dog."

"No, Joy. Just forget it. I need to go upstairs and get dressed now." Mom followed him into the hall. "Don't they see the bags under your eyes? I don't care if it's an emergency, what kind of office calls their employees in on the weekend? When you already worked every day —"

"Joy, please move out of the way —"

They went upstairs and it only took a few seconds before I heard Mom shouting followed by Dad's low murmurs. I left the cookie batter, went to the sink, and turned on the tap. I held my hands under the hot water, feeling it soak through every pore in my hand. I was so tired of this. I was tired of their fights. Their silences. The way months would pass and then suddenly, anger would explode from both sides. I was a knot on a rope being pulled in two directions. I pictured myself standing at this sink forever. I pictured myself far away, at university, with Erin and Tommy.

When I walked out into the hall, Dad was coming down the stairs in his hunting scene sweater, a red collar sticking out of the neck.

"Ask him where he goes all night," Mom said, trailing behind him.

"I told you! I'm at work!" Dad yelled.

"And every night when you come home you jump in the shower!"

I was okay until I heard the sound of the door slamming.

In the kitchen, Mom sat at the table with her face in her hands. "I thought it was all over." Her voice was muffled through the spaces of her hands.

"What's all over?" My voice sounded so much younger than it did in my head.

Mom stood up, then grabbed hold of the back of her chair. "Alicia. He's seeing her again. He promised it was over."

I stared at the cookie dough on the counter, the chocolate chips mashed into a beige lump. I was too shocked to say anything. Then I heard the sound of Mom's feet going up the stairs.

Mom had never said Crashing Wave's name before. Hearing Mom say her name made me wonder if she'd been carrying it around all this time, the weight of that name the cause of all her worries, her years on the couch. I wondered if Crashing Wave knew that she had been the shadow over Mom's life. I wondered if Dad was a better man when he was with her. For so long Crashing Wave was just an idea I kept in my head. But hearing Mom say Crashing Wave's name made her real to me all of a sudden. She was a real woman. She lived in a house, in this city. She had her own life. I thought that if I could find her, maybe I'd finally have the answers to all of my questions.

14

Later that evening, I showed up at Erin's apartment and told her everything, starting with the phone call for Dad. Talking to Erin felt like gulping fresh air after holding my breath for days. But talking, I realized, wasn't going to fix what was really wrong.

"Well, what would? I mean, what do you want to do?" Erin said.

I remembered how Mom had said Crashing Wave's name, like she understood something I didn't. "I want to find her. I want to find out if that's where my dad is going. At least I'll know then. Either way."

I expected Erin to just stare at me and smile, what she sometimes did when I offered a far-fetched idea as if it was already a plan. But Erin just nodded. "I get it. You want answers." She paced in front of her window. The snow was falling and the sky was dark. "So what do you know about her? Try to remember everything."

I hadn't thought about Crashing Wave's photograph in years, and yet it just dropped into my mind with a thud that reminded me of a can landing in the mouth of a vending machine. I saw her crown of laurels and her laughing face like the camera had caught her at the punchline of a joke. Even though I had met her, thought about her, held her in my mind for so long, she still hadn't seem real to me. She was always less than a person, but more than a ghost. She had been the background of our lives since I was eleven. But that wasn't going to help me get any closer to finding her.

"I only met her once. At my dad's AA meeting. I don't remember where the meeting was. There's about twenty every day in the city."

Erin shook her head. "Do you remember anything else?"

"She was a dancer at a club called The Right Spot. But that was a long time ago. I don't even know her last name."

"It's not much. But . . ." Erin got up and left the room and when she came back she was flipping through the city phone book. "Right Spot Chicken, Right Spot Dry Cleaners, Right Spot . . . okay, here it is. Right Spot Exotic Dancing Club. Do you want to call or should I?"

While Erin waited for someone to pick up the phone, she reached over and made a spider on my knee. I leaned my head on her shoulder. Every bone inside of me suddenly felt heavier. Erin asked if she could make some inquiries about a dancer who had worked there a long time ago, and then there was a long pause. Pauses when you want something aren't good. Pauses mean a wall. Then Erin said, "Thank you" and hung up the phone. They didn't give out any information on their dancers. It was all confidential.

"Okay, what do we now?" I wasn't going to give up.

Erin drummed her hands on the top of the phonebook. "Well,

we could *go* to The Right Spot. People have a harder time saying no when you're standing right in front of them."

I thought she was kidding. "So you want us to go to a strip club? And ask twenty questions about a person who worked there twenty years ago?"

"Someone might remember her. And we can dress up, you know, to blend in. That's the pathetic thing about our world. Nobody listens to you if you're frumpy."

That night I tossed in Erin's bed for hours, trying not to think about how Dad had stormed out of the house. Even though I'd heard Dad's car backing out of the driveway, I had held on to this fantasy that when I opened the door, he'd still be clearing the sidewalk and saying "Goddamn it" the way he always did when he had to shovel big drifts and a nerve in his back pinched him like a crab. When I pulled the front door closed behind me, I could see Dad's tire tracks, still fresh in the snow, curved around the bend. He'd left us. Just like he'd left us when I was eleven. I started thinking about all those nights he said he'd been at his meetings. Had he really been seeing Crashing Wave? What about the trips to the geriatric conventions with Marg Nutter? Or all the late nights he said he'd been working to impress his boss? I didn't know what to think anymore.

The next morning, I felt like I was sleepwalking as Erin and I skipped classes and went back to the house. Mom and Dad were both at work. The house was quiet as a snowy street late at night. The cookie dough on the counter had hardened into a stone. The note I had left on the table yesterday was still there: I tore it up and wrote a new note, *Still staying at Erin's.* Upstairs in Dad's study, I pulled the Glamour Shots album off the secret shelf. When I brought it to my face, I could still smell the strawberry air freshener.

▶

We took the subway downtown and walked to the McDonald's two blocks away from The Right Spot, so we could change and put on our makeup. The bathroom was in the basement and smelled as stuffy as used maxi pads and mop water. One of the toilets wouldn't stop flushing.

I went into the stall and pulled my costume out of my knapsack. After Erin had seen the clothes I was going to take with me from home, she shook her head and whistled, "No, you are not Jan from *The Brady Brunch*. I packed some extra clothes for you, and don't say it's too much." Erin's dress was so tight I might as well have been wearing plastic wrap, and her boots had three-inch heels. I wobbled out of the stall.

"I don't know about this," I said. "Can I wear my jeans underneath at least?"

"No, it's a good look for where we're going," Erin said. She was wearing a bustier and I could see the part of her chest where the freckles stopped and the skin looked white and fragile. "When we get there, I'm going to let you do the talking. But if you get lost, I'll jump in. Okay?"

Outside we walked east along the streetcar tracks, and the farther we went, the more the neighbourhood changed. The parked cars were stripped and wrecked, repaired with duct tape or jailed on blocks. Men with coffee-coloured beards were mumbling to themselves, pulling buggies that moved haltingly, as if their wheels were wooden squares. I felt we were moving in slow motion too. My heel kept getting caught in chunks of ice; Erin held my hand, which steadied me. I wasn't used to balancing on much more than the treads of my Converse. Erin was swinging her hips again, so I tried to walk sexily too, swinging my hips like I was rotating a hula hoop. Two guys sitting on a stoop in quilted puffy jackets whistled and asked us how much we cost.

"What do you cost?" Erin shouted back. When they didn't

respond, Erin turned to me. "Morons like that just want to say stuff first. They never have anything to say back."

The road bent slightly and when we went around the corner there were four buildings huddled against each other like they were also freezing their butts off. The first two were renovated and reminded me of The Feather Factory – sparkly and expensive, with new glass windows in the front. Inside I pictured gleaming poles and a glass stage, chandeliers and go-go dancing shot girls wearing silken bunny outfits.

"Is it that one?" I said, pointing. "Do you see a sign?"

Erin shook her head. "That's not it. It's the last one."

She pointed to a three-storey building covered in black dust, as though someone had been smoking on it for a hundred years.

"No, that place looks like a dump. Check your hand again." Erin had written the address on her hand in blue pen.

"This is it," she said.

And it was. Above the door was a neon sign of a big-breasted woman wearing a cowboy hat, with the words *The Right Spot* written underneath. The sign was losing its juice; it kept switching off and making a sizzling noise that reminded me of a deep fryer. Neon signs in the daytime were depressing. They made me think of sad people who never went to sleep because they were afraid of the dark.

I tried to imagine Crashing Wave standing on this spot, wearing her crown of laurels and her silk toga, the wind rustling up goose-bumps on her skin. Maybe she had stared at these doors and asked herself, *What the hell am I doing here?* The way I was right now.

I'd never been into a strip club before, but I'd always imagined them as glamorous places, where all the women looked like actresses and married the men who came to watch them. That kind of *Pretty Woman* stuff. But the vestibule of The Right Spot looked worse than the storage room at Moby's. A sandwich board that said, LUNCH

SPECIAL $3.99 was propped up against an usher stand decorated with frazzled tinsel.

"Who would eat here?" Erin whispered. "That's just gross."

The double doors in front of us swung open and three guys jostled out, their faces glistening as if they'd just come out of a sauna. "Hey, honey, how about a private?" I could still hear them laughing even after the door shut behind us. Idiots.

A beefy guy stayed behind. I figured he was security because he had a scorpion tattoo on his bicep and the slick pink face of a sunburnt shark. There was hardly any space between his shoulders and his ears, because he had the posture of someone who'd played football for a while. He was the kind of guy Mom would squeeze my hand about if we saw him in the street.

"Ladies, can I help you?"

"Oh, hi," Erin said, leaning in toward him as though she was going to tell him a little secret. "We were looking for work. You hiring?" She could really think on her feet.

The bouncer thumbed us toward the door. "The boss is downstairs. His door's probably shut, but you can knock."

I followed Erin into the dimly lit room, adjusting my eyes to the shades of dark blue and black, inhaling the smell of french fries and wet carpet. The stereo was playing a tinny version of Chicago's "If You Leave Me Now." While we stopped against the bar so Erin could adjust her bustier – she was getting too many looks – I looked around the room.

On a stage two feet off the ground, under puffs of bluish and silver light, was a woman rotating her hips in slow motion. Her hair was shellacked to her face and her eyes focused downward, as if she was counting the sequins on her own bikini. She dropped to the floor and started writhing around on what appeared to be a fuzzy children's blanket, pushing it around with her knees. There were six men in the audience, each sitting alone at a table. Some were eating noodles, some french fries. I glanced back at the woman onstage. The men brought their forks to their mouths rhythmically, up and down, like they were eating her.

"Come on," Erin whispered. "Let's go downstairs."

The stairs were narrow and filled with the smell of wood left out in the rain. I had to hold on to the banister to keep from tripping: my heels felt heavier suddenly, the stilettos sticking into the floor. Erin walked ahead of me and knocked on the closed door of the office. "Don't be nervous," she said. "It's just asking questions."

The manager was wearing a yellow visor and sitting behind an immovable-looking steel desk. He was punching keys on an adding machine, curls of paper like soap suds flowing out of the top of it. His shirt was open and his chest had the fuzzy texture of kiwi skin. There was classical music playing in the background. On the wall was a calendar with a picture of a polar bear on it. Except for the adding machine, it could've been my high school principal's office.

"We're only hiring shooter girls right now," he said. "Tips only." He barely glanced up at us, just kept punching the keys on his machine.

Erin cleared her throat. "We're not here for jobs, sir."

The "sir" was priceless. The manager held his fingers in mid-air above the machine and looked up, first at me, and then he gave Erin a look of appreciation I'd seen so many times before, his eyes widening like a kid's at a parade. He smiled. "Then what for?" He came around to the other side of his desk. "You didn't come to see me, did you?"

"We're trying to find someone." Then Erin turned to me. It was the moment in the race when the runner hands off the baton to her teammate, and my palms were slippery as I pulled the Glamour Shots album out of my bag. Don't chicken out, I thought. Don't you dare. The pages kept sticking as I turned to the last page.

"Her name is Alicia," I said. Suddenly her eyes were no longer laughing. Her eyelashes looked too heavy. Her smile wilted. I turned the album toward the manager. "I don't know her last name, but she worked here in 1977. This was her costume. A toga and a crown of laurels."

He glanced at her photo, then his eyes were back on Erin, first on her face, then her hair, blonde like Crashing Wave's. "You putting feelers out for your mom, Little Chicky?"

He was so dense. "Yes," Erin said in her little girl voice. "Please look at the photo and try to remember."

The manager reached his hand out and patted my shoulder. Like we were buddies. My whole shoulder stiffened as he held his hand there. Maybe the manager had put his hand on Crashing Wave's shoulder too. And she'd had to laugh at his dumb jokes, just as I had to laugh at the dumb jokes my manager at Moby's sometimes made.

The manager smiled. "Alicia, Alicia, A-lee-sha. Lemme think. When'd you say it was? Sevenee-seven? Fuck me, that was an era. I'd just put in the neon sign —"

I was afraid he was going to launch into his life story, so I thrust the album toward him. "Do you want to see her picture again?"

He really stared at the photo this time. "Look, everyone was blonde. They all went blonde for Farrah. Sevenee-seven, sevenee-seven, the new sign. Okay! Laurels. Toga. Hold on, hold on . . ." His eyes were blinking as quickly as the spinning symbols on a slot machine, and his fingers were pulling at the ends of my hair. I wanted to slap his hand away, but I thought he might throw us out and then we'd be right back where we started. "Okay, maybe this one girl. Skinny type. Girl-child type." He dropped his hand from my hair and went to stand behind his desk again. "She was here only a year. No more. She wasn't cut out for it. She wanted to talk more than dance. This isn't the talking business. One night I drove her home. Her place was in the west end, on Queen Street."

"Can you tell us anything else?" I said.

"She was into flowers. When she left, she said she was going to do a course, but I don't follow up. This isn't the social working business." He started punching the keys on his adding machine again, but I wasn't ready to leave yet. When he saw that we were still standing there, he waved us away with his hand like we were waitresses and he wasn't thirsty or hungry.

"What was her last name?" I said.

"It was like bra. But not. Lemme think." He opened his mouth and stroked one of his bottom teeth with his thumb "Alicia Brazzo. That's it."

"Can you spell it?" I said.

The sun had begun to set and the clouds were trickling freezing rain when we left The Right Spot. Erin and I walked three blocks to a payphone on the corner and looked up all the A. Brazzos in the telephone book. There were three of them. Erin pointed to the last listing.

"Let's try this one first. It's about a half-hour walk from here. I know the street. There's a chocolate factory on it."

We went back to the McDonald's and changed into our street clothes again. Then we stayed in the restaurant, killing time until the rain stopped. Erin talked the entire time, but I wasn't listening. I was imagining walking up to this cute little house with plastic birdbaths on the lawn and seeing Dad shovelling the steps. Crashing Wave would come out of the front door holding a steaming mug of hot chocolate . . . I pushed my french fries away. My stomach had started to hurt.

I guess I had been expecting a monument. A trail of breadcrumbs down the laneway. A red arrow pointing to her door. But Crashing Wave's house was indistinguishable from its neighbours, a brown-brick semi-detached with two square windows jutting out of the roof in a way that reminded me of the oversized glasses Florence wore with gusto in the 1980s. It had begun to snow. First my fingers began to tingle, then my legs.

"What if she recognizes me?"

"The last time she saw you, you were eleven. I don't think so."

"But what if she does?"

"If all else fails, make it easy on yourself and just be honest."

I looked up and down the street. I couldn't see Dad's car anywhere. I turned back to her house. It didn't look like anyone was home.

"Remember, the losing your cat story is gold," Erin said. We had come up with a story about searching for our lost cat to explain why we were going from door to door. "Lost animals just make people all soft inside. It makes them want to talk."

I believed in it less and less from the moment we started up her steps.

What if Dad opened the door? What if I saw his parka draped on the banister? What if I heard Roy Orbison's "Pretty Woman" playing from some lovey-dovey room she kept in the back? I pressed the doorbell and listened to the chime, one of those three-tone bells. All the way down her street my heart had been skipping like a stone over water, but I was calm now. I heard the sound of a lock turning.

Even though she didn't look the way I remembered, I knew the woman in the doorway was Crashing Wave. Instead of wearing high heels, she was barefoot, the cuffs of her jeans slipping down over her ankles. Her toenails were painted a bright pink. She was wearing a sweater with a drawstring at the neck. Her blonde hair was flattened against her cheeks. She smiled at us through the mesh screen. I stared at the ground. Coward, I thought, look up.

"Yes?" she said. I recognized her voice, husky with little packets of laughter sealed inside of it.

"We're sorry . . . we're sorry to be bothering you," I said. "We've, uh, we've lost our cat. We're just going around the street and asking people if they've seen him."

She was staring, and I was afraid she recognized me. Maybe she could still see the eleven-year-old girl with greasy bangs, a loose tooth sticking out of her mouth.

Crashing Wave opened the screen door, then reached out and touched my shoulder lightly. "Watch it doesn't hit you, sweetheart." Then, "A cat?"

"Our cat's an orange one," Erin said.

Crashing Wave smiled and shook her head. "I wish I could help you, girls. But I haven't seen any cats." There was an awkward silence. She bit her lips, which looked thinner than I remembered, but she was wearing that same pink frosted lipstick. I didn't move away from the door. Neither did Erin. Crashing Wave was still smiling, but now her eyes swept questioningly from Erin's face to mine. Over her shoulder I could just see inside her house. The banister was bare. Farther into the house, everything was in shadows. I couldn't hear anything except a faint radio.

Erin shuffled closer to me and quickly tapped the small of my back, as if there were a button there that would switch me on. Then she squinted at me, a sign that I should speak. But I didn't know what to say.

"Well, sorry to bother you then." Erin shrugged. "Thanks anyway."

"Sorry," Crashing Wave said. "Sorry I can't help. Good luck with finding your kitty."

I stared at her through the mesh. I had already come this far. If I turned around now, I would always wonder if this was where Dad came to whenever he left us. I had to keep going.

"Wait," I said. "Do you think we could look around in your backyard?"

"Well, it's mostly just snow, not too many places to hide, but you can try. And if you write down a description of your kitty, I can talk to the neighbours for you."

Her reaction was so genuine that for a moment I believed I had really lost my orange cat. "Thank you," I said. "You're really helping us out."

"You can go around, through the gate," she said.

Erin and I spent about two minutes pretending to search her backyard. Crashing Wave stood in the window, watching us. Then she stepped out onto her porch, and when we told her we weren't having any luck, she invited us to come inside so we could write down a description of our cat.

"And don't worry about your shoes. I've got an old carpet anyway."

My first few moments in Crashing Wave's house felt like being in a dream, in that moment right before you wake up, when everything speeds up and seems more real than real life. I followed her down the hall, looking everywhere – at the carpet, the stucco ceiling, the beige walls – for a sign. I imagined Dad walking down this same worn-down runner, past the wall of knickknacks: a yarn owl, a metal spoon, a china plate that said Niagara Falls. I could picture Dad pointing at the Niagara Falls plate and boasting about how he knew the people who ran the boat that went right under the Falls.

When we reached her kitchen, Crashing Wave turned to me and bit her lips. "Your hair's all wet. How long have you girls been walking in the snow?"

"Almost the whole day," I said.

"You're going to catch a cold like that. Here." She took a pen and paper from the counter and handed it to me. "Why don't you write that stuff down. I'll be right back. Just a sec."

After I heard the sound of her feet pattering upstairs, I went to the fridge and opened it.

"What the hell are you doing?" Erin whispered.

I'd imagined Crashing Wave filling her fridge with all the things Dad loved. More than anything, Dad loved to come home and make himself a triple-decker sandwich. If there wasn't German rye bread, cheese, salami, tomatoes, pickles, and lettuce in the fridge, he stomped around acting as if he'd been robbed.

The shelves on the door of the fridge were almost bare. There was a cloudy jar of capers, some peanut butter, and a plastic bottle shaped like a lemon. In the egg compartment were bottles of nail polish. No bread. No cheese. No tomatoes. I turned and looked around the room.

I'd expected Crashing Wave's kitchen to be modern and spotless, the kind of place a Mr. Clean commercial could be shot. Instead it was lived-in and old-fashioned. The light she flicked on was yellowish and warm. The fridge was chocolate brown, the type of appliance you see on home-renovation shows before they rip it out.

I had pictured Dad sitting at Crashing Wave's table, eating the kinds of meals that Mom had made less of over the years: his plate full and arranged with a meat, a starch, and a vegetable all in uniform shapes, the way it comes on a TV dinner tray. I saw him walking into her kitchen to find pots boiling on the stove, the lids pattering as gently as summer rain. But the top of the stove was stacked with folders and pages that appeared to be order forms. On the kitchen table were more papers, a cup of pens, and a stapler. I could tell no one had eaten there in a long time.

Crashing Wave came back into the kitchen holding a blue towel. "If you wanted to dry your hair," she said. Her voice was soft, almost apologetic.

"Thank you," I said. I took the towel and just held it. I didn't know why, but I was suddenly sure I had made a mistake. Wherever it was that he disappeared to, Dad hadn't been coming here.

"I wrote down my name and number," Erin said, pointing to the notepaper she'd fixed to the fridge with a magnet. "So if anyone sees him you can call us." Erin had written "orange cat with stripes," which sounded like Milo, then her own name and phone number.

Crashing Wave smiled. "Okay, sweetheart. I'll ask around. I'm hardly home these days, but I'll definitely talk to the neighbours for you."

"How come you're hardly home?" Erin said.

"Oh, I manage a florist shop. Wedding season begins in May, and right now all the mothers and daughters are coming in to look at samples —"

As she talked to Erin about her shop, my attention drifted to the collection of snow globes on the shelves behind her: there were about twenty of them, and inside the domes I could just make out the Eiffel Tower against a cheese-coloured sky; a teeny clog stuck to the side of a windmill; a Monopoly-piece-sized car driving through the Berlin Wall; the Statue of Liberty leaning against a small apple. I glanced at Erin's note on the fridge, which was held in place by a magnet the size of my hand and shaped like a parrot. From the parrot's mouth came a speech bubble that read, "Alicia's Kitchen, Alicia's Kitchen."

"I like your parrot," I said. "On the fridge."

"It's a riot, isn't it? I got that at Parrot Jungle in Costa Rica. Right before this parrot bit me on the arm. Right at the top of it." She made a C-shape with her fingers and clamped onto the top of her other arm to demonstrate. "Parrots don't even have teeth, but it still hurt like hell."

She started to laugh then. Her shoulders bounced as if she was shrugging off a jacket. A wisp of her hair fell onto her face. There was nothing magical about it. It was just an ordinary laugh.

Whenever I imagined seeing Crashing Wave again, I thought it would be this big movie moment when all the loose ends of our story got tied together. I was going to tell her that when I was eleven she gave me her lipstick and it had me feel so special. I was going to tell her what it felt like to sit in our cold apartment at Tivoli Towers and stare out at the skyline of the city, how when you're lonely the CN Tower looks like a big grey tooth. And I was going to ask her to tell me what it was that made her love Dad, because I wasn't sure I could love him anymore after what he'd put us through. But none of that mattered now. Crashing Wave didn't have any answers. She was just this fantasy I'd made up. Crashing Wave was just an ordinary woman named Alicia who probably worked too hard and liked to travel when she got the chance. She wasn't the problem. Whatever the reasons for our always being on the verge of splitting apart, I knew I wouldn't find the answers here.

"Thanks for letting us look around," I said. "But we should go now."

▶

When I got home, by the door were Dad's wrecked green shoes and, beside them, Mom's boots. I'd just flung off my coat and reached the first step on the stairs when Dad's voice called me from the kitchen.

Mom and Dad were sitting beside each other at the table. Dad's arm was wrapped around Mom's shoulder, and she was holding her head in her hands. Her glasses were on the table by her elbow, the arms still outstretched as if they'd fallen off her face and landed there.

"Lucy, we need to talk to you," he said. Dad's fingers tightened around the top of Mom's arm and squeezed. She sunk a little closer to him.

Here we go again.

Mom lifted her head and looked at me, her eyes pink around the edges. When Dad swallowed, his Adam's apple dipped for too long. They were waiting for me to help them deliver the bad news. They were waiting for my questions, so they wouldn't have to find their own opening lines. They were waiting for me to take responsibility.

"I don't need to talk," I said. "Why don't you just talk to each other?"

"No," Mom said. "Please, Lucy. Come sit down for a minute."

Her voice sounded as though it was coming though on a shaky long-distance line.

"I'll stand," I said. "Go ahead."

Dad drew his hand from Mom's shoulder and locked both hands into a tight ball on his placemat. "We yelled a lot yesterday," he said. "And I don't blame you for leaving. You probably needed the air. I get it. But I'm glad you're back. This is important."

He was leaving us again. I was sure of it. Only he would be the one moving out this time. He'd get an apartment worse than the one we had at Tivoli Towers because he'd be too cheap to rent a furnished place.

Mom just sat there, saying nothing. She was going to sit there and take it like they were on the same team. I wouldn't stick around for this. This was their mess. I wasn't going to be pulled into it anymore. I'd move in with Erin. I could take on extra shifts at Moby's. I'd save enough money to go away to university. It was time for me to start my own life.

"I screwed up," Dad said. "I was . . . it was just too . . . I never meant . . . I wanted to tell you –"

"Just show her, Frank," Mom said.

Dad unlocked his hands, pushed back his chair, and stood up. He pulled off his sweater. Underneath he was wearing a polo shirt with a red collar. There was an iron-patch above the breast pocket. I stared at the stitched calligraphic letters, how the word *bar* was set on its own line, the tail of the *r* dipping into a tiny decal of a mug of beer. *Kingsway Sports Bar.* All the nights Dad had come home late reeking of booze and fried food came flooding back to me.

"I walked. I walked all over the city. I photocopied my resumé maybe a thousand times. Lucy, you don't know what it's like when people look at you like you're old. Like you don't have anything to offer. After the car wash turned me down, I was too embarrassed to tell Mom that I couldn't find anything. So I told her I found this office job. But it was a job working in a restaurant. Serving old guys. Seven dollars an hour."

"You did double shifts," I said.

"He told me this morning," Mom said. She leaned forward on the table, holding her head in her hands again. "I had no idea."

"I'm sorry, Lucy. I was going to tell you when I found something better. I thought you would be disappointed."

I was still angry at him, but I was also angry at myself. For going to Alicia's house, for involving someone else. I was ashamed that I had expected the worst from Dad.

"You don't have to be embarrassed about cleaning tables. Plenty of people do it their whole lives. It's a job."

"I thought I was going to do more," he said. "That's all."

I turned to Mom. I expected her to make a joke about how Dad was a waiter now, when he was the lousiest tipper in the world. Instead, she was staring past me, the corners of her lips quivering up and down like they couldn't decide where to go, and the expression on her face wouldn't settle, making her look both very old and very young.

"Mom, why aren't you saying anything? What's the matter?"

"I went to the doctor a few weeks ago," Mom said. "He gave me the results today. I have something to tell you."

15

M om started her treatment a week later.

The months that followed were all about waiting: waiting at the doctor's office. Then waiting for the phone call every week from Dr. Burchill's receptionist, the yellow telephone cord straining as we waited for Mom to get the results of her blood work.

To give her body some time to recover, Mom decided not to go back to work in September.

"I'm the boss of this," Mom said, slipping on her Lady Shoes on the way to the doctor's office for her next round of tests. While Dad waited by the door, I held her scarf and umbrella so she wouldn't forget them. "People have *levitated* from just having a positive outlook. That's not just Florence's yoga talking either. I'm the boss of my body. And the truth is, I don't even feel any different."

Then I watched them from the living room window, Dad holding Mom's gloved hand as they slowly made their way down the steps of our house to the car. Mom wasn't levitating. She was wobbling, and I wanted to believe that was because of the shoes she was wearing and not the drugs they were giving her.

When I came home from writing the first of my Christmas exams, Dad was in the kitchen unpacking groceries. He pulled each item out of the bag carefully, grouping like items together on the counter. I'd never seen Dad be so meticulous. I imagined this was how he unpacked books from their crates at the library, organizing whatever he could into perfect piles, putting everything in its right place. I was surprised when Dad told me he had found a job at the library because he usually only went into the building when he was stranded and had to use a toilet. But more than his job at the restaurant, the library gave Dad short shifts, peace and quiet, and flexible hours so he could be at home to take care of Mom when I wasn't there.

"Well?" Dad said. "Did you beat that test or what?"

"I think so. I studied my brains out, so that should count for something."

"I don't know how you do it, all that reading," Dad said. "The newspaper's different, because you have columns, you follow them straight down." Dad pulled a loaf of bread out of the Christmas-themed No Frills bag. "Did you eat? I'm about to make Mom a sandwich. I can make you one."

"No, it's okay. I grabbed lunch on campus with Erin. But aren't you going to be late for work? I could make something for Mom."

He shook his head. "No. I need to make her sandwiches. I have time."

Dad made Mom's cheese sandwiches with the kind of focus and consideration he didn't show even when he was making his own triple-decker specials, buttering one side of her sandwich while it was still hot, so the butter melted into the craters of the bread. As I watched him slice off the crusts and cut the sandwich into quarters, I could tell it made him happy, knowing he could show her how much he cared by making this one perfect thing for her every day.

"When you go up to see Mom, bring this to her. And bring her some of Tommy's soup too. She said it was the best soup she's had in years. There's more in the fridge," Dad said, smoothing plastic wrap over a halved tomato. "And I left the magazines she likes on the stairs. The ones with all the fancy houses. The librarian just put them out."

"Okay. But you know Florence will probably bring twenty magazines over with her. Is she still coming over tomorrow?"

"I think so. And she's bringing Grandpa." Dad closed the fridge and turned to me. "I know you're busy, Lucy, but it would really make Mom happy if you went to visit him more. Otherwise, he's here, plunked on the couch and snoring his head off for twelve hours. And believe me, that's not helping anyone."

I followed Dad out into the hall and watched him zip up his parka. His face looked lost in the huge frame of his hood, the grey and white fur trim now thin and frazzled. He suddenly looked old.

"Have you eaten, Dad?"

"I had a snack. I'll just eat when I get back."

"Hold on," I said. I went to the kitchen and brought back an orange and a granola bar and handed them to him.

"If you remember, you could put on the lasagna," he said. "Then sit with Mom. It would mean a lot to her if you could do that. I'll see you in a few hours."

▶

Hazy winter light poured through the curtains in Mom's bedroom as I traced marine blue shadow around her trembling eyes. Mom was lying in her big brass bed, the ruffles of her blanket pulled up to her chin. Sitting on the bed beside her, I was doing her makeup to take her mind off the green pill, which had failed to put her to sleep, and the black pill, which made her stomach feel like it was doing cartwheels. The pill was shaped like a little missile but so large she needed coaching to get it down. As I swept the colour across her eyelids, I noticed how her skin had become so thin. Her cheekbones were sharp now. Dark circles swam around her cloudy eyes.

Mom was fifty-two years old. Her cells would not stop dividing.

It was as if Mom could read my mind – and didn't like where I was going – because suddenly she said, "I just remembered the story I want you to tell me . . ." Her voice gurgled when she paused to catch her breath. I was told this was normal once the lungs got infected, but it still kicked me in the heart. "Tell me the story of when you were eleven . . . and went off to become a hooligan."

I put the eyeshadow back on her night table, beside the plate with her half-eaten cheese sandwich. "What story?"

"The story of the gang you joined. The one that forbade you . . ." Mom paused and swallowed a few times. "To wash your hair. I kept finding a Sumo's bag behind the garbage in the bathroom. I asked Florence, 'What do young people do with plastic bags?' She said you used them . . . for deliveries. Deliveries of pot."

"Oh, right," I said. "That gang." What little light was left in Mom's blue-shadowed eyes was dancing. She knew I'd never been in a gang. She was just trying to flick on the switch so I'd start the show. Since Mom had started feeling too weak to get out of bed, we'd been trading stories to pass the time, only now I told most of them because Mom found it too tiring to speak more than a few sentences at a time.

"All the people in that gang have moved on," she said, "so you don't need to be afraid to tell me." Mom's voice was the clearest it had been in weeks.

It would've been a better story if I had been in a gang, but the musty plastic bag Mom found hidden in the bathroom at Tivoli Towers was just a makeshift shower cap I started using after I got a bad haircut. I'd wrapped it around my head when I took a shower so my curls would stay dry and not get any shorter.

"Nothing to say?" Mom said. "No mystery of the plastic bag? The gang?"

I had to think fast, but my wicker chair was scratching my butt like crazy and it was hard to think when I was hot – the heater was on because Mom was always cold now. I opened a can of Pepsi and took a long, burning swig. "The story doesn't start with the gang. It actually begins with a girl from a faroff land, and a singing trout on a wall that had a dream –"

Mom interrupted me. "You used to be good at telling stories . . . simple stories about people and their stupid choices."

"Okay. But I need a minute to think. You tell me a short one. Then I'll go."

The first time I asked Mom to tell me a story about Bulgaria was four months ago, when I was driving her to Dr. Burchill's office. I could tell she was feeling low – she wasn't telling me to get closer to the curb or keep it under thirty, like she usually did – and the only way I could think of getting her to talk without talking about *it* was to say, "Mom, can you tell me a story about growing up in Sofia?" Her mood shot up and she launched into a story immediately, as if the words had been waiting on the edge of her tongue. There was a wood cart, a donkey, and a love letter that was blank except for the salutation, *Dear Joy,* and at the very bottom of the page, *From the one who wants to be your boyfriend, Ziggy.*

Since then our trading game had travelled with us wherever we went. From Dr. Burchill's office, to her specialist's at Princess

Margaret Hospital. To the kitchen. To the living room. Now here, to her bed.

Mom's voice used to get really giddy at the high points of her stories, when someone was getting "sued for the ass in his pants" or "chopped to chop suey in a divorce." Now that her voice was weak, she had to rely on facial expressions to signal which details were juiciest. As she told me about running away from Balchik when she was six or seven – her parents had had a fight and she'd decided she would walk back to Sofia, which was five hundred kilometres away – she narrowed her eyes, as if seeing a distant beach. Then I saw it too. I saw the Bulgaria of Black Sea resorts, swarthy women with oil rubbed onto their bellies, American cars with fins humming by the boardwalk, and grandparents I had never known, floating up out of her bed. I saw Mom's short, stocky legs scissoring across the cocoa-coloured sand covered with man-of-wars. Her reddish-brown eyes gleaming from behind her Coke-bottle glasses. The underwear-filled handkerchief she'd tied to the end of a stick swinging over her back as she ran.

"Didn't the man-of-wars sting you?"

"No, I popped them with the end of my stick. When it got dark I heard a siren. The lights on the beach came up. And suddenly, behind me there were twenty policemen . . . they had been looking for me all night . . . on bicycles! Riding like wild horses, calling my name." Mom stopped and caught her breath.

"I don't know, Mom. I've never seen a bike move that fast on sand."

"It happened." Mom nodded emphatically. "Now do a story like I did it. A to B to C and kaput. New story. Can you do that?"

"Will you be happy if I do that? Tell you a story about a gang?"

"Start the story at Tivoli Towers. I was dating Robbie and you had all this time to yourself, and I trusted you."

I put my Pepsi can on the floor. "Okay. Simple, right? Once

upon a time you and your husband got split up and you started dating that mogul of slums, Robbie Roth –"

"Hey. This is your shame, not mine." Mom strained to wave her hand and her bracelets, old love letters from Hack Boyer, looked painfully heavy. "I told you. I want to hear the story about when you did strange things and for what? For a gang?" Her hand dropped to her hip, which had always been pillowy soft and full. Now I could see the bones jutting through her blanket. Suddenly her bed looked enormous, as if it had doubled in size around her overnight.

"All right," I said. "You got it. The story begins at Tivoli Towers. I didn't like you and Dad being separated. My loneliness was eight out of ten, with ten being me jumping through those green windows."

"Don't be glib."

I picked up my Pepsi can and talked with my mouth close to the open tab, like I was sending the story into a dark hole, back where it came from. "I could see this family from our window. Remember that building that faced us? Sometimes I watched them eat supper together. It was always something they had to cut up a lot, steak probably. They were like the Brady Bunch in an IKEA catalogue. They made living together look so easy. I wanted to throw a stone at their window."

"You . . . you would never throw a stone. You were too shy even to play basketball." Mom's laugh sounded like water seeping through a tube. I brought the Dixie cup to her lips and she spat. "Give me the real story."

"The truth is I had found these castanets, and I clacked them all through the apartment. The noise made the rooms feel less lonely."

Mom lifted her hand dismissively. "I won't buy a scenario where your loneliness caused you to join a gang. Maybe I was lonely too. You didn't see me swirling nunchucks at Tivoli Towers."

"Castanets! I had castanets. There's a big difference."

"What I'm interested in hearing," Mom said, "is how you . . . got initiated. Into the gang. Because as far as I know you were one minute gallivanting with Merle's daughter —"

"Diana."

Mom pushed herself up in bed. "With the red hair. Pretty, in a Jewish way."

"Yeah," I said. "She was *jew*tiful."

"And the next minute your hair is an oil spill and you're down in the garbage searching for your gang bag . . . Tell me about that bag . . . get back to it."

"You want me to get to the point? Okay. I was hanging out with Diana in her apartment one afternoon because you were out with Robbie, and I didn't want to be alone. Plus, you'd recently said to me, 'You're getting isolated and believe me when I say this will not be good for your future personality.'"

"You're a good mimic." Mom always paid me compliments in a direct but slightly teenaged and adversarial tone that used to make me feel less sure of myself than before the compliment was given. "Go on, though. You were getting to the part where you meet the gang, and they convince you to start wearing that bag on your head and not washing."

"Well, after the fight with Diana I felt so isolated, you know how it was." I kept talking as I took the phial from her night table and warmed it by rolling it between the palms of my hands. "Mom, I'm going to give you the needle now."

"Is this the fight where she defaced you?"

"No, she didn't deface me. You're totally exaggerating. Diana just told me I'd look pretty if I painted my nails." I remembered how hearing the word *pretty* from her lips had ripped up the floor inside of me. Nobody had ever said that word to me without it referring to somebody else. "Then she said, 'Put your hand on the table, I'm going to paint your nails now.' It was red polish. I was flattered by her attention. On my thumb, her hand slipped and she painted outside the nail, onto my skin. We both laughed." I uncapped the needle, pushed it through the rubberized top of the phial, and drew out 8cc. "So Diana screwed up my nail polish, but it's not a big deal. But then she started painting all over my skin, like, *wildly*, down the sides of my fingers, right down to my knuckles." I flicked the syringe to get rid of an air bubble before lowering the ruffled bedspread. Mom lifted up her pyjama top. If she still had some extra weight around her stomach this wouldn't hurt as much. "She painted up my whole hand, covering it in red. She was cackling." It was in and out and she didn't even bleed this time. "The worst part was she was holding my hand the whole time, which I thought was, like, a gesture of friendship."

"You never told me she did that," Mom said, pressing her finger to her stomach. "I thought Diana . . . was your friend. I thought she was looking out for you. When I went out at night, I worried less . . . because I knew you had someone around. To me she seemed serious and polite. Like she would become a teacher."

A few months ago I saw Diana on campus. I was walking through one of the dim hallways in the basement of University College when I saw the electric flash of her red ponytail hanging over her shoulder. We exchanged tiny nods as we passed one another by, but we didn't stop to talk. There was no point pretending we had anything to say.

Mom rolled onto her side. "Okay, so Diana painted your hand. I'm following you. But that doesn't explain how you ended up joining a gang."

I didn't want to sit in the wicker chair anymore. I got up and collected old juice glasses and stacked them by the door. "I felt horrible when I got back to the apartment, like some monster. You were out with Robbie Roth, so I watched *Entertainment Tonight* to distract myself. I thought the host, Mary Hart, was the most beautiful woman in the world. She had wispy bangs and I decided I needed those, so I took the ten bucks you'd left for emergencies and went down to the hairdresser in the concourse. But the hairdresser cut off too much. I left looking like Friar Tuck's Ashkenaz niece."

Mom mumbled. "That's why I do my own hair. Stylists do whatever they want. If they're in a bad mood it's their prerogative to give you a bad haircut."

"She made my bangs into arrowheads, mid-forehead."

Weakly, Mom said, "You looked like a cute little swamp boy."

I switched off the lamp and put the syringe back in its package and went to the bathroom to throw it out. I could feel the ache of being eleven and a half again, spending two days a week with Dad, watching the Smashing Pumpkins on MuchMusic while eating fish sticks and fries alone in the cold apartment, then checking my underwear for bloodstains. I remembered leaving the hairdresser's in the concourse of Tivoli Towers, my hands oozing sweat and my knees shaking as I wandered along Bloor Street, so dizzy I barely felt my feet touch the ground. I'd watched all the rich ladies slipping out of Holt Renfrew on their way home to peaceful families, and wished that someone would take me home with them.

I turned around and stood in the doorway of the bathroom, gazing at Mom lying in bed. Her eyes were closed, and her chest was rising and falling slowly. Then I remembered all the times when I was feeling down and Mom had told me stories – exaggerated and absurd stories – to pull me up. I finally understood what Mr. Hardaway meant when he said you're telling the right story when it scares you. He meant that when you get to that detail that makes you ache, and brings you right into the pain of the moment, you're telling the truth. But he never said it mattered how you got to the truth, as long as you eventually did. I knew the endpoint of the story Mom wanted me to tell, and I knew how hard it would be to get there without digging up a past that was painful for both of us.

But Mom's stories had always been larger than life, and now I could see the care she had taken with them. She played with the details like they were blocks so she could build us something new. Now it was my turn. If she wanted me to tell her a story about being the queen of the hooligans, I would.

I went back into the bedroom and sank into the wicker chair. The knobs on the headboard of Mom's brass bed twinkled and her eyelids fluttered.

"Are you sleeping?"

"No. But tell me, did everyone in the gang really have that same haircut?"

"Yeah, the head honcho enforced it. There was regulation. In the handbook. Most people don't know that gangs have handbooks, but this one was thick like the phonebook."

"That's good. Keep going."

"Well, before I went out to meet the gang . . . I decided to take a bath." The bathwater was gushing. I took off my pink jean skirt, my white bow-tie socks, and my ALF T-shirt, and settled into the tub: the hot water made my worries float to the top like cooked ravioli. I knew that wetting my bangs would make them curl tighter and look even shorter once they dried. Uglier. So I got out of the tub and found a plastic bag and ripped it lengthwise and wrapped it around my head like a turban — behold the Sumo's mystic! I didn't wash my hair for the next four weeks, hoping the oils would weigh down my bangs so they'd appear a little longer. I kept the bag hidden behind the garbage bin in our bathroom. I got attached to the bag, though. At the time, it was the most stable thing in my life.

"Mom, you have to understand how important it was that all the girl members smelled nice. Like roses and all that."

Mom sighed. "Finally. To me this was where your story should've started. You need to open with fireworks and close like a lamb."

"Baaa," I said. "Like that?"

"No cutesy. Get to the important part."

"I left the apartment all rose-smelling and I met the head honcho, with the low-ass pants, the chunky gold jewellery. He gave me an upgrade for my nunchucks. Then I got my gang bag for my initiation – he tied it on my head like a crown and I felt so proud. It was a warm night. The rain smelled like new lilacs, you know, just like the ones that grow at the foot of our street? For about one week in May? They fall to the road and get squashed and the road turns purple. Remember how I stuffed the buds into a jar when I was a kid?"

"You called it Eau de Road!" Then Mom looked at her hands as she squeezed them together. "But . . . when I came home you were curled up . . . on the floor in the living room. There was a bag tied around your head and you wouldn't let me take it off. I thought someone had done something to you. I blamed myself."

This was the moment Mom had wanted me to get to all along. Me with my head wrapped in a wet plastic bag as I lay face down on the carpet, crying without even making a sound. It was a moment I'd never wanted to remember, but I understood now that it was something Mom would never forget. It had broken her heart and convinced her that she had failed me. Now she wanted to know if she was failing me once more. She wanted to know if I was going to be okay if she had to leave me again.

"Mom, I know what you're thinking, but it wasn't like that at all."

Mom's eyes widened. "Then what?"

"Well, after the head honcho tied the bag around my head like a crown we walked arm in arm down Yonge Street. We were the Liz Taylor and Richard Burton of the video arcade. It was one of those sketchy ones with burnt disco lights where you can buy fake subway tickets. Out front there was all these sneaky guys hanging out, showing off their tattoos. Know which one I mean?"

She murmured happily. "Filled with drugs!"

"Exactly. And they had their nunchucks out and their Pac-Man cheat sheets and these cheese sandwiches they brought from home. They even had joints taped to the juice boxes where the straws should've been. It was all that organized. But as we were walking, this other guy saw my plastic bag crown. He was impressed, because he knew it meant I was in the club. He put out his hand out and caught me."

"Like an octopus. He caught you with his seventh arm." Mom swung her arm weakly and then it fell to the bed. We were back on track now. She laughed and the sound was oddly clear but mechanical, like a streetcar breaking the blue of the night.

"Me and the octopus walked around the block eight times and he bought me a beef pattie. The night was glittering. The street vendors had out their dollar-sign necklaces, vegetarian hot dogs, kimchee hot sauce, curried corn, and bacon bits. He said, 'You're the new Queen of Hooligans! Only, you can't wear the bag outside again. It's too exclusive. But if you take care of the bag, we'll always know you're one of us. It's your secret crown now. Don't let anyone see it.' I asked him, 'Can I show my mom?' He said, 'Sorry, no.' The last thing he said was that as soon as I got home, I should wear my crown for twenty minutes while lying on the floor. That's how I ended up in the apartment the way you found me." I took a deep breath and looked up at Mom. Her face was as smooth and radiant as the moon in a children's book. "But the most important part is how happy I was when you came home. I had missed you. That part is true."

Mom didn't say anything. I sat in the wicker chair and watched the grey light coming through the window fade to brown shadows, then to night. Time passed. I could smell the lasagna coming up the stairs, the sweetness of oregano and thyme. When her voice finally slipped out of the whorls and shapes of the dark, I could tell that she was smiling from the way the last syllables lilted upward: "Unfinished," she said. "B+."

I pulled the ruffle of her blanket up to her chin and kissed her on the forehead.

"Goodnight, Mom."

Early one February morning, Mom rode away on a royal blue Schwinn.

Sometimes when I wake up and realize she's gone, I try to imagine her riding past the lilac bushes at the foot of our street, across the bridge hidden behind the 7-Eleven, and through a gateway into a glowing room that looks suspiciously like the No Frills. She screeches to a halt beside the watermelons and taps out a hit song by Julio on the ripest ones, her Hack Boyer bracelets jangling. She whizzes up to the checkout line, nabs a pack of Big Red, and flies off to the canned goods aisle.

But I have a hard time holding on to this picture. The tinkling of her bracelets gets muffled in the Muzak drone. Her hands fade against the handlebars, then her face vanishes. By the time she's halfway down the aisle, her bike's shiny body has begun to dissolve into the cans on the shelves until it completely disappears. Then Mom's gone, and I'm left holding a plastic basket with a loaf of bread and a block of cheese inside of it, while shoppers mill around me, the world going on without her.

I guess what's hardest for me is the not knowing. I can go on the Internet and trace Amelia Earhart's last route down to the metre and I can type in our address and see our street from outer space. But I can't know for certain where Mom is. Knowing her body is buried in a cemetery on Bathurst Street doesn't explain where she *is*. Tommy is sweet to tell me "heaven," but I don't know what that looks like or where it is. It makes me feel better to think of Mom flying around the No Frills on a royal blue Schwinn. Mom knew her way around the store and she was sure of where she could find everything she needed. Heaven to me isn't a cloudy, fancy place. It should be a place where you are at home and can never feel lost. And that's where I want her to be.

➤

All that winter, Dad and I used a kind of shorthand to communicate because there were things we couldn't say just yet but wanted each other to know. I ironed his pants and folded his laundry, my way of saying, *I'm here for you*. The smoked meat sandwiches he covered in plastic and set on a shelf in the fridge was him telling me, *Don't worry, we're going to be okay*.

Dad has never been a talkative person, so I didn't expect heart to hearts. But when we were together, even though neither of us said a word, I sometimes felt a silent connection between us, as if we were thinking the same thing. And when he finally did speak, I was sure he'd been chiselling away at his words for weeks because they were perfect.

"This house feels huge," Dad said one night. "It feels like a big empty."

"A big empty what?"

"An ocean. A bottle. I don't know. I know it's not, but the kitchen seems twenty feet farther away from the couch than it did a few months ago. I swear there are more steps on the stairs. You're better with words than I am. You should tell me. What is it?"

I wished I knew what to tell him because that would mean I could see a way out of this pain. It would mean we'd be closer to getting back on our feet again. But all I could see in that moment was the two of us alone in the house without Mom.

▶

Mom had visited Grandpa at Inglewood every week until the month before she went into the hospital, when she'd grown too weak to leave her bed. "Grandpa is a talker," Mom would say, "and if we don't visit him, you know what's going to happen? He'll end up like one of those bird-feeding guys babbling to themselves in the park." This was her way of making sure I would visit him. And this is what I do.

I walk into the main recreation room and find Grandpa chatting it up with a nurse, and, no surprise, his cane is leaning against the wall a few feet away: he always tries to ditch his cane when he's flirting with "his girls." Dressed in a pink sport shirt rolled up to the elbows, bright white canvas sneakers, and a pair of linen shorts that show off his tanned hairless legs, Grandpa has that sun-baked dreamy look of a preppy teen on the cover of a Beach Boys album. He's got colour in his cheeks and a bet with another eighty-nine-year-old that he'll make it to his ninetieth birthday next April. If he loses, he has to mend the guy's suit for free. The nurse hands him a tiny white cup of pills, which Grandpa brings to his mouth and tosses back like a tequila shooter.

"Sol, you've got a pretty senorita waiting over there," the nurse says, winking at me.

Grandpa and I don't full-on hug. Instead, we perform this gesture that I think of as "shaking arms": he clasps his hands on my shoulders and slides them up and down my arms as if he's airport security frisking me for weapons. Then I do the same to him. "Oh, so you come to see me," he says, dropping his hands from my shoulders and stepping back to look at me. "You ate? I ate already so I got nuttin for you. Maybe I ask the girl for crackers."

"No, it's okay, Grandpa. I ate a tuna fish sandwich on campus. I just came from class." We sit down on a couch in the reading nook. "Do you have any mail you want me to read for you? I could go to your room and get it."

"Nah. Just stay in the couch."

An aide wearing blue scrubs with a flying sheep pattern comes by and gives him a knitted blanket for his lap. As soon as she's gone, he tosses the blanket to me. "I think she wants a husband," he whispers. "I tell her to not wear so much the long skirts."

I spread the blanket across my lap and stick my fingers through the knit. "You know what we're doing right now, Grandpa?"

"Nuttin. Just sitting."

"Yeah, but I meant back at the house. Dad and I are cleaning. We've got chachkes up to the ceiling, stuff I haven't seen since I was two. We're dust monsters over there. You wouldn't like it. The real estate agent told us to start cleaning because she thinks she'll be able to sell the place quickly once it goes on the market in June." Grandpa's hooded blue eyes are a shade paler than Dad's. They look totally blank, as if he's forgotten we're selling the house. "Is there anything you want me to bring you from home?"

He asks for a yellow juice glass that I can't remember ever seeing. "And the white sticks for ears." He always asks me for Q-tips because

he thinks it would diminish his sex appeal if the nurses knew he had
ear wax.

"Okay, I can handle that, I think. Anything else?"

"And the photo of Joy. When she's in airport."

I stop moving my fingers in the blanket. I know immediately
which photo he's talking about. It's the photo of Mom posing by the
"Arrivals" sign at the airport, decked out in her Mary Quant dress,
and grinning like her lover is a dentist. "You remember that photo?"

He raises his hands like he's holding a camera. "I make this
photo." Then, with a tailor's precision, Grandpa describes the mini-
dress, the taffeta hem, and the built-in belt with a plastic buckle.

"That photo was taken after she got off the plane. When she
arrived here in Canada. You didn't even know her then."

"No, I make the photo. One day she says to me, 'Sol, I have no
pictures of me coming to Canada,' so I say, 'Let's go in car and make
a picture of you coming to Canada!' She put on the best clothes
and she drive us to the airport. Is all."

"But Mom didn't drive on the highway. Maybe you're getting
the highway confused. With the main street."

Grandpa shakes his head. "No, she drive with me."

He tells me that right after my parents got married, Mom had
wanted to learn how to drive so she could go places on her own.
But Dad couldn't leave Glamour Shots during the day and Mom
thought driving in the dark was scary because raccoons ran wild on
our street, so while my grandma watched the store, Grandpa took
Mom out in his car. "When we start, we stay in the small streets,
near the shop, because she make like this" – Grandpa claps his hands
together – "bump, bump on the cars that are parked." Gradually,
they moved to main roads, then to the highways. "I tell her always,
'Look behind before you move,' but she move fast, doing sideways
like she making the car be a fish."

I knew Mom to drive ten kilometres under the speed limit, changing lanes with her foot on the brake, only now I try to picture her zooming past the electrical towers that resemble giant grasshoppers standing to stretch out their legs, past the woodland now paved over with malls and subdivisions –

"She was too fast. Always with stops. So the tires yell."

Except for this last detail I almost believe him. "But Mom never sped. You know, she would press the break when she went through the intersection, even when the light was green. Are you sure this wasn't some other Joy?"

He flicks his hand as if my question is as trivial as a fly. He says that Mom loved the snowbanks that formed at the top of Bathurst Street in winter, and she called them "igloos" because she thought you could cut a doorway into one of them and walk through it like it was a house. "She liked going on the highways near the airport. The ones with" – Grandpa raises his knotted finger and swirls it – "so much turning." I can't imagine Mom doing this. The turns on the figure-eights are quick and sharp, and there's one turn where you're so close to the planes as they're landing and taking off that all you hear is roaring.

"There was the stores with junk up there, near the airport," Grandpa says. "Always she is interested in clothes. But she looking for colour too much and not the quality. She likes the schmatas . . . The funny clothes."

She liked the funny clothes. Maybe what makes a story real are the details, because suddenly I can see Mom's glasses reflecting the road, hear her grape-cluster earrings clacking in the wind, even smell the scent of her hands as they clutched the steering wheel – heat melting into her rose-scented hand cream. I can imagine Mom doing what I never saw her do in real life, and I think, maybe this is what it means to set someone free.

Grandpa coughs and brings me back to the reading nook. "And bring me something for the photo," he says. "To put it in."

I want him to keep telling the story, but he's already left the highway. He's turned to watch Mrs. Bernstein cross the recreation room, her floor-length muumuu trailing behind her. "Of course. I'll bring you a picture frame next week, Grandpa."

He blinks a couple of times, grips the arms of his chair, his fingers closing around the vinyl padding, and pushes upwards to lift himself. "How you feel?"

"Me? I'm . . . I don't know."

"But you should say. Is better." Grandpa takes a breath. "I miss her too. We always love her. But we can't get stuck. We must be picking up the past and holding it, but we always must keep moving. No?"

But before I can answer, he says, "Is okay. Now go and I see you next time."

When I get home that afternoon, there's a smoked meat sandwich waiting for me in the fridge. While I eat it on the sundeck, feeling every ray of sunlight sinking into my skin, I turn back on in my head the movie of Mom driving down the highway. Only now I'm rewinding and fast-forwarding the film at the same time, splicing in photographs of the past and the future. Mom is stepping off her royal blue Schwinn, gathering her bouquet of orange flowers, opening the door of Grandpa's 1977 Cadillac, and getting behind the wheel. The inside of the car smells as salty and sweet as starch and butterscotch candies. She locks the door and waves at me through the window, pressing her hand up to the glass to leave five perfect fingerprint goodbyes. One is for Charlie Sheen, one is for Lulu, one is for me, one is for Grandpa, and the last one is for Dad. I see her flying down the highway so fast the car makes that *whhhoooooosssh* sound and dust clouds cyclone behind her. I don't know where she's going – but she looks happy. That's all I need to know.

➤

The real estate agent has told us to "streamline" the house, which I figure is code for "make the place look like a hotel." I take down the animals-with-jobs lithographs and replace them with two of Erin's "people pleasing" paintings: one's of a dog holding a stick and the other a rose floating in a bowl. Florence brings over a "modern" rug that reminds me of a grain sack and sticks it under the coffee table. Hyman mows our lawn in two directions so that when he's done the grass is as well-groomed as a country club's.

It's only when the real estate agent covers our beautiful grape velvet couch with an ugly beige slipcover that I start to see the humour in all of this: the would-be buyers tromping through with their tape measures and their mothers, and rolling their eyes when they see the wood panelling in the bathroom. Slowly, I begin to see the house as just a house. Now when I run my hand over the banister, it doesn't grab at my fingers and ask me to stay.

A few days after we get the offer on the house, Dad and I eat our spaghetti at the kitchen table, trying to act like nothing's changed. I sprinkle spices over my noodles and watch each flake hit the red sauce and sink.

"Dad, did you look at those places today?"

"Yeah. I saw a couple. One was across from a car wash that makes a hell of a noise. The other one was better. Not a rip-off either. I found it online."

I smile inside because I know that would make Mom proud.

"Is there a balcony?" When Dad and I talked about what he was looking for in his new apartment, all he had said was "a place for my new tomatoes."

"Yes. And there's a second bedroom that's a good size. It's big enough for a desk and a chair by the window. A reading chair. It will be nice for you when you come to visit."

"You know, I could stay with you for a couple of months to help you settle in. Erin and I could rent our place later in the fall."

Dad shakes his head. "No. It's time for you to get out on your own. It will feel good, believe me. You're going to feel like you're in the world. You're a smart girl. Mom and I are proud of you."

"What about you?"

Dad puts down his fork and brings his hands together, the way he always does just before he starts picking at his nails. But he stops himself and drops his hands back on his placemat. "Florence says I need a break first. She's wants me to take a trip with her. I don't know if I want to go. There's too much going on."

"But the house is sold. You've found an apartment. Maybe it would be good if you got away for a week or two."

Dad gets up and brings a plastic bag back to the table. I see a flash of the cover as he pulls a guidebook out: a lime green Plymouth with fins and a dancing woman in a red-sequined dress. I'm thinking Las Vegas in 1950. "Cuba," Dad says. Then, quieter, "How can I go to Cuba? I've never even been outside of this country. A thousand people I've told, 'Bring sunscreen 30 and above, a hat, and a fanny pack that fits under your shirt. But I've never packed my own bag. Lucy, I don't even know how to swim."

"You could get a flutterboard or just walk on the beach. I could get you one of those underwater disposable cameras so you could take pictures of fish. Fish blowing bubbles in your face."

It's been a long time since I've heard Dad's laugh. It starts out as choppily as a cough and speeds up until his shoulders are shaking and his eyes are wet so he has to take his glasses off to rub them. "I never thought I'd be buying a vacation from you," he says. "So if I do go on this trip, what do you want me to bring back for you?"

"How about some shells? Loud ones, that play different radio stations when you stick them up to your ear."

"Okay, so it's a deal. I'll bring you a Roy Orbison shell and I'll pick one up for myself. Who knows? Maybe I'll get some guts and even dip my toes into the water." Dad looks out the window and nods his head very slowly.

◆ ▬

At the beginning of July, we start packing the house. In the living room, Florence lays out bubble wrap, masking tape, and banker's boxes and shows Dad, step-by-step, how to assemble one. Even from upstairs, I can hear them squawking like a couple of sibling crows.

"Fold the tabs *in*, Frank," Florence says. "You see the tabs or not?"

"Florence, I'm not a kid. You go too fast when you're explaining. Who wins? Nobody."

I decide to begin with Mom's room. In the winter, I donated most of her clothes to the Salvation Army, keeping just a few for myself, so now all that's left to pack up are some of her drawers. Erin sits on the bed, sorting sheets and towels she's brought from the linen closet. "Let me know if you need any help."

I start with Mom's dresser. The smell of old wood hits me as soon as I open the top drawer. Inside I find a tiny plastic bag holding a dried flower. Beside it is a purse, her passport, a folded piece of paper. As I unfold it, I hope it will be something revealing. The alternative ending to the story of the gorgeous bus driver who looked like Yuri from *Doctor Zhivago*. Or a love letter from Dad. But the letter is from me. It's the one I slipped under Mom and Dad's door when I was eleven and they were fighting all the time. *I love ALF because no one expects him to make a difference. I love ALF because when he sees a problem that needs to get solved, he takes responsibility.* I fold the letter back up and hold it in my hand.

How do you decide what to throw out when everything seems important?

The day before the new owners move in, I ride my bike to the house to check that we're not leaving anything behind. I know Florence has already whirled from room to room, yanking open closet doors with the drama of a cartoon cop about to expose a robber. Even so, I want to be in the house one last time on my own.

The rooms look huge, like the walls have pushed themselves back two feet overnight. My footsteps vibrate through the hall, which is so full of light I can see rainbows flickering on the floor and dust dancing in columns and waves. I walk over to where the TV used to be. My memory of it being there is so strong that I can almost feel my calves hitting the stand, which is gone now. I walk around in a circle and finally sit down on the couch. I can imagine the TV screen flickering Mom's greatest hits mixed tape: Geraldo, at the height of his early 1990s domestic drama reign; Larry King; CNN's coverage of the O.J. Simpson trial; reruns of *Laverne & Shirley;* infomercials on vacuum cleaners and factory-reject jewellery. "Goodbye, TV," I say.

I go to the kitchen and open up the cupboards. The liners that Mom put in during a decorating kick in the 1980s are still there, curling up at the edges. I tear off a piece, so I have one last thing of home to take with me. "Goodbye, cupboard," I say.

In the sunlight of her bedroom, Mom's big brass bed frame glints the warm colour of golden sugar. I step inside the frame and just stand there, feeling the empty space. "Goodbye, bed." I walk down the hall to the bathroom and wash the dust off my hands, and as I'm drying them off I hear a voice coming from outside. At first I think it's birds, but when I open the curtains and look down onto the sundeck, Erin is standing on the lawn holding a black garbage bag. And Tommy's beside her.

"Lucy!" he calls. "Come down!"

When I walk out onto the sundeck, Erin's shaking soil out of her pink jelly shoe. Her hair is pulled away from her eyes with a sparkly headband and little beads of sweat are trailing across her forehead. "We knew you were coming today," she says, putting her arm around my shoulder, "so we wanted to help out. Tommy got his mom's car for the afternoon. We didn't want you to have to deal with all of those tomatoes on your own."

I had completely forgotten about the tomatoes.

When Florence organized our house cleanup, I'd offered to pick and bag the tomatoes, so Dad wouldn't have to. The real estate agent said the McMahons weren't so much "a vegetable family" and were thinking of putting in a pool.

"Shit. I totally forgot."

Erin grabs my hand. "Don't worry. Come see the big mess we made."

Tommy's barefoot, his tanned feet muddy. He's wearing jeans rolled up to his knees, and his T-shirt is already slicked to his back with sweat. He's converted a stretch of grass into a sorting depot for tomatoes. There are three piles and each one goes up to my shins. One pile is made up of runty green tomatoes the size of grapes. Pearls for Dino necklaces. Then there's a pile of orange tomatoes. Then a pile of bright crimson ones.

"Tommy, what are we going to do with all of these?"

He strokes his chin. "I was thinking of tomato soup. And tomato salad and spaghetti sauce. And pizza sauce. And ratatouille. And lasagna. Gazpacho."

"Yeah . . . and I guess we could pickle the green ones."

Tommy puts his arm around my waist. "Oh, I like how you're talking sexy."

Erin tosses a ripe tomato up and down in the air. "Or we could have a food fight."

"But we'd have to clean that up too," Tommy says.

Erin rolls her eyes. "Which would be even more work."

While Tommy and Erin finish picking and bagging the tomatoes, I take a last look at the mannequins. A friend of Erin's will be stopping by to pick them up later. He owns a vintage clothing store in Kensington Market, and he's paid me two hundreds dollars for each of them. Apparently they're high-quality, post-war European models with steel rod construction. With the money, I'm going to plant a tree for Mom in the park.

Mom used to take such good care of her mannequins. She washed them, dressed them, and scrubbed their toenails with a toothbrush. For Mom, in the same long shot of a way that I hoped to one day resemble Vanna White, the mannequins were an ideal family, the kind she wanted us to be. Their feet stayed planted on the ground, and they stuck together and never grew apart. But in our own way we stuck together too. I'm at least two heads taller than the child mannequin now. Her freckles have faded and her lips, those thin unkissables, have turned up in a little smile. I touch her cheek, running my finger down the rough plaster. I touch the father mannequin's cheek, then his boar bristle eyelashes. Finally, I slip my fingers into the woman mannequin's hand and just hold it.

"Goodbye you. Maybe I'll see you around."

After we carry the bags of tomatoes to the car and load them into the backseat, I remember that I've left my bike at the side of the house. When I wheel it to the car Tommy opens the trunk and I lift it up and push it in.

"All set?" he says.

When we start driving, I lean my head against the seat and reach my arm out the window, so the breeze slides through every hair on my arm and underneath my fingernails. Tommy turns up the volume on the CD player, a song in Spanish that makes me think of birds with castanets in their wings. Erin takes off her shoes and stretches her legs out between the front seats, wiggling her toes. Green trees blur alongside us, houses become flashes of bricks and siding, birdbaths and lazy lawn chairs, and then we are about to round the bend.

It occurs to me that I could turn around and take one last look at the house. But it wasn't my home anymore. So I close my eyes and stretch my arm farther out the window, grabbing the breeze and holding it in my hand, not letting go until we're through the intersection and flying.